RAVENOR

WHEN HIS BODY was hideously mutilated, it looked as though Inquisitor Gideon Ravenor's promising career would be abruptly brought short. Now, encased in a life-support sytem that keeps him alive but forever cuts him off from the physical world, Ravenor utilises his formidable mental powers to continue his investigations. Along with his retinue of warriors and assassins, Gideon Ravenor fights to protect an Imperium he can no longer see, hear or feel.

Best-selling author Dan Abnett expands the story first begun in his *Eisenhorn* trilogy with this galaxy-spanning tale of espionage, intrigue and all-out action.

More Dan Abnett from the Black Library

· RAVENOR ·

RAVENOR
RAVENOR RETURNED

· EISENHORN ·

In the nightmare world of the 41st millennium, Inquisitor Eisenhorn hunts down mankind's most dangerous enemies.

Includes the novels
XENOS, MALLEUS,
and HERETICUS

· GAUNT'S GHOSTS ·

Colonel-Commissar Gaunt and his regiment, the Tanith First-and-Only, struggle for survival on the battlefields of the far future.

The Founding
FIRST AND ONLY
GHOSTMAKER
NECROPOLIS

The Saint
HONOUR GUARD
THE GUNS OF TANITH
STRAIGHT SILVER
SABBAT MARTYR

The Lost
TRAITOR GENERAL

· OTHER WARHAMMER 40,000 NOVELS ·

DOUBLE EAGLE

A WARHAMMER 40,000 NOVEL

RAVENOR

Dan Abnett

For Marc Gascoigne

'I see comedy as a kind of amphibious landing craft...'

With, always, thanks and love to Nik for her patience and suggestions

XDX

A BLACK LIBRARY PUBLICATION

First published in Great Britain in 2004.
Paperback edition published in 2005 by BL Publishing,
Games Workshop Ltd.,
Willow Road, Nottingham,
NG7 2WS, UK.

10 9 8 7 6

Map by Ralph Horsley.

A CIP record for this book is available from the British Library.

ISBN 13: 978 1 84416 073 0
ISBN 10: 1 84416 073 4

Distributed in the US by Simon & Schuster
1230 Avenue of the Americas, New York, NY 10020, US.

It is the 41st millennium. For more than a hundred centuries the Emperor has sat immobile on the Golden Throne of Earth. He is the master of mankind by the will of the gods, and master of a million worlds by the might of his inexhaustible armies. He is a rotting carcass writhing invisibly with power from the Dark Age of Technology. He is the Carrion Lord of the Imperium for whom a thousand souls are sacrificed every day, so that he may never truly die.

Yet even in his deathless state, the Emperor continues his eternal vigilance. Mighty battlefleets cross the daemon-infested miasma of the warp, the only route between distant stars, their way lit by the Astronomican, the psychic manifestation of the Emperor's will. Vast armies give battle in his name on uncounted worlds. Greatest amongst his soldiers are the Adeptus Astartes, the Space Marines, bio-engineered super-warriors. Their comrades in arms are legion: the Imperial Guard and countless planetary defence forces, the ever-vigilant Inquisition and the tech-priests of the Adeptus Mechanicus to name only a few. But for all their multitudes, they are barely enough to hold off the ever-present threat from aliens, heretics, mutants – and worse.

To be a man in such times is to be one amongst untold billions. It is to live in the cruellest and most bloody regime imaginable. These are the tales of those times. Forget the power of technology and science, for so much has been forgotten, never to be re-learned. Forget the promise of progress and understanding, for in the grim dark future there is only war. There is no peace amongst the stars, only an eternity of carnage and slaughter, and the laughter of thirsting gods.

FOUR SUBSECTORS OF
SCARUS SECTOR
SEGMENTUM OBSCURUS
CIRCA 402.M41.
TRAILING
Spica Maxima
MERGENT WORLDS
SUBSECTOR VINCIES (LOST)
Bonmer's Reach
SPACE
OUTER WORLDS
SUBSECTOR ANTIMAR
SUB SECTOR ANGELUS
DREWLIAN GROUP
SARUM
EUSTIS MAJORIS
Vessor
Gloriecent
Vogel Passionata
Quentinus XIII
Riggion
Encage
Lenk
Fedra
Malinter
Ledspar
Flint
Bostol
Frumody
Mimoran
Tomish
Ur-Haven
Lorien
Caxton
Tancred
Brontolaph
Nova Durma
Fennis Major
Sancour
Ingeran
Lora Sen
Loki
Mirepoix
Heveron
Hasarna

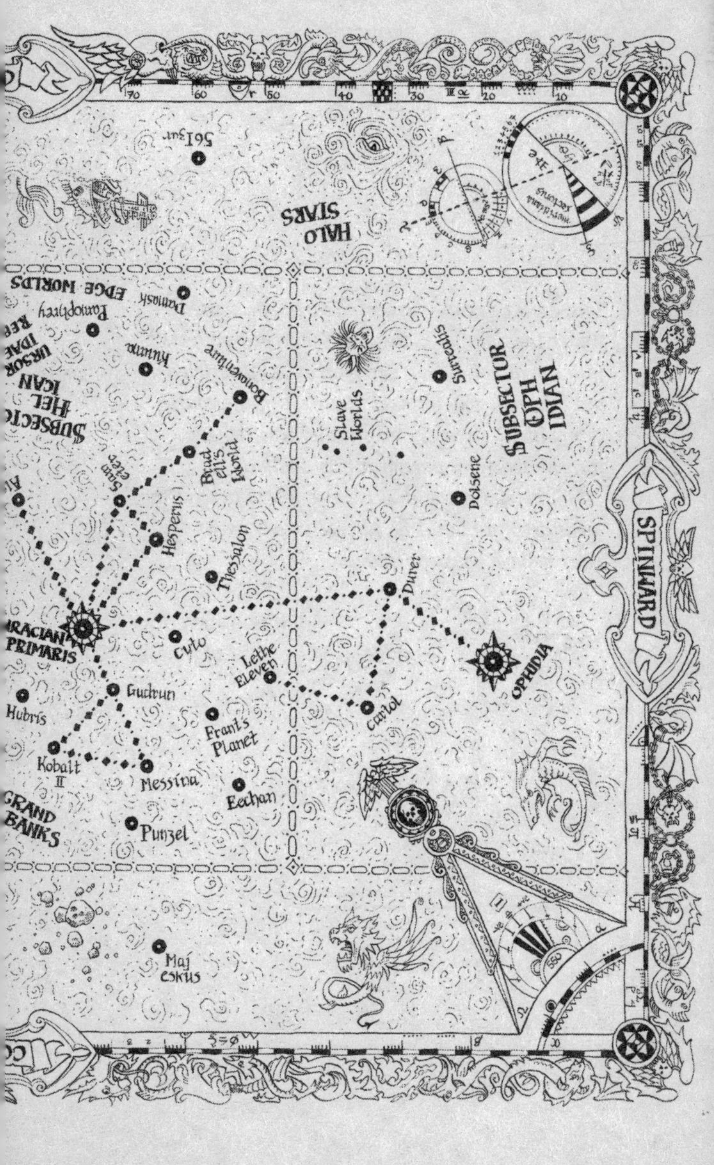

HALO STARS
EDGE WORLDS
Damask
Kuuma
Bonaventure
SUBSECTOR OPHIDIAN
Surteatis
Slave Worlds
Dolsene
SPINWARD
Durer
Bradell's World
Hesperus
Thessalon
Cyto
Lethe Eleven
carrol
OPHIDIA
Gudrun
Hubris
Frant's Planet
Kobalt II
Messina
Eechan
GRAND BANKS
Punzel
Maj eskus

THE GREAT PROCESSION *of the triumph passed under the Spatian Gate, and I marched with it, into the atrocity. That ceremonial arch, so splendid and massive, forms a threshold in the course of my life. I stepped across it and was remade, transmuted from one form into another.*

Some have said that I was crippled beyond the measure of a man. I do not see it that way.

I believe I was liberated.

– Gideon Ravenor,
preface to *The Mirror of Smoke*

THEN

Local summer time, Southern landmass, Zenta Malhyde, 397.M41

He was sleeping in his habitent when the cries of the indigens woke him.

'Ekoh! Ekoh! N'nsa skte me'du!'

He sat up fast, sweat streaking down his bare torso. He'd been dreaming about the Vents of Sleef. *Always the drop, the long drop into the bowels of hell...*

'Ekoh! H'ende! N'nsa skte me'du!'

His Cognitae-trained mind fumbled for a translation. That damned indigen argot. 'Ekoh'... that was *pay heed* or *great news*, and 'h'ende' was a formal title he was fast getting used to. The rest? 'Nsa skt'... that was a verb form. Parse it, for Throne's sake... *finding of a thing, I find, he/she/it finds, we find...*

Great gods of nowhere!

He scrambled to his feet, naked, and reached for his bodyglove, which hung like a sloughed lizard skin over the back of the trestle chair. Ambient temp was already high in the forties, and the habitent's viropump was struggling to breathe cool air into the unlit prefab.

The door-flap of the habitent drew back and the awful, prickling heat rushed in. Kyband came with it. His long black hair was lank with sweat, and the corners of his eyes and mouth were raw where he had taken too long to scrape out nte-fly eggs.

'Get dressed, Zyg,' Kyband said. Despite the weeping redness, his eyes were bright. 'The little bastards have cracked it.'

OUTSIDE, THE SHOCKING heat made him gasp despite himself. The indigens were thronging around the camp's habitents, chattering excitedly and waving their dirty fingers at the sky. Nung the ogryn had to drive them back with a lash. Kyband went to get his weapon, slapping flies away from his face.

Molotch fastened up his bodyglove. Just ten seconds in the open heat and already his sweat was pouring out inside its rubberised sheath. He set a straw hat on his head.

'Where?' he asked.

'Site C,' said Kyband.

It was only a ten-minute walk from the camp, but every step was an effort. Molotch quickly realised he'd left his glare-shades back in the tent. His eyes began to ache and tear up in the intense sunlight. The day glare seared white against the powder rock and glinted mercilessly off the shiny, ink-black cups and tubes of the fleshy vegetation.

The indigens ran around and ahead of them, urging them along, their scrawny, tanned bodies indifferent to the frying heat.

'Site C, eh?' Molotch panted. 'And there was I putting money on D. Who'd have thought it?'

'Not Nung,' said Nung, though, in fairness, there were very few things he ever thought of all by himself.

Through one last glade of stinking black tubers and they came out into the hard shadows of the pillars. Formed of white crystal, the pillars rose as high as thirty metres, like the columns of some lost temple. Boros Dias had assured Molotch they were an entirely natural geoform. The treacherous pathway wound between the pillars all the way down to the cliff face. Their feet – particularly the bare feet of the scampering indigens – kicked up sheets of white dust from the path. The clouds made Molotch and Kyband cough and spit. Nung appeared untroubled. The ogryn displayed a remarkable resilience to physical discomfort. An nte-egg infestation had swollen and necrotised the flesh of his face from behind his left ear to his eye-line, and even that didn't seem to bother him.

At site C, the servito-excavators had dug out a whole section of the grainy white cliff-face, and Nung had personally used a flamer to torch away the last of the overhanging growth. A ragged cleft had been exposed in the facing. Two weeks' worth of back-breaking labour by the indigens had cleared the cleft of rubble and revealed it.

Lynta was standing guard by the opening.

The shouting from the indigens grew louder and Molotch turned to Kyband.

'This requires privacy,' he said.

Kyband nodded. He pulled the bolt pistol from his belt holster and held it up. It had taken them a while to learn, but the indigens now understood what it did. They fled in terror, every last one of them, their triumphant whoops turning into hasty yelps.

The site fell silent but for the gurgle of sap, the whistle of insects and the buzzing crackle of the sun.

'Lynta?'

She walked over to them, mopping perspiration from her brow. Her bodyglove was set to max-chill, and rapidly thawing frost was fuming off her lean figure.

'The doc says we have it at last, h'ende,' she said.

'Don't call me that. It makes you sound like a heathen.'

Lynta smiled. 'We're all heathens, aren't we, Zygmunt?'

'After this, Lynta, we'll all be gods,' he replied and turned his body sideways to slide in through the narrow cleft.

'Zygmunt?' she called out, halting him.

'What?'

'When are you going to tell us? When are you going to tell us what it is you and the doc are after here? Me and Kyband... the rest... we deserve to know.'

Molotch looked into her bright green eyes. They were murder-hard. He knew she was right. Purchased loyalty would only stretch so far.

'Soon,' he said and wriggled into the cleft.

Boros Dias was twenty metres inside, in the darkness, and he was caked in dust. He was instructing two servitors about a painstaking method of excavation. Fan-units in the back of their distended necks whirred as they blew air into the crevices that Dias's light-wand illuminated.

'There you are,' said Boros Dias.

'What have you found?'

'See for yourself,' said Boros Dias. He raised his wand-beam over the ancient carvings on the semi-exposed wall.

'I see scratchings, and hollows plugged with dust,' said Molotch. 'Do what I pay you to do.'

Boros Dias sighed. Just eighteen months earlier, he had been magister tutorae xenos at the Universitariat of Thracian, one of the most admired academics in his field.

'I see certain structure forms,' he said. 'They have the corresponding vowel shapes and interrogative functions.'

'Is it Enuncia?' Molotch asked.

'I believe it is. But I would not dare try to voice any of it. Not without further study.'

Molotch pushed him aside. 'You're a coward,' he declared.

Molotch had spent five years familiarising himself with the basic vocatives and palate sounds. He ran his fingers over the bas-relief, and tried a word.

It sounded like *shhhfkkt*.

The cranium of the servitor unit next to him burst in a splatter of gore, brain-matter and spinning metal fragments. Molotch's mouth began to stream with blood. The other servitor went berserk and started to beat its forehead against the far wall of the chamber. It carried on until its head smashed and came off.

Molotch staggered backwards, retching up blood. He spat out one of his own front teeth.

'I said it was too dangerous!' Boros Dias cried.

Molotch grabbed him by the throat. 'I haven't come so far, and suffered so much, to throw this away! For frig's sake, doctor! I lost eighteen good men cutting my way through that tau cadre just to be here!'

'I think maybe the tau knew this was forbidden,' Boros Dias ventured.

Molotch punched him in the face, knocking him onto the narrow cave's dusty floor.

'Know, doctor, my basic tenet is that nothing is forbidden. Zygmunt Molotch has lived his life by that philosophy.'

'Then Zygmunt Molotch is damned,' whimpered Boros Dias.

'I never said I wasn't,' Molotch said. 'Get on. I need some air.'

* * *

MOLOTCH PUSHED HIS way back out of the cleft into the appalling sunlight.

'What the hell happened to you?' Lynta asked when she saw his mouth.

'Nothing,' Molotch answered. Kyband and Nung stood nearby, gazing into the forest. Emmings joined them. The leathery Imperial Guard vet was cradling his trophy pulse rifle and muttering with the other two in a low voice.

'What's the matter?'

'We might have company,' Kyband said, looking round. He gestured towards the black, fleshy stalks and fronds of the surrounding jungle beyond the pillars. 'Out there.' Molotch followed the gesture and winced. The world was too bright to look at except through a squint.

'Nung can smell it,' Nung said.

'Company? What sort of company?' Molotch snapped.

'Bad company,' said Lynta, pulling out her snub-las. 'Throne agents.'

'The doctor needs more time,' said Molotch. 'Rouse everyone. We'll deal with this.'

KYBAND VOXED THE camp and Hehteng joined them quickly. The fur on his muzzle was spiky and dank and his tongue lolled with the heat. When he spoke Low Gothic, it sounded like a scavenger snaffling at a marrow-bone, but Kyband had known him long enough to get the gist.

'Salton and Xuber are still too sick to come,' Kyband relayed. 'The maggots are in Salton's gut now. He's bleeding out.'

'So noted,' Molotch replied. Hehteng had brought the drone monitor handset from the camp and Molotch took it from him. He studied the little screen display. None of the sentry drones ranged around the camp area and site zones had triggered at all.

'Seems like a false alarm,' Molotch said. 'But we'll check them all by hand.'

He led them back up the baking white track between the pillars to the stinking wall of soft, black vegetation. He longed for his glare-goggles. His eyes were aching. The flare-bright sun was high in the colourless sky, and mirrorkites were turning slow circles on the thermals far overhead.

They entered the noxious miasma of the jungle. Bars of sunlight stabbed down between the glossy black tube-forms and puckered cup flowers. The rancid air was seething with nte-flies, and larger, bottle green crawlers writhed in the oozy sap of the cups or dangled from the swollen nectaries. There was a scent of gangrene.

They spread out, their boots squelching through the smaller, ground-covering tubes, bursting some and spilling their fetid juices. Molotch looked up at the canopy – a lattice of white light and black growths – and took his straw hat off to wipe a hand across his dripping scalp.

There was a flash, a whoop of superheated air, and the world tumbled over on its end.

Molotch found himself lying on his back. His face was wet. A dull, concussive numbness was in his brain, a raw ache in his right thigh. The canopy above him continued to form a lattice of light and darkness. As he watched, two incandescent bolts of las-fire, each shaped like an elongated spearhead the length of an adult human forearm, squealed overhead.

He could hear frantic shouting around him – Nung bellowing, Kyband yelling – and the throaty *boom* of a bolt pistol. Then, on top of that, the high-pitched *zap-spit* of a pulse rifle on rapid/auto.

Molotch sat up. He was spattered with root sap. There was a bloody hole the size of a bottle top through his thigh. Mulch worms and flies were already invading it.

'Oh God-Emperor...' he breathed. He crawled behind a fat, drooping tuber. More las-fire whined past. Several bolts punched into foliage, vomiting sprays of sap and chunks of black plant-meat. Kyband was in cover nearby, squeezing off shots with his bolt pistol. Beyond him, Emmings was hosing the forest with rapid fire from his precious pulse rifle. To Molotch's certain knowledge, Emmings had killed forty-five men, eleven tau, twenty-three greens and five eldar. He'd accomplished that score with a battered Guard-issue long-las. Ever since he'd picked up the handsome tau weapon as spoils of combat, he'd been itching to use it.

Nung was finally making a response to pain. Like Molotch, the ogryn had been caught by the first salvo. He was bellowing, blood was squirting out of a scorched hole in his side.

Molotch struggled over to Nung's aid, shots shrilling above his head. The ogryn was in bad shape. A secondary wound, just a glancing injury, had burst open the infested tissue of his cheek, and larval grubs were pouring out down his neck and shoulder. Molotch stuck Nung with a one-use tranq-blunt from his belt pack.

'Come on! Come on, Nung!' he urged.

The ogryn stopped bellowing. He glanced at Molotch with an unreadable expression that might have been gratitude, and then rolled his massive bulk over onto all fours. So arranged, he shuffled over through the ooze as far as the next main tuber growth, and then unshipped the Korsh 50 assault cannon from the syn-hide boot on his back. Nung wore three heavy drum magazines from his waistbelt the way an ordinary human carried water bottles. His fat fingers fumbled to connect the belt feed.

Then he had it. The cannon shook into life, tongues of flash-fire dancing like an afterburner around the rotating multi-barrels. It roared out a great blurt of noise, undercut by the metallic grate of its cycling mechanism. A cascade of spent cases flew into the air and pattered down onto the ooze.

The cannon-blasts stripped away the vegetation before them, pulping it into matted, wet debris and a sticky mist of sap-vapour. The las-fire ceased abruptly.

'Go!' Molotch ordered. 'Get to the camp!'

They all started to run, splashing and tearing through the mulch and undergrowth. Molotch couldn't see Lynta at all. Emmings was in front. He was first out into the open glare.

'Come the frig on!' he shouted, turning back to wave at them.

Emmings's head snapped sideways, whip-cracking his reedy neck. The shockwave travelled down his bony body and twisted it violently. Before his feet left the powder-white ground, his head began to deform, to wrench out of shape, to lose all semblance of Emmings. Then it burst, and Emmings folded like a snap-shut clasp knife. He fell sideways into the dust. Molotch glimpsed a lean figure with a bolt pistol duck back into cover behind one of the pillars. Just a glimpse, but Molotch recognised him.

That bastard interrogator, Thonius.

So, they'd found them. Thonius, his cronies – and their thrice-damned master.

Nung trampled clear of the undergrowth and peppered the nearest pillars with his cannon. Stone dust and quartz shrapnel blizzarded off them in a long, stippling line.

Molotch ran out beside him and pulled the blood-flecked pulse rifle out of Emmings's still-clenched hands.

'Where is he?' Lynta was behind him suddenly, her snub-las raised. 'It was that runt-freak Thonius, wasn't it? I saw him.'

'Over there...' Molotch pointed.

'Hose it!' Lynta yelled to Nung, and started to run.

Nung loved Lynta as much as he could love anything. He obeyed without hesitation, raking the pillars again and showering the ground with spent cases. The chalky impact spume wafted up, clouds into a cloudless sky.

Lynta disappeared behind the nearest pillars. Molotch started to move again. Kyband and Hehteng emerged from the jungle.

'The camp!' Molotch screamed at them. 'Nung's with me!'

Kyband and the lupen started to run up the track. Hehteng used his backward-jointed, powerful limbs to leap ahead of the human.

Molotch edged down into the pillars. It was hot and quiet again suddenly. The sun glared down, almost overhead, and he ignored his pouring sweat and the burning of his skin. He'd lost his straw hat somewhere. He moved from shadow to shadow, hugging the scant shade at the base of the pillars. Nung shuffled after him. The ogryn's breathing was loud and ragged.

Abruptly, two figures whirled into view around the side of one of the columns: Lynta and Thonius. Somehow, they had disarmed one another. Their desperate combat was extraordinary, almost too fast for the eye to follow. Kick, jab, kick, evade, duck, slice, jab. Two perfectly trained killers unleashed. Molotch raised his rifle and tried to draw a bead on Thonius, but Nung knocked his aim aside.

'Zygmunt hit her!' he wheezed.

It was true. He might. The combatants were a blur of circling bodies and scything limbs. There was no way to separate them.

Molotch ran past them instead, tracing his way down the sunburnt track towards site C. He quickly left Nung behind.

Molotch paused beside the last of the pillars, panting, and gazed down at the cliff-face and the cleft. There was no sign of life; in fact, there was no sign of anything except the disengaged excavator modules cooking in the sun where the servitors had left them.

He took a step forward. Something hard and hot pressed against his temple.

'Drop the rifle,' said a woman's voice.

Molotch hesitated.

'Drop it, Molotch, or I drop you.'

Molotch tossed the tau weapon into the white dust. 'Is that you, Kara Swole?' he asked.

'You better believe it, you frig-wipe ninker.'

She let him turn slightly, so the barrel of her laspistol was in his face. Of all the bastard's band, she had always been his favourite. A dancer-acrobat, short, well muscled, womanly. Her body was tightly packed into a cream skinsleeve, and her red hair pressed down under a hood. She wore glare-goggles. Her small, expressive mouth and wide cheekbones were as attractive as he had remembered.

She was not smiling.

'I always did think you picked the wrong side, Kara,' he said. She spat, and banged the nose of the pistol into his throbbing, gap-toothed mouth so hard it made him whine.

'So help me, I'll kill you for what you did on Majeskus. So help me, I'll–'

She halted and stiffened, as if hearing some invisible command. 'All right, all right,' she protested to someone not there at all. 'Alive.'

'He's with you, isn't he?' Molotch said. 'Tell him... tell him I'll see him in hell.'

Nung had finally caught up with his master. He slithered down between the last of the pillars, howling Molotch's name and firing the cannon.

Molotch threw himself down as the fusillade of fat-cal shots went over him. He saw Swole leap the other way, turning an expert but desperate handspring in the dust. She cleared the fire zone as far as one of the excavators, and ducked down as rounds spanged off its bodywork. Then she ran, lithe and fast, into the jungle. Molotch wondered if Nung had hit her. He doubted she would still have been moving if he had.

Molotch snatched up the pulse rifle and fired a few blurts after her, splattering tubers and cups.

'Nung! Stay guard here!' he instructed, and ran towards the cleft.

In the crooked, sweltering dark, he met Boros Dias coming the other way.

'Back!'

'I heard shooting...'

'Back, doctor!'

Boros Dias retreated into the excavated chamber. The organic parts of the mangled servitors were already beginning to rot.

'What's happening?' Boros Dias demanded plaintively as Molotch pushed past him. 'Molotch?'

'The justice of the Imperium of Man, swaggering with its own self-importance, has come to interfere with us.'

'The Imperium? You mean the Inquisition?'

Molotch took an expensive larisel-fur brush from Dias's kit and began to brush dust away from the frieze.

'You mean the Inquisition?'

'Shut up, Dias.'

'Oh great throne of Man...' Dias whimpered and slid down the wall onto his backside.

'Shut up, Dias.'

The brush was too fussy, too slow. Molotch upturned the xenoarcheologist's field kit and began to pick through the items that had spilled out onto the gritty chamber floor. He found the hand-flamer Boros Dias used for frying off lichen and algae.

It ignited with a single pump of the trigger, and Molotch wound the nozzle up to full. The flame was blue-hot. He ran it along the lines of the carving, frying out dust, blasting away loose matrix. The narrow chamber filled with the acrid stink of cooking stone.

'You'll damage the relic!' Boros Dias yelped, seeing what he was doing. 'It's priceless!'

'I know,' said Molotch, agreeing with both points. He burned away more dust and sand, heedless. 'How long would it take you to reveal the rest of this frieze, doctor?'

'A week...maybe two...'

'We don't have an hour.'

The flamer was no good against the thicker coverings of ancient rock that caked the base and upper left quadrant of the relief. Molotch snatched up a sample hammer and started chipping the layers of rock away with brutal strokes.

'Stop it! Molotch, stop it!' Boros Dias cried, getting to his feet. 'You're destroying–'

'Shut up, Dias,' Molotch said, cracking away more splinters with fierce, fluid blows.

'Sir, you pay me to advise you. You pay me well for my expert opinion. We have an understanding, a compact. I only agreed to join you because you said the excavation work would be done with rigorous attention to formal practice.'

'Shut up, Dias.'

'Molotch, you are brutalising the treasure of the past! You are vandalising the most important–'

Molotch turned, sweating and short of breath. He lowered the sample hammer. 'Doctor, you are completely correct. This is sacrilege, and I have contracted you at great expense to oversee this project in all formal particulars.'

'You have, sir,' Dias agreed. 'If we preserve the find, perhaps the Inquisition will take that into account.'

Molotch smiled. 'You really don't understand what the Inquisition means, do you, doctor?'

'I–' Boros Dias began.

'Doctor, I think it only fair that we conclude our professional arrangement here and now. Consider yourself freed of the terms of our contract.'

Boros Dias began to smile. Then his face melted, just as it had started to scream. His bared skull cracked like pottery and he fell onto his back.

Molotch dropped the hand-flamer. 'I never liked you,' he said to the smouldering corpse. Then he turned back to the relief and resumed his frantic attack. The smell in the chamber was now much, much worse.

He only had time left for another few savage blows. There was so much more hidden. Perhaps if he'd had a power drill...

He tossed away the hammer and located the portable brass picter from amongst the late doctor's overturned kit. Two or three wide angle shots of the whole, then a series of close-ups, one section at a time, with as much overlap as he could manage.

His thigh throbbed like hell.

Molotch tucked the picter into his bodyglove and squirmed his way out of the cleft.

NUNG WAS DEAD. Blood-loss from the ugly gunshot wound had finished him. He lay as he had fallen: propped up over one of the excavators. Nte-flies foamed around his face and the hole between his ribs.

Beyond the massive pillars, wretchedly thick black smoke boiled up from the direction of the camp, staining the bright, empty sky. Molotch could hear the distant chatter of exchanging gunfire.

Running as fast as he could in the heat, he followed the eastern path out of the cut of the cliff, away from the pillars, and into the emerald shade of the adult tubers. These were monsters: their trunks were five metres in diameter, their cups like basins, and their boughs and fleshy leaves arched up twenty metres. Poison-bees hummed around him as he ran. Viscous sap-pools splashed under his feet.

Only his most trusted – Kyband and Lynta – knew about the escape plan. Where they'd first made planet-fall, over to the west of the sites they'd hidden a way out. They'd done this even before they'd established the habi-camp.

His heart was racing. He knew it would take months to recover from this ordeal. But he pushed himself on.

At first, he missed the spot. Burned out and panicking, he fell down on his hands and knees and began to cry. Then his Cognitae-schooled intellect took over; the mind that encompassed noetic techniques, polished and refined by the great and abominated academy. He sat up, and breathed deeply to slow his panic. Then he methodically consulted his wrist-mounted locator. Over to the north, a hundred metres.

Molotch got up again and ran in that direction. Sunlight invaded the clearing where the drop flier sat. It was a handsome little thing, a Nymph model recon flier, removed surreptitiously from a Guard munitions depot in the Helican sub. It crouched on six long hydraulic legs, its wings folded back. It looked like a giant metal mosquito.

Molotch had left it under canvas. The camo-tarp was now heaped up on the mucky ground.

He stepped forward. Lynta appeared from behind the tail boom.

'Throne, you scared me,' said Molotch.

'I have that effect on most people,' she smiled. 'It's all gone to hell, hasn't it, Zygmunt?'

Molotch nodded. 'It has. But all is not lost. We can escape, you and me. This bird can get us clear. We'll fire up a beacon. Brice can send a shuttle down to meet us. We'll be gone before the fighting's over.'

She shrugged.

He popped the cockpit door and leaned in to fire up the engines. The vector fans began to whine into life.

'Thonius. Did you kill him?' he asked.

She replied, but he couldn't hear her over the mounting fan-chop.

'Thonius? I said, did you kill the bastard? Last I saw, you were deep in it.'

'That was all for show,' she said. She was pointing her snub-las at his face.

'Lynta?'

'Game's over, Molotch.'

'God-Emperor no!' he mumbled in dismay. 'I trusted you... you've been with me for nearly a year! Lynta! We even–'

'Yeah, I know. Makes me sick just to think of it. Drop the pulser.'

'Tell me this isn't true, Lynta...'

'My name isn't Lynta. It's not even Patience Kys, but that's how I'm known these days.'

'Patience Kys? But she's one of that bastard's–'

'Exactly. Toss the tau gun.'

The murder-hardness had not left her green, green eyes. He threw the long, square-ended xeno-weapon into the mud at his feet.

She gestured with the snub. 'Now kill the engines.'

With his gaze fixed on her, he reached over into the cockpit, keeping his hands visible, and took hold of the throttle.

And rammed it forward.

The engines screamed into max-thrust. They stripped wet, black flesh off the tubers around the clearing, blew a rippling crater in the ooze beneath the flier and threw Patience Kys onto her back.

The Nymph rose, wings unfolding, and wallowed sideways, crushing into the tuber stands and threshing them into mush with its veetol jets. Molotch clung on, and scrambled up into the cockpit, screaming out with the terrible effort. Twice, he nearly fell off.

He seized the controls and calmed the yawing flier. Las-shots bounced off the nose. Kys was on her feet below, blasting up at him. Molotch veered away and started to climb hard, leaving the traitorous bitch behind.

He circled over the black jungles and white scarps, getting his bearings. He slammed the canopy shut. The pall of smoke from the camp rose to the east.

'Brice! Brice! This is Molotch!' he shouted into his vox-link. 'I need evac now!'

The signal crackled. 'Understood. Five-eleven-three nine-six-four rendezvous lock. Make it fast!'

Molotch punched in the coordinates and slammed the flier west over the gloss-black rot-forests. He could do this. He *would* do this...

'Where you going, Zygmunt?' a voice suddenly crackled over his link. Molotch knew the voice. It belonged to Harlon Nayl, the most dangerous agent in his bastard-adversary's private cadre.

'Does it matter where I'm going, bounty hunter?' Molotch said, cueing the vox to 'send'. 'I don't see you being able to stop me now.'

'Oh, you know me, Zygmunt,' the voxed voice replied. 'You bring a blade, I bring a cannon... you bring a flier...'

Noiseless, arch-winged, ominous, a Valkyrie assault carrier rose from the forest before him, washing the canopy growth back in a wide, concentric ripple. It was dressed in black camo paint, its Imperial Guard insignia removed. Its chin-turret began to flash.

Molotch's Nymph lost a wing in a shower of splintering metal. It began to descend hard, auto-rotating. Multi-laser shots burst its belly and exploded its leg assemblies. The 'crash' alarm was blaring. Fire swirled up into the cockpit and roasted his legs.

Molotch screamed.

Then the first rocket struck home and blew off the flier's tail boom. More followed from the Valkyrie's under-wing pods, snaking out on curling spits of smoke. The Nymph came apart, burning, and dropped like a stone towards the inky forest cover, scattering casing fragments, engine parts and glass specks as it fell.

Zygmunt Molotch, ablaze from head to foot, was still alive when the hull finally met the ground.

A firestorm rushed out from the impact point, sucked back in again with the shockwave overpressure, and left a scorched circle ten hectares across in the undergrowth.

NOW

Local spring time, Petropolis, Eustis Majoris, 401.M41

TIRED, I MAKE myself comfortable. Not in any physical way. The sustain-field of my chair accommodates my rudimentary body-needs. I settle and adjust mentally, according to the psykana rituals.

A soft-edged trance allows me to open up. I can hear hectic noise from the ship around me, but I muffle it out. I am weary from the long voyage.

I concentrate. I resolve. I see nothing. I feel everything. Everything that makes up Eustis Majoris. Bloat-world, obese with cities. Filthy with a crust of dirt I can taste. It is like examining a putrefying corpse.

My fingertips feel contaminated already, though I have no fingers.

Eustis Majoris. It makes me gag. Old world. Rain-eaten world. Sub-sector capital. The smell of tar and slime and ouslite on its consumptive breath. The dry odour of trade, the stale stink of vice.

It is hard for me to bear. My gorge rises, my stomach turns.

I resolve. There is too much data, too many signals from too many lives. I have to focus. They are down there. My people, hard at work. I must not lose them.

Specifics. I look for specifics. I hunt for the glints of the wraithbone markers. I whisper through lives, from one to another, as if walking through the rooms of an endless mansion.

I am a courtesan called Matrie, beautiful but spurned by my lover-protector, dreaming of a rich, new patron. My skirts are heavy with lace.

I am a drunk called Tre Brogger, counting out change on a bar top to see if I can afford one more snifter of amasec.

I am a footpad without a name. I am running, out of breath. My estoc is slippery with blood. I think I belong to a clan, and I think the clan will be pleased with the pocket-chron and credit wafers I have just acquired.

I am a washerwoman, crying over the son I once gave away.

I am a hab super, dry heaving as I force entry to a stack apartment where flies fill the air. Three weeks since the old man was last seen. I will have to call the marshals. I might lose my job for this.

I am a bird. Free.

I am an administry clerk called Olyvier, tapping at the keys of my codifier, the screen reflecting green phantoms at my augmetic eyes. I have awful halitosis because of an abscess in my gum. I cannot afford the medicae fees unless I put in extra shifts all month. I have a scheduled break in one hundred and nineteen minutes.

I am a servitor, stacking boxes in a stock-house. I had a name once, but I have forgotten how to say it. It takes an effort just to remember to stack the boxes the right way up. The boxes have arrows on their sides.

I am a pardoner called Josev Gangs. I am waiting nervously for the court doors to open.

I am a rat, and I am gnawing. I am a rat.

I am a gamper called Benel Manoy, crouching under the shutters of a sink-shop, waiting for the rain to come and bring me business. I am nine. My gamp, furled, is taller than I am. It was my father's, when he carried the service. It needs new skinning, because it is sorely worn. The name on the gamp is still my father's. When I get it reskinned, I will have 'Benel Manoy' writ upon it.

I am a wherryman called Edrick Lutz, pulling on the oars of my skiff as I sing out for business. The water is murky and smells of piss. I was married once. I still miss her. The bitch. Where is all the trade today? The quays are empty.

I am a sheet-press worker called Aesa Hiveson. I am sound asleep in my one-room hab in the stacks of Formal K. The double-shift left me exhausted, so I fell asleep the moment I sat down. The feeble shower I intended to get under is still running. The water pipes are thumping and banging. They do not wake me. I am dreaming of a fine custard dessert I once tasted at a distant cousin's wedding. He was a wealthy man. I will not taste its like again.

I am a nurse in the Formal G medicae hall. Everything smells of contraseptic. The lights are too bright. I do not like the way the starchy uniform constricts my upper arms. It reminds me that my upper arms are too fat. The name on my badge is Elice Manser, but my real name is Febe Ecks. I have no qualifications. I lied to get this job. One day they will find me out. Until then, I intend to make the most of my unchallenged access to the post-partum hall. The cult pay well, especially for healthy babies.

I…

I am anonymous, gender uncertain, a very long time dead, undiscovered behind a false wall in Formal B. I am two girls in PDF youth uniforms, left in shallow graves in the north end flowerbeds of Stairtown Park, behind a row of acid-browned bushes. I am a man hanging from a rope in room 49/6 of a condemned hab-stack. I am the family of a girl who vanished on her way to lessons. I am a fab-worker who keeps pict-shots of young men in the same bureau drawer as a whetted combat knife. I am a rubricator, felled by a heart attack on my way home on a transit mag-lev. I am a tree that is withering in High Administratum Square.

I AM AN IMPERIAL inquisitor called Gideon Ravenor.

The realisation makes me start. I had almost lost sight of myself in the discordant psyk-noise. Slowly, out of the mass of fidgeting data, I lock down the signals. One at a time, each one is almost drowned out by the polyphony of living minds. It is like trying to single out a lone voice from a choir of ten billion.

Focus, Gideon. Focus…

There! There's Thonius. And Kys the telekine, too. Together, in a bustling commercial street, surface level, two vital life-beats in a mosaic of millions.

And there's Kara. Bright as a pulsar, shining up from deep in the sink levels. I feel her tense. Her heart rate accelerates. I smell the dining house around her. Oh shit, the god-damned ninker is going for it–

Lost her!

Too much, *too many*. The acid rain drenching the upper level streets burns my skin, though I have no skin. The sensation is delicious. I wish I could linger on it.

No time for that. I taste Nayl. Pure muscle and testosterone. Hugging the shadows of a deep, sink-stack slum.

And then…

What's this? Who's this? Beloved Emperor, this one hurts to touch. Hurts so very much…

From inside his head, I hear his name. Zael…

PART ONE

Burn City

ONE

He used his first flect the summer he turned eleven, but he'd seen them before. Seen the users too. Scrap-heads, burn outs, wasters. Then he found out just how crap life in the sink-stacks could get.

Four months before his eleventh birthday, the Departmento Munitorum shut down two fabricatories in the district. Nineteen thousand indentured workers were, in the Munitorum's words, 'decruited'. No reason was ever offered for the closures. But it was common knowledge that there was a trade slump right across the sub. Stories went round that new, automated plants had been opened in the northern-most zone: plants where a single servitor could perform the work of twenty indents without the need for sleep shifts. Other rumours said the fabs had lost a navy contract to manufactories on Caxton. Whatever, the work was gone. The fabs were shuttered up and boarded. Nineteen thousand able indents were hung out to rot.

Zael's parents had both died in a hivepox outbreak years before. He lived in the stacks with his granna and his sister, Nove. She was eighteen, a flat-frame rigger, and the family's only wage earner. Nove was one of those decruited.

It got hard, fast. Welfare and subsist tokens couldn't feed them. Zael was forced to cut scholam sessions to earn money, by doing errands for local traders. Some of them were less than clean. He never asked what was in the brownply carriers he delivered to scribbled addresses in the stacks. Meanwhile, granna killed her worries with the fumes from spent glue-wands that she gathered from the trash spills behind the hemming fab. And Nove looked for work.

She found none. But somewhere in the looking, she found flects. Zael didn't know how she paid for them. He got used to her glassy look and the vacant smile.

'Should try one, little,' she said once. He'd always been 'little brother', but now 'brother' seemed too much like an effort.

He'd come home after an errand job with a sweaty fold of notes in his pocket. Nove hadn't been expecting him back so soon. She started up from the little dinette table in the hab's tiny kitchen, and pushed something away under a grubby dish towel. Zael stood in the doorway, fascinated by the glint of whatever it was she was trying to hide.

Nove relaxed once she realised it was him. She'd been afraid it was the marshals, or a surprise knock from the ministorum temperance division. They'd been working the stacks in Formal J that week, going from door to door bearing pamphlets and disapproving expressions.

Zael stepped into the kitchen, forked the bills out of his pocket, and dropped them onto the rusty drainer.

'Good one, little,' Nove said. 'Good little little, working hard.'

Zael ignored her and looked for the last of the citrus-flavoured drink he'd hidden in their larder.

Nove had already found it and drunk it. He set a pan on the stove to boil water for a dehyd soup mix instead.

His sister slid the dishtowel back to reveal a small chunk of glass, irregular and no longer than a thumb. It lay in a crumpled sheet of pale red tissue paper.

He tried to look busy so she wouldn't notice him sneaking a glance. The water pinged in the pan as it boiled. The kitchen smelled of soured meat stock and granna's glue.

Nove smoothed out the edges of the tissue wrap and stared down into the sliver of dirty glass. She blinked, then shivered. Her lips were trembling. She rocked back against the chair rest, and put her hands flat on the tabletop.

That's when she said it. 'Should try one, little.'

'Why?' he asked.

'Makes everything seem better.'

The soup in the pan boiled over, and drowned the burner's flame. Zael had to twist the tap quickly to prevent the room from filling with escaped gas.

A WEEK LATER, Nove was dead. The marshals collected up her body, marked the scene, and hosed down the sink-alley. They said she'd fallen from an upper landing while under the influence of a proscribed substance. No one was ever able to explain why she'd landed face up. Backing away from something. People backed away when they were scared.

Eighteen storeys. Only the medicae mortus's report established which way up she'd been at impact.

YEARS OF WATCHING his granna inhale fumes from discarded wands, years of watching her sneeze up blood-stringed snot and piss herself in her armchair had made Zael damn sure he would never try her particular poison.

But there was something different about flects. They were just bits of glass. Little, grubby chunks of glass wrapped in pale red tissue. He saw dealers on dark block corners handing them over in exchange for cash. He'd heard of parties where a dozen eager users had shared the same, large pane.

The summer he turned eleven, he'd done a run for a local type called Riscoe. Nove had been dead three weeks. Riscoe, a bloater with his very own atmosphere of stale sweat stink, ruffled Zael's hair with fat salami fingers, and remarked he was clean out of bills. Did Zael want to wait for cash, or would he take a look as payment? Zael took the look. A tiny bundle of pale red tissue was fished out of Riscoe's coat and passed to him underhand, like a card sleight.

'Lose yourself,' Riscoe said. He hadn't meant 'go away'. It was just user advice.

Zael kept the flect in his pocket for eight days. Finally, one night, when his granna was unconscious, he went up to the stack-hab's deserted service level, unfolded the tissue, and looked.

And never looked back.

HE WAS TWELVE now. Or fourteen. He couldn't be sure, but he was certain it was an even number. He ran full time, and took his wages in flects – or money that he used for flects. Either way, it worked. The only recent memory that stood out was the removal of his granna's body by the Magistratum.

'How long has she been dead?' the Magistratum medicae asked him, pulling a gauze mask down from his grimacing mouth.

'My granna's dead?'

'Choked on her own vomit...' the medicae faltered. 'She's decomposing. Must have died weeks ago. Didn't you notice?'

Zael shrugged. He'd just scored a flect and wanted to use it. It itched in his pocket. These men and their questions were keeping him from it.

'Everything will be fine,' the man said, standing back as his colleagues wheeled a shapeless bodybag out through the kitchen onto the stack landing. He was trying to sound reassuring.

'I know,' Zael said.

ZAEL WAS LOOKING for a look when he saw the guy.

The guy was trying to blend, but he wasn't making it. Tough-looking knuck-head: tall, wide in the shoulder and heavy in the arms. He could almost have passed for one of the Stack clan's moody hammers – which he was clearly trying to do – except that he was a little too washed and his matt-black bodyglove was too new. Zael had been intending to score a flect from his usual dealer, a flat-brained tube addict called Isky who worked out of a stack hab on the lower northsink. But when he sussed the guy, he made new plans.

The guy followed him, all the way down through the stacks of Formal J to the river bridge. Zael loitered a while on the bridge's wrought iron walkway, gazing down at the polysty garbage bobbing in the murky water. A steam train rattled over the boxgirder elevation above him, strobing carriage lights down at the unlit river. Coal-tar vapour shrouded the walkway for a few seconds, and Zael took his chance to slip.

Two streets later, heading into the hab-stacks of Formal L, he spotted the guy again. No mistake. The matt black bodyglove, the shaved head, the dark goatee that hadn't been sink fashion for several seasons.

At Crossferry, Zael split west, hoping to shake. The guy was good. Really good. A double-back, a jink, and still he was there, hanging back.

Zael started to run. He ran back along Crossferry, through the stalls of the weekly cheap, and along a gloomy underpass below the triangle stacks. He turned to look back over his shoulder, and ran smack into an open hand.

The guy clamped him around the throat and pushed him back against the wall.

'You're a looker,' said the guy, his voice edged with an off-world accent. 'I was trying to make this easy on you, but you needled it. Your dealer. I want your dealer.'

'Screw you,' Zael said, laughing falsely.

The grip tightened, and wasn't even remotely funny any more.

'WHY D'YOU WANT my dealer so bad?' Zael asked when the guy let him go.

'Because.'

As if that explained everything.

'You a marshal?'

The guy shook his head.

'What then?'

'Worst thing you can imagine.'

Zael breathed hard. He was scared now. He got hassled every day in every way, but not like this. This guy wasn't a user looking for a dealer to rip off, and he wasn't a moody hammer out to fix the competition. He was hardcore. Zael wasn't about to lead him to Isky, but he knew he had to give this guy something actual. There were some other dealers he knew of, over in the Formal L stacks. He had no qualms about giving them up. It was his damn neck in the vice.

'You got a name?' Zael asked.

The man paused. 'Yours or mine?' he asked, as if speaking to an invisible person beside him. A pause. The guy nodded.

He turned to Zael.

'Call me Ravenor,' he said.

It started to rain. A brisk westerly had thickened the cloud cover over the district, and precipitation alarms fixed to the street posts began to bleat.

Carl Thonius didn't seem to hear them, so she pulled him by the elbow and gestured towards the cover of the tintglas walkway.

'I hate this frigging planet,' he said.

Two dozen centuries of dirty industry had poisoned the atmosphere of Eustis Majoris. Ninety per cent of the time, the immense city-state of Petropolis stewed under a roof of toxic stain cloud, its streets choked with hydrocarbon smog. Every now and then, the clouds burst and drenched the surface quarters with acid rain. The rain ate into everything: stone, tiles, brick, steel, skin. Epidermal cancer, a by-product of exposure to the rain, was the planet's second biggest killer behind pollutant-related emphysemas.

The moment the rain-burn alarms started to sound, gampers flocked out of alleyways and sink shops and began loudly offering their services to passers-by. Each one flamboyantly unfurled the long stemmed, telescoping umbrella he carried over his shoulder like a spear. Some gamps were treated paper, others steel-silk or plastek or cellulose. Almost all had been hand-painted in eye-catching ways and inscribed with details concerning hourly rates and the gamper's unimpeachable character.

The two off-worlders shooed them away and kept themselves under the walkway. They could hear the corrosive rain pattering on the tintglas, and sizzling on the open flags of the street.

Carl Thonius kept a linen handkerchief clamped coyly over his nose and mouth. He had soaked it in oil of osscil.

There had been a look of fastidious distaste on his face since the moment they had arrived on the surface.

'You look like a complete pussy,' Patience Kys told him, not for the first time.

'I don't know how you can begin to suffer this foul air,' he replied scornfully. 'Every breath brings a lungfull of pestilential filth. It is quite the most loathsome frigging arsehole of a planet I have ever known.'

Thonius was a man of unremarkable stature but remarkable poise. He stood or walked or sat just so – always with a perfect mix of elegance and composure. An ankle turned thus, an elbow crooked. He was dressed in a red velvet suit that screamed of good tailoring, with expensive, black buckle-shoes and white lace cuffs, and a mantle-slicker of oxidised grey plastek. He was twenty-nine years old, standard. His heavy blond hair was brushed back off his high forehead and he had dusted his face with white foundation. With the pasty pallor and the kerchief to his nose, he looked like a classical school statue – 'Gentleman about to sneeze'.

'Pussy,' she repeated. 'Reminds me of home.' Patience Kys had been born on Sameter in the Helican sub: another dirty, smoggy, deluged hab-stacked world. The Imperium was full of them.

They made an odd couple. The dandy and the vixen. Taller than him, athletically slender, she walked with an exaggeratedly casual roll that seemed to slide her along the pavement. Her chocolate-brown bodyglove was detailed with scales of silver and left nothing to the imagination except the risks involved. Her black hair was coiled up in a tight chignon secured by two long silver pins, and her face was pale and angular. Her eyes were green.

'Lost him,' she admitted.

Thonius glanced at her and cocked a plucked eyebrow. 'The blue one,' he said.

'And how can you tell?'

The walkway and street before them was a bobbing sea of gamps in the downpour. In the midst of them, a blue one stood out.

'No markings. No inscriptions or hourly rates. He's rich. He doesn't use a public gamper. He has his own man.'

'The stuff you know...' she mocked. 'Though you're still a pussy.'

Thonius snorted, but he didn't deny it. Anyone shy of an Adeptus Astartes in full Terminator plate was a pussy compared to Patience Kys.

They moved through the midday crowd, following the blue shade. It was morbidly fascinating to see how many pedestrians around them had skin burns. Some old and faded, some raw and new. Some - and Carl Thonius pressed his fragrant kerchief tighter still - no longer burns, but discolouring into lethal melanomas. The received remedy was faith paper. You could buy it from street corner vendors and stalls in the sink-shop arcades. Tissue-thin and gummed, it had been blessed by various ecclesiarchy somebodies and infused with palliative serums like thistle, milkroot and flodroxil. You cut it to shape - usually into little patches - moistened it, and stuck it to your rain-burns. Faith, and the God-Emperor of Mankind, did the rest. The civilians around them were speckled with faith paper patches. One old man had his entire neck and forehead wrapped in it, like papier-mâché.

A whirring sound passed over them through the lethal rainfall. Kys looked up in time to see a flock of birds turn overhead and dart as one up into the high reaches of a city spire, hazed by the drizzle.

'How do they live?' she wondered aloud.

'They don't,' said Thonius.

She didn't know what he meant, but she didn't care. It was too miserable for a Carl Thonius lecture.

At the crossroads on Lesper Street, the blue gamp turned left and bobbled away down the wide boulevard of St Germanicus into the ceramicists' quarter. The rain continued to hiss down.

'Where's he going now?' she muttered.

'It's his only vice. He collects klaylware.'

'Not his only vice,' she ventured.

Thonius nodded. 'The only one he admits to.'

Under iron awnings and heavy jalousie blinds, the artisans and dealers of the quarter had set out their wares on wooden stalls. Blue gamp lingered around those that displayed bowls and vases of a fat-lipped, heavy style, with rich earthy colours and gleaming glazes.

'They say he has the finest collection of antique klaylware in Formal B,' Thonius said.

'You say that like it's something to be proud of. Or even something that makes sense,' Kys said. 'I'm getting bored, Carl. Let's slam him.'

'No. We'll never get his guard down if we push him. He's far too clever for that.'

'His orientation is hetero, isn't it?'

Thonius paused and looked at her. 'That's what the briefing notes said. Why?'

She pulled him by the arm and fast-walked him until they were well ahead of the blue gamp. It was hesitating around another pot-monger's storefront.

'Kys? What are–'

'Shut up. He'll be here in a few minutes.' She gestured to the ceramics display of the shop nearby. 'This place any good?'

'I… uh… yes, I think so. Some fine quality pieces from the late third era.'

'Pick me something.'

'What?'

'You know this stuff. Because you're a pussy. Now pick me something. The choicest thing they have.'

UMBERTO SONSAL, SECOND director of the Engine Imperial manufactory in Formal B, was an unpleasantly portly man with soft, full lips and lidless eyes. The rain alarms had stopped – the downpour had abated – and as he approached the ceramics shop he adjusted the dial of his signet ring. The anti-acid scales that had loricated his skin retracted into the slit pockets behind his ears and under his eyebrows. His personal gamper furled the wide blue rain-shield.

Sonsal dabbed his forehead with a lace handkerchief and wandered in between the rows of shelves, occasionally pausing to lift and examine a particular piece. His assistant, his shader and his two bodyguards waited in the doorway of the shop.

The dish on the third shelf was particularly exquisite. No more than late third, perfect in all dimensions, and with a sought-after crackling to the glaze. He was about to reach in and lift it up, when a hand came and scooped it away.

'Oh, so beautiful,' murmured the girl as she held the piece up to the light.

'It is,' he said, his voice a rich whisper.

'I'm sorry. Were you about to look at it?' she asked.

She was stunning. Her eyes so green, her slender form so striking, her love of klaylware so evident.

'Be my guest,' Sonsal said.

She turned the piece expertly in her hands, noting the maker's stamp on the base, and the little disc of paste-paper showing the import serial.

'Late third?' she mused, casting a glance at him.

'Indeed.'

'And the stamp. It looks like Nooks Workshop, but I think in fact it might be Solobess, before Nooks bought him out.'

She held the piece out to him. He patted his fat lips and blinked. 'I would concur. You know your ware.'

'Oh no!' she said hastily, smiling an intoxicatingly fleeting smile. 'Not really. I just... I just like what I like.'

'You have extraordinary taste... Miss?'

'Patience Kys.'

'My name is Sonsal, but I would be pleased if you called me Umberto. Patience, your eye is excellent. Will you purchase the item? I recommend you do.'

'I'm afraid I can't stretch to something like this. Really, Umberto, my dabbling is confined to appreciation for the most part. I have a few pieces, but I seldom have the capital to buy.'

'I understand. Does anything else take your eye?'

+THONIUS!+

The call-thought hit him between the eyes like a flung brick. He was on the other side of the street, observing from the awning-covered shop front of a faith paper vendor. Fuming water from the seared roofs shuddered down the old, iron gutter pipes nearby. Thonius cranked up the magnification of his pocket scope.

+Quickly now. Something good!+

'Are you seeing this?' Thonius asked. He received an assurance, far softer and quieter than Kys's crude mind-jab.

'Suggestions?' Thonius said.

He listened to the reply and then said, 'Just to your left, the wide-mouthed urn. No, Kys, your other left. There. The brown one. It's early fourth, but the maker's a good one. Marladeki. It's favourable because the proportions are especially good, and Marladeki died young, so his output wasn't huge.'

+How young?+

'I'll ask. How young? Uh huh. Patience... he died at twenty-nine. Made mainly bowls. An urn is rare.'

+The stuff you know. Okay.+

'THIS IS NICE,' Kys said, stroking her hand around the rim of a tall wine flask that had been finished with an almost treacle-black glaze. 'But this...'

She feigned a sigh as she picked up the wide-mouthed urn ever so gently. 'Glory, this is a fine piece. Early fourth, I'd say... but what do I know?'

Sonsal took it from her, his eyes as much on her as the urn. 'You know plenty, my dear. Early fourth. Who is the maker now? I can't quite make out the stamp...'

Sonsal fixed a delicate jeweller's lens to his right eye and examined the urn's base.

Kys shrugged. 'It couldn't possibly be Marladeki, could it? I mean... he made so few objects that weren't bowls.'

Sonsal put his eyepiece away and turned the urn over in his hands.

'It is,' he said, softly.

'No!'

'By the God-Emperor, Patience, I've been looking for a piece like this for years! I'd have passed it over as a fake but for you.'

'Oh, come now,' she said with a diffident shrug. The man was loathsome. It was damn hard to remain civil, let alone play the part.

'I must have it,' Sonsal said, then glanced at her. 'Unless you...?'

'Far and away out of my price range, Umberto,' she demurred.

Sonsal held the piece up and the storekeeper hurried forward to take it, wrap it and write out the bill of sale.

'I am indebted to you, Patience,' Sonsal said.

'Don't be silly, Umberto.'

'Would you... would you do me the pleasure of being my guest for dinner this evening?'

'I couldn't possibly–'

'I insist. To celebrate this acquisition. Really, Patience, it's the least I could do to acknowledge its finder... and how could you be so cruel as to deprive me of a supper with a woman of such extraordinary good taste?'

'Umberto, you really are too sweet.'

'BY THE THRONE, he's disgusting,' Thonius muttered. 'Great golden throne, you're such a whore, Kys.'

+Shut up, pussy.+

'Just be careful, Patience. Just be careful.'

THE RAIN-BURN ALARMS had begun to sing again. As Sonsal's party moved away up the street, his gamper opened the blue umbrella and Sonsal and Patience sheltered beneath it together.

'Yes, I'm watching them,' Thonius said tartly, in response to the nudge in his head. He was tailing the blue gamp. 'I'll stay with her, don't worry. If Kara or Nayl are free maybe–'

Nudge.

'Oh, both of them busy? Very well. I can handle this. Yes, I can handle this. I said so, didn't I?'

Nudge.

'Good. Relax, Ravenor. I am ever your servant.'

GOD DAMNED NINKER was going for it.

The reach into the jacket. Always a giveaway. What had he got? A snub? A slide-away? A frigging bolter?

Kara Swole didn't wait around to find out. She turned a back flip and let a hand-spring carry her over the brushed-steel service counter.

Shots slammed into the heated racks above her, throwing trays of braised meat and steamed veg-mash into the air. Wax jars of preserved fish and pickled cabbage burst and sprayed their noxious contents down the rear of the counter. Someone was screaming. Probably the waitress with the stupendous rack, Kara decided. Let her scream. She had the lungs for it, evidently.

Kara ran along on all fours, quick as a felid, and popped the top three buttons of her waistcoat, allowing access to the shoulder rig she was wearing. The flatnose Tronvasse compact virtually fell out into her waiting hand. At the end of the service counter, she sat down on her bottom, her back to the warm steel, and racked the gun's slide.

The shooting had ceased for a second. All she could hear were the yells and howls of the patrons flooding for the exits.

'Where is he?' she whispered, testily.

+Five metres to your left, coming forward. A sense of high anxiety about him.+

'No crap. He's just drawn down on me. High anxiety doesn't even begin to cover it.'

+Please be careful. It would be expensive to replace you.+

'You're all heart.'

+I was about to add... we don't want the trouble. Not here. Too many complications. Can you defuse?+

'Defuse?'

+Yes.+

'A maniac with a gun?'

+Yes.+

'Let's see...'

She raised her head slightly. Two more shots nearly scalped her as they came whining over the counter top.

'That's a no.'

+Um.+

'Look, I can try. Let me see, would you?'

+Close your eyes.+

Kara Swole shut her eyes. After a moment, a clear, slightly fish-eyed vision appeared to her. The service parlour of a dingy public dining house, as seen from somewhere up near the ceiling vents. Every few seconds the view blinked and jumped momentarily, like a badly formatted pict-track. She saw the tables and chairs lying where they had been overturned in the stampede, the litter of broken crockery and food bowls. There was the counter, its greasy surface gleaming under the hood-lamps. Behind it, in cover, a short, heavily muscled girl in soft gymnast slippers, gorgeous japanagar silk harem pants and a sleeveless leather waistcoat. She was holding a compact auto tight to her splendid cleavage. Under the fringe of her short bleached hair, her pretty eyes were closed tight.

Never liked the bleached look. Must go back to my natural red.

+Concentrate. That's not helping+

'Sorry.'

And there was the ninker. Other side of the counter, edging round towards the far end. The extended magazine projecting down from the pistol grip of his auto was so long, it looked like he was holding a T-square by the top of the rule.

+Apart from anxiety, I can't assess anything. He's smoked obscura some time in the last thirty-five minutes. It's blocking everything.+

'So he's not likely to fold if I get a good drop on him?'

+Unlikely, I'd say.+

Kara took a deep, pulse-calming breath, her nose filling with the pungent aromas of spilled food and stewed caffeine. Then she snapped upright, aiming the Tronsvasse compact at the ninker.

Who was no longer there.

'Where the frig–?'

+He has, I believe, fled. Rabbited, to use your term.+

A sprung service door behind the counter was gently flapping to and fro. Kara ran to it, keeping the auto at full extension in front of her – the trademark 'ready' position of armed marshals. Kara Swole had never been in the Departmento Magistratum, but a hardnut chastener, name of Fischig, had taught her the skills some years back.

She eased open the swing door. Beyond it was a gloomy little walkway with a sloped, worn lino floor. Crates of freeze-dried noodle bricks and tubs of mechanically recovered cooking fat were stacked along both walls. A hot, bilious stench drifted up from the kitchens below.

The establishment was called Lepton's, one of a chain of family-run public dining houses in the Formal D district of Petropolis. Like all the independent bars and eateries, it was in the sinks. Eighty levels of habs and manufactories weighed down upon it and neither the wan sunlight nor the burn-rain ever penetrated this deep. Only the grim, Munitorum-subsidised canteens could afford higher-level positions on or near the surface streetways. All of the public places were open round the clock, and catered for the constant shift-work. People came to eat breakfast at tables beside other workers chowing supper and getting addled on cheap grain liq at the end of a hard shift. Down here it was a dark world of artificial lighting, metal decks, flakboard walls and an indelible layer of grease that coated everything.

Kara ran down into the kitchen. Heedless servitors laboured at bulk skillets or broiling vats, and there was a constant clatter of utensil limbs. The air was thick with steam and food smoke, trapped and stirred by vent extractors that had ceased to function properly generations before. The handful of actual humans working the food line were just emerging up from hiding places behind coolers and workstations. They all jumped back into hiding in terror at the sight of another armed body passing through their infernal realm.

'Where did he go?' she demanded of a terrified undercook who was trying to hide himself behind the frying pan he was clutching. He mumbled something unintelligible.

'Where?' she snarled again, and put a round through a nearby fryer for emphasis. Scalding fat began to leak and spurt out of the puncture hole.

'The loading ramp!' the undercook meeped.

She left the kitchen area and hurried into a broad corridor where the mesh decking was mounted with a trackway for narrow gauge carts. On either side were walk-in larders, bottle stores, hanging pantries and – distressingly – an overflowing employees-only latrine that proved to be the real source of the kitchen's underlying smell.

The hatch at the end was open. Cool air gusted up at her. She slid flat to the wall for the last few metres.

The loading ramp was a battered metal platform jutting out from the hatch over a dank, rockcrete chamber. Access tunnels, large enough to take carts and freight vehicles, ran off to left and right, lit by pulsing amber lumo-panels. Overhead, dirty air, dripping acid-water and the faintest daylight filtered down through a vent shaft that went right up to the surface levels. Huge, corroded airmills grated around in the shaft.

Kara went to the platform rail and leaned over in time to see her quarry disappearing up the left hand tunnel. She leapt down and ran after him.

By the time they came out into an alleyway, fumed by the yellow light of sodium lamps and crowded with trash-crates, she had closed the distance between them. He looked back, saw her coming, thought about trying to fire in her direction, but ran again.

'Halt!' she yelled.

He didn't.

Kara dropped down on one knee, aimed, and fired the auto from a braced double-handed grip. The single shot punched through the back of his left thigh and he fell sideways, awkwardly. He hit the face of a trash-crate so hard that he dented the scruffy sheet metal.

He was sobbing as she dragged him upright and threw him against the crate again.

'That was downright rude. I wanted to have a little talk with you,' she said. 'Let's start again.'

He moaned something about his leg.

'I'll try not to make that worse. I want to talk to you about Lumble.'

'I don't know any Lumble.'

She kicked him in the thigh-muscle above the bullet hole and made him squeal.

'Yeah, you do. You were happy to talk about Lumble and his business to those pals of yours in the public.'

'You must have misheard.'

'I didn't hear at all, chump. I read your mind. Lumble. He's the man. You want it, he can get it. Good price too. Grinweed. Yellodes. Baby blues. Looks. He can sort the lot.'

'I don't know! I don't know!'

'You don't know what?'

'I don't know what you want!'

+Kara.+

'Not now. Chump, you so know what I want.'

'I don't!'

+Kara.+

'Not now. Listen, you little ninker, I want an intro. I want an intro to Lumble. I want a serious in with the man.'

'That could be arranged,' said a voice from behind her.

Kara let the wretch go and he slid down the crate side, weeping. There were six big friggers in the alley behind her, all leather smocks and studded jackets and vat-grown muscle enhancements. The leader had acid-burns across his face, tracing out deliberate designs in scar tissue. Clansters. Moody hammers. Stack muscle.

'You might have warned me...'

+I tried.+

'Help you, gentlemembers?' she asked, flashing a grin.

They all smiled back. Their teeth were filthy reefs of steel dental implants and craggy amalgam. Several had lip piercings or secondary teeth woven into their tongue tips.

'Well, aren't I just the frigged one here?' she said. She did a rapid risk-assess. Two had slingblades, two had long-handled industrial mallets and one, the leader, had a chain-fist. It buzzed menacingly as the oiled blade-tracks idled.

She had her auto and her wits. It was even odds in her book.

+It is not even odds, Kara. Do not try it. We will devise another way out of this.+

'Yeah? Like what?' she snapped sarcastically.

'Who you talking to, knuck-bitch?' the leader asked.

'The voices in my head,' she replied, hoping that at least might give them pause. Even in a town as grievously messed-up as Petropolis, folks didn't like to tangle with the psyk-touched or the demented.

She head-calced that her best starting gambit was to sort the leader with her auto. That would open an account and remove the chain-fist from the equation. From there, it would be a matter of improvisation.

It would have worked too. But as she brought the auto up, the frig-damned ninker on the ground behind her kicked her hard with his good leg and she fumbled forward. One of the work-mallets came down nasty-fast and smashed her gun away into the gutter.

+Kara!+

Somehow she dodged the chain-fist. It scythed a hole through the trash-crate behind her. She jab-punched at the leader's ribs and felt something give as she dived through, but a slingblade ripped a long cut in the baggy flare of her favourite harem pants. Then a mallet caught her a glancing blow across the left shoulder and she stumbled over onto the gritty rockcrete.

'Shit! Shit! You gotta ware me! You gotta ware me right now!'

+The distance is too–+

'Screw the distance! I'm dead meat unless you ware me!'

He obliged. She knew he hated it. She knew she hated it. But there were times when only it would do. The little wraithbone pendant around her neck crackled, and lit up with psyk-light. She convulsed as he took hold and everything that made up Kara Swole – her mind, her personality, her memories, her hopes and desires – folded up and went away into a little dark box made of solid oblivion.

Kara Swole's body, blank-eyed, leapt up from prone by arching its back. It deflected a mallet-swing with an under-turned hand, and then side-kicked one of the slingbladers in the chest so hard his sternum snapped like a dry branch.

The sling-blade flew up out of his limp hand, spinning in the air. Kara Swole's left palm lunged out to connect with it – not to catch it but to slap it away, altering its trajectory and greatly increasing its momentum. A clanster dropped his mallet with a thump, and groped up to feel the brand new piercing in his forehead. Then he fell over onto his back.

Straight-legged, bottom out, Kara Swole's body bowed low to avoid a swing from the other mallet, and then it leapt up, spinning horizontally in the air, and delivered a kick with both feet to the face of the mallet wielder.

She landed on her feet, grabbed the other slingblader by the lower jaw, her fingers gripping inside his mouth, and threw him right over onto his back. A back-stamp with her left heel crushed his windpipe. The leader came in, chain-fist shrilling. One of the abandoned mallets was now turning in her hands. She swung it out so the head of it met the punching glove-weapon coming the other way. The mallet-head was completely abraded away in seconds, but it was a duracite tip, and eating it up burned out the drivers of the chain-fist's mechanism. Smoke gusted out of the seized device. Kara Swole's body jammed the splintered end of the mallet-haft into the leader's chest with both hands.

Surrounded by the bodies of the dead and crippled, Kara's own form began to shudder and shake. It dropped down onto its knees, gasping.

Fierce spotlight beams framed it abruptly. Her eyes didn't react to the light.

'Magistratum! Magistratum! Don't make another move or we shoot!'

Pinned in the spotlights, Kara's hands slowly rose in a gesture of surrender.

Armoured and ominous, belligerent figures swept into the light around her, handguns aimed, power-mauls raised.

'On your face! Down! On your face!'

'I have authority,' Kara Swole's voice said, though it wasn't her own voice at all.

'You do, huh?' crackled one of the Magistratum troopers through his visor-mic. 'What kind of frigging authority explains this?'

Her face, blank-eyed and expressionless, turned up towards him. 'The authority of the Ordo Xenos, officer. This is an officially sanctioned operation and I am Inquisitor Gideon Ravenor. Please think very carefully about what you do next.'

TWO

ACCORDING TO ZAEL, there was a good place down at the south end of Formal L, on the overfloat. Genevieve X ran all the serious business on the overfloat, mostly from semi-legit fronts, but there was a place you could go if you wanted to see her yourself.

Zael had never been there in person. He'd never met Genny X nor, as far as he knew, done business with her clan, but it sounded like the sort of big deal the guy was looking for. At first, Zael had thought of taking the guy to one of the smaller dealers in L, but he didn't see that ending happily for him or the dealers. That's when he'd got 'The Plan'.

He was witchy for a look now, shaking a lot, and that made his brain rat-sharp and nasty. The plan was a nice one. No one, not even a big knuck-head like this guy, came down Genny X's place looking for mood. Zael would lead him down there and let the X's hammers do the rest. According to the Plan, Zael would slip away during the mayhem or – and this was where the Plan got clever – he'd make such an impression with Genny X for selling out the guy to her, she'd be grateful and generous. Maybe give him a freebie look, maybe even offer him a job. Shit, wouldn't that be a step up? Even if Genny X wanted him to be her new gamper, that was prestige. Hanging with the X. That put him stacks away from running for the likes of Riscoe and flat-brain Isky.

Zael was so bloody pleased with the Plan, he had to remember to keep a smile off his face.

You COULD SMELL the overfloat long before you reached it. Waste outfalls, garbage slicks, estuary mud, all burned by the rain. It was always low tide under the overfloat.

Sometime way back in the whenever – history was not Zael's thing – Petropolis had outgrown the patch of land it had originally sat down on. It had spread, like a fat arse on a bar stool. Up in the north, in Stairtown, it had invaded the hills. In the south, it had bulged out over the river bay. Originally, stone piers had been built out into the estuarine flats and over the water, their wide bases sunk deep into the ooze by the guild masonae. Then, as demand grew for cheap habs, elevated prefab sections had been constructed between the radiating piers, creating a whole city slum-quarter, forty storeys deep, suspended twenty metres above the silt and water.

It was always sick-damp in the overfloat. Moss grew rampant on every surface, and you were never far from the sound of gurgling bilges. Deep below, railed hatchways led down through the sink-bottom decks into the gloom of the water level, where you could hire cab-boats and wherries to get you from point to point under the slum.

The rain alarms were ringing by the time they got down to the rotting boardwalks of the overfloat, but that didn't matter much because most of the surface streets there were covered over with pitched storm-roofs. In winter season, the overfloat got the worst of the ocean gales.

'Lovely part of town,' the guy said, in a funny, mannered way. Zael decided the guy was being sarky and meant 'this town is so knuck-nasty it hasn't even got a lovely part, but even by its own low standards this is bad.' Typical snooty off-worlder. By then, that's what Zael had decided the guy definitely was. An off-worlder. The name was a dead-give away. 'Ravenor'. Shit! Why not just call yourself 'Imperial aristo from a much richer planet than this' and have done with it?

They wandered down the upmost deck of the Nace Street sink, past the stalls of the jettison-sellers and the drift merchants. Tide-treasure was on offer all around, most of it stinking and caked with black ooze. You could choose yourself a bargain, or – for a few coins extra – get the vendor to hose the thing off with his spigot for a better look. They passed a couple of mech-riggers examining a cylinder block as the vendor's hose spattered the mud away onto the deck. Another merchant was offering IDs, pocket-watches, dentures, tie-pins and buckles, all of them cleaned up and laid out on a box cart. Quality merchandise that, dredged up from the down-below.

'People throw the strangest stuff away,' Zael commented, with a nod to the cart.

The guy said nothing. Just a shrug. Zael knew the guy was down enough to recognise that IDs and dental plates didn't end up in the silt under the overfloat by accident. The thick mudwater down there in the dark was a useful disposal facility for clansters and footpads.

An ecclesiarchy preacher was haranguing the world from a push-pulpit on a street-corner, informing the passing crowds that their souls would corrupt and die unless they mended their ways and followed the light of the

God-Emperor. No one was paying him much notice. Maybe it was his metaphor that was at fault. On Eustis Majoris, exposure to the sky did not equal redemption. It equalled faith paper, weeping sores and premature mortality.

On the next street, between the stalls of two more flotsam-sellers, an old woman was tending wooden cages. The sign above her stall asked for charitable donations towards the upkeep and preservation of sheen birds. The things in the cages ranged from the size of a crow to the size of a piphatch, and all of them looked weak and sickly, if not dead. Plumage had been torn or broken off, or eaten away, and eyes and limbs lost. Metal was exposed in many places, delicate wired mechanisms succumbing to rust and acid-gnaw.

'A coin for the poor birds, sir?' she called out to the guy as they went past. 'Just a coin for the poor birds is all I ask.' She wore a plastek smock and had a mag-lens taped over one eye. On the bench in front of her, a sheen bird was stretched out and pinned down for cleaning in the manner of an anatomical study. Its neck filaments buzzed as its head jerked around, and it piped piteously out of its tiny metal beak. Another bird, much larger and totally devoid of implanted feathers, perched on her shoulder. It was quite a splendid thing, its wing blades and chassis polished chrome.

The guy ignored her and shoved Zael onwards.

THEY WALKED DOWN the stairs to the sink-base crossroads at Wherry Dock. Thirty-six levels of stack towered above them.

'Where now?'

Zael gestured.

'You sure? I'm having trouble believing anyone of clout could be found in this part of town. This better not be your idea of a trap.'

Zael flinched. Was the guy on to him? Had he cottoned on to the Plan?

'Honestly,' Zael said, trying to sound credible. 'There are some class places. Genevieve X's place is in one of the piers. Old money. Trust me.'

'Trust you?' The guy laughed. A nasty, grown-up laugh. 'How old are you?'

'Eighteen standard,' Zael said.

'Try again,' the guy snorted.

Zael didn't say anything. He didn't want to admit that, at some point since his eleventh birthday, he'd forgotten how old he really was.

GENNY'S PLACE WAS a six-storey mansion rising from the centre span of one of the old pier vaults, deep in the under-sink darkness. Even though the walls were dank and mossy, by the light of the deck lamps it looked impressive, and this seemed to silence the guy's doubts. If there was any class at all on the lower overfloat, it would be here.

'She's the deal-engine this side of town,' Zael said confidently. 'They say she has links high up in the Munitorum.'

'That so?'

'Uh huh. A little backhand lolly every month and she can fix any colour of favour you want. Ident wipes, fake papers, travel permits.'

'I'm surprised the entire population hasn't come to her then,' said the guy, doing his insufferable sarky thing again.

'She...' Zael began, and then checked himself. His enthusiasm to whet the guy's appetite had almost made him say the first thing everybody said about Genny X. That she had so much moody hammer weight watching her action she was best avoided. Now, saying that would ruin the Plan.

'She what?'

'She deals,' Zael improvised. 'Looks especially. That's what you want, isn't it? Looks?'

'That's the idea.'

'Okay, then. We go round to the side door, and I'll make an introduction. Then we–'

'Exactly how stupid do you think I am?'

'What?'

'I'm not going to walk in through the front door – or the side door – and let you do the talking, just like that. You think I got this old not knowing how to stay alive?'

'Then what?' asked Zael, feeling the Plan slipping away out of his fingers.

'I have a plan,' the guy said, which was exactly what Zael had been afraid of.

On the second hard knock, the door opened. It was a simple but hefty wooden door, and it swung in on a mechanical bracket. The real door was the shimmering void-field behind it. Through the glitter of the energy screen, Zael could see a moody hammer glaring out at them. The man was big, his face-flesh decorated with acid-burned motifs and metal studs. South Overfloat Shades, by the concentric pattern.

'What?' the hammer asked.

'Got a bit of business,' said the guy.

'With who?'

'With the X.'

'Concerning?'

The guy nodded down at Zael. He had Zael locked in a double arm-clamp. Zael's eyes must have looked terrified enough as it was, but the guy gave his locked arms a painful little wrench and he squeaked for good measure.

'This piece of knuck,' the guy said.

Frig-damn me, Emperor, this was so not the Plan.

'Not interested,' the hammer said, and started to wind the mechanism that closed the outer door.

'Okay. I'll just let him get on with what he was doing. Hell, I'll even show him to the Officio Inquisitorus myself. That's in Formal A, isn't it?'

The hammer stopped. 'What's the frigging Inquisition got to do with anything?'

'That's something I'll discuss with the X and not her porter.'

The hammer drew a grease-black pivot-gun from his belt and then turned his head and shouted something away into the darkness behind him.

The void-field crackled and died. The hammer waved them in with the snout of his pivot-gun.

Just before they stepped into the dark hall, Zael heard something. Three words.

+Be careful, Nayl.+

'What?' Zael asked the guy.

'I didn't say anything.'

THE ENTRY WALK into the pier tower was long and dark. The air was humid. Stinking like cattle, eight massive moody hammers – three South Overfloat Shades and five East K stackers – moved in around them as escort. They didn't bother to frisk the guy. After all, what was he going to do?

A hatchway ahead, beyond it a translucent pool of green light. The hammers led them into an anteroom and vanished. It was super-cool in there. Huge chrome vents crafted into the wall decoration pumped clean air in and stale air out. The floor was polished jet, inlaid with repeat fish patterns, and the high arched roof was lit by electro-lamps with turquoise shades. This was serious good living, the first Zael had ever tasted. It seemed a shame he was getting this first good taste at the same time as a shoulder-crunching, elbow-breaking arm-clamp.

'Could you let me go now?' he asked.

'No.'

The guy looked around. Three tall, arched doors, all closed, led off the anteroom, besides the hatch behind them that had let them in.

+Three heartbeats, closing from the left.+

'What?' Zael asked.

'What what?'

'You said something about heartbeats–'

'I didn't. Shut up.'

The left hand door opened. A man wandered in, flanked by two more bulky hammers who took up sentry positions either side of the doorway. They were both Shades – senior members, by the pattern of their ritual-inflicted acid tattoos – and both held wire-stocked lasrifles.

Zael had never seen a lasrifle before. He blinked his fear away. The man was far more terrifying.

He was over two and a half metres tall and extremely thin. Not even stick-thin like Jibby Narrows, who everyone said could get good money working part time as a noodle. This freak was emaciated-thin. He wore a beautiful housecoat of vitrian glass, floor-length, and his arms hung from the sleeves like twigs. Twigs coated in gold foil, that was. His head was a skull with the merest hint of skin. His eyes were augmetic plugs; sutured in, multi-facet insect jobs. He smelled really good – a classy cologne or maybe even a flesh-wired pheromone aura. He didn't walk. He hovered.

Pausing under the green lamps, he turned his reed-thin neck and regarded Zael and the guy.

'What is the nature of your business?' he asked. His words had sound and meaning, but absolutely no flavour to them.

'Who's asking?' said the guy.

'I am Taper. I am the Mamsel Genevieve's seneschal.'

The guy hunched his shoulders, diffidently. 'What we have here is an organ grinder/primate situation. Go fetch the X.'

'I think not. You are very good at this whole, rugged machismo thing, but you really don't understand the layers of protocol. The X doesn't want to have to talk to you. The X doesn't even want to have to deal with you. Mamsel pays me a great deal of money to process matters for her. I am her eyes and ears. I decide what she will or won't review. Do you understand?'

'Maybe,' said the guy. 'What if I act up and start throwing my weight around?'

Taper smiled. He hovered over to his waiting hammers, and held out a bony hand. One of them obediently drew a gang knife and put it into Taper's palm.

Taper turned and snapped the blade. He didn't even use both frigging hands. He simply snapped the twenty-centimetre steel with a flick of his twig fingers.

'I am significantly augmetic, my friend. I chose to be elegant and slender because I despise obvious physical threat-postures. A massive torso, thick arms, a shaven head... such as yours, for instance. But I did not stint on strength. I could poke your bastard heart out with my tongue.'

'I see,' said the guy.

'I think you do. Now. Explain the nature of your business. To me.'

The guy relaxed his grip on Zael and stepped forward, suddenly modest and unassuming. 'Look, Sire Taper, sir,' he said. 'I'm a newbie to this world. Just got in a few days back, pulled the long haul from Caxton.'

'And I should care why?'

'I've got the slam in me. I can work and make action. I'm looking to get employment, but this frigging city is all sewn up by the clans.'

'It is. So go elsewhere.'

'Easy said. I can't afford another out-ticket, not even a freezer bin. So I decided I needed to prove to the great and good here that I was worth having around. Worth having on the payroll.'

Taper slowly tilted his head and stared at Zael. 'And you thought this would somehow impress us?'

The guy looked round at Zael too. 'Well, not to look at, I grant you. But I got wind of what this little knuck-head was up to.'

'And what was that exactly?'

'I wasn't doing nothing!' Zael exclaimed.

'Shut it,' the guy told him. 'This little knuck was out to make his mark. He was out to make his big splash. One way or another he knew about Genny X, and he had decided the Inquisition might pay well for the inside track.'

'I frigging didn't!' Zael yelled. 'For knuck's sake, he's making this up!'

'He would say that,' said the guy, grinning in a mean way.

'I suppose he would,' agreed Taper.

Knuck's sake, they were all pals together now.

Taper looked at the guy. 'So what did you have in mind?'

The guy shrugged. 'I brought him to you. I made it easy for you, before the Inquisition got a sniff. I covered your arses. I thought you might look on that kindly and give me a job.'

'What kind of job?' Taper inquired.

'A hammer action. A body job. I can do plenty.'

Taper looked the guy up and down. 'I see. How very enterprising of you.'

'So? You'll give me a place? Put a word in with the X?'

Taper shrugged. 'Let me get this straight. You've brought a fink to me in the hope that in return I might reward you with a job. I could just waste the fink here and give you that job. Or I could waste both of you and spare myself the effort.'

'I guess...'

'I like economy of effort. I favour the latter.'

Taper looked round and nodded to his hammers.

The guy just smiled. 'Oh well, it was worth a try.'

The hammers by the door brought their lasrifles up, slicking off the safeties and making the cells hum. Zael saw his brief, stack-waste life flash before him and wondered vaguely if he had time to run for the door.

He heard two hard, dry bangs. The hammers slammed back against the doorposts, their rifles tumbling from their hands. Both had blackened, bloody holes in the centres of their foreheads and no backs to their skulls any more.

The guy suddenly had a gun in his fist. A great big Navy model Hecuter 10, the muzzle smoking. Taper was gaping at him, absolutely stunned by the speed of what had just happened.

The guy was still smiling.

He put two more rounds into Taper's chest, point blank.

Oblivious, Taper flew at him, twig arms outstretched.

'You really don't understand who you're dealing with!' Taper wailed, his bony fingers closing in a vice.

But the guy had somehow sidestepped him. Despite his bulk and size, the guy moved like lightning. He came up around Taper's lunge and kicked him in the back, sending him sprawling into the corner of the room.

The guy threw something small and black at Taper. 'Sire Taper, it's the other way around. *You* don't understand who *you're* dealing with.'

Instinctively, Taper caught the small black thing. He looked at it for a split second. A split second was all he had.

The grenade's blast vaporised him and brought down the wall behind him.

Before the dust had settled, the guy was up and running.

+Three heartbeats in the hallway outside!+

'Three heartbeats in the hallway!' Zael screamed out.

The guy was already firing through the doorway.

'How did you know that?' he yelled.

'I heard it...' Zael said.

'How did he hear it?' the guy asked no one at all.

'Don't leave me here!' Zael cried.

+Don't leave him.+

'You're kidding me!' the guy snorted to the invisible voice.

+I never kid. You know that. Don't leave him. I want to know how he's picking me up.+

The guy glanced round at Zael.

'Come on,' he said. He wasn't happy about it. Not at all.

HIS PISTOL HANGING in his hand in an alarmingly casual way, the guy went out into the hallway with Zael behind him. The guy's shots had made a mess of two more hammers who were sprawled on the tiled floor. One was still twitching. Just death-spasms. The last jerks of a ruined body.

A few metres on, at the end of a smeared trail of blood, the third hammer was trying to crawl to safety. The guy casually shot him once in the back of the head.

Zael swayed and turned to face the wall. His mind was a mess. The guy probably thought he was queasy because of the killing, but Zael had seen plenty. This was withdrawal. A look was long overdue. Throne, how he needed one! Just a little cheapo splinter even, to calm his nerves.

'What are you doing?' the guy snapped.

Zael had been stroking the cool wall with his palms and resting his sweaty forehead against it. He glanced round, aware that the muscles in his face were beginning to tick.

'God-Emperor, look at you. Don't skid out on me now, or I will leave you.'

Zael flinched, hoping to hear the invisible voice again, sticking up for him. But there was nothing now. The guy seemed to notice it too.

'Ravenor?' he asked. 'Ravenor? You with me still?'

Zilch. 'Ravenor?'

'I thought *you* were Ravenor,' Zael said. The guy sneered at him. He was about to say something, probably something impolite, when the invisible voice came through again. Just a hiss. Just a whisper, as if it was under great strain.

+Kara.+

'Kara? What about her? Ravenor?'

+In trouble.+

'What sort of trouble? Are you waring her?'

Nothing. The voice had gone away again.

'Shit,' breathed the guy. 'I should get out of here. They might need me.'

'Getting out of here,' Zael shrugged. 'Now that's a good idea. I remember where the door is.'

'No,' said the guy. 'We're too committed. We stick to this.'

None of which was what Zael wanted to hear.

The hallway turned into a lounge area with big, red satin sofas and three fabulous hardlight sculptures. The blinking, neon-bright structures of the art utterly captured Zael's attention so the guy had to drag him on by the hand. Ahead they could see yellow-robed household staff fleeing before them.

A moody hammer came running towards them down a corridor to their right. He was hugging a sack to his chest, and skidded up hard as he saw them. His eyes grew.

He dropped the sack and started to run off the way he'd come. The guy aimed his pistol at him, but thought better of it. Instead, he went over to the sack and emptied it onto the floor. Dozens of little parcels fell out, each wrapped in red tissue paper.

Flects.

'Throne, let me have one! Let me have one, please!' Zael blurted out, realising at once how frigging pathetic he sounded.

Kneeling, the guy sneered at him, and tossed a single parcel towards his hands. Zael almost dropped it.

'This stuff is filth. Filth you can't imagine. You know about the Ruinous Powers?'

Zael shook his head.

The guy sighed. 'Just use it. If you're coming with me, I'd rather have you sussed and sorted than witchy-edged.'

'I'll be fine. Fine. Really. Fine,' Zael replied. He wanted to prove to this guy that he wasn't just some scrap-head, some burn-out, some waster. But he put the flect in his pocket all the same.

THEN IT GOT really nasty. It went down so fast, Zael wished he'd taken the look while he'd had the chance. Genny X's hammers – those that hadn't run – put up a last effort to defend their boss. They were all East K stackers, a clan notorious for not knowing when to quit. Shades and Jack-Ls had a rep for being meaner, but the stackers were famously brute-stupid and stubborn.

Zael and the guy came up some stairs into another room: a gloomy gallery with paintings and hololiths on the walls. It seemed empty, but the hammers were hiding behind furniture and wall panels. They came out like devils, howling, baying. Most of them were knucked out of their minds on baby blues and redliners. They were crazy-mad. Kill-hyped.

Everything became a blur to Zael. Overload. He froze, stock still, and screamed aloud as the frenzy exploded around him. It was too much. It was much too much.

He distinctly saw a hammer with rake-hook spin over onto his back, blood puffing from an exit wound the size of a dinner plate. He half-saw another drop to his knees, his entire face crushed by a curt little slam-punch of astonishing force delivered by the guy's left fist. Another hammer flew past him at head height. Zael wasn't sure if the hammer was travelling under his own momentum, or if he'd been thrown.

He heard four distinct shots, three of them the throaty roar of the Hecuter 10, one a small-cal sting-blunt. He saw a hammer down on his hands and knees, choking on his own blood, and another stagger spastically across the room to crash into a framed hololith, which he brought down on his head as he fell.

For a brief moment, Zael saw the guy, spinning on the spot, on one foot, his body bent over. His other leg was cocked out at right angles. The heavy boot snapped a hammer's jaw as it rotated. Broken teeth ejected from the hammer's mouth.

A hammer came right at Zael. A stacker with acid-tats like smile lines and a sow's rib through his septum. He was shrieking so loud Zael couldn't hear him. The hammer's mouth was wide open and his uvula was wobbling. A grind mace cased his right fist and he was swinging it at Zael's face.

The guy thundered into the hammer from the side, deflecting his weapon. There was a brief mist of blood, and something small and soft bounced off Zael's stomach. The guy floored the hammer, broke his arm, yanked the disarticulated limb backwards, and slammed the still-spinning grind mace into the back of the hammer's skull. Zael closed his eyes just before the hot, spattery mess drenched his face.

It was all still and quiet suddenly. He opened his eyes. Eight moody hammers lay dead around the trashed gallery. The guy was sitting on his backside in front of Zael, nursing his left hand. Little jets of blood were zipping where the guy's left middle finger had previously been.

'Well, shit this,' the guy said, genuinely upset.

The finger had bounced off Zael's stomach, and was now lying on the floor at Zael's feet.

'Damn,' the guy added, pulling a little surgical clamp out of his thigh pocket and jamming it down over the digit stump.

'You're a first,' he told Zael as he got up. 'Never lost a body part until today.'

The guy seemed completely oblivious to the fact he had just taken out a room full of moody hammers, single-handed, in under ten seconds. Zael knew he'd cost the guy that finger. The guy had been saving him.

THE GUY PUSHED open the heavy tethwood doors and yelled out 'Genevieve? Genevieve X? My name is Harlon Nayl! I am a certified agent of the Inquisition!'

The X did not respond, nor did Zael expect her to, somehow. He could feel cold, exterior air blowing at him, and that was odd. Had she opened a window and run?

They went into Genny's sanctum. The guy led the way, pistol raised, blood still dripping from his clamped left hand.

Huge, floor-to-ceiling windows of stained glass threw coloured light down onto the expensive tappanacre rug.

Genevieve X sat behind her desk, staring at them. There was pretty much nothing left of her except her bloody skeleton and little torn ribbons of tissue and flesh. It looked as if her clothes, skin, body fat and muscle, her lips, her eyes... had all been ripped away. Denuded, her skeleton seemed pitifully small. The bare bones, shockingly white, were patched with blackening clots of gore and sinew.

'Damn,' breathed Harlon Nayl.

IT WAS HARD to tell beyond that black wall of smog whether the actual daylight had gone or not. Still, another day was over. Billions of lights sparkled into life across the great, black city: from the highest points of the inner spires to the skirts of the suburbs. Out of the city's heart, the Administratum clerks flowed in a monotonous grey tide. Along walkways and pavements, across pedestrian bridges and stack-level galleries, ten hundred thousand pale men and women in sombre rain-coats of emerald and black made their routine way homeward in slow procession. Many had shaven heads, or the scalp or neck punctures of neuro-link sockets. Most wore tinted goggles. None wore any kind of expression at all.

Eustis Majoris was capital-world of the Angelus subsector. Its heavy manufacturing industries may have begun to slump, and its fabricatory districts fall into decay, but it had one ancient craft that still thrived. It was the bureaucratic hub of two-dozen Imperial worlds. Here, in the massive ouslite towers of Formal A and Formal C, the minutiae of Imperial life was recorded, processed, evaluated, stored, examined, compared, scrutinised for levy and, ultimately, filed. There were more clerks and scribes, and more processing codifiers, in this ten kilometre square slab of city than in all the other sub-sector worlds combined. In gilt letters above the hallway doors of the administry towers were the proud rubrics of their function: 'Knowledge is power', 'Data equals assessment, assessment equals insight, insight equals control', 'Know your codes', 'Information is truth'. All workers were encouraged to repeat such adages as mantras during work shifts.

Locally, there were other phrases that had come into coin, phrases the administry did not encourage at all. 'If something's worth doing, it's worth doing in triplicate', 'Those who shred history are doomed to repeat it' and 'I file everything, therefore I know nothing' were three of the most popular.

ANONYMOUS IN A hooded rain-cloak, Harlon Nayl still stood out. This was because he was moving against the flow. Tugging the boy along by the sleeve, he was heading into the central districts against the night's outpouring of scribes and administry functionaries. In places, he had to move aside where the rows of marching workers refused to break to let them pass. Sometimes he simply had to push his way through. But not once did such an affront provoke anything more than a slight scowl from the pale, shave-headed workers.

This was a new world to Zael. He gawped at it in a state of mounting unease. It was less than seven kilometres from the formal where he'd grown up and spent all of his however-many-it-was years. The streets and people here were cleaner than the dirty sink-stacks he thought of as homeground, but they seemed darker and totally drained of any spark. Formal J was a dump, full of no-hopers and filth, and condemned stack housing with yellow repossession notices pasted to the doors, but at least it had some sense of life and colour. The flicking neon of the bar signs, the fire tubs, the street musicians in their gypsy finery and the smile-girls in their scabby silks.

This was different. Soulless, bitter, grimly routine, depressingly quiet. How could so many people make so little sound, Zael wondered? Just the tramp of feet, the tinny tannoy announcements from the transit stops.

'I'd like to go home now,' he said to Nayl.

'Home? To that hole?' Nayl replied, about to laugh. Then he looked around and sighed, as if to say he knew what Zael meant. To both of them, there suddenly seemed to be a huge and distinct difference between a life where hope had been crushed and a life where there had never been any hope to begin with.

THE SILENT CROWDS were thinning. They entered a very grand but depressing plaza of cold stone flags and wrought iron lamp standards. Statues lined each side of the space, acid-eaten worthies of the Imperium of Man that Zael had never heard of. Ahead was a mighty building faced in streaked black slate, its lit windows tall and very slender. It seemed big, but it was dwarfed by the gargantuan towers of the administry behind it.

There was a golden aquila on the building's solid front, its wing tips forty metres apart. Superimposed across it was a set of scales, like the zodiac rune.

A lone figure waited for them in the centre of the plaza, made tiny by the emptiness. He stood self-consciously, as if aware he was being watched. He was adjusting his hair with the aid of a hand mirror.

'There you are,' he said as they came up. Then he paused and looked Zael up and down. 'And there you are,' he added in an uncertain tone. 'And you are?'

'This is Zael.'

'My dear Harlon, you haven't gone and found yourself a little friend have you? How absolutely darling! There's hope for you yet.'

'Shut the frig up, Thonius,' Nayl snapped. 'He's only here because the boss wants to examine him.'

Carl Thonius pursed his lips and shrugged. 'I see. I didn't think he really was your type. Not enough breasts by a factor of two.'

'Can we get on?' Nayl snapped. 'I take it she's in there?'

'That's what we think. The local info-systems are damned hard to wire into. Actual decent Arbites cryptography for a change, wouldn't you just know it? But we're pretty sure she's still here. And we know who to talk to.'

'We do?'

'A deputy magistratum called Rickens. He's got the case.'

'We could just go to the top–'

Thonius shook his head. 'Only if we have to. Remember why we stealthed ourselves onto planet in the first place? This place is administry central. We go on record, the data's in the system and we're compromised. No matter how careful we are. Potentially, there's too much at stake for that.'

Nayl nodded. 'Let's go then. Where's Kys?'

'Busy,' said Thonius, with a shrug. 'Maybe onto something. You?'

'Something and nothing all at once. A zilch, probably, but an interesting one.'

'What happened to your finger?'

'The zilch I was talking about. Come on.'

With Zael in tow, they walked towards the main steps of the gloomy building.

'How do you want to play this?' Nayl asked.

'Like we did on Satre?'

'Okay, but don't namby about this time...'

TAP... TAP... TAP...

The base of a steel-shod walking cane struck the polished wooden floor. It announced the man wherever he went. People straightened up respectfully when they heard the tap approach.

Deputy Magistratum First Class Dersk Rickens came down the gloomy, panelled hallway on level nine. The two officers on duty went straight-backed smartly and opened the tall double doors for him. He acknowledged their salutes with a brief nod. They could tell he was tired. He was leaning heavily on his walking cane.

His secretary, Limbwall, hurried behind him, laden with a pile of report slates and ribboned case-folders forwarded during the course of the day from duty processing. Limbwall was a young man, prematurely bald, his underwhelming looks ruined altogether by the heavy augmetic optics implanted into his eye sockets. He'd been an administry scribe for seven years until his request for transfer/promotion had happily coincided with the deputy magistratum's written application for a scribe who could file.

Limbwall said a cheery hello to the guards as he passed by, but they ignored him. Limbwall wore the uniform – badly – but he wasn't a real marshal in their opinion. Just an ink-monkey.

Beyond the great doors of panelled oak lay Ricken's domain. A looming wooden mezzanine lit by cream-shaded electrolamps that hung on long chains. Files and slates were heaped up on the floor under the tall windows, and piled high along the tops of the battered filing chests. Mam Lotilla was dutifully processing case files at her old-model codifier, and Plyton, the savvy young junior marshal narco had sent his way, was pinning crime scene pict-stats of disembowelled bodies onto the wall boards. Beyond the mezzanine, wide wooden stairs led down into the main vault of the department, where hundreds of his officers worked at console stations or long rows of desks. A penetrating background murmur rose from the great room below.

Rickens had a headache. He'd been in budget meetings all afternoon, and they'd run over like they always did.

Sankels, the bull mastiff from interior cases, had been up to his tricks again, and had managed to get all the finance additionals from narco, homicide, xen-ops, special and prohib-pub thrown out in favour of booster funds for his own office. There was cleaning to be done, he had told the chief magistratum, and the chief magistratum had agreed.

Which was all nonsense. The chief magistratum had only agreed because he knew Sankels was nose-deep with Jader Trice, the first provost of the newly formed Ministry of Sub-sector Trade, a man Rickens knew well from his numerous pict-channel interviews but had never met in person.

And that meant that Sankels had a direct line to the lord governor himself, because Trice's Ministry was the lord governor's own idea. If the chief magistratum hadn't made nice with Sankels, the chief magistratum would have been back on stack-beat in Formal X come morning.

In all truth, Rickens wondered why the city bothered with a Departmento Magistratum at all. The interior cases division was fast becoming the lord governor's own private police force. Such were the powers of a lord governor sub-sector.

His, he reminded himself, was not to reason why. His was to get the knuck on with his job and run his department to the best of his ability with increasingly limited resources.

'Good evening, deputy magistratum,' Plyton said, looking up from a close-up pict of an intestinal mass she had been turning over. She was trying to decide which way up it was supposed to go.

'Is that meant for us?' Rickens asked. 'Looks like homicide should be dealing with it.'

She shrugged. She was twenty-two years old, thick-set and fine featured. Her black leather uniform suit was always perfectly turned out, the silver marshal's crest always polished. Her dark hair was cut short to fit under her duty helmet. 'Sent it to us, sir. Said it fell into special's purview.'

Rickens headed up the Department of Special Crime. The smallest of the hive's Magistratum divisions, it was a catch-all division, designed to investigate anything that didn't neatly fall into the remits of the other departments. Special was looked on as the misfit member of the family, the unpopular cousin. The shit they got sent...

Limbwall plonked his armful of slates down on a desk, and wiped a hand across his mouth. 'Anything else, sire?' he asked.

Rickens shrugged. He was a small man in his early one-fifties, with a permanently put-upon expression. For seventy-two years, he'd walked with a limp caused by a ball-shot from a hammer's pivot-gun that went through his hip. Seventy-two years, tap... tap... tap...

'It'll have to wait,' Rickens said, tapping the pile of slates.

'Actually, I don't think so, chief,' smiled Plyton. 'This fell into our laps because the perp claimed she was an Imperial inquisitor.'

'She what?'

Plyton shrugged. 'And there are some people in your office. Waiting to talk to you about it.'

RICKENS'S PRIVATE OFFICE was a quiet space of dark wood and soft illumination screened from the mezzanine and the rest of the department by a panelled wall with frosted glass mullions. As he entered and closed the door behind him with a soft click, the two men waiting for him rose to their feet. Rickens tapped his way over to his carved cathedra, settled himself down and punched in a private code that brought his cogitator to life. The screen glowed green and sidelit his face. He gestured for the two men to resume their seats on the leather bench facing him.

By then, he had already made an assessment of them. Off-worlders both: an over-dressed youth and an older man, probably muscle. The youth's body language betrayed confidence. The older man was unreadable, but then muscle usually was, in Rickens's ample experience. Until the split-second it decided to act.

He called up the file onto screen, and carefully set his half-moon spectacles on his face.

'What we seem to have... a female, lacking citizen validation, work dockets, status codes or visitation permits... physical age twenty-five years standard by approximation, though some traces of juvenat procedures... apprehended in an undersink of Formal D this afternoon having just killed or crippled seven individuals, all local males. The female refuses to answer any questions, but on apprehension she identified herself as Inquisitor Gideon Ravenor.'

Rickens took off his spectacles and looked up at the two men. 'This is an old fashioned world, perhaps behind the times with cutting Imperium fashions, but I believe Gideon is still a name reserved for the male gender?'

'It is,' said the well-dressed youth.

'So, this female is lying?'

'Yes,' the youth replied cordially. 'And no. We request you release her into our custody.'

'She is a friend of yours?' Rickens asked.

'A colleague,' said the youth.

'A friend,' the muscle said quietly.

'Given her crimes, I really can't see how–'

The youth leaned forward, interrupting Rickens, and set a small black wallet on the table in front of him. Rickens flipped it open. The light of the electrolamps glinted off the Inquisitorial rosette.

Rickens didn't react. He took a scanner wand from his jacket and played it across the badge.

'Stackers have been known to fabricate this sort of thing out of tin and glass,' he said. He sat back and regarded the wand's readout. 'This, however, is genuine. Which one of you is Ravenor?'

'Neither,' said the younger man. 'Like the female in your custody, we both work for him. I repeat my request.'

Rickens drummed his fingers together. 'It's not that simple. Not at all.'

'You would impede the operation of the Holy Inquisition, deputy magistratum?'

'Throne of Terra, of course not.' Rickens looked at the young man. 'But there are protocols. Procedures. I know the Inquisition has the power to run rough-shod over every law and statute on Eustis Majoris. It may demand the release of an accredited agent. But... I would expect such a demand to come from the Officio Inquisitorus Planetia itself. Formally. Not like this.'

'Inquisitor Ravenor does not wish this matter to become formal at all, deputy magistratum,' said the older man softly. 'It would... I'm sorry, it might... jeopardise the entire nature of our investigation here. We want our colleague returned to us, and all data surrounding her arrest erased.'

'That is beyond my power.'

'Not at all,' said the younger man. He leaned forward again. 'I see the case file on your display still has a green tag. It is pending, subject to you processing it. You could erase it here. Now. With a touch of your keypad.'

'I would be betraying my office,' said Rickens.

'You would be serving your Emperor,' said the younger man.

The other man said nothing, and that's what did it. Deputy Magistratum Rickens was not easily intimidated, but there was something about the unreadable face of the older man. Rickens had a sudden image of himself, dead in his old, carved cathedra, while these two ominous servants of the Inquisition slipped away into the night. And all for what? For sticking to his tired principles?

Rickens believed in Imperial justice, and these days he got damned little chance of taking legal action at all thanks to the powers that be. Who was he to stand in the face of the real thing, however unorthodox?

'Very well,' he said and tapped an erasure code into his cogitator. 'You may collect your colleague from holding pen nine at the south entry.'

'Thank you, deputy magistratum. Your efforts will not be forgotten.'

THE TWO MEN had only been gone ten minutes when Plyton knocked and entered the office cautiously.

'Sir?' she asked. 'All my files on that Ravenor case have... uhm... gone.'

'I know.'

'What did those men say to you?'

'Forget it, Plyton. Erase it from your mind.'

'But sir–'

'Do as I say, Plyton. No good will come of it.'

ONE OF SONSAL'S staff had voxed ahead to inform the house of his master's dinner plans. When the motor-carriage swept them in under the rain-proofed portico, servants were waiting for them in the courtyard. Sonsal descended from the carriage and courteously handed Kys down to the pavement.

The house, like those of all Petropolis's worthies, was on the surface level. Despite the burning curse of the rain, it was thought improper for the wealthy and the respectable to dwell in the deep sinks. Sonsal's house was in Formal B, one of the three core districts of the city-hive, and the only one given over exclusively to residential buildings. To the north and west rose the many massive towers of A and C, the hub of sub-sector bureaucracy and government.

Sonsal conducted Kys into the atrium, where floating glow-globes cast a shimmering yellow light. The walls were lined with hand-printed paper showing a repeat print pattern of the holy skull-cog in gold leaf. More iconography of the Adeptus Mechanicus decorated the iron staircase. Engine Imperial was proud of its association with the machine cult. Like other incorporated commercial firms, it leased tech processes and construction secrets from the guild, and manufactured them under license. The great financial return made it worth the huge lease fees and the pressure of regular inspection.

Ewer bearers waited for them, and they washed their hands and faces clean of air-pollution in silver dishes of clean water.

Sonsal invited her to wait in the inner chambers. 'I have a small piece of business to attend to, then I will be with you.'

'I'll be waiting,' she said, tense with the terrible effort of being suggestive.

ALONE, KYS RELAXED and paced in an ornate apartment. A carpet of woven silver thread filigree covered the black tile floor, and the pink-upholstered furniture had heavy, gilt feet and arms. Lead-glass cabinets displayed various pieces of klaylware, and there were a number of ugly oil paintings and hololiths on the walls

'You with me?' she said quietly.

+I am.+

'You're very faint. Why is that?'

+I'm tired. That, and the landspar. Very heavy, very dense. Most of the residences in Formal B are made from it. It is particularly resistant to the acidic rain. A rich man does not want to lose status by having his house crumble around him, after all.+

'So?'

+It's psi-inert. Dead stone. It's all I can do to hear you and let you hear me.+

She frowned. 'All right, don't wear yourself out. I'll call if I need you.'

She strolled around the room, thought-feeling for niches, hidden panels, hiding places, though she doubted Sonsal would be foolish enough to keep anything in a public room. There was a panel, however, in the west wall, the size of a small door. She could sense its hollowness. She traced its catch mechanism delicately with her mind, and then popped it open. The panel swung inward. Behind it was a small, private study, lined with shelves of books, slates and wafers. There was a desk, and a leather suspensor chair.

She turned her head slowly, feeling around. A particular density in the third drawer down on the left side of the desk.

The drawer's lock was significantly more complex than those of the other seven drawers. It refused to pop with a simple, blunt thought-thrust. She was forced to analyse it, component by component, comparing and matching tumblers and pins. The intense mental effort made her perspire. Finally, with a triumphant blink, she turned the last drum and heard the lock click.

Kys reached out a hand and started to slide the drawer open. She saw three, small red-tissue packets lying on top of several envelopes.

She heard a door handle turn. She slammed the drawer shut and dashed back into the public apartment, taking a seat by the heavy, leaded window just before Sonsal came in.

'My dear, are you all right? You look slightly flushed.'

'I'm fine,' she said. He was coming towards her. She saw that, in her haste, she had not pulled the panel door into the study fully shut. Another step, and he would see it.

'Just a little warm,' she smiled, standing up quickly and undoing the top four clasps of her dark brown bodysuit. His hungry attention was immediately focused on the exposed V of white skin. Kys took advantage of his distraction and hooked her mind around the lip of the panel door, snapping it flush.

'Dinner is served,' he said. 'Shall we?'

THE FOOD WAS excellent. Little bowls of spiced goshran, followed by stuffed pettifowls that had been imported from off-world, then a kuberry sorbet wrapped in a parchment of filo pastry. The sommelier kept their glasses filled with a series of fine wines that matched each course to perfection. When Sonsal wasn't looking, Kys glanded an antioxidant to keep her head clear. His conversation was poor. He kept telling her about the various vintages, how difficult some had been to procure, how hard it was to import decent pettifowl these days, the secret of the spices that made the difference between good goshran and great goshran. He wanted to impress, and like many wealthy, empty men, his conspicuous wealth was the only thing he could think of using.

She nodded and smiled, and hung on his every word through sheer force of will. Her act was working. They both drank too much, but where she was glanded against it, he became loose-tongued and over-familiar. Gently, she mind-stirred the air-molecules around him, heating him up and making him sweat. Then she started to custom-build her own pheromones to suit his very-readable templates, and steer them towards him. By the end of the meal, he was intoxicated in more ways than one.

He ordered the sommelier to pour them a large amasec each, and then dismissed him and all the serving staff.

Sonsal raised his glass, dabbing his sweaty neck with his other hand. 'My dear Patience,' he said. 'This evening has been a delight. The entire day too. I have placed my purchases in the vault. Perhaps we could go and admire them later? I have some other pieces you might find most enchanting.'

'That would be nice,' she smiled.

'I want to thank you again,' he said.

'Please, Umberto. There's no need. This fine meal has been more than enough. You're spoiling me.'

'Impossible!' he declared. 'Nothing could spoil a woman of such infinite beauty.'

'Umberto, you will turn my head with such compliments.'

'Such a fine head. Of such infinite beauty,' he said, getting up badly and sloshing his drink.

She kept a smile on her face, but watched him carefully.

'How is your amasec, Patience? It's forty year-old Zukanac, from the mountains of Onzio.'

'It is wonderful, but I fear I have drunk too much already. Any more, and I might forget myself.'

He leered.

'My tolerance for good drink is low these days,' she continued. 'It dulls the senses, don't you find? I have travelled widely, and know there are other intoxicants that freshen and clear the mind most wonderfully. Sadly none are available on such a proper world as Eustis Majoris.'

He considered this for a moment. 'You never did tell me what you do,' he said.

'I have a modest, private income. I travel. I explore. It is most... liberating.'

He nodded knowingly. 'Then you are open to experiences. How delightful. Set your amasec aside, Patience. I have something else you might enjoy.'

He walked unsteadily over to the hidden panel door, opened it and disappeared for a moment. When he came back, he was cupping something in his hand. 'I think you'll find Eustis Majoris is less proper than you thought. This will clear our heads. It will relax and refresh us. So that we might enjoy the rest of this perfect night.'

Kys made sure the smile she gave him showed nothing but total approval of that prospect.

TWO, SMALL HARD shapes, each one wrapped in red tissue paper. He led her by the hand over to a chaise and set the red parcels down on the lacquered top of the low table nearby.

Then he kissed her.

'What are these?' she asked. It had taken a great deal of resolve to accept the kiss and not kill him with a sternum punch.

'They are flects. Have you heard of them?'

'No,' she said. 'Umberto, I thought you might have been talking about obscura or lucidia.'

'Obscura is far too addictive and debilitating for a man of my station,' he said, sitting down beside her. 'And lucidia is too coarse. It has an unpleasant low, I find.'

'These flects then... what are they?'

'Like nothing else. Wonderful. Liberating. New. You will not be disappointed.'

He began to unwrap one, slowly teasing out the tissue paper.

'Where do they come from?' she asked. He shrugged. 'I mean, how do you come by them?'

He finished his amasec and set the glass down. 'I have a contact. A fellow who provides. It is very unofficial. Now then–'

She reached out a hand and set it on his. Then she leaned forward so her mouth was very close to his ear. 'There's something you should know, Umberto,' she said.

'What... what is that?'

'I am an agent of the Imperial Inquisition, and you are in very big trouble indeed.'

SONSAL STARTED TO cry. Sobbing at first, then deep bellows of despair woven up with anger. He curled up on the chaise like a child, kicking his feet.

'Shut up,' she said.

His weeping became so loud, the apartment door opened, and a houseman peered in.

'Go away,' Kys said, slamming the door shut with a stern blink.

'Please! Please!' Sonsal sobbed.

'Shut up. I won't lie. This is not good for you.'

'My office! I will be disgraced... sacked! Oh, God-Emperor, my life is at an end!'

She stood facing him. 'Disgrace? Yes, most likely. An end to your illustrious career with Engine Imperial? I should think so. A prison term, with hard labour? You can probably bet on that. But if you think this is the end of your life, you are sadly mistaken. You have no idea how bad life can get before it ends. Trust me.'

'P-please!'

'Umberto? Are you listening to me? Umberto?'

'Yes?'

'Stop sobbing and pull yourself together, or I'll introduce you to the nine principles of real pain. You believe me when I say I can do that, don't you?'

'Yes.'

'Good.' She crouched down facing him, and he shrank away, wiping snot from his nose, his eyes puffy and red. His scale lorications had partially extended across his face, triggered by his weeping. 'You are in the hands of the Inquisition now, Umberto Sonsal. It requires information from you. Your real fate depends upon the fullness of your answers.'

Sniffing, he sat up. 'H-how do I know you're not lying?'

She reached into her thigh pocket and fished out the rosette.

'See?'

He started to cry again.

'Oh, shut up! Umberto, picture the near future... the many possible near futures. On one extreme, I walk out of this room and leave you here to get on with your empty, privileged life. You never see me again, and the Inquisition never comes to your door. To reach that future, you have to answer every question I ask you to my satisfaction.'

'All right...'

'Here's the other extreme. You answer badly. I kill you, here and now, and drop your fat corpse into the river.'

His lip began to tremble and his eyes filled with tears again. She could tell he was fighting hard to stay in control. As hard as she had done to pretend to like him.

'In between those extremes, there is the future where I expose you, drag you to the marshals, get you charged and locked up and generally ruin the rest of your miserable frigging existence.'

'I understand.'

'And there's one final extreme. An extreme extreme. Far worse than me just killing you and dumping your corpse. I call my superiors and they take you away. What happens to you after that is, I can assure you, far worse than a quick death.

'So... which future do you like the look of best?'

'The one where you walk away.'

'Good. Who is your dealer?'

Sonsal rocked back on the couch. 'He'll kill me,' he said.

'Futures, Umberto, extremes...'

'All right! His name is Drase Bazarof.'

'And who is that?'

'One of my line chiefs at Engine. He's sink-scum. But he knows people.'

'Where does he live?'

'I don't know! A sink-stack somewhere! I don't socialise with scum like that!'

'But his residence will be logged on your personnel manifest, right?'

'I suppose so.'

'We'll look in a moment,' she said. She walked over to the dining table and took a slug of her amasec. 'Who does he supply? Besides you?'

'He keeps his business out of the workplace except for me. The machine guild inspects our premises so often. But he's said things to me about his stack. He sells there, I think.'

'He has a supplier. I mean, he must get these things from somewhere. He doesn't make them.'

'I have no idea who. You'll have to ask him.'

'I will. Calm down, Umberto. You're quaking like a leaf.'

'I'm scared. I'm scared of you. I'm jumpy. Would it be all right if I just used this look to calm my nerves and–'

'You're kidding, aren't you?'

He hung his head and gazed at the tiled floor.

'Where's your manifest?' she asked.

SONSAL ACCESSED HIS work database using a codifier in the corner of the apartment. His hands were shaking. The codifier was a curved valve screen set over an intricate mechanism of brass tubes and wires. The enamel keys of the touchboard had long, stiff arms.

Sonsal pulled up the Engine Imperial info-strata, opened the various document files with his personal codes, and decompressed the manifest. Then he left her to read it and wandered back to the couch shakily.

Kys used an alphabetiser to locate Bazarof, punched up his address, and memorised it. For good measure, she skin-wrote it too, on her left forearm, gently mind-nudging pores open and closed to form a pattern visible only by microscope.

She checked her chronometer. It was late.

'Ravenor?'

Nothing.

She sighed. She was about to get up when she heard a snuffling noise.

At first, she couldn't work out what it was. An insect caught in the windowlights, maybe. A poor piece of plumbing. She looked around.

The noise was coming from Sonsal. He was getting to his feet, jerking and twitching, and shuffling backwards, sliding the chaise across the tiles.

She knew at once he'd used a flect while she wasn't looking. Damn him! Damn her! She should have kept an eye on him. He'd been so scared, so dreadfully strung out that he'd looked for an escape, even a temporary one.

'Sonsal? Sonsal!'

His head was bucking around, dystonically. His eyes had rolled back. Shit, was this normal? Was this what flect's did? Sonsal kept backing away so violently that the chaise overturned with a crash.

'Sonsal!'

He seemed to hear her voice. He staggered away, moving backwards as if in fear, and slammed through the panel door into the study.

'Damn it!' she cried.

The main doors pushed open and two of Sonsal's bodyguards looked in.

'Sire? Are you all right?' one called

'Get the hell out!' Kys yelled, and with a nod of her head slid the entire dining table down the length of the room, crockery and glassware tumbling off it. It slammed into the doors and pushed them shut. Outside, the bodyguards began hammering and kicking at the blocked entrance.

Kys ran into the study. The desk was askew, and several drawers had been pulled out. A door out into the hall stood open.

'Sonsal!'

She ran out into the hall. The glow-globes were set to low burn. As soon as she appeared, the bodyguards ceased their hammering and ran at her. She deflected one with a rolling kick and punched the other off his feet into the wall.

Sonsal, still jerking and twitching, was backing up the grand staircase away from her. Blood was leaking out of his mouth and one eye had closed. Terrified household staff members appeared in doorways and peered out. They all vanished, shrieking, when Sonsal started shooting.

It was a small-calibre slide-away, a sleeve piece. He must have got it from his desk. Blindly, he fired it down the staircase as he went up backwards. Shots pinged off the marble treads and twanged away from the iron rails.

Kys had no gun to return fire with. She ducked into cover and crooked her left wrist backwards, drawing the long, handle-less kineblade out of her bodyglove sleeve with a jerk of her telekinesis. The twelve-centimetre blade hovered in the air.

'Put the gun down, Umberto!' she yelled.

He fired back at her, blowing out a dusty hole in the wall's plasterwork beside her head. Another shot took a huge mirror off its wall-hooks. It splintered on the landing floor.

With a fierce burst of directed telekinesis, she leapt out into the open. The kineblade zoomed up the stairs and pinned Sonsal's left sleeve to the banister rail. At the same moment, she plucked the slide-away clean out of his hand and whipped it through the air.

She caught the gun neatly, and aimed it back at him.

'That's enough!'

He was still shaking and vibrating, frantic. His pinned sleeve seemed to distress him more than anything, and Kys realised it was because he could no longer back away.

'Right, Umberto! Right! I'm coming up there! Calm down and I'll–'

Sonsal pulled at the pinned sleeve, tore it away, and staggered backward at the same moment. Suddenly freed, he slipped and went over the stair rail, shoulders first.

Two storeys to the marble floor of the atrium.

She looked away. Even the bone and mush sound of impact was bad enough.

'Shit,' she said. Alarms were ringing right through the house. People were screaming.

She retrieved her kineblade, went to the south exit, and let herself out.

THREE

SHE MELTED AWAY through shadows, through the city darkness. I kept watch over her as soon as she was clear of the house's blinding landspar. From the mosaic of her raw, surface thoughts, I reconstructed the events up to Sonsal's death. Her mind presented an indifference, but I could tell it was forced. She was troubled, alone, and a little scared. Patience Kys hid many things well – her true name, for example – and all who met her thought her hard and callous. But I knew better. Not because I could see her vulnerable side – she wouldn't allow that – but because I knew it was there. I could hear its hollow echo when I tapped gently against her mind, as a man might knock to hear the leaden sound of a hidden alcove behind a wood panel.

Alarm protocols had drawn the marshals to the neighbourhood of Sonsal's house, along with other, less identifiable officials. My mind lingered with her for some minutes as she hid in a temple porch while fast-dispatch cruisers and prowl-trucks scoured the streets. The Petropolitan authorities took the security of their richest and most privileged citizens very seriously. This was the second time in the space of a day my people had run foul of the Magistratum.

At the warning sirens from Sonsal's house, the other residences in the street fortified themselves automatically, like herd animals reacting to the distress signals of one of their number. Gates and doors were mag-locked, window shutters furled into place, and roof armour, designed primarily to guard against rain, clattered out into full extension. I could feel the tense sensor-cones of alert-ready sentry servitors, taste the ozone stink of electrified wall-tops, and smell the stirring heat of suddenly armed anti-personnel mines.

Sonsal's terrified householders had already furnished the marshals with a description of a single assailant. Thirty-five minutes after she had quit the south entry, Kys was still no more than a half kilometre from Sonsal's house, and seven hundred and seventy-three armed officers were hunting for her.

It was time to even the odds a little. I directed her north, towards a high-rise section of Formal B known as the Staebes, where wealthy young professionals lived in their own, opulent version of the city's lamented hab-stacks. The architect had had a keen sense of irony.

Kys plied the shadows, forced to keep to the surface streets because the crime-alert had locked out all the descender wells into the sub-levels. I wanted to speed her on her way with minimal fuss and attention. Distractions were needed.

I left her and drifted on to a transit control office on Staebes circle. There, with a little effort, I planted the image of a lone female, running scared, in the mind of the shift supervisor. He would later swear on the aquila that he'd seen the woman on a security pict transmitted from the outbound platform of the Gill Park mag-lev station. His urgent call swarmed the manhunt in that direction.

Continuing west, I located by chance three Munitorum contractors performing after-hours repairs on an electrical supply sub-station behind Lontwick Arch. I rested gently in the forebrain of one of them for a few minutes, figured him out, and guided his hands. By the time I departed, he had misconnected two street-quarter grids and caused a blackout across eight city blocks. It took the trio seventeen minutes to repair the fault and restore power. They spent a good ten minutes of that time in fierce argument as to which of them could have been damn fool enough to cross-wire in the first place. The blackout, suspicious to say the least, surged the manhunt round again, splitting it, confusing the searchers.

By then, Kys was crossing the pedestrian footbridge across the hydroelectric canyon that divided B from E.

There, she was nearly caught. A Magistratum flier, cruising overhead, caught her on pict. I got into the observer's mind just in time to block his recognition. The flier moved on, stab-lights scissoring, blind to her.

Kys was now moving south, down through Formal E. Under the ironwork walkways and tintglas roofs the streets were busy. Surface E was a popular zone for bohemian dining houses and drinking parlours, frequented by the rich from the high rent neighbourhoods over the canyon. Here, the marshals had ditched their transports and were moving through the crowd. Many were covert officers. The patrons of surface E did not take well to armoured marshals tramping through their midst.

It was hard to watch them all at once. Hundreds of minds, hundreds of personalities, some of them intoxicated, some of them high. The minds of the non-uniformed marshals were disguised by their well-rehearsed cover idents.

+Get into that cafe. Buy a drink and sit in the far end booth.+

Kys obeyed. I had to get her off the street. I'd just sensed two detective chasteners closing through the crowds towards her.

The cafe-bar was small, and lit by glow-globes so tar-stained they shone orange. Kys bought a thimble of sweet black caffeine and sat where I had instructed her. There were nine other customers, all middle-aged, sallow men in black clothing. They chatted in low, tired voices. Each one had ordered a large mug of foamed milk-caff.

They seemed sinister. For a moment, I feared I'd directed Kys into a den frequented by some form of secret police.

It was not so. Three doors down from the cafe-bar was the Elandra crematorium. The custom on Eustis Majoris was for sombre, evening funerals. The men were all paid mourners and hearse drivers, taking a respite during the long service before returning to perform their duties on the way to the wake. They sipped cheap amasec and grain liquor covertly from cuff-flasks, and smoked short, fat obscura sticks with hardpaper filters. When they departed, the cooling milk-caffs were left untouched on their benches. The bar owner cleared them without a shrug. The mourners were regulars, the untouched caffeines their way of paying for a seat out of the evening chill.

'Where now?' she asked, stepping into the cold night again.

+Follow the street down to the mag-lev station, and take the second through train to the Leahwood end stop. I'll join you again shortly.+

I was confident she was clear now. I wanted to back-track and see what I could learn from those hunting for her.

THE MAGISTRATUM MANHUNT was running out of steam. I touched mind after mind, and felt only the spectacularly ordinary sensations of everyday marshals. Wariness, weariness, gripes about too-tight boots or too-loose jacket armour, worries about pension prospects, longings for the end of the evening shift. Occasionally, I brushed by the thoughts of a more senior officer, and felt the agitation of failure, of crime-solution quotas not met.

I circled back as far as Sonsal's house. The psychic contour map of the city was still lit up, livid with recent trauma. There were flavours of pain and shock, worry and hysteria in the air here. I filtered out the sobbing house-maids, the damaged pain-throb of the bodyguards, the job worries of the butler, the seen-it-all dismissal of the medicae mortus scooping Sonsal's ruptured cadaver into a linen sack.

I found the officer in charge, a marshal called Frayn Totle. He was afraid, and that surprised me. He was standing in the atrium, gazing down at the awful splash of blood on the marble. The dominating strands of his thought processes were as obvious as the layers of a sliced cake. An unsolved crime against one of the formal's most respected was foremost of his worries. His wife, eight and a half months pregnant, was a distracting layer just under the icing. But he was afraid too.

What of? Why?

I waited to see. Three men walked over to join him, and his fear level rose. I tried to see them through his eyes, but he was resolutely avoiding them. I skipped away, and entered the mind of a mortuary attendant, who was waiting nearby to ship the gurney.

Three men. All dressed in tailored grey suits of the finest murray. One was tall and imposing, very wide, bigger even than Nayl, but he held back. Stepping forward was a well-made, more slender man with a combed chin-beard and tied-back black hair. His face was lean, hard-set, dangerous. The third man was a little, thin wretch with a balding blond scalp and fierce blue eyes.

'D'you know who I am?' the slender man with the tied-back hair asked. His voice was slick, like flowing honey.

'Yes, sir,' replied Totle. 'I recognise you from the news-picts and–'

'Well, that's great,' the slender man said. 'You can, I'm sure, understand why we have an interest here?'

'The flects, sir.'

'Yes, the flects. The death of an august citizen like Sonsal is grievous enough, but the dissolute manner of his life that has consequently been revealed...'

'I'll keep the press out, sir,' Totle said.

'Yes, you damn well will!' said the slender man. He paused, staring at the marshal. 'What's the matter with you?'

'I'm... I'm surprised to see you here, sir. Dealing with this matter personally.'

'I take my duties seriously, marshal,' the slender man said.

Who the hell was this? I wanted to know. I slid out of the mortuary attendant, who sighed gently as if waking from a dream, and moved closer to Totle and the trio. I reached out.

I got a brief taste of cold metal and power, a caustic spittle of danger and ambition. I got close enough to read the surface thoughts of the big man and know his name was Ahenobarb and he was hired muscle of the most dangerous kind. Then I reached out towards the slender man's mind.

The little blond wretch turned and looked at me. I wasn't there, but he saw me anyway. Saw my face, into my mind, my body and my soul, my birth and the lives of the generations before me. He was a psyker of appalling power. With just one look, he ripped into me and almost exposed me altogether.

'Kinsky? What is it?' the slender man said suddenly, seeing his companion stiffen.

'Thought pirate,' Kinsky replied. He was still staring at me, his blue eyes burning into my head.

I started to retreat. I threw up three mind-walls to cover my escape, but he punched through them as if they were paper. He left his body and came rushing after me.

As I soared up into the roof of the atrium, I saw his body go limp and fold. The big minder – Ahenobarb – caught him expertly before he fell, as if well practised.

Kinsky came up after me. Non-corporeal, he took the form of a ball of fire, fizzling the same blue-white as his eyes. I could feel the steel-hard lattices of his thought-traps closing on me and blocking my escape.

'What is your name?' he demanded, without words.

'Screw you is my name,' I replied, and thrust out at him with a charged mind dagger that formed, sharp and scarlet, in the air before me.

The ball of blue fire knocked it aside and chuckled. 'Is that the best you've got, screw you is my name?'

I had been inhabiting a small, fragile sylph of white light, but in the face of the oncoming blue fireball, I resolved my non-corporeal self and became an eldar *kon-miht*, furious, winged and golden. I had been tempted to become an aquila, but I didn't want this mind-warrior to gather any clues.

The fireball balked slightly at the sight of me renewed. Then it surged on, forming ectoplasmic skins of milky flame around itself. I could feel it pressing at my heart, reaching for my home form.

Circling away, up through the atrium ceiling and out into the night air, I raised more fundamental barriers. Thorn-walls, memory-barbs and dense, delaying layers of crackling deja-vu.

This Kinsky was good. Frighteningly so. He did not even begin to sidestep my countermeasures. He went through them, disintegrating them. The psi-echo shattered the glass roof of the atrium and all below scattered for cover from the cascading debris.

Kinsky dragged his trap lattices shut around me. I broke through the first, and then struggled to find a chink in the second. He was laughing. He spat darts of pure pain into my golden flanks.

With sheer force of will, I broke out of his trap. The psi-shockwave burst windows down the entire length of the street, and ripped security shutters off their hinge-mounts. I doubled back and started to flee down the road, feeling the dazed Magistratum officers picking themselves up from the asphalt. Kinsky, whirring now with the guttural throb of the warp, pursued. The bow-wave of his mind sent Magistratum vehicles and officers flying on either side. Cruisers overturned, buckling and exploding. Men flew backwards into walls and armoured windows.

He was fast. He was faster than me. Stronger than me. His mind was like a daemon-engine.

I soared like a comet out over Formal B into the dark streets of Formal E. He closed on me, like a murder-star, blazing through the heavens. Windows cracked and roof tiles rippled away in the wake of our chase. I went low under the iron bridge at F crossing. He punched through the girder bars, leaving ectoplasm crackling along the handrail. At Tangley Tower, I banked left. He came right through the huge building, filling the minds of the sleeping occupants with nightmares. Two of them had terminal heart attacks. I could feel their lives shutting off as I climbed away through the steep ranges of the administry towers.

With a blue-flame wink, he closed another vice. Beartrap jaws of agony bit into the trailing limb of my gracious eldar form. I lurched to a halt. My inaudible screams of pain rattled windows and dislodged slates in the city below me.

Kinsky was closing, the blue fireball now transmuting into the form of a black-pelted predator with a gaping maw.

When an animal is caught in a trap, it often gnaws its own leg off to be free. Anguished, I severed a part of myself, left a part of my soul quivering between the brutal teeth of the vice, and fled.

I could not fight him. Extended like this, I had nothing like his power. Wounded and hurting, I dropped like a stone into a busy manufactory in E. The furnace pits were blowing sparks, and sweating figures with shroud masks were drawing up the smelting ingots. I fell directly down into one of the workers, a second-line boss called Usno Usnor. I made myself him and hid in his heat-raddled brain.

The blue fireball came down through the roof, hesitated, and hovered slowly along the work line. It examined each mind one by one. It probed close. I forgot myself, forgot Gideon Ravenor, and became Usno Usnor. My back ached. My hugely muscled arms glistened with sweat as I wrenched another ingot out of the flames. White heat in my face. Another half-hour until the whistle blew shift-change. I was Usno Usnor, torso stung with heat, arms tired, worried that the foreman would dock my pay for being three minutes late on platform today, worried about my wife who had the ague, worried about my son who was mixing with the moodys and had just got an acid-tat, worried about the food-pail I had left under number five alloy-finer. The others would eat it if they found it. There was good pressed meat in there, and bread, and a cup of pickles…

The blue fireball hovered over the work line for several minutes, and then, frustrated, flew up and away out through the roof.

MUCH LATER: A vacant lot between hab-stacks in Formal M, a deep pit of jumbled rockcrete and collected pools of rainwater exuding the acrid stink of sulphur.

M was an especially decaying sub-borough, famished by a forty year long downward arc in trade. Many of the six century-old stacks had been cleared by optimistic landlords hoping to raise new cheap pre-habs and cash in on the worker influx to the petrofactory combine when new contracts came through. But the promised contracts had never been honoured. The combine had closed. The razed sites – some cleared to their sink levels – remained as gaping pits between crumbling stacks.

Kys walked out across the bottom of the open hole, gazing up at the mouldering rockcrete shells around her. The only light came from oil-drum fires in some of the neighbouring ruins that warmed dispossessed families. She could see them flicker at high, ragged holes that had once been windows until the glass and metal frames had been robbed and sold.

'In one piece, I see,' said a voice. She didn't bother to turn. Carl Thonius appeared out of the shadows to her left, screwing up the lid of a silver hip-flask.

'In one piece,' she replied.

Kara Swole appeared to her right, looking tired and haggard. 'I understand you've caused as much hoo-ha as me,' she said.

Kys shrugged.

'Now we're all here, I suggest we don't waste any more time,' Harlon Nayl said from the shadows behind her. Kys sighed. She'd been able to sense Thonius and Swole waiting, but Nayl had fooled her, as usual. He looked grumpy. He was dragging a scruffy street kid along by the wrist.

'Who's that?' Kys asked.

'This is Zael. He's coming with us,' Nayl said curtly. He looked over at Thonius. 'Bring it in, would you?'

Thonius walked over into the centre of the derelict lot and produced a guide beacon from his coat. It was a chrome cylinder no larger than a spice grinder. He twisted the top of it and set it on the ground. A pattern of tiny green lights flashed in repeats around its sides. Kys could just feel the sub sonic pulse.

As they drew back to the edges of the lot, Kys said, 'So what? A pick up? He wants us back at the ship, does he?'

'No,' said Nayl.

She heard the gentle hum of cowling-suppressed landing thrusters from above them. A black shape appeared overhead against the dark froth of the clouds. The lander descended slowly, vertically, into the demolition cavity.

The vehicle was unlit. Even the running lights were off. The only illumination came from the faint green instrumentation behind the canopy and the hot-blue bursts of exhaust from the jets. As it came in, skeletal landing gear unfolded from the belly with a hydraulic moan. For the last few seconds before touchdown, they had to turn their faces away as the jets lifted grit and dust and created a vortex in the squalid confines of the pit.

The jets died away to nothing. Like a squid's beak, the nose hatch articulated open. An object rather than a figure emerged, gliding down the ramp on silent anti-grav suspensors.

'By the Throne,' Kys said, 'When was the last time he came in person?'

'WE'VE NOT HAD a good day, have we?' Gideon Ravenor said. His tone was tired, but it was impossible to assess his actual demeanour. The voxponder system of the force chair that did his talking for him washed out inflection.

'Not bad, exactly,' said Harlon Nayl.

'No, not bad,' echoed Thonius.

'Though not entirely great, either,' admitted Kara Swole. Her voice was husky, and there were dark rings around her eyes as if she hadn't slept in a month.

'Bad enough for you to come,' Kys said pointedly. The sealed chair unit, matt-dull and intimidating, rotated slowly to face her.

'Indeed,' replied the colourless voxponder voice. 'Looks like I won't be able to protect you effectively from orbit. I feel a more intimate range is necessary. Let us get into concealment before we talk further.'

There was a muted acoustic click from the chair as Ravenor sent a vox-signal they couldn't hear to the waiting lander. Two figures emerged at once from the hatch and strode over to them. Then the jets cycled up again and the unseen pilot steered the lander up and away into the dark.

The inquisitor had brought Zeph Mathuin and the blunter named Wystan Frauka with him. Ravenor clearly wasn't taking any chances. Mathuin – tall and dark-skinned, with long ropes of tightly braided hair hanging down the back of his leather storm coat – was muscle, plain and simple. He'd been part of the team for three years, and no one knew much about his past, except that – like Nayl – he'd once operated as a licensed bounty hunter in the outworlds. His eyes were little coals of red hard light framed in the slits of his lids. He had a hand-gun already drawn, stiff at his side in his right hand, and his left hand was pushed into his coat pocket to brace against the weight of a heavy kitbag slung over his shoulder. He nodded a brief acknowledgement at Nayl as he came up – out of professional respect, mainly – but ignored the others. Mathuin didn't mix well, so Ravenor usually held him in reserve, but he liked to bring him along when he had to act in person; there was no doubting the ex-hunter's skills.

Kys sighed when she saw Frauka. Considering he never played any physical part in their activities, Wystan Frauka was a hefty man – big-boned and broad, with a louche, diffident manner. His hair was dyed black and neatly trimmed, his clean-shaven face craggy, mocking and lazy. Technically, he was almost sexy in a weather-beaten, exotic way, but the basic essence of him repelled Kys. The blankness, the nothingness. As he approached, he took a pack of lho-sticks from the hip pocket of his well-tailored, sober suit. He slowly tapped one out and lit it. Then, with a fork of blue smoke exhaling carelessly from his nostrils, he nodded at Kys, a little appreciative nod, his eyes wickedly narrowed.

She turned away. For now, at least, Frauka was wearing his limiter, but there would be a time, probably quite soon, when that limiter would be deactivated, and she'd have to tolerate the numbing void of his being. The attribute made him indispensable as well as unpalatable.

Under Nayl's lead, the group left the pit and entered a sub-level of the rotting hab adjacent to it. The place had been gutted. Seeping rain-burn had eaten away the plyboard tiles of the suspended ceilings to reveal cavity spaces of corroded wiring, decomposing insulation and scabby stonework. The beams of their lamp-packs stabbed through the dripping gloom, revealing rust-streaked, mould-blotched wall boards with sticky folds of shed lining paper concertinaed at the skirting, piles of trash, nitrate-burned carpets, doorless holes.

Once they were deep inside the ruin, Ravenor selected a usable room. It had been a communal lounge shared by all the habs on that landing, larger than the individual living spaces and – because it was at the centre of the block – more intact. Wet rot had got into it, blackening the ceiling, covering the now skeletal furniture frames with fungal growths, and curling the barely readable paste-boards and notices away from the wall. Washroom rosters, rent association announcements, hiring lists, uplifting motto cards and scriptural quotes distributed by the ministorum.

They entered, and assembled loosely around Ravenor as he illuminated the chamber with a wash of yellow light from his force chair's lamps.

'Wystan, if you wouldn't mind?' the voxponder said. Frauka nodded, switched his lho-stick to his other hand, and reached into his jacket. This was the moment Kys had prepared herself for.

Wystan Frauka was one of those rare beings known as a blunter or 'untouchable'. It wasn't just that he was a non-psyker – like the majority of humans – he was the antithesis of a psyker. His mind was psi-inert. It could not be read or probed by a psyker, nor could it even be detected. Moreover, it totally inhibited psychic activity in his immediate location. The moment the limiter was switched off, Kys felt her telekinetic powers ebb away, felt even the essential vibrancy of her mind stifled. It was almost intolerable, like being blindfolded and muzzled. She wondered how the inquisitor – a profoundly more powerful psyker than she – could bear it.

Whatever the discomfort, it was useful. With Frauka's cold blankness loosed around them, and with the anti-snoop devices Mathuin had set up, they now enjoyed virtually seamless privacy.

They began to talk. Kys willed them to get it done quickly. She wanted to be rid of Frauka's company, even though she knew his presence was vital if a psyker like Ravenor was going to operate without detection on Eustis Majoris. Untouchables had first been utilised by Ravenor's mentor, the legendary Eisenhorn, who had built up a cadre of them known as the Distaff. Those times were as long gone as Eisenhorn himself, the Distaff disbanded, but Ravenor carried on some of his old master's traditions.

One by one, they reported their activities. Nayl briefly spoke of the gang maven he'd hunted in the overfloat, and of her bizarre fate. Kara described the way serious clan muscle had cornered her when she probed too hard after the dealer Lumble. Then Kys recounted the unfortunate matter of Umberto Sonsal.

'I got a lead on his supplier,' she said. 'Drase Bazarof. A line chief at Engine Imperial. I have a residence address.'

'What a mess,' muttered Frauka, with amusement in his voice. He was lurking in the corner of the room, leaning against the wall and lighting a fresh lho-stick from the smouldering paper filter of the one before. Nayl and Kys both shot him dirty looks.

'Just my thoughts,' he said, with a shrug.

'I see no reason to reproach my agents,' Ravenor said. 'The circumstances they each encountered could not have been predicted.' Kys knew there was resentment behind the comment. Prediction was a mind-skill that Ravenor had long tried to master, without success. It was pursuit of that secret that had made him tolerate the eldar for so long. 'I myself have faced the unexpected tonight. A psyker, level gamma, perhaps higher.'

There was a murmur. Ravenor's own latent ability hovered somewhere between high delta and low gamma, an extremely potent capacity that he was able to boost to truly scary levels using the psi-amplifiers laced into his chair.

'I aim to discover who he is, and what his status is. He appeared to be operating as an agent of some kind of private Magistratum unit, but the psykana register shows no one licensed to operate anywhere on Eustis Majoris except at the Guild Astropathicus.'

'Unlicensed... or secret,' Thonius said.

'I have not discounted the possibility that he is the agent of a rival inquisitor in Petropolis, Carl. I'd like you to spend the next few days finding out what you can about him. His name is Kinsky. He was accompanied by a minder called Ahenobarb and a third man, unnamed. I'll burn likenesses of all three into your short-term memory later.'

Thonius nodded.

'Immediately, we need decent transport and secure accommodation. Harlon, Kara, that's your job. We'll follow up on your avenues of investigation later. For now, I believe our most promising line lies with Patience's clue. This man Bazarof.'

ONCE NAYL AND Swole had gone, Ravenor turned his attention to Zael. The child was clearly terrified – of the people he had fallen in with, of the events he had been dragged through in the last several hours.

'In Genevieve X's house,' Ravenor said, 'you could hear me. Yet you weren't boosted like Harlon.'

'I don't know what that means,' Zael said. He was visibly shaking, and trying not to look at the strange, sealed machine that hovered before him.

Ravenor had Frauka re-engage his limiter for a short while, and switched his chair's voxponder off, speaking directly into the boy's mind. It seemed to calm the boy considerably but now, relaxing, he became washed out with exhaustion and near to collapse. Ravenor let him curl up on the ratty seat cushions of an old armchair and sleep.

Thonius went through his pockets. 'What's this now?' he said, producing the red-tissue parcel.

KARA SWOLE WOKE, and found herself crooked up in a foetal position on a shabby settee. She yawned, tasted her own wretched morning breath, and then hesitated. In the dimly lit room, Wystan Frauka sat opposite her on another settee. He was smoking, and looking at her. All she could really see was the amber coal of his lho-stick.

She sat up fast, and pulled on her waistcoat. 'You're a creepy little ninker, aren't you?' she murmured. 'See anything you like?'

Frauka opened his eyes – or rather, Kara realised that until then his eyes had been closed.

'Sorry, what?' he said, taking a drag of his lho-stick.

'You were looking at me. While I slept.'

'No,' he said, with little conviction. 'I came in here for a rest. I didn't mean to disturb you. I was asleep.'

'Right. With a lit smoke in your hand.'

He tilted his head to look at the lho-stick between his fingers.

'Ah. That's a bad habit, I know.'

'Ninker,' she said, and got up. She scooped her shoulder rig from its resting place on the top of a cloth bale and pushed her way out through the hanging drape that served as a door. Frauka made no move to follow her. His eyes were closed again.

Outside the store closet, it was noisy and bright. The large factory space had a rockcrete floor across which pale daylight shafted down through skylights. Heaps of cloth bales and material rollers twice as high as Kara almost filled the place. She could hear the rattle of the thread machines coming from the adjoining hall, and the whine of the burn-alarms out on the street. Up in the rafters, by the opaque skylights, a few wild sheen birds roosted.

Thonius had told her all about the sheen birds. *Machine birds.* Centuries before, the original architects of Petropolis had commissioned them from the Guild Mechanicus – simulacra of bird life, programmed to flock and sweep around the city spires as an adjunct of the architecture. Time and pollution had dwindled their numbers just as they had eroded the face of the towers. Now few remained: feral, uncared for, unloved.

Like so many things in this city, Kara thought.

Patience Kys was leaning against a wall nearby, eating some kind of meat off a spit-stick. She didn't look like she'd slept at all.

'What's up, Kar?' she asked.

'Frauka,' Kara replied.

'That frigging slime.'

'He was watching me sleep.'

'Frigging slime.'

Kara walked past her into the main factory hall. It had been the best she and Nayl had been able to manage the night before. A clothing manufactory in the busy garment district of Formal D. Decent vehicle access, basic amenities, an owner who was as afraid of crossing the Inquisition as he was glad to get some extra income for letting out the back store.

The boy Zael was fast asleep on a pile of insulation padding. He kicked gently in his slumber, like a dog. Nearby, Mathuin was working under the propped hood of the eight-wheeled cargo they'd bought for next to nothing from a drunken stevedore. Mathuin emerged, wiping his greasy hands.

'Piece of shit,' he said, but not to her. Mathuin seldom directed any comment at anybody. Kara liked him, even with his stand-offishness. Studly build, achingly gorgeous dark skin. She particularly liked the way his hair was bead-plaited right across his scalp away from a left side parting. She liked asymmetry.

'Can I help?' she asked.

He looked at her as if he'd never seen her before. 'Know anything about carbide engines?' he asked.

'No, I believe I don't.'

'Then no.'

Kara grinned, helped herself to his polysty cup of caffeine and wandered on. Sex on a stick, that Zeph Mathuin. A way with the lay-dees.

'Wha'cha doing?' she asked Thonius as she strolled up behind him. He was sitting on an off-cut roll of lining cloth, poring over something, and jumped when he heard her.

'Nothing.'

'Doesn't look like nothing.'

'I'm making notes. Detailing the case,' he said huffily, showing her his chapbook.

'What's that you're hiding in it?' she teased.

'My pen,' he replied, revealing it.

'Right,' she said. He was really bristling. What had he done to get all guilty about? 'I was just asking.'

'Well,' said Thonius, 'well, just don't.'

What the hell was up with everyone this morning?

Kara finished Mathuin's caffeine and tossed the cup aside. To her left was a bay area screened off by a half-height wall of chalky rockcrete. A rattling frame of pipes and shower roses hung over it, spitting out water. It was a wash area, built for fabric workers to shower in after long shifts in the dye-house. Kara leaned her arms on the half-wall and looked over. She smiled to herself

Nayl was standing naked under one of the shower-heads, water streaming off his hard, scarred body. He looked as if he was in a trance.

'Looking good, bounty,' she called, mockingly.

He looked up to see her, but made no attempt to cover himself. They'd been soldiers together in this war for a long time. Gender distinctions and sexuality had long since reduced to a dense layer of loyalty and unspoken devotion. They had been together for a while, since the early days, when they answered to Eisenhorn. It had been fun. Now, they were like brother and sister.

'Missed a bit,' she said.

He looked round.

'That looks like blood,' she added.

'Yeah,' he said. 'Mine. Me and Zeph went knocking for that Bazarof chump this morning., early. We'd have taken you too, but you were out for the count and the boss said you needed sleep.'

'Boss wasn't wrong. How'd it go?'

'Shitty,' Nayl replied, scrubbing the last of the dried blood off his calf with a shred of wet cloth. 'He'd got wind of Sonsal and done a runner. Left a homemade pin bomb in his lodgings for those who came knocking. I was too slow.'

'You intact?'

'Just about. Tap.'

She reached in over the half-wall and knocked the rusty faucet shut. The water pipes shuddered and stopped their output. Nayl splashed through the draining water to the wall and grabbed a dank towel.

'Got a lead, then?' she asked, as he dried himself.

'His workmates said he has family up in Stairtown. They think he might have run home to hide. We're going to try some addresses there this morning. You up for it?'

'Sure,' she said.

Nayl walked out of the shower bay past her, and reached for his bodyglove.

'Where's the boss?' Kara asked.

Nayl jerked a thumb.

She hadn't seen him, but there he was. A lightless armoured shell lurking between cloth-roll piles at the far end of the warehouse. He'd even killed his anti-grav. The force chair sat on its runners.

'What's he doing?' Kara asked.

+I'm thinking.+

'He's thinking,' said Nayl.

'Yeah, got that, thanks.'

THEY ROCKED UP north in the cargo-8 once Mathuin had got it running. Nayl drove, with Kara beside him. Mathiun sat silently in the cabin behind them, his heavy kitbag at his side on the tatty rear seats.

On the broad, inter-formal routes the going was excellent. These were great raised roadways of crumbling rockcrete with siding baffles of chaincage and ballast-filled plastek hoppers. They slid through the grimy morning traffic, adding a billow-wake to the greasy exhaust pall. Kara watched the huge hive-city glide by the window. Stacks, manufactories, broken lots jailed in chain-link, a transit station with an elevated track-section that ran along the inter-route for six kilometres, retaining ouslite walls daubed with illegible slogans and peeling posters, smokestacks, the low, pale sun strobing through the posts of a long roadside fence like a zoetrope.

Occasionally, through the smog, the looming forms of the distant inner-formal towers emerged, like primeval leviathans rising briefly to the surface light. Sunlight struck hard, starry glints off faraway fliers. Dry lightning twinkled over the estuary.

Off the inter-routes, in the tight surface streets of the formal boroughs, progress was a slack crawl. Traffic was dense, and the constantly shifting daily street-marts impeded their way. Kara saw the ratty frontages of shops and trade-dens roll past; dangling neon signs and wrought iron script placards, flocks of pedestrians, faith-paper booths, hollow-eyed indents queuing at the labour halls, peddlers with their barrows, and spry kerb-dancers tumbling for coins.

She heard music from a dozen sources, the booming unintelligible sermons from the street corner speaker-horns, the rise-and-fall whoop of an Magistratum siren. She smelled spit-fat, sausage and skilleted bushmeat from the gutterside cook-stalls. She watched the gampers flood out of the sink-shops every time the burn-alarms sounded. As they unfurled their umbrellas, it looked like a time-lapse reel of forest mushrooms blooming.

'Eyes up,' said Nayl. 'We're nearly there.'

Ahead of them, the city rose abruptly, as if it had been folded at right angles. The stratum of stack floors and landings climbed away into the murk.

Stairtown.

FOUR

Here, Petropolis met the hills and conquered them. Here, the city shelved up and became a vertical borough. Mist had gathered in the deep wells of the formal, and the rain-alarms were ringing. Vast spiral stairways of iron, lidded with tintglas so they looked like vast models of genetic double helixes, rose out of the vapour into the upper levels. Powerful pendant lamps hung down on rusting chains three kilometres long, like shackled stars.

They left the cargo-8 in a pay garage under the west nine stack and climbed spiral five into the habs. All the pedestrian screw-stairs were bustling with citizens, moving up, moving down. Their combined voices filled the huge misty well like the rustle of gigantic paper sheets. The spirals were stepped streets, broad enough for twenty people to a tread. Hawkers and cook-stands had set themselves up on parts of the wider outside curves. Some vendors hung their wares out over the guardrails on long frames so that ascending citizens could admire them from floors below. Gymnasts and acrobats, some of them enhanced with poor quality mechanical augmetics, twisted, rotated and swung from scaffold structures suspended off the sides of the staircase, defying the fathomless drop. Kara pulled on Nayl's sleeve so she could watch them for a moment. Mathuin waited, glowering with impatience, two steps up, the kitbag slung over his shoulder.

That had been her life before this, spinning and dancing between the thorny iron bars of the circus arena. She admired the techniques. Taut wire, trip trapeze, solid bar work. The augmetics were cheats though. Three-sixty differential wrists and auto-lock digits made some of the moves too easy, too safe. She could have done it all, aug-free. She peered over the rail into the ghastly void of the sink below.

Maybe not with that risk.

'Coming?' said Nayl.

They went up past two more level stages and, with Mathuin leading, they turned left onto a landing, passing under a corroded sign that read 'hab west nine eighteen'.

A makeshift trader grotto had clustered itself around the landing stage exit off the stairwell, the way worm-feeders gather around an ocean-floor black smoker. The grotto thrived on passing trade. It offered contraband, tariff-free lho-sticks by the carton, reheated pasties of mechanically recovered meat product, low-quality erotica slates, dubious mech-ware, knock-off copies of small calibre urdeshi weapons, cheap clothing, promise-bonds.

'No thanks,' Kara said to a grubby trader who offered her a new ident and a facial re-sculpt for the price of three courses with wine at a Formal B trattoria.

They entered the stack warrens. Rows of hallways, rows of identical doors, rows lined with failing strip-lighting that looked like luminous vertebrae. Trash littered the hallways. There was a strong smell of stale urine.

Mathuin walked ahead, pausing to read off a plak-board notice listing the addresses of the residents.

'Bazarof, eleven ninety,' he said.

'A sister, we think,' Nayl said.

The hallway carpet had been worn back to the matting by the constant foot traffic. Many of the wall panels had crumbled or been damaged, and most repairs had made use of cheap blue insulation tape, which gave off a sickening smell of rotten citrus. The doors to some habs stood open and inside they glimpsed squalor. Hunched hab-wives talking in doorways or just standing, arms folded, looking out blankly into the corridor; dirty children running from hab to hab; the sound of poorly-tuned vox broadcasts, the smells of rancid food, decomposition, grain liqour, toilets.

Eyes followed the trio indirectly but no one approached them. They didn't want the trouble... they were too tired to deal with trouble. But by now someone would have tipped off whichever clan operated this hab.

Eleven ninety. The door was open. An ugly, unwashed reek emanated from the hab. The walls just inside the door were shelved, and those shelves laden with bric-a-brac that was so dirty and broken it was impossible to identify individual items. Nayl led the way.

The interior was semi-derelict. Exposed bunches of electrical trunking bulged like a goiter into the room where the plasterboards of the west wall had collapsed. Garbage covered the floor and the crippled furniture. Two heavy tanks of lead glass with iron frames stood over by the eastern wall, full of filthy brown fluid that bubbled occasionally. The smell came from them. The only real illumination came from an old pict-viewer set in the corner, distorted black and white images dancing and flickering on its cracked valve screen. A woman sat watching it.

Nayl cleared his throat.

The woman glanced round, and looked them up and down. Then she went back to her viewing. She was old, Kara thought. Not a sister, a mother. A grandmother, even.

'Looking for your brother,' Nayl said.

'Take your pick,' she said, and gestured to the tanks. Kara looked again and saw that inside the glass tanks were pallid, deformed lumps of flesh. Limbless, formless, supported by the filterpipes and the chem-pumps. She saw a single, pitiful eye.

'Shit!' she recoiled.

'Your other brother,' Nayl said.

The woman got up and faced them. If she was the sister, life had ridden her hard and worn her out.

'Drase,' Nayl said. 'It's probably not to your advantage to protect him.'

'I won't protect him,' she said, somewhat surprisingly. 'Knuck-head. He come here earlier, but I sent him away. Way he was acting told me whatever was after him was going to kill him, and anyone what helped him. And I didn't want part of that. Not for me, or my brothers.'

Mathuin suddenly tensed and turned round. A heavy set, acid-marked clanster stood in the doorway, looking in at them. Four or five more loomed outside in the hall.

Mathuin reached for his weapon, but Nayl stopped him with a look.

'You all right, Nenny Bazarof?' asked the clanster.

'Yes,' she said.

'You don't want them escorting out?'

'No,' she said. 'Drase was always bad news. I won't be sucked down with him. I got my brothers to look after.'

'What happened to them?' Nayl asked.

'Metal poisoning. Industrial accident. They got workers comp, but it's not much. Ten years I cared for them. Can't even afford to flush their tanks as often as I'd like. Drase never gave me nothing.'

She looked at the hammer in the doorway and shook her head. He backed out and left them alone. Then she looked at Nayl, and thought for a moment as if summoning up a great measure of courage.

'Hundred crowns,' she said.

'What?'

'For a hundred, I'll tell you where he is.'

Kara looked away. A hundred was paltry, pocket change. Not to the Bazarof sister, though. More than she'd see in a year. She had to pluck up the bravery just to suggest such an extortionate sum.

Nayl reached into his jacket and counted out a hundred from a fold of local currency. The woman's eyes fixed on the fingers and the money. There was a flash – pain or anger – as she realised she could have asked for much more.

'Drase has a friend,' she said as she took the money. 'Lives up Stair, in the deadlofts, last I heard. West twenty, I think.'

'I'd like you to be sure,' said Nayl.

'West twenty,' she confirmed. 'Right up there. His name's Odysse Bergossian. They've known each other since growing up. Neither one good for the other.'

'What's this Bergossian do?' asked Kara.

The Bazarof woman looked at her, as if only now aware of her. 'Little as possible. He's a waster. Got a serious gladstone habit, last I saw him. Sometimes does a spot gamping, other times odd labour jobs. I heard Drase talk about Odysse working at a meat packers in a freight zone up in K, and sometimes in the circus silos.'

'Which circus?'

'The big one. The Carnivora, in Formal G.'

'Thanks,' Nayl told her. 'We won't be back.' Nayl nodded, and Kara and Mathuin followed him out of the hab and left the woman to her flickering picter and atrophied kin.

THE VOX-SET BLEEPED. Frauka was reaching for it, but Kys pushed past him to get it first. Even just brushing against him made her flesh crawl. Frauka stood back with a false, laconic 'after you' gesture.

'Kys.'

She heard Nayl's voice through the tinny burble of the encryption circuits. The channel was as safe as they could make it.

He told her their progress. Ravenor, who had heard the vox-chime, slid his chair over. She knew he was tense. With the unidentified psyker out there, they couldn't risk switching Frauka off so the inquisitor could shadow the team mentally. Circumstances like this were a cruel reminder to Ravenor how helpless he really was.

'They're going up Stair,' she relayed. 'They think they've got a trace on my guy.'

'Tell them to be wary, and to check in regularly,' Ravenor's chair-speakers whispered tonelessly.

Kys talked to Nayl some more, and wrote down the details of their destination. Then she hung up the vox-horn.

'Got a feeling in my bones,' she said. 'They're going to need help.'

'Wystan, could you prep some weapons for us?' Ravenor asked. The chair rotated slightly to face Kys. 'Patience, I think the factory owner has some vehicles. Go and see if we can borrow or rent one from him.'

As Frauka knelt down and unclasped one of their equipment cases, Kys strode away across the factory hall.

She was tense too, and edgy. A sound from above made her start, but it was just the mangy birds up in the skylight, knocking their rotting wings against the glass.

She saw the boy, Zael. He was awake, crouching against a rusted loom-block, sipping dehyd soup from a plastek bowl. They'd offered him proper rations, even foods from one of the street stands, but it seemed he liked dehyd. He was a sickly little thing. His undergrown body was so strung out by self-inflicted abuse, he probably couldn't take anything more than dilute, freeze-dry broth.

He was watching Thonius. The interrogator had set up his portable cogitator set, and spliced the data-leads into one of the municipal communication conduits. A branch of them ran down the alley beside the hall, and Thonius had used a sniffer to find their voltage and a uni-plug on the end of an extension lead to hack in. The risk of detection was minimal. The whole of the hive was wired up, and given the city's state of decay there were breaks in the system all over the place. Finding his splice would be like identifying one hole in a fishing net.

And Thonius was a fine operator. He had a slew of whisper programmes and encryption tools, some of them ordo issue, some of them self-written. Through his spliced link, he was rifling the data-blocks of Petropolis for information.

The portable cogitator, leather-bound, was the size and shape of a passenger trunk and so heavy only Nayl could carry it any distance without help. Thonius had got it up onto a pair of packing crates and it now formed a makeshift knee-hole desk. Skeins of wires ran out the back to the junction point with the extension feed. Three more wires ran up into the sockets behind his right ear. The lid of the trunk, which formed the screen, was propped open with a little brass elbow joint. Thonius was typing slowly using the oiled mechanical keyboard.

'How's it going?' she asked as she came up.

He shrugged. An amber rune appeared amongst the screen's rolling data columns, and he tutted, pressing a key.

'Slow. As might be expected of an administry world, the info-systems are vast and well governed. I have to watch every step for fear of detection as an unauthorised user.'

Another amber rune. Another sigh and a tap.

'See? The city datacores are divided into discrete sub-blocks, which means separate encryption protocols and user codes. I've already burned out one decrypter. I've had to rescribe the Geiman-rys paradigms from memory.'

'The stuff you know, Look, we may roll soon, to back up Nayl. You staying here?'

'Yes, there's a lot to do.'

She nodded and walked away. Zael was now watching them both, she noticed.

Zael put down his bowl as she walked away. He'd heard most of their exchange and wondered why the foppish man had lied to the woman.

Until she'd walked over, he hadn't been working on the cogitator at all.

THEY WERE HIGH up at the top of west twenty. They could hear the wind moaning, and the actual fabric of the massive tower creak and give. The rotting hallways were deserted. It was creepy, like being on an abandoned ship at sea.

This was the upper realm of the Stairtown towers, a place called the deadlofts, six kilometres above sea level. Originally, these levels had been luxury habs and penthouse apartments, but then Stairtown – like so many other boroughs – had fallen into slump. Without maintenance, the summit levels had succumbed to decay. Wind, acid rain, regular fires generated by lightning strikes, vandalism. The rich and beautiful people had moved out years ago. Now the deadlofts – the top six or seven floors of every Stairtown stack – were lawless places where the homeless, the poor, the fugitive and the insane claimed their own spaces. And even they did not number many.

It was a sparse and inhospitable zone. There were no amenities. No power, no plumbing. Some areas were entirely exposed to the lethal ministry of the rain. Others had lost their tintglas and were traps for murderous radiation and ultra-violet light. Where the window ports were broken, the high-alt gales could get strong enough to rip people right out of the tower or rupture them with extremes of atmospheric pressure.

It had taken the three of them two hours to cross between the Stairtown towers on foot to west twenty, and another whole hour to climb to the loft level. No working lifts. Two double-backs because of blocked accessways, two more due to screwstairs that had collapsed from corrosion.

They saw only a smattering of life. Ragged vagrants huddled in corners; shadows that darted away as they approached: a naked man clad only in faithpaper, his body hideously blotched with acid burns, cooking moss over a candle; a semi-dismantled cleaning servitor, dead except for its left function limb that mindlessly circled a buffing mop in the air.

They had to sidestep acid drips from the roof, and check the flooring where it had been eaten into soft pulp. Draughts whined down abandoned halls. Nayl had drawn his pistol and the other two followed him closely. Kara was especially unnerved by the absence of Ravenor. She had to remind herself that back in the old days, with Eisenhorn, she'd happily functioned without a telepathic nursemaid. But she'd become so used to Ravenor's presence since then.

They'd questioned a few of the inhabitants. Some refused to answer at all, and most that did claimed not to know any Odysse Bergossian. But one old woman, hunched on a mat in an empty hab, had mumbled a few directions. The windows behind her were cracked and broken, and hard light and cold air streamed in. The back of her head and neck were burned raw. She hadn't moved for a long time. She was eating beetles when they found her.

Through those cracked windows, Kara saw the poisoned glare of the sky, the cloudbanks, the dropping view through the tower tops towards the vast expanse of the smog-covered city. This was the brightest, lightest place in the whole of Petropolis, pushed up out above the pollution cover. And it was also the most wretched.

They followed the instructions she'd lisped through bad teeth flecked with broken wing cases and leg segments. Two halls on, they heard music.

Kara drew her compact and checked the load. Mathuin put down his kitbag and unfastened it. He pulled the rotator cannon out and settled its bulk over his left shoulder, buckling the support frame around his torso. The weapon was about as long as a man's arm, a counterweighted cluster of ammunition hoppers from which a swathe of six aluminium barrels projected. The cannon actually depended from a gyro-balanced armature that extended from the harness frame under his left armpit. Mathuin took off his left glove and revealed the polished chrome augmetic connector that replaced his left hand. He clunked the connector into the receiving socket on the back of the cannon so that it became an extension of his arm, and brought it to life. The autoloading mechanism clacked and shifted the first of the ammo hoppers into place. The swathe of barrels test-rotated as one with a metallic whir.

'I'd like to be able to talk to him before you paint the walls with his body,' Nayl said.

'Just a precaution,' Mathuin said.

'In that case, you get to be backstop.' Nayl made to walk on, then turned back. 'You kill me or Kara with that bullet hose, Zeph, and we'll come back to haunt you to the end of your frigging days.'

'I know what I'm doing, Nayl,' Mathuin said. He did. Kara knew that. He really did. In this trio, despite her years of experience, she was the amateur. She'd learned her trade since recruitment as an ordo auxiliary. These two had both been doing it since they could walk. Bounty men, hunter-killers, so hard-bitten teeth broke on them.

But when Nayl offered her point, she felt flattered, even now. Stealth was her thing. She moved like silk, and had a nose for surveillance. Those skills had been why Eisenhorn had chosen her for his retinue in the first place.

She led the way, Nayl a dozen metres behind her, Mathuin out of sight down the hall. Sunlight blazed down through the skylights, mobile and distorted by the fast motion of passing clouds. She could smell acid.

The music was louder now. Thumping, tinny. It sounded like bootleg pound, the music of the twists. Mutant club sounds were all the rage with younger types.

At the end of the hallway, a door was shrouded with opaque plastek sheeting stapled to the jamb. Hard daylight shone out around it. That was where the music was coming from. She thumbed off the safety and edged forward. Handwritten in paint by the doorway were the words GET OUT.

Ordinarily, she'd have had Ravenor tell her what was behind the sheeting. Now she had to sidle close and peer through a slit. A large penthouse chamber, part of a suite. Bare floorboards, bare flakboard walls, huge tintglas windows through which the sunlight blazed.

Kara waved Nayl flat against the wall, and took a breath. Then she pushed through a gap in the plastek sheeting, her weapon raised, and panned it left and right.

There was no one there. A stained mattress roll, some empty wine bottles, drifts of discarded, soiled clothing, a battered old four-speaker tile player covered in club stickers from which the music was raging. There were open doorways to the right and the left.

Beside the mattress roll was a polysty tray full of gladstones. The Bazarof woman had said Bergossian had a habit. The smooth stones, mined on a distant outworld and strictly prohibited, were slightly psyk-reactive. Held in the hand or put under the tongue, they produced a warm, blissful sensation. The sense of euphoria and well-being could last days apparently. They were popular in the twist clubs down in the undersink.

These, strangely, were dusty, as if unused and untouched for weeks.

The floor around the bedroll was covered in screwed up hanks of red tissue paper.

Nayl came in after her, his heavy pistol up and ready. She pointed to the player to suggest she might turn it off, and he shook his head. He kept watch on the right hand doorway as she checked the left. A galley kitchen, unlit. It stank. With the power and water cut, it had no function any more except as a dump for trash. Heaps of discard rubbish and crap rotted in there. Craproaches scurried in the gloom.

She re-emerged and moved towards the window to be out of line-of-sight from the other door. With Nayl covering her, she went through.

Another large room, also well lit thanks to the vast expanse of tintglas. This one was also empty. There was a broken toilet stall to the left, and another doorway in the right-hand wall. Originally, this had been where the apartment finished. The doorway had been opened through the flakboard partition with a sledgehammer, allowing access to the neighbouring apartment. More plastek sheeting covered it.

Kara waved Nayl in. Immediately, he saw what she'd seen. Someone had used a charcoal or graphite stick to write on the bare walls, the ceiling and the floor. The markings seemed insane. Some were patterns and geometric designs, dividing up the sections of the room. These were annotated by odd, scrawling texts, some of which were written directly onto the walls, others on sheets of paper taped to them. There were drawings too: men, cherubs, monsters, all primitive but carefully rendered.

'Ninth heaven of truth...' Nayl whispered, tracing a finger along one annotated space.

'The place of atonement. The zone of understanding. The fifteenth heaven, where men rest from their travails...' Kara looked at him. 'What the frig is this?'

He shook his head, and pushed his way – gun raised – through the plastek-covered doorway.

ODYSSE BERGOSSIAN HAD taken over nineteen apartments in the top of the deadlofts. All of them were stripped and almost scrubbed clean and all linked by holes he'd smashed in the dividing walls. Each one was an annotated diagram of insanity. The markings and writings became more and more complex as they edged their way on. Increasingly, the creator of the markings had used colour – wax crayons – to decorate the walls and ceilings and floors. They found discarded lump ends of crayons underfoot, and more scraps of red tissue.

By the tenth apartment, the designs had become manic, and extraordinary. Fully rendered views of the city in full colour, as good as any limner could have managed. Lifelike faces. Unearthly beings that made Kara's skin goose to look at. Intricate captions rendered in gold leaf and paint, naming such things as the 'Hall of Sublime Healing', the 'Domain of the Sane', the 'Fifty-First Heaven of Lesser Gods' and 'Somewhere New'. Some of the murals had blood and body fluids caked into them. Kara and Nayl were both on their nerve ends. The music, far behind them, was a distant pulse. They could hear the creaking of the high-alt wind.

In the nineteenth apartment, they found Odysse Bergossian.

He was naked and hunched up, drawing on a wall. A basket full of broken crayons, paint pots and mucky brushes lay beside him. He had half-covered the room with designs. The contrast between the decorated half and the bare walls was oddly distressing.

He didn't look up as they came in. They only knew it was Bergossian because he jumped when Nayl said his name.

He looked at them. He was young, no more than twenty-five, and his face and neck had nasty burns on them. He covered his face with paint-smudged hands and rolled over in a heap.

'Where's Drase Bazarof?' Nayl said.

Bergossian moaned and shook his head.

'Harlon!' Kara called. Nayl went over to her, keeping his eye on the trembling man.

She pointed at the wall, and Nayl looked. This was the drawing Bergossian had been halfway through when they interrupted him. In full colour, beautifully captured, was the likeness of Bergossian. Standing over him, half-finished but unmistakable, were the figures of Kara Swole and Harlon Nayl.

'Emperor preserve me!' Nayl whispered.

* * *

Zeph Mathuin decided he had waited long enough. He was about to move when he heard footsteps coming up the hall behind him. Silent, he backed into the shadow of a doorway.

A thickset young man in labourer's clothes walked past him, carrying a pail of hot riceballs and meat sticks, and three polysty caffeines on a preformed tray. He disappeared in through the plastek drapes.

Mathuin keyed his voxer.

'Nayl. I think Bazarof is coming your way. Want me to intercept?'

'Follow but hold back. We'll get him.'

'Odysse? Odysse? I've got lunch,' the young man called as he walked through the connected, decorated chambers. 'Odysse? Where are you?'

'Busy,' said Nayl, stepping out of a doorway and aiming his weapon.

The young man gasped and yelped, and dropped the foodpail and the drinks.

Kara appeared behind Nayl, dragging the whimpering Bergossian by the wrist.

'Drase Bazarof?' Nayl asked, lowering his gun. The young man clearly saw this as a chance to flee, and turned. Mathuin stood behind him, rotator cannon aimed at his chest.

'Uh uh uh...' Mathuin hissed.

'I'm not Bazarof!' the young man implored, looking back at Nayl. 'I'm not! My name is Gerg Lunt.'

'And that makes you what?' Nayl asked.

'A friend! Odysse's friend! Shit, I knew Bazarof would get us into trouble...'

'He's here?' Nayl asked.

'Three cups of caffeine,' Mathuin noted.

Lunt looked twitchy.

'Up,' said Kara suddenly. She'd heard the creaking of the roof before any of them.

Mathuin swept his weapon up to aim at the ceiling.

'No!' Nayl cried. 'I want him alive.' He looked at the skylight. 'Boost me, Kara,' he said.

'You're kidding, right?' she answered. 'You boost me.'

Nayl was about to argue.

'Wasting time!' Mathuin growled and placed himself under the skylight with his free hand cupped. 'Move it and do what you do,' he said to Kara.

She used Mathiun's cupped hand as a stirrup for one foot, and his shoulder as a shelf for the other. He was rock steady. Nayl glared at him.

There was no clasp or catch – the light had not been designed to open – but the seals were rotten and Kara pushed it out of the frame with the heel of her hand. Then she hoisted herself up and through from Mathiun's shoulder.

Nayl looked at Mathuin a moment longer. 'Guard them,' he said, pointing at the two men, then hurried from the room.

OUTSIDE, IT WAS bitingly cold and painfully bright. The air was thin. Kara edged her way along the roof, testing every step. Years of acid rain had turned the fabric of the roof into a damp, flaking landscape.

She put on her glare-shades and pulled up her hood. The gables and wings of the roof section projected before her. Behind her was a tower of old comm-masts and cable-stays, a vertical nest of rusting metal and faded plastics. She looked around. There was no sign of anyone. Maybe it had just been the wind.

The world was huge. She could see for many kilometres in every direction: an immense raft of curdled black cloud cover out of which the massive towerheads of Stairtown poked like islands. The sky above the cloud layer was a bright, watery smear. She didn't want to be out here for long, especially if the rain or wind picked up. She could already feel the skin of her face tingling. She fastened the neck of her hood up to her nose.

She walked along further, getting nearer to the edge. It was treacherous underfoot. Kara held onto a stay-cable for support and saw smoke waft out where her glove clasped the dripping steel. Fumes from acid reaction was also puffing out from under her feet.

Over the steady buffeting of the wind, she heard a noise, turned, and almost slipped. Then she realised it was her vox-link.

'What?'

Nayl's voice sounded like it was coming up from a deep drain. '–are you?'

'On the frigging roof!' she answered.

'No... where on roof?'

She looked around, trying to translate the stark roofscape into something he would understand from beneath. It wasn't easy.

'Just turn on your locator!' he snapped.

Stupid. Obvious. The precariousness of her state had made her forget basics. She was light-headed. The thin air was making her pant. Kara pulled back the cuff of her jacket and activated the little tracer sewn into the lining.

'Got me?'

In the deadlofts below, Nayl came out of Bergossian's rooms into the hall. There was a rune flashing on the fold-out screen of his compact auspex. 'Yeah,' he called back. 'I'm almost under you.'

She moved on. The wind was gusting stronger and it smelled wet and corrosive. There was a flapping, rattling sound, but it turned out to be a series of tatty old mills along the edge of the roof, their vanes spinning as the air moved.

Thirty metres away to the west, a gaggle of sheen birds burst up into the air, wings beating, and curled away over the lip of the eaves. They'd been disturbed. Kara saw a figure scrambling along the lower slope of the next roof section, clinging on to a tension cable.

Arms out for balance, she paced down the pitch of the roof like it was a high wire, and then leapt down onto the flat top of a ducting box. The bare metal of the box's top dented like a tin drum under her weight and splashed up moisture from the pool gathered there. She saw a smatter of burn-holes appear in the strengthened cloth of her leggings.

He'd heard her land. She saw him look her way, and then continue on with more animation.

Ninker was going to slip, if he wasn't careful...

'Bazarof!' she yelled. It was hard to project her voice over the thump of the wind.

He vanished out of sight behind a flue stack. She dropped down off the ducting box and scurried over the coping of the lower wing. Almost at once, she slipped over and began to slither down the hip of the roof. She caught a projecting truss-cable and arrested her slide.

'Kara?'

'West of me! About forty metres!'

In the corridor below, Nayl broke into a run, calculating her guess on the auspex screen. He had to kick open a door that had been locked for decades and pick his way through a dark, stinking apartment withered by the encroachment of the rain. Through another door, ajar and decayed to the consistency of wet paper, and he was out into a service corridor. It was littered with rusting junk and as dark as the room before it. A derelict servitor, decomposed down to bone and bare metal, decorated the next junction. It was lying on the bonded floor as if prostrate in prayer. Nayl turned left, groping now; it was so dark. Slimy tendrils of filth dangled from the ceiling and got in his face. He spat and wiped them away. There was another door. It gave beneath his shoulder.

Sunlight, bright and dangerous, streamed down through broken skylights into another corridor. The floor had almost rotted and burned away. He had to step his way on the exposed cross members. Below his feet, gnawed holes showed the drop into the darkness of the floors below.

Nayl paused, legs braced wide between two mouldering joists, and raised his pistol to cover the skylights. The wind was creaking the superstructure, but it sounded like someone was up there.

Kara followed her quarry's path along the lower roof, using the tension cable as he had done. By the time she reached the flue stack, her gloves were ruined. She could feel spot-burns on her legs from the splashed rainwater. She was out of breath and dizzy.

The metal flues, like the pipes of an organ, had been burned almost blue by the climate. She swung around them. The end gable of the roof wing was immediately beneath her, then the gulf itself: the flank of the tower dropped away into the cloud cover below. It looked a long way, even to the clouds. Much less to the ground itself.

There was no sign of Bazarof. Had he slipped and fallen? If he'd managed to scramble around the gable-end – using only the rotting fascia as a foothold – he might have made it onto the adjoining roofwing – a wide mansard that abutted the central rise of the tower. Beyond that was a flat roof section fitted with broken skylights.

Kara chose her grip and spidered her way around the gable. Mushy pieces of verge boarding came off in her fingers. She leapt the last of the distance onto the edge of the mansard, trying to ignore the prospect of the drop behind her, and ran up it on all fours to the crest. There, she slithered down onto the flat section. Her heart was pounding, and her breaths came in rasps.

Gun drawn, she reached the skylights and peered down. Nayl and the barrel of his gun were looking up at her.

'Damn!' she panted. 'Didn't he come that way?'

'No sign here.'

She looked round. 'I'd have seen him if he'd doubled back. Maybe he did fall off...'

'What?'

'Just stay there,' she said, and circled back away from the skylights. Debris and junk fallen from the inner tower littered the inward part of the flat roof. She picked through it. The pieces of flaking metal siding, that were bent and collapsed like fallen window blinds, were large enough to conceal a man. In fact, they concealed nothing except pools of slime water and rot.

The rising elevation of the inner tower was smooth travertine, streaked with orange stains of corrosion. As she got closer, she realised the stains marked out where iron rungs had been set into the wall. They were loose and unsteady, but they supported her weight. She went up with her gun tucked in her belt.

The end of one of the rungs popped out in a puff of floury mortar. She skipped it, stretched, and pulled herself up onto the next few. The extra exertion made her head swim.

'Kara?'

Nayl ached to know what was going on. With his feet braced wide between the joists, there was no way he could launch himself up far enough to get out of the roof lights.

'Kara!'

There was a ledge, ten metres up, underbraced by eroded arcature. She got up onto it. It was only a metre wide and ran along the face of the tower to the corner. At the head of the rungs, lichen had been scratched and torn away recently: she wasn't the first to make this climb.

She went along the ledge to the corner. The turn of the central tower looked out over another jumble of roofs. Bazarof was scrambling over them, into the face of the gale.

'Got him! South-west! The next wing!' she voxed and jumped off the ledge. It was a five-metre drop, down onto a flat section of coping that ran along between the beehives of six air-exchangers. Bazarof was still going. He hadn't heard her.

She ran down the coping, stepping wide over iron roof ribs, and jumped down again. She was coming up the slope of roof behind him. Stay-cables swung loose from stanchion brackets and the wind moaned through the few strands that remained under tension. He looked back and saw her, then darted left sharply along the line of the roof, his feet slipping on the loose tiles.

'Stay put!' she yelled. He reached another cluster of air-exchanger domes and disappeared from view.

She drew her weapon again, and edged between the first of the metal beehive casings. She winced as a squall of rain spattered down out of the pale sky, then she advanced a few metres more, around the next two domes. Another flurry of rain. This time she turned her head aside and raised an arm to shield her face.

He hit her from behind, slamming into her hard and banging her sideways into the nearest dome. She dropped her shoulders and flinched in time to evade his follow-up punch. His fist cracked hard against the dome's metal.

Bazarof squealed with pain. She brought her gun up, but he lashed out blindly and chopped her across the inside of her elbow. At the same moment her right foot came out from under her on the wet leading. She fell back against the dome again, and he kicked her hard in the belly. She was coughing, spitting, cursing, so winded she couldn't move. Bazarof – bigger and tougher than he'd seemed from a distance across the roofscape – reached down and tore the compact from her hand. He moved to aim it at her head, but had to fiddle with the unfamiliar design. She rolled hard, sweeping his legs away with a desperate scissor kick.

He crashed over heavily, the gun skidding away down the guttering. They rose together, Kara extending an open palm in time to stop his first punch dead and a forearm in time to block his second. Bazarof had physical strength, but no combat training, except maybe a diploma in basic brawling. His third strike was a hooking punch that she stepped back out of, turning her back step into a full rotate that delivered a backward spin-kick to his chest. He was thrown back against another of the domes, but came back for more, his eyes bright with fear. She pivoted back on her right foot and, straight-legged, brought her left heel down into his shoulder. The blow broke something and folded him into a heap.

She reached over to grab him, but wobbled badly. The effort of subduing him had really made her head spin, and she had idiot stars of nausea dancing across her vision.

He put an elbow into the side of her left knee and Kara folded, hitting her head a glancing blow against the side of the air-exchanger as he went down.

A blur. Colour. Shapes. The smell of blood in her sinuses and the taste of it in her throat. She shook herself. Bazarof was gone.

As she was getting to her feet, she heard a sharp cry above the wind.

'Bazarof? Bazarof?'

He had tried to flee, but the thin air and effort had made him dizzy too. He'd slipped on the edge of the coping and gone over the side, sliding down the hip of a steep catslide roof almost to the edge.

Kara peered over and saw him. A terrified white face looked up at her. His hands were wrapped around a rain-spout. His feet were milling in empty air, the sheer drop of Stairtown below him.

She couldn't reach him. She leaned out and tried, but knew at once that she was likely to slide right down after him. She looked around and found a broken length of pipe, but it was too short. He squealed again, his hands slipping, acid fumes rising from between his fingers.

Kara ran back along the coping and grabbed one of the slack stay cables. It was heavy and awkward, and coiled against her grip like it was alive. Grunting with effort, she dragged it back to the edge and spilled it out down the catslide. It writhed open and down, flopping over the gutter near to him with a weighty metal snap. Then she worked it along so it was right beside him. The cable squeaked along the guttering.

'Grab it! Come on!'

He moaned that he couldn't.

'Come on!' Kara was damned if they were going to lose another source before he could be questioned. Their record during the Petropolis op so far was dismal.

'Grab it!'

With a frantic lunge, Bazarof grabbed the cable. He started to slide again almost at once. Kara cried out with the effort of bracing against the cable.

With a shriek, Bazarof went over the edge.

Kara cursed aloud, but the cable was still dragging heavy. He hadn't fallen. He was still holding onto the steel line, dangling out of sight. She heaved once, twice, her teeth gritted, her straining hands slipping on the wet cable. He was too heavy. She couldn't – Patience Kys appeared beside her.

'Where did you come from?' Kara gasped.

'We thought you might need a hand.'

'Help me, for frig's sake, before he falls!'

Kys didn't move to take hold of the cable. She just looked down the catslide towards the gutter, her brows furrowing.

Kara felt a sudden slack on the line, as if Bazarof's weight had gone. Ninker had fallen after all...

But no. He slid into view, hands first, then his face, then his body. He was still gripping the cable, but it was Kys's telekinesis that was dragging him up. Face down, the whimpering man slithered up the tiled slope like a snail, until he was close enough for them both to grab and pull onto the coping. Kys stood back, exhaling softly from the effort. Bazarof writhed and moaned at their feet.

'Enough!' Kara told him, dragging him to his feet. He was shamming. He clawed at her, so she rammed his head against the side of an air dome with enough force to dent the dome's casing.

'Enough!'

And at last it was.

SUSPENSORS GENTLY HUMMING, the inquisitor moved through the chambers of Bergossian's deadloft at a slow, frictionless glide, scrutinising the intricately marked walls one centimetre at a time.

Frauka walked beside him, smoking another lho-stick. They looked like sedate visitors at a public gallery.

'Important?' Frauka asked.

Ravenor's chair-speakers responded with a soft, non-vocal click, the equivalent of a pensive human 'hmm'. The chair swivelled round and the sensors regarded the opposite wall. From deep inside the chair-body came the faint whirr of recording pict-ware.

'Acts of insanity,' Ravenor said at last. 'Random scrawls, showing signs of tertiary stage derangement, yet sub-ordered with specific or quasi-specific symbolism. The product of a trance-state, I think. An altered state, certainly. No way to tell if there's any consistency to the inscriptions. The maker could be mad, or illuminated beyond the remit of sanity.'

'Surely not,' Frauka said. The voxponder's cadences were created only by the generative combinations of artificial speech. There was no inflection to the rise and fall tones, so it was impossible to tell when the inquisitor was joking.

'I'm joking,' Ravenor said. 'Probably.'

Nayl walked into the room behind them. 'They've got him,' he reported. 'Just dragged him back.'

'Then let's talk to them. Wystan, if you please?'

Frauka stubbed out his smoke and activated his limiter.

THEY WOULD NOT need much breaking. I could tell that as I rolled into the room where Mathuin had them under guard. Their surface thoughts were all but shouting out. Bazarof was dazed and terrified, and Lunt was scared and at a loss to know what was going on. Odysse Bergossian was a mess of tics and withdrawal spasms.

They were frightened enough by the armed members of my team, but the sight of me chilled them into silence. My chair has that effect, I know. Faceless, armoured, cold, as unforthcoming as a polished stone block.

At first, I didn't even have to ask questions. Lunt's mind was the most open. He was a friend of Bergossian's, and sometimes – like now – stayed with him in the deadlofts when work was thin and he didn't have the cash for flop-house rates. He was a labourer, poorly schooled, but intelligent enough. Bazarof, known to

Lunt but not considered a friend, had shown up that morning desperate for a hiding place. He had refused to elaborate, but Lunt thought it likely the authorities were after him.

Lunt had advised Bergossian not to take him in. Bazarof was not good news. The pair had found trouble together before. More importantly, Bergossian was in no fit state. For years now, he'd slithered from one addiction to the next, spending great swathes of time out of his head. It had been obscura for a long while, then pills, then gladstones.

In the last few months, Bergossian had been using flects too. A few at first, relying on gladstones for his base fix, but then more and more. Bergossian had really lost it. He'd forgotten about gladstones, and used flects every day. That's when the drawing had started.

Lunt was worried about his friend. Lunt was no user – a little lho, sure, sometimes a puff of obscura, but nothing hardcore. He wanted his friend clean. Bergossian wasn't taking care of himself. He wasn't eating properly and he certainly wasn't working enough. Strange thing was that he seemed happy. Blissful, most of the time, muttering with delighted but barely comprehensible enthusiasm about the designs he was making.

He'd become so obsessed with them; he'd knocked through room after room with a sledgehammer to open up more space to work in.

I drifted out of Lunt's mind. Bazarof was tougher-edged, even though his head was still throbbing from the crack Kara had given it. He'd heard about Sonsal, and was running witless.

+You're right to be scared.+

Bazarof's head snapped up and he stared at me, blinking.

+Everything you tell me now will encourage me to press for leniency in your case. Where do the flects come from?+

I knew he wasn't going to tell me, not just like that. Under verbal interrogation, he'd spin lies for hours until there was nowhere left to go. But the moment I asked him, the answer he didn't want to give came right to the forefront of his mind as he concentrated on not letting it slip.

Bazarof was no user either. A line chief at Engine Imperial, he pulled a decent enough wage, but supplemented it with black market dealings, usually narcotics. He couldn't afford to use. The guild mechanicus kept a tight watch on their franchised workforce, with random urine sampling and blood tests. If he used, he'd lose his job. Likewise, if he dealt at work. But he did a nice little off-book business in his home stack.

As a line chief, he knew people, and had plenty of contacts in supplier manufactories and haulage consortiums throughout the city. He had good travel papers too, which gave him the luxury of free movement. Most of all, he had a lot of old friends like Odysse Bergossian who lived and earned in the shadows of the hive's economy.

Bergossian had been Bazarof's line of supply for three years, on and off. He could get most things, mainly because he craved them himself. What he got depended on where he was working. Yellodes and gladstones when he packed meat in K, grinweed when he gamped the sink markets, though he hadn't done that for a while.

The good stuff, like the flects, came from his links at the circus.

I switched my attention away from Bazarof, and directed my thoughts towards Odysse Bergossian. His mind was like rubber.

+Odysse. Tell me about the circus.+

Bergossian blinked and laughed out loud, looking around like a child for the source of the voice. Lunt and Bazarof both looked at him in alarm.

There was no tricking Bergossian's mind into the truth the way I had done with Bazarof. There was no guilt or secrecy to trigger, no hidden truths to tease out. His thoughts were a miasma of unfocused light and colour.

I probed a little deeper. I felt Kys start as she sensed the tingle of increasing psyk in the room. A little pattern of frost flowers bloomed along the window.

I went deeper still. Uncomfortable, Kys walked out into the hall. Blunt as they were, Kara, Mathuin and Nayl could feel it too now, their wraithbone markers glowing slightly. They stood back warily. Bazarof and Lunt trembled and tried to distance themselves from Bergossian. He was sitting in the middle of the floor, chuckling to himself. They pulled away towards the kitchen doorway. Behind me, feeling none of it, Frauka lit another lho-stick and started to hum a tune.

+Odysse.+

Another laugh, but it was followed by a slight wobble of the lower lip. I extended into his surface consciousness, surprised by the manifold waves of bliss and contentment I found there. His mind was a warm soup, a thick, reassuring, fluid space.

+The circus, Odysse. Tell me about that.+

'The circus, the circus, the circus!' he giggled. This made everyone jump. It was the first thing anyone had said since I had entered the room.

+Yes, Odysse. The circus. That's where you get the flects, isn't it?+

'Yes, yes. On reflection, yes!' he gurgled and started to laugh hard at his own awful joke. He rolled over on the floor and pawed at the air.

+Who sells them to you, Odysse?+

Bergossian snorted. 'Duboe!' he cackled. 'On reflection, Duboe at the cavea!'

'For frig's sake, Odysse!' Bazarof shouted. 'They'll frigging kill you if you sell them out!'

+Shut up, Bazarof.+

'Duboe! Duboe and the game agents!'

'Don't, Odysse!' Bazarof yelled again, moving forward. I had no time for that. I kicked out a little psi-slap that slammed Bazarof off his feet and back into the kitchen wall.

Then I rolled forward until the giggling Bergossian was right in front of me.

+That's very helpful, Odysse. What else can you tell me?+

He started to shake his head, as if he was tiring, like a man who has been on a wild circus ride which had been fun at the time but had left him feeling sick. Like a drunk who has drunk too much. I could feel the bitter tang of his nausea rising, the wild disorientation of a mind and body spinning out of control.

May the Emperor forgive me, it was delicious. Any extremes of physical experience, even the most unpleasant, are so alien to me that I cherish them.

But this was getting worse. It was as if the blissful, warm fluid of his thoughts was draining away. Shapes rose out of the liquid like submerged rocks exposed by the tide. The warm light in his head dimmed and a black dawn rose up around the rim of his mind.

+Odysse.+

The shapes were around me now, twisted, calcified, bone-brown, slick with the last of the warm fluid as it spattered and gurgled away. On the floor in front of me, Bergossian was starting to have some sort of seizure.

From behind, I heard Nayl hiss. 'Get out of him. Boss, get the hell out of him!'

I realised... that I could not. I was sliding forward into the black-light landscape of his blighted, burned-out mind. For a moment, it seemed almost comical to me: as if I was perched, not in my suspensor module, but in an old-style, non-powered wheelchair, which had been set on a slope and I was rolling, rolling down, gaining speed, rushing headlong, without hands or feet or brake to stop me.

+Odysse. Let me go.+

Bergossian was thrashing around, cracking his head, heels and elbows against the floor. There was a screaming, but I could no longer tell if it was his physical vocalisation or some keening threnody surging across the scorched earth of his thoughtscape.

I plunged on, unable to stop. Before me, a vast wasteland of jet cinders and blackened material, twisted, bulbous, shattered, crusted. The sky was domed and full of rushing, splintered cloud. A sun, as red as a blood-shot eye, rose and climbed across the flitting heavens and set again in the space of a single breath.

The howling increased. The black landscape cracked open into a stinking abyss. A pit of skulls. Billions of human skulls, every single one tainted by the echo of its own death-scream. There were buildings before me, towers and spires and cyclopean citadels, all ruined, all made of solidified night. A burned city. A murdered hive. Was this Petropolis? Was this the future?

I fell between the vast towers, and saw their countless windows, row upon row, tier upon tier, deadlights like eye sockets, giving back no reflection, stained by unimaginable ages spent in consuming darkness.

Then I was stationary. The howling had stopped. I was alone in the silence, the ruins rising around me, the air heavy with ash and decay. There was broken glass underfoot and–

Underfoot.

Underfoot.

I started to shake. I was standing. I was whole. Feet, legs, torso, arms, fingers...

I looked down, and saw with eyes instead of photoreceptors. The crazed black soil under my naked feet was covered in a myriad shards of broken glass. Imperfectly, like a deranged mosaic, they reflected back my perfection.

I saw my face. The face I had once had. Gideon Ravenor, young, strong, determined. How I had missed that face...

Something was coming. I could hear it behind me. Something heavy, something fast, skittering and crunching the glass underfoot. Snorting. Growling. Spitting.

I wanted to turn. My remade body refused to move. In the broken reflection at my feet, I saw the hulking, hairy shadow of some great thing loom up behind my shoulder. Teeth flashed.

In the last second, the numberless glass fragments showed my reflection change and become true again. My true self. A knotted, bulging sack of scar-tissue and old burn-smears, the stumps of limbs, the ragged useless lump of a head, healed up and pink-smooth like a badly-sewn bag.

And entirely helpless in the grip of Chaos.

FIVE

You COULD HEAR the circus from twenty streets away and see it from ten. The horns, the sirens, the deafening come-ons from tannoys, the dancing light beams and the popping flares. It lit the city night of Formal G like a bowl of fire.

The approach streets and ramps were packed: jostling multitudes, laughing and drinking, and the peddlers, tricksters, hawkers and smile-girls who fed off them. It was a game night.

The circus drome was a colossal domed amphitheatre, its tiered and arcuated outer walls towering ninety metres high. But the great ouslite substance of it was just a shadow in the smoky night, lost behind the flash and dazzle of the raging lightshow. Red stablights on the tops of the walls crisscrossed the exuberant crowd. Screamer rockets banged up from the upper arches and fizzled into showers of green and white sparks. Twenty metres above the street on the main facade hung a massive wiron sign that flashed out the name CARNIVORA in letters three times the height of a man. The orange light tubes blinked out the word whole, then pulsed it in syllables – CAR-NI-VOR-A – before blazing out the whole again. Caged fires and glowglobes lit up the stadium's exterior columns, and blue-white electric discharge danced up and down cathode filaments over the horseshoe arches of the public turnstiles.

Factory-grade hooters sounded above the roar of the crowd, and speakers blasted out the bass-beat hook of a popular pound number at inhuman decibels. In time to the music beat, even louder, the vox-horns played a recording of a male voice bellowing 'CAR-CAR-CAR-NIVORA!'

Above the wiron sign, pulsing in time to it, and the beat, and the voice, a massive pict screen projected a loop of fast-edit images. There was a split second of a naked woman, body-painted gold, turning an aerial cartwheel, that smash-cut to a fragment of two armoured male fighters clashing chainswords. The screen smash-cut again to a violent half-second of some lidless, yellow-toothed saurian lunging at the camera, followed by a final smash-cut to a bloody, blurry decapitation that segued to white noise/pict-out as if the camera had broken. Bang! Bang! Bang! Bang! CAR-CAR-CARNIVORA! CAR-CAR-CAR-NIVORA! Over and over and over until the assaulting repetition was one numbing adrenal rush.

Patience Kys let the crowd crush sweep her along to public gate IV. She was gnawing on a meat-stick she'd bought from a ramp vendor, and openly drinking from a liquor flask. She laughed and joked and flirted with the moody hammers and indentureds in the crowd around her, posing with some, and gently dissuading the over-eager advances of others with subtle tweaks of telekinesis. In her tight black and emerald bodice and long net-lace skirts, and with her hair loose, she was just another smile-girl out to shout herself hoarse and drink herself blind at circus night.

Already, she was in with a group, a bunch of tanked-up clansters from the meat-pack sept. They were big men, noisy, filthy, their vat-muscled bodies rippling with studs and piercings and the distinctive acid-tats of their clan. One of them – Lesche – kept passing her his grain-liqour for a swig, and he insisted on paying for her at the turn-stile. He thought he was in. His brothers certainly believed Lesche had pulled a high-formal party-girl who was slumming it in the sinks of G for the night.

The hammer's hands were all over her, and she let him, up to a point. They flocked en masse through the gate, pressing forward past the stadium stewards towards the wooden stalls in the attic levels. The cheap seats.

There was a weapons check at the entrance to the attic levels. The stewards let the hammers through anyway – they knew better than to question the drunken, rowdy clansters with that many piercings. But the doorway flashed red as Kys went through. The stewards closed on her, despite the protesting roars from Lesche's group.

'I got no blades,' Kys said, straight-faced. 'Shush, you,' she added to Lesche with a wicked grin. She raised her arms high as the stewards aimed hand-scanners at her body, deliberately accentuating the corseting of her top, her pinched waist and elevated bosom. 'See? It's just the wiring in my bodice.'

The hammers roared approval. Realising they were on to nothing, the stewards waved her on. She laughed as she ran through, and Lesche grabbed her around the waist. She kissed him as they rambled up into the attic stalls and found a row with a good view over the primary stage.

The circus was filling up. Searchlights swept back and forth across the terraces, illuminating a raving mass of the populace. The pre-game show was just getting under way. The main arena filled the bottom of the stadium's bowl. It was an oval measuring fifty by ninety metres, and it was surrounded on all sides by the rising terraces of public seating. It was not a single showground, but resembled rather the oblate cylinder of a revolver: there were six, circular cavities around the edge of the oval arena, and one large one in the middle. Massive hydraulic systems deep underground could raise or lower performance stages – logeums – into place in any of the cavities. The central one was for the night's headline fight. Right now three of the outer logeums were hissing up into place, venting steam through their exhaust outlets. On two of them, twenty paired teams of knife fighters with silver fish-head helmets were putting on a display of speed bladework with hair's-breadth accuracy. The crowd gasped. Knives in each hand, whirling like windmill vanes. Sparks sliding off meeting blades. Not a single scratch.

On the third outer stage, four twist clowns were pantomime fighting with mallets. They were all big, lumbering mutants, hunch-backed and ogrish, their disfigurements accented by white face-paint, rouged mouths and striped pantaloons. The audience loved them. The whole arena rotated so that everyone could get a decent view of the outer stages.

The out-stage displays continued as more siren fanfares sounded. A huge scaffold cage descended over the main logeum, winched down from the massive lighting gantries and over-stage platforms above the arena. The acrobats dropped down into the cage space, like coins into a collecting box, freefalling for heart-stopping distances before grabbing crossbeams and trapeze struts. They were all female, naked, painted gold. A mighty applause rang out across the stadium as they swung, caught, pulled full-ins and struellis, walked over flat bars, spun on wires, somersaulting and flipping. There was no net. The hard arena was thirty metres below the bottom spars of the performance cage.

Lesche slavered at the sight of the nubile gymnasts. He took a tug on his bottle and looked round to pass it to the girl.

But Kys had vanished.

CAR-CAR-CARNIVORA! CAR-CAR-CARNIVORA!

'You! You'RE LATE!' Mamsel Scissors squalled. Her voice was high-pitched and imperious, as befitted the circus's troupe-mistress. She pulled up the hem of her long lace skirts and petticoats and stomped across the suspended boarding with her walking cane. It was twilight up here, under the stadium roof and amongst the lighting gantries. The swell of the crowd's roar came up from seventy metres beneath. Gantrymen ran back and forth, hauling tension wires and adding sand-sack counterweights to the pulley systems. Reflected light speared back up through the board cracks in the staging under their feet.

Kara Swole, wearing a flesh-tight bodyglove so transparent she might as well have been nude, was smearing the last squeeze of a tube of gold dye over herself.

'I'm sorry, mamsel,' she said.

'Sorry doesn't bring in the punters! Sorry doesn't put on a show!'

'I know, mamsel.'

Scissors peered at her, her ancient lined face taught and inquisitive.

'Do I know you?'

'Yes, mam. I'm Kara, mam. You hired me last week.'

'Last week? I don't remember...'

'You did, mam.'

'I doubt it. You're not right. Too short. Too much bust and hips.' Scissors poked a gnarled finger into the giving softness of Kara's left breast.

'But you did, mam. You thought my handspring and diamond combo was particularly fine, and you liked my wire work.'

Mamsel Scissors stepped back, her withered hands folded over the knob of her cane. 'Show me the move again.'

Kara breathed in, and lunged into a handspring that she flicked out of, spun a body-length fly-away in the air and came down stuck. The gantry boarding shuddered under the impact and swung very slightly.

Below, the crowd roared again, but not at her. They were out of sight up here.

'Good,' muttered Mamsel Scissors. 'Where did you learn that?'

'The Imperial pits, Bonaventure,' said Kara.

'I still don't remember hiring you,' Scissors went on, 'and you're late for the pre-show anyway. I won't have that from my girls. You're sacked.'

Kara shrugged. She'd got this far into the circus by passing as one of the acrobat troupe. It was enough. Frankly, she'd got herself up onto the gantry late deliberately. She hadn't fancied risking her neck in the over-hung cage. Once, maybe, she could talk and pass as a dance-crobat, but perhaps, these days, the exertions of the lissom girls spinning below was a bit beyond her.

Still in the part, she frowned. 'Sacked?'

The mamsel thumped her cane on the boarding. 'Sacked! You heard me! Get dressed and get out!'

Kara walked over to where she'd left her belongings and gathered up her clothes.

'Go home!' Mamsel Scissors screeched.

Kara picked up her kitbag, palmed the compact autogun into her left hand, and headed for the ladders.

She was in now. That's all that mattered.

CAR-CAR-CARNIVORA! CAR-CAR-CARNIVORA! came the roar from below.

HARLON NAYL LEANED on the horn of the freight-rig as he edged it down the concrete slip towards the service ramp. The crowd parted slowly to let his ten-wheeler through. Every few seconds, the crossing stabs of the searchlights blinded him and lit up the drive-cab blood red.

He adjusted his microbead. 'Coming up on it now,' he whispered. 'This better go good.'

'Relax, Harlon. Piece of piss,' Carl Thonius crackled back.

The shutter ahead was locked down. Stadium officials headed towards him up the ramp, pointing flashlights. They had to push their way through huddles of ecclesiarchy puritans protesting against the barbarity of the circus.

'Now, Thonius...'

Nayl wound his cab window down as the stewards waved at him.

'What's this?' yelled one.

'Meat truck for the spoliarum, sir!'

'Yeah? What outfit?'

'Buckanold's Bushmeats, sir...'

'Let's see the slate,' the steward said, holding up a hand.

Nayl handed out the data-slate. 'Thonius...' he hissed into the bead.

'SCANNING NOW,' CARL Thonius said, sitting back from his cogitator. 'Five points, three points, one point... we're up. I'm reading the guy's slate coding now... decoding... decoding...'

'Hurry the frig up!' Nayl's voice rasped.

'Got it. Code's clean. Feeding it through to your slate.'

* * *

'SOMETHING WRONG?' NAYL asked, peering out of the cab.

'No,' said the steward. 'No, nothing. A slight registration delay.' He handed the slate back to Nayl. 'You check out. Go through, bay number fifteen. Open the gate, vehicle coming!'

The shutter clanked up into the arch. Nayl gunned the engine and rolled the freight-rig down into the stadium's choragium. He could feel the thumping handclap and bellowing of the audience above his head.

'Too close, Carl. Too close,' Nayl whispered.

'WAS IT TOO close?' Ravenor asked.

In the back of the cargo-8, Thonius glanced round nervously from the cogitator at his master. Space was cramped. Between the cogitator set-up and Ravenor's stowed force-chair there was barely room for the interrogator to sit. Frauka and Zael were exiled up front in the dingy cab. The boy was looking back at them through the chipped clearplex divider. Thonius decided he didn't like the boy. His eyes seemed to be everywhere. Thonius didn't like that at all.

'Was it too close?' Ravenor asked again.

'No, no,' smiled Thonius. 'This is non-wired hacking. I had to wait until Nayl's slate was close to the steward's so I could get clean reception.'

'And he's in?'

'They're all in, sir,' Thonius said. He looked at the sleek casing of Ravenor's force-chair.

'You're wondering if I'm all right, aren't you?' Ravenor said.

Thonius jumped. 'I thought Frauka was switched on!' he declared. 'How could you read me like–'

'Frauka is switched on,' the inquisitor's voxponder said expressionlessly. 'But I have eyes... and can read body language. You keep looking at me, Carl.'

Thonius shrugged. 'That thing with Bergossian. It wasn't good.'

'No, it wasn't. It hurt. I was unwise, and it scarred me. I'm recovering fine.'

'But–'

'But nothing, Carl. I probed an insane mind, and almost got caught in it as it collapsed. But I got out. Three days have passed. I'm healing.'

Thonius shrugged. He hadn't been there, but Kys had told him how Odysse Bergossan had gone into spasm and then... well, exploded. Messily, she'd said, as if there was any other way. Kys said Ravenor had howled as he struggled free of the collapsing mind. A voxponder shriek. A sound she'd never forget. Monotone. Anguished.

'Fine,' Thonius said. 'That's good.'

He paused and adjusted the wavelength setting of the voxcaster.

'Getting signals. Kys is in. Kara too. Nayl is still mobile.'

'Let's get on with this,' Ravenor said.

CAR-CAR-CARNIVORA!

The booming declamation came from above her, shaking the walls. The audience was joining in, stamping their feet and clapping in time. Bam-bam thump! Bam-bam-thump!

Patience hurried along the dim stone passageways under the seating, watching the glow-globes twitch as the walls vibrated. As she ran, she unfastened her skirts and let them fall, revealing the tight black and emerald bodice to be the top part of a bodyglove. Now she could move more freely. She adjusted her microbead headset, and pulled on her gloves.

Someone was coming. She sidestepped into the shadows of an alcove. Two stewards ran past, on urgent business.

Up ahead was the hatch entrance to the choragium. A short but heavy-set twist with horns sprouting from his mottled flesh was watching the hatch. Kys slid back against the wall and crept towards him. She picked out a broken bottle on the floor of the passageway and, with a gentle sigh, caused it to skitter and tinkle away from her, past the twist, and past the hatch.

The mutant heard it and turned. His thick, grey fingers raised the power-maul that had been leaning against the wall next to him, and he bent down, searching for the source of the noise.

As soon as his back was turned, Kys danced forward and slipped away through the hatch, flying down the wide metal stairs into the vast understage chambers of the Carnivora.

THERE WAS NO time to get dressed. Kara dumped her clothes and kit on the landing platform of the ladder-climbs, and continued on down, a gold phantom with a gun in its hand.

The sound coming up at her from the arena below was like a physical force: a beating, deafening solid thing that made the wire-supported ladder-climbs sway. Lights were strobing. She looked down. Thirty metres below her and to her left, the stablights were illuminating the main show stages as the dance-crobats finished their amazing performance and slid down glide-ropes to the central logeum. That stage disk was already beginning to descend into the underfloor, and outer logeums were rising to present the next entertainment: a roped saurian and five drug-numbed twist clowns. She looked away as the biped saurian, maddened by goads and skin-implant agonisers, scored an early point, tearing one of the bemused clowns in two. The crowd, now a quarter of a million strong, bellowed their appreciation. The ladder-climb shook. The whole arena shook. It was a predator-roar, the exultation of a blood-hungry mob.

The ladder-climb wobbled. Gantry men were coming up from below to help the overhead crews winch back the dance cage.

Kara looked left and right, made a quick estimation, and leapt off the landing platform, her weapon gripped between her teeth. She fell five metres and caught one of the guy wires with both hands. The snap made her grunt. She accelerated her pendulum swing and then got her legs up over the wire and slid down it. Quite a show, if the lights had been on her. But she was out in the dark, above the radiance of the lamps.

A few metres from the end of the wire, she let go and dropped into space. She turned a neat cartwheel and smacked down onto the landing of another ladder-climb.

She took the gun out of her mouth and wiped her lips, tasting gold body-paint. The western terrace was ten metres below her, a mass of writhing bodies and waving arms. She unwound a support rope from the landing's bracket and tested it for give. Then she kicked out and swung from the landing across to the roof-spars of the attic tiers. The swing wasn't quite going to do it. She let go and flip-flopped the last few metres, landing on a rafter barely thirty centimetres wide.

Kara teetered on her feet for a moment, arms spread.

Then she ran along the rafter and jumped off, dropping onto a crosswise beam two metres below. When she reached the end of it, she vaulted over a stone divider and landed in a service gallery above the attics.

Two clansters looked round in surprise as she flew in and landed with a slap. They had left their seats for the cool gloom of the upper walk, to share some grin and 'lax out' before the main show.

They could scarcely believe their eyes. A voluptuous girl, painted head-to-foot gold and, as far as they were concerned, butt-naked, had just flown in through the frigging window.

'The circus gets better and better…' mumbled one. They stepped towards her.

Kara was suddenly glad of the cacophany from below.

NAYL ROLLED THE freighter to a halt, expressed the air brakes and pulled on the parking lock. The chamber was like a cavern, dark and damp. Five other trucks were parked beside his. The noise of the circus audience was like remote thunder overhead.

This was the choragium, the understage. For all its size, the circus had more private parts than public ones. Immense cellars and subdecks existed to service the arena. Nayl could hear the hissing clank of the rising and falling logeum platforms as he got out of the cab. The air smelled bad. He could taste the ash-burn of the ustrinum, where they cremated the bodies and waste products from the pit fights.

Nayl walked the length of his freighter and hammered on the backdrop. The tailgate slammed open and Mathuin leapt out. He was carrying a pistol, but Nayl knew the murderous rotator cannon was zipped up in Mathuin's kitbag.

'Put it away.' he said, nodding at the pistol. 'We've a way to go yet, without attracting notice.'

Zeph Mathuin frowned and put the handgun into the pocket of the filthy plastek smock-coat he was wearing. Nayl had one on too… crusted with dirt and dry blood.

They hurried across the chamber, through the bustle of the stewards and crewmen. The floor shook with the transmitted shudder of the crowd. They stood back as three cavea handlers led a muzzled, thrashing ursid through to the stage-gates ready for the next show. Nayl found the chained beast's angry whimpers strangely affecting. He felt sorry for it. Win or lose, it would be bushmeat by dawn.

They crossed a stone pier over a rancid waste-sluice, and passed under a heavy portcullis gate into a warren of understage tunnels. There was activity all around: stage-men shouted for cues, labour muscle wound the chain winches, engineers ran coke carts to stoke the furnaces of the hydraulic engines, and gladiators oiled their bodies in the chrismatories.

They came down another narrow stone corridor into a wide underfloor hall. The spoliarum was to the left, a dank, foetid pit where all the bodies were dumped. Mech-anised ploughs swept each descending logeum clean of debris and cadavers, and they ended up in the spoliarum. There, the dead were recycled. Armour and weapons were recovered, and rings and trinkets looted. Human bodies were carted away to the ustrinum for burning. Non-human flesh was sold off by the kilo to buyers from the food markets. Bushmeat was a cheap and ready source for the hive's provisioners. Bear, lizard, twist... it all looked and tasted the same once it was macerated, spiced and roasted on a street-vendor's stick.

A few other meat brokers had arrived before them, and were lounging around, smoking, waiting, under an arch nearby. Nayl wandered across to the spoliarium overseer and signed his name in exchange for a numbered paper chit. At the end of the show, the overseer would draw the numbers randomly. The winning broker got first pick of the spoils, the second got to choose from what was left and so on. A butcher's lottery. The waiting brokers had buckets and carts, soiled aprons, saws and surgical masks. In their filthy plastek smock coats, Nayl and Mathuin looked the part.

'Lucky seven,' said Nayl, walking back to Mathuin and flashing the chit.

'What now?' Mathuin asked.

'Now we lose ourselves in the mix. Hang on.' He strolled over to the waiting brokers, and nodded a few curt hellos. Mathuin heard him ask them where a man could get a drink while he waited. A couple of the brokers pointed and mumbled.

Nayl rejoined Mathuin. 'Now they won't even miss us,' he said as they fell into step.

The underhall was packed. They had to weave their way through the crowd. A team of chainsword fighters shared a group huddle as they waited to enter the caged walkway onto one of the lowered logeums. Weaponeers trundled carts of swords and pikes over to the traps. A pit-bull cracked his lash across the backs of a chain gang of convict fighters, desperate men hoping to win a state pardon through an arena victory. Rumour had it the lord governor himself was here tonight, enjoying the show from his executive belvedere. That would certainly explain the number of marshals on the prowl. Gold painted dancers ran by, perspiring and swearing. Two trainers were having a stand up row about marquee billing. A professional gladiator, huge, oiled and armoured, knelt and bowed his head as the circus's appointed priest blessed him in expectation of death. Tipsters and bookies were everywhere, eyeing up form and gathering last minute advice for their clients. Servitors lumbered past with crates of water and ale for the fighter pens. Musician bands tuned up against the constant din. Money changed hands, debts spiralled or were wiped clean, letters of pledge were signed. Medicae surgeons knelt in a pool of blood around a twist clown who had come off stage minus an arm.

Two animal handlers hurried past with long pole-goads. They were heading through the crowds towards a heavy shutter on the far side of the hall.

'Follow them,' said Nayl.

THE GALLEY HALLS were rattling with activity. In a hellish, smoky environment, squads of cooks and their underlings and servitors slaved to cater for the paying customers in the stadium. Most of their fare was savouries or pies that were taken up by box lift to the vendor stalls in the stands, but there were sumptuous feasts to be prepared for the dignitaries in the exclusive belvederes – meals that would be shipped up by hand and served by impeccably mannered attendants in circus livery.

Kys held back in the main doorway for a second. Unless she went all the way around the outside underwalks of the circus-drome, the only way to the cavae was through the galleys. And no matter how many telekinesis distractions she created, she'd not manage that without being seen. She breathed in, remembering one of the inquisitor's training dictums: 'If you can't hide, don't. Bluster.'

If nothing else, Patience Kys had boundless confidence. She adjusted her microbead and whispered, 'Carl? Who's head chef tonight?'

As the reply came, she straightened her bodice demurely, adopted a haughty stance, and marched into the kitchens.

A few underchefs glanced at her, perplexed, but they were too fearful of their head cooks to stop what they were doing and challenge her. Kys strode right down the line between brushed-steel workstations, and paused to lift the lid on a large stockpot simmering over a galley range.

'Who the hell are you?' yelled a senior cook, spotting her. He was a fat man – always a good sign in a cook, Kys believed – but he was meatily powerful and over two spans tall. His apron was cinched around his great girth. Red faced, he marched over to her, pushing several slow-moving undercooks out of his path.

Kys ignored him. She elegantly extended the index finger of her gloved left hand and stuck the tip of it into the pot's contents. Then she withdrew it, and made a business of studying the moonstone ring she wore on it.

'I said–'

'I heard,' she cut him off, and looked him in the eye. 'Are you Binders?'

'What?'

'Binders, man, Binders. Are you Binders? I was told he was cook in charge tonight.'

The senior backed off a little. 'No, mam, I'm Cutcheska. Senior Binders is away in the cold store, but I can get him if–'

'No matter. Cutcheska. Your name was mentioned too. I've heard fine things of your work. Fine things.'

The senior blushed. 'Mam…'

Kys walked past him to another range where underlings were pan-frying marinated terrapins. 'You understand that not just anything can pass the lord governor's lips?'

Cutcheska balked. 'The lord g–'

'His food must be inspected rigorously for tampering.'

'I… I know that, mam!' the senior exclaimed, hurrying after her. 'But his tasters and personal dietitian have already examined the kitchen and–'

'I know they have. But an unscheduled inspection keeps you on your toes, does it not?' Kys leaned past an undercook's shoulder and pressed the tip of her left index finger against the tenderised belly of a frying terrapin. Then she studied her ring again. As if noticing the way Senior Cutcheska was staring at her hand, she held it up towards him.

'Augmetic,' she said. 'The index finger is a micro-calibrated poison snooper. If it detects any trace venoms, the result is displayed in the ring screen.'

'I see,' nodded Cutcheska.

Kys raised the little finger on her left hand. 'This digit cases a tight-focus digi-weapon. If I find any food tampering, I am authorised to use it to incinerate the line chef responsible for the contaminated area.'

Cutcheska started to tremble. 'I can assure you–'

'I'm sure you can. Walk me through.' Kys started off again, with Cutcheska hurrying to catch up. She paused for a moment to glance back at the undercook frying the terrapins. 'Too much nutmeg, by the way.'

Cutcheska took her down the line, waiting nervously while she poked her finger into all kinds of food. He brought her a glass of wine, and she poked her finger into that too, before nodding and knocking it back. He introduced her to four other seniors, who fell in step behind them like an anxious chorus.

Finally, she turned to face Cutcheska. 'Through there,' she said, indicating over her shoulder with a thumb. 'That goes through into the cavae, am I right?'

'Indeed, mam.'

'I'm very troubled. Livestock... including xenos-breeds... penned this close to the main food manufactory.'

'We are scrupulously, clean, mam–' Cutcheska began.

'My dear senior, xenos germs and bacteria travel in ways unknown to science. I will have to examine it.' Kys took off one of her pearl earrings and handed it to Cutcheska. 'Hold that up, please, between finger and thumb. No, arm straight, Higher. That's it.'

She started to walk away.

'What am I doing?' he called.

'That's a relay sensor for my augmetics,' she said. 'I'll enter the cavae and take readings, and then compare them to the delayed response of that module. Be careful, it's very delicate. Arm straight, please. This should only take about ten minutes. You can stand there for ten minutes holding that up in the air, can't you, senior?'

'Of course, mam.'

'Good. Arm really straight, please. Do try not to move.'

THE KNUCKLES ON her right hand were badly skinned. Threads of blood ran down the back of her hand and along the gold-painted skin of her forearm. The second clanster's jaw had been more solid than it looked.

Laying them out had slowed her down. Kara was running now, along the attic upper walk, and then down the stone screw-stair, the emergency exit that led right down the side of the building into the subdecks. She took them three at a time, hip-surfing off the handrails and leaving streaks of gold paint behind. The stadium was still shaking with noise. Through a window-slit, she glimpsed the night's first headline bout beginning on the main logeum. The outer stages had sunk down into their pits, awash with gore and littered with bodies, victorious champions raising their arms and bloodied blades to the baying masses as they descended from view. To a fanfare and a tumult – CAR-CAR-CARNIVORA! Bam-bam-thump! – the evening's first primary spectacle rose up on the central stage. Chained at intervals around the main stage's edges were four professional pit fighters, armed and gleaming, and four inhumanly massive greenskins, glanded out of their minds on spika and slavering at their leashes. A thorn-bar cage rose up to surround the main logeum. Then the chains released.

The crowd roared, louder than ever before.

Kara kept on running.

She came down into a choragium sub-deck where sooty spade workers were shovelling body parts into the furnace hatches of the ustrinum, and sprinted west, through the tunnels of the fighter pens towards the cavae.

A pair of stewards at the entrance tried to stop her.

'Where you off to in a hurry, dancer girl?' asked one.

'Not that we mind you running, at all,' smiled the other. 'Makes your body jiggle real nice, if you know what I mean.'

No time left. Certainly no time for subtlety. 'My frigging boyfriend just got eaten by some frigging carnosaur!' Kara yelled. 'I gotta get in there!'

'If he's eaten...' one of the stewards began.

'He had my nanny's diamond ring as a keepsake! I gotta check the dung for it, or nanny'll kill me!'

There was no arguing with that. They let her pass.

'Uh, some keepsake,' one of the stewards called after her.

RANKLIN SESME DUBOE, accredited handlerman-chief of the Imperial pits, ran the cavae. He was two hundred years old, standard, and had benefited from judicious juvenat work. He looked forty-five, was strong and well muscled. His grizzled face sported a bushy salt-and-pepper moustache. He never seemed to have to raise his voice. Just a look sent his handlers scurrying. He was a force of power in the circus understage. Without his say-so and his skill, the show would simply not go on.

He knew what to buy and where to buy it. He knew how to source the most interesting and deadly beasts for the show, and how to cage them and keep them fit, and how to get them dandered up just right for the spectacle.

Of all the great understage sections of the circus stadium, the cavae smelled the worst. Worse than the kitchens, worse than the fight-waste furnaces, worse even than the reeking spoliarium. In a long, semi-circular series of dank chambers under the drome's western end, the pit animals were caged and prepped. The air was wretched with the sharp bite of piss-ammonia and fecal matter. Blood too. And the humid musky scents of penned creatures, most of them predators, most of them anguished and goaded.

A cue-man ran a slip over to Duboe. He read it, tossed it away, checked with the logeum control via his headset, and then pointed across the paved stone floor to a team of handlers around a trap cage in which a mature fighting struthid was clawing and clacking.

The handlers obeyed at once. They pulled the slot-hatch open on the logeum entry, and then cranked back the cage door. The flightless fighting bird – four metres tall and with a beak the size of an Space Marine's power axe – came rushing out up the penway, driven by the sparking jolts of the handlers' electro-goads.

Overhead, the crowd thundered approval.

Pulling off his headset, Duboe walked over to the group of game agents assembled around an upturned pack-crate they were using as a table. A smile-girl in a short skirt had fetched them liquor and grin from upstairs, at Duboe's expense. She was serving them now.

Duboe approached, and shook hands with a few of them, accepting a shot-glass of amasec from the girl.

'Budris... good work, that struthid. Worth the wait, I'm sure.'

Budris, a sallow man with two lean bodyguards, nodded his satisfaction.

'Skoh. What can I say?' Duboe slapped hands with a heavy-set, square-jawed man with sandy-white hair. Skoh's bulky figure was sleeved in leather armour. 'Perfect saurians as always.'

'I may have some long-tusks come winter,' said Skoh. 'Interested?'

'Only if they're the aggressive kind. The dociles play really bad here. Yeah, I'm looking at you, Verdendener. I haven't forgotten that crap-fest last summer.'

A bespectacled agent turned his head, miffed. 'I was assured of their quality–' he began querulously.

'Take another drink, Verdendener,' Duboe smiled. 'You've redeemed yourself with those ursids. Never seen bears so nasty. Leave the long-tusks to Skoh here.'

Skoh nodded appreciatively.

Duboe looked over at another game agent. 'Murfi... stop bringing me shit crocodilians, or I'll turn them back.'

Murfi hung his head. 'Sorry, Duboe. They seemed class to me.'

'They weren't class. They were shit. Doped.'

'I had to dope them to get them in transit.'

'Next time load them with a spike to get them kicking. Those bastards just lay there in the frigging pool, like it was midsummer with nothing to do.'

'Sorry, Duboe.'

Duboe finished his drink and set the glass down. 'That's all for tonight, gentlemen. I've work to do. Pick up your fees from the drome office. I've stamped your dockets. Get on with you.'

The group broke up. Duboe tugged Skoh by the arm and drew him aside.

'Post-match, we'll talk. I've got demand. Can you deal?'

'I'll talk to Captain Thekla,' Skoh said.

CAR-CAR-CARNIVORA!

The main stage slid down out of sight. An outer rim logeum rose with two raptors from Quinze on it, slavering at their chains.

In the underpits of the cavea, Harlon Nayl walked up behind Duboe and fell in step with him. Duboe was busy shouting out at a team of gangers who were about to let a bull-cat out of its cage.

'Duboe?'

'Who are you?'

'Let's take a walk and talk.'

Duboe stopped and looked at Nayl. They were eye to eye. Duboe was a big man and he didn't take shit from anyone.

'I don't think so,' Duboe said.

'And yet... I think so,' said Nayl. 'There's a Tronsvasse 50 in my coat pocket, and it's looking at you.'

Duboe frowned. 'Just a word, and my staff will have you over. Gut you. Feed you to the animals. I don't know who you are, but get out of my frigging way.'

Nayl smiled. 'You want to go for it? Look to your left. Catwalk. See the big guy? He's watching out for me. That's a rotator cannon. Let's see your staff deal with that.'

Duboe shrugged. 'So, you're heavyweight. Hardcore. I'm impressed. What do you want?'

'Cooperation,' said Nayl.

Duboe nodded. 'Look, mate, if I don't release these cygnids, the circus master will have my guts,'

'Go ahead.'

Duboe aimed a control wand and frothing dog-beasts dashed out of their cage and up the trap towards the stage.

'You said cooperation,' Duboe said. 'Concerning what?'

'Flects. You deal. I know. I want a source.'

Duboe laughed.

'Funny?' asked Nayl.

'Like I'd tell you. You'd need more than a gun in your pocket to get that out of me.'

'And there I was being nice,' smiled Nayl.

'I'm sure you were,' Duboe said. He looked back at Nayl. 'Rip-fish. What do you know about them?'

'What?'

'Rip-fish. Are you familiar with them?'

Nayl frowned. 'They're from Antigula. Antigula, right? Like eels, but voracious. Strip a human to bones in a second...'

He paused.

'Why the frig are you asking me that?'

Duboe grinned and raised the control wand. 'Because you're the one standing on the trapdoor.'

The hatch parted under him and Harlon Nayl fell.

Below, the water chute was a frothing madness of famished rip-fish, boiling the water to hell.

AMID THE CAVAE's din and activity, no one seemed to notice what had happened for a moment. But Mathuin had his eyes on Nayl, and started forward along the catwalk with a cry.

Duboe, hurrying on his way, clapped his hands and roared an order. A mob of waiting handlers immediately unlatched a main pen, and herded horned grazers out towards the central up-ramp. They were big, jittering beasts, designed to be the third party distraction in a large-scale man/predator showfight.

Mathuin cursed. Surging forward, the grazers suddenly created a flowing wall of haunches, bellies and hooves between him and Duboe. He ran along the catwalk further, to where suspended steps gave him access to a higher walkway.

'Duboe's running,' he voxed as he moved. 'Duboe's running and Nayl's down.'

Duboe himself moved quickly across the main floorspace of the handling chamber. He was talking fast into his headset, making it look like business as usual, but in fact he was calling in his inner circle. Already, three or four veteran handlers were heading after Mathuin. Two others were heading across the understage to check the rip-fish had done their job and to close the tank shutters.

The pair of them approached the deck-hatch and heard the wet thrashing from below. One of them went towards the winch-post that manually controlled the hatch.

Upright, a slightly surprised look on his face, and his hands at his sides as if to keep balance, Nayl rose up out of the tank-pit, suspended on empty air. He wasn't even wet. Duboe's goons blinked at him. Nayl landed on his feet, gently, on the edge of the tank in front of them.

'Where did Duboe go?' he said, as if nothing untoward had happened.

Scared more than anything else, the goons drew out short-bladed estocs and lunged at him. Nayl delivered a backhand slap across the face of one whose headlong charge became a disorientated backward stagger. Then he sidestepped the other. The second man was only wrong-footed for a moment. He turned, to come in at Nayl again.

But he cried out in alarm. Although his feet had stopped moving and he was willing his body around, he was continuing to surge forward. His feet dragged and pumped weightlessly on the pit edge and then he was suspended out over the tank itself, held in space by some soft, invisible force.

A force that went away again as suddenly as it had come.

With a shriek, he dropped out of sight.

The other goon rallied at Nayl, who grabbed his knife-hand, snapped the wrist and punched him so hard in the face that he fell down and didn't get up again.

'Thanks,' Nayl said. 'I thought I was fish-bait there.'

Kys walked into view, breathing hard. 'Sorry it was a bit last minute. You've put on weight.'

Together, they started to run across the chamber. Many of the handlers and pit-crews had seen the brief, violent altercation, and had stopped work, glancing around in confusion. Some were calling out for Duboe.

'To the left. That way,' said Kys, running ahead of Nayl. Pit-men got out of their way in a hurry.

'Mathuin?' Nayl voxed.

'Busy,' the link answered.

Mathuin was up on the higher catwalk by then. Duboe's hefty teamsters, a couple of them twists, were coming up ladders at either end. The bounty hunter slid to a halt, looked up and down the walkway, and then swung the cradle-brace around so the cannon's multi-barrels covered the west end of the walk.

Two men ran up into view. One had a drawn stub pistol.

'Drop it!' he shouted.

'You're kidding, right?' Mathuin replied. He tipped up the barrels with a slight tug and fired off a blurt. The sound of it boomed across the chamber. Hyper-velocity shots howled over the heads of the two men in front of him. The one with the stub pistol fell down the steps in an effort to duck, and knocked the man behind him off the stepway entirely. Falling, the man tried to grab a suspension strut, but missed and landed badly on a cage-roof below. The small, biped saurians in the cage began to leap and snap up at him. The man struggled to balance on the curved roof-bars and yelled out for help.

The sound of Mathuin's cannon had caused other trouble. There was genuine panic in the cavae now. The penned animals began struggling against their cages. Several others in the process of being moved, including a spiger and the grazers Duboe had signalled, went berserk and broke free. The spiger – a three metre long felidform with eight legs and a furred, segmented body – snapped its leads, brought a servitor crashing over and started to chase pit-men across the floor. The grazers stampeded in all directions, crashing into cages, into chute-walls, into guardrails, into crates and barrels, into men. Six of them, in a tight, galloping pack, broke all the way round the saurian lockers and trampled two handlers on the loading ramp behind them. The grazers had big, V-shaped horns growing up from thick bone-masses above their flaring nostrils, and when they ran, they put their heads down. There were marrow-mashing crunches. A body was tossed up into the air, terribly gored, and came down on the locker roofs. It lay there, leaking blood through the bars and driving the caged saurians into a frenzy. More handlers ran in, firing scatter-guns, and cracking lashes. Other workers fled for the exits.

From his vantage point, Mathuin glimpsed Duboe running through the pandemonium towards the northern cargo-docks. He voxed the sighting to the others, then ducked shots at him from behind. Several pit-men, firing small-arms, were rushing along the walkway after him.

Mathuin turned and felt the rotator-cannon shudder against his hip. White flame danced around the muzzles. His pursuers pulverised explosively in puffs of blood and meat and several shots tore into the catwalk itself, shredding the decking and shearing support cables. A whole section of catwalk tore away and plunged twenty metres to the floor below.

Mathuin turned grimly to continue on his way when something of extraordinary force struck him on the left shoulder and wrenched him off his feet. He spun off the walkway and into the air. He blacked out for a microsecond, then woke in time to black out again when he smashed, face first, into a cage roof.

Fifty metres away across the cavae's crowded, chaotic floorspace, the game agent, Skoh, lowered his custom-made long-las.

'Thank you,' said Duboe. 'Now come on.'

'This is my neck on the block here too, Duboe. Who are these people?'

Duboe smiled at the game agent, pushing pit-men out of his path. 'They're dead,' he said.

MATHUIN WOKE WITH a start. Before he had even tried to remember where he was, he knew he was hurt bad. Broken ribs, seriously frigged arm and shoulder.

He was face down, suspended across the bars of a cage roof. His head, right leg, right forearm and the business end of the rotator-cannon were all hanging limply down through the iron rungs. He tried to move, but it seemed too painful, and the bars were so widely spaced that if he rolled too far, he might well slip down between them entirely. Slowly, he raised his right hand to clasp the nearest rung, then his right leg, hooking his foot around a rung for support. Then he tried to raise his head. Pain made him close his eyes. Whiplash, maybe, from the fall, combined with the damage the las-load had done punching through his shoulder.

For a second, Mathuin felt hot, damp, stinking air blow up at his face, and wet droplets spatter him. There was a sound like two heavy wooden boards being smacked together.

He opened his eyes.

Four metres below, the cage's occupant, a mature crocodilian, looked up at him with lidless yellow eyes. It lunged vertically again, its great maw wide open and, pain be damned, this time Mathuin pulled his head up. Another hot blast of breath and saliva. Another hollow smack as the jaws closed empty.

The thing slithered round beneath him. He pulsed the trigger of the cannon to rake it to pieces, but got nothing except the pinging misfire tone. The fall had screwed the cannon, jarring the munition feed out of its lock.

The crocodilian powered up again, driving itself against the cage floor with its massive tail. This time it got him. The tip of the massive jaws closed around the dangling end of the cannon barrels.

'Oh shit...' Mathuin gasped as the gigantic weight began to pull the cannon down between the bars, and him with it.

FOR A MOMENT, across the heads of the milling crowd, Nayl saw Duboe. Then he was gone again, and trouble was rushing Nayl and Kys from all sides. Pit-men and twists, paid well to be loyal, piled in with fists and blades and goad-staves.

Nayl was in no mood now. With a snarl, he lashed into the first one, crushing a nasal bone, and chopped an elbow elsewhere into a throat. An electroprod stung him a glancing blow on the right hip, but the armour of his bodyglove soaked the worst, so he tore the prod out of the man's hands and stung him back into the air with it. Then he brought the crackling prod round one-handed like a sabre and felled the next.

'Patience!'

'Right with you,' she said, making her words audible over the commotion by way of a little T-nudge boost. Two pit-men were already on their hands and knees at her feet, coughing blood. She straight-armed the heel of her left hand into the solar plexus of a third, catching the barbed pole the man dropped with a little telekinesis and then spinning the pole straight into the face of another. A twist with a cleaver swung for her, but she did a nimble three-sixty walkover to get out of his way and then TK'ed the floating pole round in a fast circle and cracked the twist around the back of the skull with it.

Kys stepped forward over the twist and drew four kineblades that had been concealed as boning in her bodice. The four sharp slivers began to orbit in slow circuits around her. Nayl tossed aside the now buckled electroprod, and tackled another handler using an armlock, and pushed the yowling man out of their way.

Duboe had already disappeared through the shutters into the northern cargo-docks.

RAW AGONY TORE through Mathuin's shoulder and neck. The crocodilian was beginning to shake its snout. He couldn't reach around far enough with his right hand to release the cannon's harness straps. He felt himself beginning to slide.

'Help… me…' he gasped.

'GET OUT OF here,' Duboe told Skoh as they crossed the cargo-dock. Skoh had just used his long-las to cut down a maddened grazer that was bucking and jerking across the deck. 'I've got things to do. Get out and I'll meet you at the usual place.'

Skoh nodded and hastened off towards his truck. Duboe turned and went the other way towards his private offices under the north-end terraces. By then, the whole stadium knew something was amiss in the understage. There was a lot of discontented noise from upstairs. A squad of six armoured marshals came pounding out of the stair access to his left. Regularly posted at the circus, the officers recognised Duboe at once.

'In there! The cavae!' Duboe yelled. 'Reckon it's some of those frigging anti-blood sport maniacs. They're armed, so watch it!'

The marshals pumped their shotgun grips and spread out towards the cavae hatchways. Duboe reached his office, punched his code into the door plate, and was felled from behind by a hefty blow.

He looked up, dazed. One of the frigging dance-crobats. She was pointing a compact at his face.

'What the hell…' he growled.

'You're coming with me,' she said. 'Right now. Before this gets any further out of hand.'

Duboe grinned. 'Ekkrote,' he said.

'What?' said Kara.

Ekkrote was one of the Carnivora's headline gladiators, something of a local hero in G. Two and a half spans tall, an ex-clanster, formed like a mountain range from grafter muscle, he was blessed, oiled, armoured in gold monobond ceramite armour, armed with a chainsword, and loyally in the pay of his friend and dealer Ranklin Sesme Duboe.

He was also standing right behind Kara Swole.

NAYL AND KYS came up out of the cavae into the dock, and straight into the path of the Magistratum squad. They saw the heavy pistol in Nayl's hand and aimed their riot-guns and red laser-taggers.

'Where you are! Drop the handgun!'

Nayl glanced sideway at Kys. She didn't even break stride. The four kineblades zipped away from their orbit around her and flew into the open barrels of the four nearest pump-guns. Two misfired on the spot, blowing their users back hard. A slamming wave of telekinesis and the butt of Nayl's pistol left the rest sprawled and disarmed.

Nayl and Kys broke into a run.

FACED WITH A choice between keeping her gun or keeping her head, Kara opted for the latter, and threw herself into the longest impromptu dive of her life to avoid the gladiator's scything chainsword. She had no time to prep for a decent landing and the compact bounced out of her hand as she sprawled over and rolled.

Ekkrote was also fast. She rolled hard and then had to back-flip just to evade the singing edge of the sword as he stormed after her, swiping at her.

His blade tip cut a groove in the rockcrete floor, then nicked a pillar. Kara ducked and did a handspring sideways, landing neat and next to her fallen compact. She snatched it up and fired off four or five shots. Ekkrote's armour and surface muscle stopped them all. The chainsword mangled the muzzle of the compact and she ditched it, turning a backwards somersault as the gladiator closed the distance between them again.

Kara was out of breath. Her muscles burned. How much longer could she stay out of the bastard's reach?

THERE WAS A shot – something chunky like a las-carbine – and the crocodilian let go and flopped over onto the cage floor, leaking black ichor from its split brain pan.

Mathuin sagged as the weight released. His left arm felt like it had been torn out of its socket. He saw the barrels of the rotator were twisted and deformed.

He peered around, upside down. Carl Thonius was staring up at him from outside the cage, carbine slung in his hands.

'You alive?' he called.

Mathuin moaned, nodded and slid slowly back along the roof bars. Then he flopped over until he hit the ground. When he landed, he just stayed there, too hurt and exhausted to move.

Thonius walked up to him. The cavae around them was still in uproar.

'You're here,' panted Mathuin.

'Yeah. Sounded like you needed the whole works.'

'So he's here too?'

'Oh yeah.'

* * *

RUNNING ACROSS THE cargo-dock, Nayl and Kys saw Kara fighting to stay out of the big pit-fighter's way. Any second now, the chainblade was going to unzip her.

'Kara!' Nayl yelled. He was still fifteen metres away. He raised his heavy pistol and opened fire, striking the gladiator's back armour several times.

Ekkrote lurched under the hi-cal impacts. He wheeled away from Kara, not interested in her any more, and took another bullet in the cheek-guard. He charged Nayl and Kys. Kys met him with her telekinesis, but he was too massive for her to lift. All she could do was stop him in his tracks for a moment. Ekkrote struggled against the invisible barrier and Kys wobbled back a step.

'God-Emperor!' she wailed with the effort. 'Drop him, Nayl!'

'Trying!' Nayl replied. He'd slapped home a fresh clip and was busy emptying that. The pit-fighter was clearly hard-wired against pain and hyped up on some serious glanding frenzy-maker. Nayl was inflicting serious tissue damage to the gladiator's chest, but still he was fighting to reach them, his face a rictus of kill-hate.

'Can't hold him!' Kys barked. Her telekinesis stalled, exhausted, and Ekkrote thundered towards them. Then a huge force lifted the gladiator off his feet and drove him hard against the chamber wall. He continued to thrash. The force, invisible, slammed him into the wall three or four times until the stone facings cracked and he went limp.

The inquisitor's force chair powered towards them across the dock. Frauka – his limiter clearly active – walked behind it. Zael was in tow.

Nayl pushed on, past Kara, who was on her knees panting, and into the handlerman's offices. The floor was littered with papers, slates and other belongings that had been overturned in Duboe's frenzy to cover his tracks.

Duboe was behind the desk, a heavy-grade tube-charge in his hands.

'Uh uh!' he warned, his hand ready to twist the arming dial. 'Back out!'

As if alive, the tube-charge leapt out of his hands and crunched hard into his nose. Duboe fell on the floor, hands clutched to his bloody face. Kys stepped up behind Nayl and took the charge out of the air where it was floating.

Together, they bundled him out onto the dock where Ravenor was waiting with Kara, Frauka and the boy.

+Get him to the transports.+

They all started to move, then stopped when they heard the inquisitor send the word, +Wait!+

His mind-voice seemed to falter.

There was a rush of air. The main dock hatches around the outer edges of the bay were hissing open. Units of Magistratum and PDF troops were streaming in, and amongst them were several men and women dressed in simple grey suits.

Two were already heading right towards them. One was a very big man indeed. The other, small and thin, was regarding them with piercing blue eyes.

It was the psyker, Kinsky.

SIX

'YOU WANT I SHOULD...?' Frauka began.

'Not yet,' I said. I was ready for Kinsky now, whoever he was. To my team, he was just a scrawny, grinning wretch. To me, he was ablaze from head to toe in lambant psi-flame. His big minder – Ahenobarb – stood ready to catch him the moment he went bodiless.

I didn't want a mind-fight. I certainly didn't relish the prospect of going up against this one again. But I would if I had to. And I was on the ground now, face to face. He'd find me more of a match.

+Let us pass.+ I sent.

+(Laugh) I don't think so. Several of the people with you are armed. I want to know who and what you are.+

+Not without some notion of your authority and jurisdiction,+ I sent back flatly.

Kinsky pursed his lips. Marshals were closing in around him, weapons aimed at us. Others spread out through the cargo-dock and through into the choragium proper, rounding up the scattering circus workers. I heard weapons discharge. Some more of the poor, loosed animals brought down, I supposed.

Kinsky reached into a pocket of his grey suit and flipped open a wallet, showing us the official seal.

'Lomer Kinsky, Ministry of Sub-sector Trade, by the authority of the lord governor himself.'

He used his voice for this, so we all could hear him.

I'd heard of the Ministry, of course. A soft, bland title for a powerful regulatory body. The lord governor's secret police. Not a force to be trifled with. Kinsky's presence at Sonsal's house, and the way the marshals had deferred to him and his colleagues, now made sense.

But, as the saying goes, I had one better. The time for subterfuge had gone... or at least, had been stolen from us by circumstances. The nature of my operation on Eustis Majoris was about to change irrevocably.

I sent a mental impulse into the display mechanism of my chair, and a small flap slid open on its armoured prow. A fish-eyed projector lens flipped out, flush to the smooth bodywork, and glowed into life. I displayed the hololithic version of my rosette.

+I am Gideon Ravenor, inquisitor, Ordo Xenos.+

It was worth it just to see the look on Kinsky's face.

THE LORD GOVERNOR's palace was a bratticed tower rising from the side of the gigantic administry monoliths in Formal A, like a pier of coral from a main reef. Heavy rain lashed through the night as we were escorted in armoured vans to the palace undercroft. We all went: myself, Kara, Nayl, Patience, Frauka and Zael. Duboe was carted off into custody by the Departmento Magistratum. Carl and Mathuin had not yet been rounded up, and I trusted they could stay out of harm's way.

Kinsky, Ahenobarb and a female in grey whose name I wasn't told escorted Frauka and me up to the cap levels of the palace. We left the others waiting in an anteroom off the undercroft.

Kinsky was clearly nervous. His psi-force had ebbed a great deal; it was just a flicker now. I could tell he remembered our clash at Sonsal's house. He'd cut loose there. Now he knew I was an inquisitor, he was worried how things might go for him.

The elevator doors slid open and we emerged into a high hallway lined in wood veneer and beam lighting. At the far end, more doors opened into a wide, softly-lit apartment whose tintglas windows overlooked the entire western part of the hive.

'Wait,' said Kinsky, and the three of them withdrew, leaving me alone with Frauka. Frauka wandered across the room between armchairs and settees, and opened an inlaid box on the writing desk under the windows. He took out a lho-stick – a more expensive brand than the one he smoked – and lit it.

'Should I contact the ordo here?' he asked.

'We'll see,' I said.

A man walked in from a side door. He was dressed, like Kinsky, in soft grey murray, and was slender, with a chin-beard and tied-back black hair. The third man from Sonsal's house. The one with the power. Not power like the psyker. Real power.

'Good evening, inquisitor,' he said, bowing slightly to my chair. He ignored Frauka, which seemed to suit Frauka fine.

'Good evening,' I replied, using my voxponder.

'My name is Jader Trice. I am first provost of the Ministry of Sub-sector Trade. I would like to start our conversation by apologising for any unpleasantness this evening.'

'Unpleasantness?'

'At the Circus Carnivora. You found yourselves caught up in a routine crime-raid.'

'A routine raid? I thought you were responding to an altercation in the cavae.'

Trice shrugged. He was handsome, and immaculately groomed and manicured. A real operator. I noticed he had one brown eye and one blue. There was something else about him. An essence. A hint of something I was desperate to put a figurative finger on. But at this stage, under these circumstances, it would have been rude to probe, however discreetly.

'Our raid had been planned for several weeks, and we'd brought in sections of Magistratum and the PDF. Fairly major scale. The Carnivora is a hotbed of crime and smuggling. We were intending to move in towards the end of the night, but the – altercation, as you put it – forced our hand. I understand this... altercation... was set off by your own investigation.'

'I had reason to examine the circus. The criminal elements objected to my interest.'

Trice smiled. 'Can I get you a drink?' he asked.

'A little malt liq with a shaving of ice,' replied Frauka, helping himself to another lho-stick.

Trice looked at him.

'I don't,' I said. 'But please indulge my companion.'

Trice fetched Frauka's drink from a stand on a sideboard, and poured himself an amasec. 'The lord governor was most upset to hear that an inquisitor had been caught up in tonight's operation.'

'I'm sure.'

'He extends his best wishes, and asks me to offer my services to you.'

Trice handed the drink to Frauka and looked at me. Like everyone else, he was put-off by the unforthcoming nature of my enclosed chair.

He sat down, facing me, and swirled the amasec in his balloon. 'The Ministry of Sub-sector Trade is a newly created body. I don't know if you're aware of our purview.'

'I am,' I said. 'I'm very familiar with the writings of the lord governor. A perceptive man, a reformer, an innovator. His election to office last year was a thing to be welcomed.'

I meant what I said. Oska Ludolf Barazan, who had been in his time hive mayor, senator plenipotentiary, and, since 400.M41, lord governor of the Angelus sub, was an erudite and forward-thinking politician whose reformist attitudes I much admired. Given the segmentum-wide trend for such offices to fall to under-achievers via nepotism and birthright, Barazan's election seemed like a miracle of liberalism. Generally stagnant men inherited control of stagnant sub-sectors and thus further stagnated them. The Ministry had been part of his election platform. He had wanted to create an active, sharp-toothed instrument that would oversee the workings of Imperial bureaucracy on Eustis Majoris and beyond. Clean them up. Cut the crap. 'Reform' was not wide enough a word.

'I'll pass your comments on to the lord governor,' Trice said. 'He'll be flattered. He is an avid student of your own work.'

I had written a few things: a number of treatises, an extended essay or two. They had been well received. If I'd had a visible face, it would have been blushing.

'He is troubled, however,' Trice went on. 'His central doctrine is openness. Clarity.'

'Full disclosure,' I remarked.

'Quite so. And yet, you chose to operate on the capital world... clandestinely.'

Frauka snorted. Trice looked round at him and he raised his glass. 'Don't mind me,' he said.

'I'm sure,' I said, 'the lord governor is not unfamiliar with the workings of the Inquisition. Our success in preserving the purity of Mankind relies entirely on our unquestioned power. The Inquisition does not have to ask, or obtain permission. It may look where it wishes, and do what it wishes. It is the most absolute power in the Imperium of Man, save the God-Emperor himself.'

'Oh, quite,' said Trice, swirling his drink some more. I notice that he had not touched it. Keeping his mind sharp. 'There is, however, an inference that you did not inform the lord governor of your activities here because you suspected the authorities as well.'

'Of course I did. No offence to the lord governor, but corruption is everywhere. Is that not why he created your Ministry, Provost Trice? To clean the house from the top down? Consider me to be cleaning from the basement up.'

'May I enquire the nature of your investigation?' he asked.

'You may. Prompted by my ordo masters, I have undertaken an investigation into the nature and origin of the addictive substances know as flects.'

Trice frowned. 'Narcotics are an Magistratum matter, and smuggling...'

'The flects are not narcotics, provost. Not in the chemical sense, whatever their characterising traits. They are most definitely xenos in nature.'

'Xenos?' he breathed, uneasy.

'They are artifacts. Tainted artifacts. Their abuse has spread, these last two years, down through the Angelus sub, into the Helican sub and the Ophidian too. All signs indicate the root of that trade is here on Eustis Majoris.'

Trice got up and set down his untouched drink 'We... we are on the same side, inquisitor.'

'I'd hate to doubt it, Mr Trice.'

He smiled at me. 'I mean to say, we are aware of the flect problem. It is rife here. We... uhm... we know we are the source of it. The fact pains the lord governor greatly. It is, consequently, uppermost in my Ministry's list of actions. Tonight's raid on the Carnivora was part of our ongoing war on flect-distribution.'

'You had identified the circus as a source?'

He nodded. At last, he took a sip of his amasec. 'The Imperial pits are a focus of contraband crime on many worlds, inquisitor. The staff has powerful contacts with rogue traders and commercial outfitters, all licensed to import xenos-breeds on-planet for the games. It is an obvious source. A trader imports a snarl-cat from Riggion for the circus, under license... What else does he bring in the snarl-cat's cage? Grinweed. Gladstones. Phetamote thrill-pills baggy-packed into the animal's intestine.'

'And flects,' I said. 'The ship traders and outfitters are moving flects through the circus businesses. Through other outlets too, I'm sure. Wood, metals, weapons perhaps. But the Imperial pits are key. They have the most open trade permits, necessarily, to cater for the creatures they bring in.'

He nodded again, sagely. There was a click-clacking sound. By the desk, Frauka was trying to light another lho-stick from an ornamental desk igniter that refused to spark. He became aware of us staring at him, and put the igniter down.

'Sorry,' he said and pulled a match book out of his jacket.

Trice looked back at me. 'You detained a man tonight.'

'His name was Duboe. Chief handlerman at the cavae. A dealer.'

'My Ministry had suspected as much.'

'I'd like him returned to me for questioning.'

'Of course!' Trice smiled, as if anything else was unthinkable.

'And I'd like to continue with my work... unimpeded.'

Trice nodded. 'I have a request. From the lord governor. He asks that we pool our efforts.'

'How so?'

'We have information that may assist you... You have the force of the Inquisition behind you to empower it. I have to admit, Inquisitor Ravenor, my Ministry – for all it is newborn and fresh – is hard stretched. We would like to combine our efforts with yours and close off the flect trade at source.'

I slid my chair a few centimetres forward towards him. 'Your information. Try me.'

Trice pursed his lips. 'Our investigations have shown that Duboe's source was a game agent from the outworlds called Feaver Skoh, one of a famous dynasty of xeno-hunters. Skoh operates from a rogue trader called the *Oktober Country,* captain of which is one Kizary Thekla. The *Country* runs the lanes up through our sub to Flint, Ledspar and beyond, sometimes as far as Lenk, every half-year, to buy choice stuff from the beast-moots there. Sometimes they go on into Lucky Space so that Skoh can hunt for himself on the rip-worlds up there. We believe they're sourcing flects, maybe from the moots, maybe, from Lucky Space.'

'Trice. Why are you telling me this?' I asked.

'In the spirit of cooperation. Full disclosure,' he said.

'And?'

He knocked back his drink in one tug. 'The *Oktober Country* broke orbit fifty minutes ago, without permission from ground traffic. Its last vectored course was up the line to Flint.'

* * *

NAYL, KYS AND Kara were waiting for me on the palace pad. Zael was hanging back behind them, and they had Duboe in manacles.

As the drop ship came down out of the night on columns of spitting flame, I rolled out onto the pad to join them, Frauka at my side. Behind me came three figures in soft grey cloth-suits, their crewbags slung over their shoulders: Kinsky, Ahenobarb and a female called Madsen.

Nayl looked at them.

'Who the hell…?' he breathed.

'Say hello,' I replied. 'They're coming with us.'

PART TWO

Lucky Space

ONE

He'd been on wherries down the overfloat, trucks and cargo-8s a few times and, once, a train over to Formal R to visit a cousin or some such. He'd been pretty young at the time; he barely remembered the cousin, let alone the train.

He'd never been off the ground for more than a few seconds, never flown, not even in a lifter. He'd certainly never been on a starship.

The guy (Zael still thought of Harlon Nayl as 'the guy' even though he knew his name – it was kind of a comforting thing to cling on to) told him the ship was called the *Hinterlight*. Meant nothing. Might as well have been called *Yer Momma is a Smiley-Girl*, Zael still hadn't heard of it. But he was sort of impressed, and funny-excited. It was a starship, and it was all that word implied. Off-dirt, the void, distant worlds whose names he couldn't spell.

The big deal, as far as Zael saw it, was that they were taking him too. Where, he didn't care. Had to be better than the J stacks. His little, knucked-up life had just taken an interesting swing.

It occurred to him to wonder why they were taking him. The Chair had talked to him several times since he'd hooked up with the guy, said a few things that seemed to indicate that he thought Zael was special somehow. Well, that was fine. The Chair was the big shot in this little gang, and if The Chair thought Zael was special, it probably meant he was.

Though he kind of wanted to know *special how?*

The Chair's gang had been scaring the life out of him since he'd met them, but they were sort of cool too. He'd seen the guy do his thing, for a start. The guy was a piece of work. Then there was Kys. She was as scary as the guy, but in a different way. Zael tended to look aside when Kys glanced his way. Kara was nicer. She always asked if Zael was doing okay. She was sexy. Kys was probably sexy too, in a blade-thin, dangerous sense, but her scariness got in the way. Kara was just nice, simple as that. And she had these killer curves that made him feel tingly.

Thonius was a freak, though. Unpleasant and sneery. Zael got the feeling Thonius didn't like him much. Well, that was fine. And also mutual. There was Mathuin, who was simply a surly bastard. He reminded Zael of the worst kind of moody. But Zael had to feel a little sorry when the flier stopped to pick Thonius and Mathuin up. The bastard had been hurt bad. There was a lot of blood, and a spew-making smell of crispy flesh. Kara and the guy carried Mathuin into the rear compartment to patch him up.

Zael sat in his seat as the flier rose up out of the city. There were window ports, but he couldn't see much. He could feel it, though, in his stomach. A little up and down. So this was flying. It made him queasy.

The other member of the gang sat down next to him. His name was Frauka, and there was something weird about him. Every time Zael got near him, his head started to hurt. And Frauka smoked all the time.

'Something the matter?' Frauka said, exhaling lho-smoke through his nostrils.

Zael shook his head.

The smoke smelled pretty good, actually. It reminded Zael of the drink-clubs in the stacks. It had been days now since he'd taken a hit of anything. He'd been really witchy-twitchy for a while, but he was better now. He wouldn't have said no to a flect, just a little look, but he didn't crave one. He had the distinct feeling that The Chair had done something to his head. Nothing bad, just... eased it. Cradled it. Taken out the sting.

The Chair could do that. It wouldn't surprise Zael to find out that The Chair could do anything. He really wanted to know what was inside that smooth, matt-black form. He didn't even know what an inquisitor was, not actually, although he knew that everyone he'd ever known got terrified at the mention of the word.

The Chair didn't seem all that terrifying to Zael. Not like Kys, or Mathuin, or the guy. The Chair was more like what Zael imagined the God-Emperor to be. Quiet, faceless, potent, benign.

Or maybe that was just something else The Chair was doing to his mind.

Zael looked down the companionway towards the forward seats of the flier's main compartments, and wondered about the others. The newcomers. One, haggard and blood-flecked, sat on his own, his chain binders anchored to a seat restraint. Zael knew he was called Duboe, and had witnessed the final moments of his apprehension in the Carnivora. That had been another first. Zael had never been to the big circus before.

Zael wondered what Duboe had done. He certainly felt for him. With Kys and Thonius and Mathuin around, Zael sure as hell wouldn't have wanted to be a prisoner here.

Then there were the other three. They kept themselves apart from The Chair's gang. They were dressed in identical suits of fine-quality grey cloth, but they were far from identical themselves. One was very large, bigger than the guy even, his muscles stretching at the cut of his jacket. His skin was dark, though not as black as Mathuin's, and he had a little trimmed moustache line and clan-style piercings in his left eyebrow. His black hair was short and downy. There was something primitive about him, something coarse. He was very still. He reminded Zael of picts he'd seen, picts of huge lizards sun-basking on rocks, stock-still and blank for days at a time, jaws agape. Waiting, waiting to explode into fury and eat something alive.

The woman seemed to be in charge. Her name was Madsen – Zael had heard her introduced to Kara. She was white-blonde and slender, with a hard, pinched face that would have been really pretty if it hadn't been so tight. She spoke to her two companions now and then in a low voice that no one could overhear.

The other one, the stringy man, was more alarming. Zael had an impression of a balding, blond creep, but for some reason, every time he looked at him, Zael saw nothing but a sort of blur. Like the creep wasn't really there. Or like he was twice, and the two-ness of him was making him appear distorted.

Once during the flight, when Zael was looking at the creep, the creep had turned and looked back at Zael, as if feeling his eyes on him. The creep's stare was like hot wires. It said *look someplace else, you little freak.*

Zael had looked away fast.

He peered out of the window. The flier shivered as it climbed. Zael suddenly saw spots of fire in the dark and cried out.

'What the frig's the matter?' Frauka asked him, petulantly.

Zael pointed.

'Stars. They're stars. Haven't you ever seen stars before?'

Another first.

HE'D EXPECTED SOME grand fanfare and ceremony – this was a starship after all. But there was simply a thud, and a scraping sound and the flier's hatch had opened to reveal another hatch, which had opened to display a dank, greasy metal corridor.

And everyone had just got up and got out.

Zael felt cheated. He'd wanted to see the starship and understand where he was going. This oily deckhall could have been the back stacks of J, anywhere.

The Chair slid past him.

+Find our friend a cabin and make him comfortable.+

The guy nodded, and turned back to Zael.

'Come here, boy. I've got to–'

'Find me a cabin and make me comfortable,' Zael said.

The guy faltered. 'Yeah... that's right.'

Zael was busy lifting his feet one at a time and putting them back down on the deck grille. The strange, fluid sensation made him smile.

'What?' asked the guy.

'Weird,' said Zael.

'A-G,' said the guy.

'What's that?'

'The ship's artificial gravity. You'll get used to it.'

'What's... gravity?'

* * *

A RECORDING OF sweeping orchestral music was being broadcast at high volume across the bridge of the *Hinterlight*. Somebody or other's Ninth Symphony, laden with strings, brass and kettle drums. It was one of shipmistress's idiosyncrasies, a little ritual. She liked to break orbit with something appropriately stirring blasting from the vox. Besides, she claimed, it helped the Navigators compose the course.

'Down three,' she said as she saw me enter the bridge by the after hatch. The music muted appropriately.

'Thonius tells me we're off to Flint.'

'To begin with,' I replied, using the voxponder. I did this out of respect. For some reason, she had always objected to me mind-speaking. 'It could be a long run. Right up the lane to Lenk, if needs be.'

Cynia Preest pouted. 'No bugger goes to Lenk any more.'

'Some buggers do. The sort I'm after. I hope to catch them before that. Certainly before they hit Lucky Space.'

She tilted back her head and laughed. Then stopped. Then looked at me with narrowed eyes. 'You're joking?'

'It's been known, but not at the moment.'

'Shit!' she said, and turned away and then said it again, with equal vehemence. 'Shit! I am not... categorically not... going to take my darling into Lucky Space.'

'Cynia...'

'No. No way, Gideon. Flint's bad enough. It's only borderline Imperial these days. But Lucky Space? I am not taking the *Hinterlight* out of sub territory, especially not there. There are pirates out there, dark kin, brigands, death worlds, rip-worlds–'

'The people we're shadowing have a particular interest in rip-worlds,' I said.

'Well, lucky them. They can enjoy them on their own.'

She walked away from me, cussing my parentage, and leaned over the pilot console, resting her hands on the spoked brass wheel. I knew what this was about: Majeskus. I'd enjoyed a fine working relationship with Shipmistress Preest until Majeskus. God-Emperor, it still haunted me. I have never – will never – forget the desperate voices of Will Tallowhand, Eleena Koi and Norah Santjack as they crackled over the vox in the moments before their doom. Nor have I forgotten the damage done to the *Hinterlight*. How many was it? Fifty, sixty per cent of the crew? May the Throne of Terra keep the soul of Zygmunt Molotch burning in agony forever. Sometimes I wished that bastard was still alive so I could kill him all over again.

But he was dead, incinerated on Zenta Malhyde, and my friends and allies were dead and gone also. And that was then, and this was now.

Cynia had ramped the volume up to full again. The bridge space shook with symphonic pomp.

'Cynia!'

She pretended she hadn't heard.

+Cynia.+

She snapped round to glare at me. 'Not to put too fine a point on it, I'm bloody unhappy about this.'

+Cynia…+

'Don't mind-chat me! Talk like a regular human, or get off my deck!'

'As you wish,' I said, switching back to voxponder.

'Better,' said Cynia Preest, and dimmed the music. 'Throne, Gideon, I'm afraid.'

'Afraid?'

'It'll happen again, won't it? Sooner or later. We'll meet a bastard tougher than us and he'll hurt us bad.'

'Zygmunt Molotch was a genius-psychotic. A Cognitae-schooled freak. An aberration. Yes, he hurt us. More than hurt us. But he's gone now. Get Harlon up here and he'll relish telling you how he flamed Molotch's arse on Malhyde. We're after safer game, Cynia. Crim-smugglers who've hooked up with game agents. They scour the ripworlds and everything else out there for viable circus beasts. There's very little risk.'

Mistress Preest scowled at me. 'That's what you said last time.'

She turned back to the helm position and studied it for a while. The *Hinterlight's* bridge was surprisingly small for such a large vessel, essentially because it had been rebuilt in drydock after the Majeskus incident. Six months' expensive reconstruction, courtesy of the Guild Mechanicus, who'd only agreed to touch a rogue trader because of the influence I'd brought to bear through the Ordos Helican. A compact strategium well contained the actuality sphere. Behind it, a double hatch let into the shipmistress's ready room. Fore of the strategium, a simple, sloping bay contained the helm stations and the Navigator's socket. Bridge crew and servitors scurried round. Oliphant Twu of the Navis Nobilite was already plugged in to that socket, his lids shut, reading ghost stars on all three retinas.

'I have a course, mistress,' he reported in a slow, lazy voice. 'Flint. To orbit, four days.'

'Hold it ready, if you please, Navigator.' Preest looked at me.

'Cynia...'

'Don't you bloody "Cynia" me!' Cynia Preest exploded again. 'Be at your beck and call, fine! Carry you and your band of killers around the known stars, fine! But this...'

Cynia Preest was mistress of the *Hinterlight*, and my pilot. She was two hundred and eighty-four years old, although she always gave her age as 'twenty-seven and a bit'. Clad in a gold-suede bodyglove and red velvet robes, she was an imposing figure, womanly but robust, and just now becoming stocky and matronly. She had cropped, bleached hair, heavy make-up shadow over her eyes, and favoured excessive dangling earrings. I always thought she could have passed as a tavern hostess or a smile-girl madam, but for the tracery of fibre-wire inlay that ran down the left side of her face.

'Lucky Space...' She spat out the words.

Elman Halstrom, Cynia's deputy and first officer, had wandered over to join us while we had been talking. Modestly built, with a genial, heart-shaped face and slightly down-turned, put-upon eyes, he was a Navy veteran, and always immaculate. His thinning black hair was oiled back fleet-fashion, and he wore the formal uniform of Battlefleet Scarus, though every insignia, pip and crest had been removed from it. Even the embossed buttons had been replaced by plain bone disks. I understood he'd been a captain once, though I knew nothing about the circumstances surrounding his exit from service. Cynia had engaged him – like so many of the crew – after Majeskus.

'We are fit and running free,' he reported. Halstrom was precise and clipped when it came to duties, a legacy of his years in the Fleet, but he was not beyond informality. I liked him. He could yarn a good tale and deliver a fine jest. 'Eustis Majoris control has cleared us for system exit. Course is ready and held. Enginarium reports jump speed at your discretion.'

Preest nodded.

'I couldn't help but overhear,' he added. 'She's mentioned brigands, I take it?'

'She has,' I said.

There was a twitch of a smile on his small, rounded mouth. 'Dark kin? Death-worlds?'

'All noted, Mr Halstrom. The shipmistress has made all her objections abundantly clear. I will endeavour to make sure our voyage has to go no further than Flint.'

'Well then, that's excellent.' Halstrom glanced at Cynia. 'Mistress?'

Preest glared at me again, and then walked away to the main throne in the centre of the bridge. There she sat down and oversaw final preparation for warp translation.

'A word, if I may?' Halstrom said to me. He leaned over as he spoke, as if my three-sixty degree audio receptors wouldn't catch his confidence somehow, as if craning for an ear to whisper into. The gesture touched me.

'Of course.'

We left the bridge and proceeded down the midships companionway. Halstrom walked slowly by my side.

'I understand we have guests?'

As first officer, it fell to Halstrom to supervise matters of shipboard security.

'We have. I've told them to make themselves available for induction interviews at your convenience. For now, they're restricted at my instruction to the quarters I've provided in my deck.'

'Do you want them to remain restricted?'

'Not unduly. Not so that we appear rude. Standard prohibitions, I think... no access to the enginarium, the arsenal or any private cabins. I feel it is up to you and the mistress to decide what rules you set for them.'

'I see. And, though I will interview them, what can you tell me about them?'

'Not a great deal at this stage. They are agents of an official department known as the Ministry of Sub-sector Trade, and answer directly to the lord governor sub-sector himself. They have influence and power. A mis-handled situation could cause a rift between the ordos and sub-sector government.'

'We wouldn't want that,' smiled Halstrom. 'And might a situation arise that could result in mis-handling?'

'It might,' I replied. 'One of them is a potent psyker. I suggest you have Frauka present when you interview him.'

Halstrom was silent for a moment. We had almost reached the end of the long companionway. Ahead, it split into the through-deck corridors and the main dorsal elevator bank.

'Obviously,' Halstrom said, then, gently, 'I know only what you and the shipmistress care to tell me about your work, on Eustis Majoris. But I know enough to understand that you deliberately conducted your operation on the planet clandestinely. As it was explained to me, you felt you could trust no one. Not even the authorities.'

'That's still the case, Mr Halstrom. I'm attempting to locate the source of a material that is undoubtedly warp-tainted. It is used as... as a drug, essentially. Recreational. But it is no narcotic. It is heretical. To obtain it, and smuggle it onto the sub-sector capital world and elsewhere... that requires friends in high places, I believe. So I tried to keep my business quiet. Unfortunately, fate decided otherwise.'

'So these guests are here under sufferance?'

'Quite so. They're here because it is diplomatic to cooperate with them, not because I trust them.'

A buzzer sounded and amber lamps began to flash along the length of the corridor. Halstrom stepped back and took careful, experienced hold of the nearest handrail, and I cut my chair's lift and maglocked it down to the deck. There was a slight tremor, then twenty seconds of vibration combined with a flickering, time-lapse impairment to my vision. The rumble of the main drives grew louder.

Then the buzzer stopped and the lights ceased. We had passed the translation point. Now the *Hinterlight* was travelling at something close to maximum velocity, outside realspace, traversing the treacherous oceans of the warp.

'I should return to my duties,' said Halstrom, releasing the handrail. 'Thank you, inquisitor, for your time and candour.'

'Mr Halstrom?' He paused and returned to me.

'How long will I keep Preest?' I asked.

He closed his eyes and shook his head. 'I can't answer that, sir. Only the shipmistress decides. It would not be out of turn for me to mention that she has complained to me many times about the risks involved in continuing to act as your contracted conveyor. She is scared. That business six years ago. It's fair to say it destroyed her faith in you.'

'I know,' I said. The toneless voxponder did nothing to convey the sadness in my words. 'Cynia and the *Hinterlight* have been part of my operation for... well, it will be thirty years next spring. I can't bear the idea of sundering that arrangement, or the idea of having to find another shipmaster to trust. But the last few years have been difficult. She's spoken of breaking our contract?'

He shook his head. 'Mistress Preest would never be so unprofessional. But her agreement with you and the ordos is up for renewal on the anniversary. She has mentioned that it might be time for a change. Time to return to free trading, perhaps in the Ophidian sub, where merchant business is said to be booming. Of course, she will miss the security of the ordos stipend and retainer fees.'

'But not the danger?'

'Not the danger, no, sir.'

'I understand how you feel,' I said, turning my chair towards the nearest elevator.

'Me, sir? No, sir,' he said. 'The mistress has been hurt once, and perhaps has lost her nerve. I can sympathise. But a little run up into Lucky Space, hunting for heretics? That sounds rather exciting to me.'

* * *

THE CABIN, BADLY lit and untidy, was pretty much the only place in the Imperium Harlon Nayl thought of as home. In a long, bruising life extended by juvenat treatments – Nayl was just over a hundred, standard, but looked a robust late-thirties – he had known a number of homes. Loki – cold, hard, unforgiving Loki – was his birthworld, but he'd outstayed his welcome there pretty much the same day he decided to follow his brothers into the bounty-hunting business. Loki hadn't been home for a long time now. He'd wandered for some years, not so much in pursuit of work but because pursuit was his work. Then he'd crossed paths with an inquisitor called Eisenhorn.

As part of Eisenhorn's band, he'd had residence in a number of places, and remembered most fondly the Ocean House of Thracian Primaris and Eisenhorn's estate, Spaeton House, on Gudrun. Both of those were memories now, just as Eisenhorn himself was. No one had seen the inquisitor since the affair on Ghul back in the eighties. Nayl often wondered if Eisenhorn was dead. So many of them were from that time... Fischig, Aemos, Tobias Maxilla, Eleena Koi. That's what this life did; it killed you, sooner or later. Serve the ordos of the Holy Inquisition, and eventually that duty got you dead.

Nayl pressed the hatch-stud and closed the door behind him. He moved through the gloom, and snapped on a few glow-globes. A status monitor by the door showed a pulsing red light. They were warp-bound now. He'd felt the shudder.

His cabin was quite small and situated on the end of a corridor. The shipmistress had bequeathed an entire deck to Ravenor and his entourage as their own private, sovereign state. The *Hinterlight's* crew never came here, except by invitation. It was even off-limits to the cleaning servitors, which probably explained why his room smelled of socks.

To his left, in an alcove, an unmade bunk, surrounded by scattered clothes, data-slates and books. Various pict-shots decorated the wall over the cot like a shrine. Most of them were faded, the emulsion peeling. In the main part of the room stood a small table and three chairs, a codifier terminal linked to the vessel's data system, and a row of recessed cupboards built in between the bulkheads. To his right was the sliding door into the head and the upright washroom.

Nayl dropped his kitbag on the floor, where it became one of many. The main area was littered with equipment packs, rolled-up body gloves, boots, pieces of armour, tools, and various weapons that he really should have returned to the arsenal. One of these days he was going to get up in the night for a piss and tread on a loaded hand-cannon. Then he'd have to do some frigging explaining. And, most likely, go hunting for some missing toes.

Nayl wandered across to the bulkhead cupboards. He was limping. He ached. The free-for-all in the Carnivora had been less than fun. Reaching out to the cupboard latch, he noticed how skinned and raw his knuckles were. Grime-black, caked in dried blood, the calloused skin torn. He needed a shower. The effort didn't appeal to him.

He raised his left hand and held it out alongside his right. The missing finger seemed like a smack-in-the-mouth slur, an offensive lack. Ironic... that finger had once been his favourite insult. Now its very absence seemed obscene. All these frigging years, he been shot and stabbed and left for dead but he'd never lost a part of himself. It was like an omen. He'd never needed augmetics. He thought of Gregor Eisenhorn, replacing and supporting his battle-torn body bit by bit. Then – shit – he thought of Ravenor.

Was this where it started? Was this the beginning of the end? First a finger, then what? An arm? A leg? A major organ...

He'd liked that frigging finger. It had been on his top ten list of favourite fingers.

He poured himself a drink, amasec, from a bottle in the cupboard. It took him a while to find a glass, and longer to decide that the glass didn't actually have to be clean. Sipping it, he reached out to press the activator stud of the player unit in the cupboard. Nothing happened. So that's what that finger had been for. He used an existing finger this time, and low volume melodies flowed out into the cabin.

He'd have to go and see Antribus, get himself a new finger, augmetic, whatever and–

Nayl paused. Antribus? Ravenor's medicae was six years dead. One of Molotch's victims at Majeskus. The *Hinterlight* had a new medicae now. Nayl couldn't remember the fellow's name.

He sat down at the table, looking for a space to put his drink down. A carapace armour unit occupied most of the table top. He'd been repairing it on the way to Eustis Majoris, and the job was unfinished. He pushed aside powered drivers and stinky pots of lube.

The music was good. It was an old tile, one of his favourites. He hummed along, taking off his shoulder rig and disarming his pistol.

He took off his boots. He was hungry. He was sleepy. He was pissed off.

He was old.

He was thinking about the guests as he walked over to the bulkhead cupboards for a refill. He didn't like it, not at all. Didn't like them. Something about them, probably no more than the fact they were intruding into his work, into the inquisitor's work. Kinsky was dangerous. The other two... who knew? Nayl reckoned he could take Ahenobarb out, if it came to it. Madsen, though. She was a blank page. And only the inquisitor could handle Kinsky.

He heard a little noise outside his cabin door. Just a little noise. A glance reminded him he'd left the hatch unlocked.

Nayl put down his drink and picked up a sleek Tronsvasse 38 from under a pile of soiled clothes. Its tiny red tell-tale light showed it was loaded and armed.

He walked towards the door, gun raised, and popped the stud.

Zael as good as fell into the room.

'What the hell are you doing here?' Nayl asked.

'I got scared,' the boy said.

A LITTLE AMASEC calmed him down. The drink made him flushed and smiley. He lolled on the edge of Nayl's bunk, holding the glass in both hands.

'What's this frigging music?' he asked.

'It's frigging bouzoukis playing frigging reels from my frigging homeworld,' said Nayl from his seat at the table.

Zael thought about this. 'It's a bit plinky-plunky, isn't it?'

'Not to me.'

'Just saying.'

'Don't.'

'Okay.'

The boy swung his legs and looked around.

'When do we set off?' he asked.

Nayl looked at him. 'We've been in transit for about thirty minutes already.'

'Oh.'

'Didn't you feel the translation?'

'No. What was that, then?'

Nayl sighed. 'The moment we went warp. A vibration? A shaking?'

'Oh, that's what it was. I thought–'

'Thought what?'

'Nothing.'

'Thought what?'

Zael smiled a weak grin. 'I thought it was withdrawal. I've been getting witchy-twitchy now and then.'

Nayl snorted and knocked back some drink.

'Where are we going?' Zael asked.

'Never you mind.'

Zael pursed his lips and rocked back and forward. He looked around. 'You've got a lot of guns in here.'

'Don't touch anything.'

'Well, duh!'

Nayl frowned. 'And don't tell Ravenor I've got a lot of guns in here either. He'll only fret.'

'Okay.'

Zael took a sip from his glass and flopped back on the bunk so he was looking upside-down at the picts Nayl had stuck on the wall there.

'Who's that?'

Nayl looked across.

'That's Kara.'

'She looks different.'

'Her hair was black then. It was a few years ago.'

'She's nice.'

'Yeah, she is.'

'Who's that?'

'That's Will. Will Tallowhand. And the girl is Eleena Koi.'

'They look nice.'

'They were the best. Friends of mine.'

'Are they on board?'

'No, Zael. They're dead.'

'Oh.'

His feet stopped swinging for a moment, but he still lay on his back and stared up at the picts.

'My mumma and pappa are dead. And my granna. And Nove.'

'Who's Nove?'

'My sister. She fell off a stack.'

'I'm sorry about that.'

'It wasn't your fault.' Zael pointed. 'Who's that?'

'Kara again.'

'She looks so different each time.'

Nayl leaned back and smiled. 'That's Kara. But she's always Kara.'

'Is she your girl?'

Nayl laughed. 'I wish. Once, almost and sort of. Kara and me are friends now.'

'She's laughing a lot on that pict. She looks pretty. Why is the bottom half of it folded up?'

Nayl frowned and leaned forward to look at the pict, then grinned and leaned back again into his seat. 'Because I knew one day I'd end up with a maybe-teen boy in my cabin who'd ask all sorts of frigging stupid questions and get over excited at the sight of bare bosoms.'

Zael sat up, maintaining his gaze on the pict.

'Her bosoms were bare?'

'Yeah, they were.' Nayl cupped his glass and looked down into it. He remembered the night. Fooling around, drinking, laughing, making love. Kara had brought the picter along. Nayl wondered if she'd kept the pictures of him.

'I bet they're really nice...' Zael whispered.

'I'm not even going to have this conversation,' snarled Nayl.

There was a painfully long silence.

'Yeah, they really are,' Nayl admitted at last. They both started laughing. Really laughing. Zael rocked back and forth, snorting and wheezing.

God-Emperor, it was the best laugh Nayl had found in a very long time.

'Understand me,' said Nayl, fighting his laughter, 'you ever take that pict down to look at the fold, I'll kill you.'

'That's fair,' giggled Zael. 'You have lots of guns. Probably worth it, though.'

'Oh yeah.'

They burst out laughing again.

'Who's that? He looks like a real hard knuck.'

'Who are you pointing to? Oh, yeah. That's Eisenhorn.'

Zael looked at Nayl. 'And he is?'

'Dead, I think. My old boss. Another inquisitor.'

'The Chair's not your first boss then?'

Nayl smiled. *The Chair.* Funny, and obvious the kid would think that way. 'No, I worked for Eisenhorn before.'

'He looks like a double-hard bastard.

'He was.'

'So how long have you worked for The Chair?'

Nayl had to think about it. It had been a fluid thing. He'd been in Eisenhorn's band for a long time, right up until the infamous mission to Ghul, really. But by then he'd also been working with Ravenor. When Eisenhorn disappeared, that arrangement had sort of become permanent.

'Since the late eighties, pretty much. Nearly fifteen years.'

Zael nodded.

'Who's that?'

'That's Ravenor.'

Zael sat up and peered hard at the pict. 'He's really handsome. Is that what he looks like now, inside that chair?'

'No, Zael, it isn't.'

'What happened to him?'

'Thracian Primaris, back in '38. The Triumph. A great procession of the great and good. The forces of the Enemy struck, and caused a... a... well, it's been called the Atrocity. Ravenor was caught in a firestorm and burned really badly. He's been in that force chair ever since. His mind is the only thing left to him.'

Zael considered this. 'That's really bad,' he said.

'Yes, it is.'

'And who's that?'

Nayl leaned forward to see.

'Now, that's–'

He stopped. 'Damn,' he said, 'I've forgotten to do something important.'

ZARJARAN. THAT WAS the new medicae's name. Zarjaran. Nayl nodded to him as he swept Zael through the infirmary towards the cryo-stacks.

The hatch opened. Cold air fumed out.

There she lay, sleeping like she had done ever since '86.

'Is she dead?' Zael asked.

'No, she's not.'

'Alive?'

Nayl frowned. 'Not that either.'

'She's very beautiful.'

'Yeah, she is. Look... every time I come back aboard, I make a point of saying hello to her. Maybe she can hear me, maybe not. She's been in this... state for fifteen years. She was Eisenhorn's most loyal ally, and a good friend to me too.'

'What was her name?' Zael wondered.

'Alizebeth Bequin. Lizebeth? Hi. It's me. Harlon. Just come to say hello.'

'She's frozen!' Zael said.

'Yeah. She's not dead or alive, just preserved here. Maintained in the cold-hold of the *Hinterlight* for a decade and a half. Maybe she'll live again one day. Maybe she's dead. I like to think she can still hear us.'

Zael leaned forward and pressed his hand against the armaglas cover of the cryo-bin. His fingerprints remained as frost-blooms.

'Hello lady,' he said. 'My name is Zael.'

TWO

'SCREW THIS,' SAID Madsen, turning and climbing back down the grassy slope. 'It's a waste of time.'

Carl Thonius nodded. They'd missed this beast-moot by several weeks. The vast stock yards were empty. A bitter gale swept across the derelict pastures where the tents and cage-pens had been pitched. Some rusting iron pegs and hoops and a copious amount of dried, white dung were the only signs that this area had seen any life in years.

The sky was grey and fast: sliced strata of cloud hurtling west across the salty margin, beyond which the dark ocean boomed and rattled.

'We'll push south,' Madsen said. Thonius nodded again, but realised she had been directing the words at Ahenobarb and Kinsky. They were wandering the sparse moot-space. The psyker was saying something, but his voice was hindered by the wind. Ahenobarb hovered close to Kinsky, waiting, watching.

'What did he say?' Thonius asked, squinting.

Madsen looked at him. The wind tugged at her white-blonde hair.

'The usual psyker crap, Mr Thonius,' she said.

THE WESTERN BANKS was hard, saline country, a ragged hem where the great plains of Flint's largest continent met the uncharted sea. The planet boasted a few thriving colony cities down in the temperate south, but it was out here in the unforgiving west that the trade on which Flint prospered was conducted: stock, beast-flesh, meat.

Dynasties of stockmen, drovers and herders inhabited the great plains, dutifully following routes and trails established by their ancestors, driving the super-herds. Straight-horn, flange-horn, demi-pachyderm, the behemoth tuskers. Drove-dynasties specialised in one breed or another, catered their skills and disciplines to that breed, but all for the same purpose: driving them west each season for the beast-moots along the Western Banks.

Moot-towns studded the broken coastline like buckles on a tangled belt: Droverville, Salthouse, Trailend, Huke's Town, West Bank, West Trail, Endrover, Fleshton, Slaughterhouses, Ocean Point, Mailer's Yards, Beastberg, Great West Moot, Tusk Verge. To each one, at the close of each season, the stock was brought in to market. Off-world traders thronged around each moot, landing their fliers and bulk-lifters on the scorched commerce fields to inspect the best of the merchandise.

Nayl and Kara had headed up towards Huke's Town and all points north. Thonius's team was covering the southern reach of the Banks.

The wind off the foreshore was picking up.

Kys was waiting for them by the half-track they'd leased from a drove specialist in West Bank. Thonius and the three Ministry agents trudged down to join her on the bleak roadway.

She was looking out to sea. The dark ocean was crashing in onto the rudely worn rocks, each wave impacting with a sound of shattering glass.

THEY DROVE SOUTH along the coast highway, the sea on one side, the slipped, craggy land on the other. The road was unmetalled and raw. Several times they had to slow to overtake work gangs on foot. Some were freelance drovers, shabby in treated hides, trudging with decorated herd-poles held aloft towards the next moot. They looked like troglodytes to Kys: skin-clad, caked in dung and clay that had dried white, their leaders decorated with skulls and antlers.

Other work gangs were slaughtermen, dressed in long, button-front black coats, and carrying the ritual chain-blades in engraved biers stretchered over their shoulders. Their shaven faces were marked with finger-drawn patterns of blood.

Kys slowed and leaned out of the cab to question them. 'Beast-moot?'

Their answers were contradictory and useless.

THEY PASSED THROUGH empty, wind-blown coast towns: Endrover, Western End, Tally Point. The places had been scarred and eroded by the ocean's eternal blast and now, out of moot-season, were almost devoid of life. Tall grasses grew in the moot-yards; the buildings were shackled up and boarded. Paint peeled. The great raised stock-boards over the highway displayed fading chalk-scrawls costing last season's going rate for tusk-bison.

The towns were an odd mix. Big or small, wealthy or struggling, they followed the same essential pattern: wide tracts of commerce fields for the off-world ships to land, wider and greater moot fields where the stock was penned and displayed, and little clutches of buildings, the town itself. Taverns and barter halls, constructed in the local style, using great, curved beams as both wall posts and rafters, with a wattle-and-daub of mud-straw and flakboard in between, sat alongside more modern, rockcrete-built rendering silos. Kys wondered aloud where on this treeless plateau the locals had found the timber to raise the old barter-halls.

'Not timber… tusks,' Thonius said. 'Some of these buildings are very old. Traditionally, they use the tusks of mature animals as frame ribs.'

Kys was driving. She slowed right down as they passed through Tally Point. The bare, yellowed ribs forming the superstructure of the weatherbeaten town hall were twenty metres long.

'What kind of animal carries–'

'None. Not any more,' said Thonius. 'The real big, mature bulls were all slaughtered centuries ago, during the early colonisation. A bull has to live a good few hundred years to sport tusks like that. We'll not see their like again.'

Kys looked across at him. 'But they still herd these things here?'

Thonius nodded. 'It's the key to Flint's economy. The big placental herbivores grow fast, put on a lot of mass. The great plains are lush. A demi-pachyderm can develop enough bulk to be worth slaughtering in under five years. But their tusks don't grow half as fast. Given the rate of supply and demand, this world will never see another giant bull with eighteen metre tusks.'

'The stuff you know,' she chuckled.

He smiled back. 'I know what every trade economist worth his salt knows… and what every slaughterbaron on Flint chooses to ignore… at this rate of slaughter, Flint will be wasted out in another century.'

She realised there was nothing but grim finality in his smile. 'The stuff you know,' she murmured again.

They pressed on south, through several dead towns that trade and life had already disowned: Fleshton, West Walkaway, Ling's Berg. The yards there were totally overgrown, the drystone pen walls collapsed. In each town, the buildings were faded and abandoned. Kys saw crumbling jetties and fallen-down piers half-overwhelmed by the ocean spray. Once the trade had come by sea, shipping the meat down to the southern cities on barges.

Not any more.

THERE WAS A small moot in Mailer's Yards and another in Hidebarter. They spent a while in both, checking the moot's record books and ledgers for off-world buyers. The locals were far from compliant. Flint had no centralised record of its visitors. The moots compiled their own archives. Space traffic was deregulated. High orbit above Flint was filled with thousands of trading spaceships, none of which advertised its identity with a transponder. Only the ledgers of a town's baron could say who was around. Any trader who wanted to do business at a moot had to register himself.

In the crowded market places, amid the jostling, shaman-like drovers with their clay-caked flesh and antlered heads, and the armoured finery of off-world traders, sober-suited agents from the Departmento Munitorum went from dynast to dynast, performing the never-ending task of assessing trade for the purposes of Imperial levy. There was noise everywhere: the chattering bark of the drovers bartering, the shouts of the stock auctioneers, the clatter of tallyboards, and the constant background lowing of the vast flange-horn herds in the moot yards.

Neither moot had any record of the ship they were after. In Mailer's Yards, Thonius and Madsen went into the barter-hall to inspect the local baron's own archives. Kys waited outside on the ivory decking with Ahenobarb and Kinsky. The scrawny psyker went to the bone rail and stood, looking out across the jostling market towards the fuming sea. Kys could feel a pin-prickle of psi-use, but it was not directed at her. She wondered how many minds in that marketspace Kinsky was idly rifling through.

The facade of the barter-hall glittered brilliantly every time the sun came out from behind the chasing clouds. It was covered with thousands of silver disks, each one about a thumb-span in diameter, no two identical. They were all nailed in place. Fish scales, she realised, from some pelagic giant. They were as hard and simple as everything else on this beleaguered frontier, but somehow had a beauty that Flint did not.

Ahenobarb had seen the scales too. He reached out to take one down as a trophy, and then snatched back his hand. He glared at Kys, sucking blood from sliced finger tips. The scale edges were razor-sharp.

Kys unhooked three using her telekinesis, and floated them across to her. They glinted in the air. She hung all three over the top button-stud of her body glove using the nail-holes in their centres. They shone like a badge of office at her throat.

Thonius and Madsen emerged from the hall. They had learned nothing to their advantage.

'Except,' said Thonius, 'the Tusk Verge moot begins tonight.'

THE TUSK VERGE moot was amongst the biggest held on Flint, almost on the scale of the Winter Great Moot and the Spring Drove. They drove the sixty kilometres to Tusk Verge through the late afternoon, and while they were yet some distance from the town, they saw the first signs of it.

Initially, contrails in the cold, bright sky. Criss-crossing lines of vapour that spoke of heavy inter-orbit traffic. Then a few fliers, shuttles, zipping over, then a pair of battered bulk-lifters that grumbled along overhead and blotted out the sun.

The traffic on the highway got denser. Herdsmen, slaughtermen, a few troupes of entertainers. Then caravans of slow-moving, high-sided wagons drawn by oxen or traction engines. The wind trailed back a chalky dust from the caravans that carried the sour bite of ammonia. There was money to be made from collecting up a herd's droppings and selling it on for phosphates and fertilizers. Colonies on mineral-poor worlds paid generously for Flint's excrement.

Just five kilometres from the town, they saw greater clouds against the horizon, billowing from inland. They were white, like low-mist rolling in banks, but they were dust. The dust of the super-herds coming in down the ancient drove roads.

THE HIGHWAY ENTERED Tusk Verge over a stone viaduct two kilometres long. Beneath its broad arches, spread out on the wide coastal plains, was a portion of the moot's pens and gated yards, a giant patchwork of drystone enclosures through which animals could be driven, penned off, separated, counted. High-walled droveways led up to the commerce fields where the cargo haulers of the orbiting trade ships lined up to be filled. In the failing light, blue and yellow flares came intermittently from the direction of the commerce fields, the afterglow of landing jets and atmospheric drives.

The stock was pouring into the town locale through the drove gates along the eastern perimeter. The ancient trackways and drove roads, scoured into the Great Plains by generations of herds, had been dug down through the coastal cliffs, forming high-flanked cuttings and gorges that funneled the incoming livestock down into the pens of the moot yards. Stockmen hauled on massive iron swing-gates, directing one herd or herd-portion into this pen, another into that. One dynast's animals were kept from another's, or a major herd was portioned down into commercial parcels. Brandsmen went from pen to pen, checking flesh-brands and ear slashes for provenance and ownership, while tallymen collected up bronze tally rings of appropriate value from drove men, and clattered them onto the abacus-like tally boards they carried. The rise and fall of stock values and the going rates for certain beasts of a certain weight was set by the slaughterbaron and his cartel, based on the accumulated tallies, and then chalked up on the massive boards overlooking the auction arenas.

Beyond them, lit by oil-drum fires, stood the long halls where buyers could inspect sample animals, and then the long, grim silos of the rendering plant. Some traders bought dead meat and salted or froze it for shipment to the cheap food-marts down sub. Others bought live and shipped it – sometimes in stasis – to more discerning clients on the wealthier hive worlds of Angelus. Some bought low quality in bulk, others high quality animals, individually chosen and purchased. Some came for the mechanically-recovered meat products of the rendering plant, others for phosphate dung. A ten tonne demi-pach might fetch twenty crowns a tonne, get turned into thirty thousand meat patties to be sold at half a crown a time in the food-stalls of a hive's slum-hab. A sixty kilo shorthorn might fetch five times as much, because it was destined to sell as a prime imported delicacy in the uphive restaurants of Eustis Majoris and Caxton at fifty crowns a pop.

The firedrums lit the evening with greasy flames. The air was heady with the autumnal stinks of blood, dung, fire, herbivore gas and baled feed. They pulled off the viaduct, parked the half-track in a rockcrete yard where other trucks had been left, and went looking for the slaughter-baron.

INEVITABLY, THE LIVESTOCK trade up and down the Angelus sub overlapped the pit-game business. Traders shipping a hold full of pachs might as well make some extra fees carrying more dangerous animals for the Imperial pits, and game agents in need of transport often hired stock traders because they already had a lot of the specialised holding equipment.

The beast-moots of Flint were primarily livestock oriented. Occasionally drovers brought a great plains predator to market for extra cash, but the commerce of the Western Banks was essentially about meat. Further up the line, out towards Lenk and the rip-worlds, that was where you found the specialist beast-moots, the ones held entirely for the pit-trade.

Even so, Flint's beast-moots were frequented by the game agents. Some were passing through on their way to Lenk. Others came to buy cheap meat-cuts for bait and feed: many of the pit-favourite carnivores grew too placid if cargoed in stasis, and a full grown taurosaur ate its own weight in meat several times over during six weeks live-haul. Some agents came to Flint to purchase big herbivores that could be goaded into violence for specialised bouts and others yet came because they were travelling as paying passengers on livestock trade ships and had no say where the shipmaster put in.

Baron Julius Karquin had run Tusk Verge for sixty years. In his rich, off-planet robes and lime-clayed animal hide cloak, he seemed a man caught between two worlds, part businessman, part shaman. During the moot, he held court in one of the tusk-frame pavilions in the town centre.

An entourage of slaughtermen, tallymen and dynasts surrounded him, along with market advisors and record keepers. Distinguished far traders were admitted to his presence, many were greeted like old friends. Baron Karquin had done business with just about everybody.

There seemed small hope of getting close to him, certainly not without causing an altercation and revealing their authority. Already, from the wary behaviour of officials at the smaller moots, Thonius had realised the folk of the Western Banks did not take well to Imperial dealings. It was a free market, which depended on the good will of the rogue traders. The authority of the Throne was not welcome.

Kys tried to bribe a junior ledger-keeper for information, but it hadn't worked. The baron had great power here, particularly during the time of the moot. He wielded Imperial authority by proxy. During a moot, a slaughter-baron had more power in his town than the lord governor sub-sector.

Karquin's face was craggy, and his frame big, made bigger by the weight of velvet, chainmail and hides. His teeth were bad, his eyes hooded. On his head, he wore a circle-crown of bronze mounted with two polished rams horns, an ancient badge of office. The crown was mostly lost in his unruly black hair, so it appeared the horns sprouted from Karquin's own brow. He had four of his many bodyguards by his side at all times. They were big men, dressed in the high-button coats of the slaughterman guild, but their chainblades were designed for combat, not rendering. They wore bleached antlered beast-skulls on their leather caps. The bodyguards saw to it that none but the most important clients got close to the baron.

'We're screwed at this rate,' said Madsen. Thonius didn't think he'd ever met anyone so pessimistic.

'Let's press the issue,' suggested Kys.

'And get in a fight?' Thonius said.

Kys shrugged. Ahenobarb, just a big shape in the firelight, seemed to approve.

'There are ways!' Kinsky said sarcastically. He glanced at Ahenobarb and immediately the big man reached out to catch Kinsky as he fell.

'What's he doing?' Thonius hissed.

Kys took a couple of rapid steps backwards and covered her mouth in shock. The raw, unleashed surge of psipower had taken her off-balance.

'Shit!' she gasped. 'He's gone... left his body...'

'What?' Thonius said.

Kys pointed through the bustling crowd towards the great gaggle of people collected around Karquin on the baronial dais at the end of the hall. 'I can feel him... hunting...' Kys said.

'Get him back here!' Thonius said to Ahenobarb.

'Kinsky knows what he's doing,' Madsen said stonily. 'If we leave this up to you, we'll be here all week.'

'This is the inquisitor's operation,' Thonius growled. 'You three are here under sufferance.'

'Whatever,' said Madsen and looked back into the crowd. Thonius stared too, but he could see nothing out of the ordinary. What was Kinsky doing?

'That ledger keeper, just behind Karquin, on the left,' whispered Kys.

Thonius found the man. Pale, old, wearing long, limecaked robes and a necklace of bulls' teeth. The old man had turned from a trencher of food and was leafing through the tanned skin pages of one of the massive ledger books. Each volume took two men to carry. They sat on ivory stands around the baron's dais. The ledger keeper speed-read each page he turned with blank eyes.

Abruptly, the ledger keeper backed away from the volume, blinking and disorientated. Kinsky lurched and opened his eyes.

'They're not here, but they were expected,' he said.

'What?' asked Thonius.

'Captain Thekla of the *Oktober Country* is a regular visitor to this moot. The baron had prepared accommodation for him, and reserved several herd parcels that he believed Thekla would be interested in.'

'So we are wasting our time here…' Kys began.

Kinsky grinned at her. 'There is an interesting part to this. According to the records, the baron knew Thekla wasn't coming this season, because Thekla's apologies and regrets were passed on to the baron this morning by a stock trader called Bartol Siskind.'

'Who is?'

'Master of the rogue trader *Allure*, and currently in the auction pens, bidding for flange-horn.'

THEY SPREAD OUT into the crowds and the firelit night. Moving into the shadows of a doorway, Thonius touched his wraithbone pendant and made contact.

'The *Oktober Country* isn't here and it isn't coming, but we've got a lead on another shipmaster it may have had recent dealings with.'

+Details?+ Ravenor replied.

'Bartol Siskind, of the *Allure*. Kinsky got the information out of a local mind.'

+I felt it from here. We will be asking Mr Kinsky to be more circumspect. He is powerful, but also crude. An incident here would be regrettable.+

'Indeed,' said Thonius. He glanced round. A couple of ragged drovers had just gone by, glaring maliciously at the off-worlder in the shadows talking to himself. 'I'd better go. We're going to see what we can get out of this Siskind once we find him. You'd better recall Harlon and Kara to the ship.'

+I will. Be careful, Carl.+

Thonius made his way through the crowd. Despite the gale off the sea, the night was warm. Four hundred thousand head of stock generated a significant amount of heat.

And smell. Already Thonius's favourite buckle-back boots were ruined from the dung swilling the streets. He wafted his kerchief in front of his nose.

Staccato shouts echoed from the vast bowls of the auction arenas. Bidding was in progress. Confident, experienced-looking shipmen in winter coats, cloaks or body armour leaned at the bone rail and held up numbered cards as a dozen of the hugest quadrupeds Carl Thonius had ever had the misfortune to smell were circled in the paddock below.

But there was another source of commotion, above the chatter of the crowd. It was coming from behind him, back from the direction of the baron's pavilion.

Casually, Thonius took up a place on the nearest arena's overstage. The man next to him was a brawny red-head in a bodyglove and heavy cloak.

'What's that about, do you suppose?' Thonius asked idly, nodding back in the direction of the pavilion.'

The shipman scowled. 'Some frigger brought a psyker. Got into the head of one of the baron's people. Karquin's gone frigging nuts, so the whole moot's gonna slow right down until the fuss dies away.' The man swore again. 'I'm meant to be in Caxton in eight days with a hold full of sirloin,' he complained.

'A psyker,' said Thonius. 'That's not good.'

'Of course it's not good!' the shipman blustered. 'Everyone knows they're banned from the moots! Moot-law. No psykers, on account of unfair trading. Always been that way. That's why the baron's got his warlock.'

Of course, that's why the baron's got his warlock, Thonius thought. Of course, of *course*, and *everyone* knows that psykers are banned from the moot by ancient decree. Of course they do. Of frigging *course*.

He could hear Kys saying it. *The stuff you know.*

Well, it turns out *this* wasn't one of them. Come to that, he hadn't even seen a warlock.

'What the hell have you done?' the shipman asked him suddenly. Thonius started. Was the look of dismay on his face that obvious?

But that's not what the shipman had meant. He looked down, over the ivory rail, into the street. One of the baron's bodyguards was down there, chainblade in hand. Two ragged drovers were busy pointing out the man they'd seen talking to himself.

'Oh shit,' said Thonius.

TRIPLE SHUTTERS SECURED the holding cell. I waited as they opened in series. Vertical doors, then horizontal barriers, then an inner skin of verticals again, all sliding back into the recesses of the armoured frame. Then I moved through into the dingy cell.

Duboe looked up at the light and at me and groaned. He was tethered to the floor by a long chain that was fixed to his bracelet cuffs. The chain had enough length on it to allow him to lie on the straw pallet in the corner or use the chemical toilet. He was dirty and unshaven. A tray lay by the door, a half-eaten meal on it.

'You again,' he said.

Me again. Get used to it, I thought. But for the information he might yet yield, most inquisitors I knew would have had Duboe executed by now. He was criminal scum, exploiting the systems of Imperial society just to corrupt it.

He was also a strange one. He had no discernible mind-talents, but parts of his brain were unreadable. I had interviewed him a dozen times in the six days since we'd set out from Eustis. His mind had become ever more impenetrable. It also seemed as if he had been getting stupider.

'What do you want me to confess to now?' he asked, getting up on his knees.

I made no response.

Duboe stood up, tired but somehow triumphant. 'Okay,' he slurred, 'okay... I admit it. I'm Horus, reincarnated. I am the arch-enemy of the Golden Throne. I am–'

+Shut up.+

He fell silent and stared at the floor. To begin with, cavae-master Duboe had been quite forthcoming. He had owned up to his part in the narcotic trade, explained how he had abused his position as an importer to circulate contraband into the subculture of Petropolis. During our second interview, he had been quite forthcoming on the subject of his sources. A number of rogue traders who had dealings with the Imperial Pits supplied him with prohibited substances along with pit-beasts. The *Widdershins* secured him obscura and gladstones at a decent rate. The *Fontaineblue* brought in grinweed and yellodes. The *Macrocosmae* had been good for both. Duboe had been perfectly placed to distribute, thanks to his connections with the moody clans and the gamesters. I had already passed all three names on to my masters in the Ordos Helican. Others could deal with it.

It had taken longer to fox the *Oktober Country* out of him. That was where the flects were coming in from. Duboe finally sold out his contact, Feaver Skoh, and the complicity of the *Oktober Country's* master, Thekla. But he insisted he didn't know where Skoh and Thekla were getting the flects from. That was where the mind-wall went up.

I probed him for a moment. For the third or fourth time, all I got was a mysterious memory-echo... 'Contract thirteen'.

+Tell me about the *Allure*.+

He winced. 'The what?'

+The *Allure*.+

He shrugged. 'It's a ship. It does the Lenk run. It's brought me beasts a few times.'

Hovering, I circled around him slowly. 'Its captain… a friend of Skoh's?'

'No.'

+Thekla, then?+

A shrug. 'Yeah, Thekla. Old ties. Trader bonds. All buddies together. They're allies. That's how rogue traders work.'

+Did the master of the *Allure* ever supply you with flects?+

'Siskind? No?'

+Did the master of the *Allure* ever offer to supply you with flects?+

'No.'

I stabbed a mind-lance into Duboe's mid-brain and he swayed, in pain. It was like pushing a sword into wet paper. His mind seemed so… mushy.

+What else can you tell me about Siskind and the *Allure*?+

Duboe rocked. 'Siskind is Thekla's third cousin. They're both related by blood to Lilean Chase.'

I was momentarily stunned. Lilean Chase had been an abominable blight on the Imperium eighty years before. A radical of the Recongregator philosophy, she had forgone her ordo loyalties and founded the Cognitae school on Hesperus. There, for three generations, she had hard-schooled the brightest and best that had fallen into her clutches and formed them into sociopathic monsters, driven by a will to undermine the fabric of the holy Imperium. The Cognitae had only come to an end thanks to a purging raid led by Lord Inquisitor Rorken, now

Grand Master of the Ordos Helican. Damn! Molotch himself had been a product of that deranged academy!

I became aware that my contact alarm was piping. I retreated from the cell and keyed the hatches to shut after me.

Medicae Zarjaran was waiting for me outside.

'What's the trouble?' I asked him.

'I'm concerned, sir, only for the prisoner's welfare,' he said.

'And so?'

'Duboe's mind is fraying,' he said. 'He is dying. I'm afraid it's because of the repeated interrogations.'

'Medicae, I've gone easy on him. A dozen interviews, no more than that.'

'I understand, but when Mr Kinsky's sessions are added in–'

+Mr Kinsky's sessions?+

I had forgotten myself. My frank mind-clause had quailed him. The short, olive-skinned medicae cowered back from me.

'My apologies,' I said. 'Please confirm... Kinsky has been interviewing the prisoner too?'

'Yes, sir,' said Zarjaran timidly. 'He and Mamzel Madsen, twice a day.'

What the hell was this? I turned my chair automatically to roam up to the bridge and demand answers out of Preest. But Halstrom was standing directly behind me.

+Yes?+

'My lord inquisitor. I summoned you out of your interview. There's a... situation... down on the surface...'

PATIENCE KYS SHOULDERED her way through the massing crowds, thankful of the camouflaging flicker of the firelight, looking back and forth for Thonius.

+This is bad,+ she sent, but instead of Ravenor's voice she got the gruff mind-drawl of Kinsky.

+Yeah, it's bad. Get your ass in gear. We're leaving.+

+Where are you?+

+The ride. Get a move on.+

Gongs and what sounded like kettle drums were sounding out now from various parts of the torchlit town. The noise caused a stir, an agitation in the already unsettled moot crowds.

Everywhere she looked, slaughtermen were moving through the throng. The baron's bodyguards, their strength supplemented by regular meat-cutters from the rendering silos.

+Carl? Where are you?+

No response. She repeated the query using her pocketvox. Still nothing. She hurried down Tusk Verge's busy main street in the direction of the highway viaduct. Overhead, the night sky was underlit amber by the smoke and canfires of the town. A large, slender, sickle moon hung high in the west. A slaughterman's moon, it was called, announcing moot-time because it resembled both a butcher's stripping blade and a long ivory tusk.

Carl had told her that. The stuff he knew.

The drumming became more incessant. Then she heard a fierce, rasping *whoosh*. She looked round.

A blood-red full moon seemed to be rising above the town, rising fast. But it wasn't a celestial body at all. It was a globe balloon, trapped in a thick woven net that stretched down beneath its spherical bulk to suspend an ivory basket. The rasping, whooshing sounds came from the brief, bright squirts of flame from the burner as it rose. The basket trailed a cable down to the ground. There was a man in the basket, a dynast drover by the look of him. His body was caked in white clay except for dark kohl rings around his eyes, and he wore a headdress of antlers. He had a bone rattle in each hand, and he shook them and pointed them down into the crowd.

Kys had seen this man before, in the barter-hall. The baron's warlock, his shaman. Evidently a psyker himself – Kys could feel her flesh goosebump – he had gone aloft to locate the interloper. The balloon rose no higher than ten metres. Its tether was fixed to a cart that the baronial bodyguards were wheeling through the streets to move their warlock bloodhound around.

Kys started to run. She reached the rockcrete yard where they had left the half-track. The three Petropolitan agents were already aboard, and Madsen had the engine running.

'Come on!' Kinsky called.

'Where's Thonius?' she asked.

Kinsky shrugged. 'Like I give a damn. We've got to leave town now before things get ugly.'

'We're not leaving him behind!' Kys said.

'You want to take the whole frigging place on?' Madsen called. 'Look, I don't like leaving a body on the ground either, but frankly, sister, better him than all of us. The baron will have us ritually shredded if he gets hold of us. Shit, Thonius is probably already dead. Where will your precious inquisitor's mission be if we all end up as dog-mince?'

'Are you frigging well gonna get aboard or not?' Kinsky asked.

'No,' said Kys. 'And if you drive out of here now, next time I see you, I'll kill the lot of you.'

Ahenobarb laughed. Madsen threw the half-track into gear. 'You stay here, Kys, and there won't be any next time.'

Kys stepped back as the vehicle lurched forward. It pulled a wide turn and then thundered away across the torchlit viaduct.

Kys watched it go and then turned back into the town.

* * *

THONIUS STARTED TO run. He could see the balloon and the ghastly capering freak in its basket. More importantly, he could hear the shouts and cries in the crowd behind him as the slaughterman bodyguard pushed his way through to reach him.

His heart was pounding. This wasn't fair. It just wasn't fair. He didn't deserve this.

He knew running was making him stand out. He might as well have been holding up a sign saying, 'Here I am, the guilty one'. But still he ran. The bodyguard had got a good look at him. All he could see in his mind's eye were the polished teeth of the man's chainblade.

Most people got out of his way. Nobody wanted a piece of this trouble. A few, tallymen and stock-men mostly, cried out and pointed, alerting his pursuers.

There was a junction ahead. Straight on was the bustling main street, to the right a short drystone alley that led to a staircase down into the moot pens. He kept going straight. If he could get to the street, then he could reach the yard, reach the vehicle. They'd be waiting for him. With the engine running.

Hands grabbed at him. Three filthy drovers had decided they weren't just going to stand by and watch some outsider get away with breaking their most inviolable laws. Shouting out, they clawed at his coat. One had his left arm pinned.

'Get off me!' he wailed. One thumped him across the side of the head to shut him up. The drover had bone rings on his dirty fingers and the hard edges stung and drew blood. Thonius could feel it dribbling down the side of his face.

Carl Thonius hated physical combat. He didn't look like much of a threat either. He appeared too fragile, too slight, especially compared to combat specialists like Nayl and Zeph Mathuin. Certainly, he saw himself more as a thinker, a tactician. He tended to leave what he called 'the fisticuffs' to his more brawny comrades. But, in truth, Carl Thonius was a trained Throne agent, an ordo interrogator. The fact that Harlon Nayl could kill him with a single cough obscured the fact that Thonius was still far, far more capable than the average man on the street. This street included, it was to be hoped.

The drovers holding him were whip-thin and strong. The pursuing bodyguard could only be a few paces off now. Thonius was not physically powerful, but he fought with a canny combination of brains and vicious dexterity. He went limp, and his assailants relaxed slightly, assuming him to be submitting to their efforts.

It was easy, therefore, to snap himself sideways, freeing his pinned arm. He back-kicked the drover behind him in the shins and jabbed his fingers into the eyes of the dynast breathing rancid halitosis in his face. The man screamed. Thonius danced away, ducked a flying fist from the third drover, and pirouetted neatly to kick him in the gut. Two were down – one doubled over and retching, the other on his knees, hands clamped over his injured eyes. The third came in, roaring hoarsely, slashing with an ivory dagger. Thonius dodged to the man's right, caught his stabbing wrist with his left hand and broke the drover's humerus against his right forearm with a scissoring block-and-yank.

Some of the off-world traders in the immediate vicinity cheered. They didn't care about the outcome. A decent street fight was an entertainment to be enjoyed.

There was a revving sound, the noise of a chainblade kicking into life. In his high-buttoned black coat, the pursuing bodyguard stormed into view, his powered, ceremonial weapon whining as it swung and circled in expert hands.

Thonius jumped backwards and the alarmed crowd retreated wide to avoid the oscillating chainblade.

Thonius could hear the warlock-freak up in his basket, shaking his rattles fit to bust, screaming that the rogue was found.

The bodyguard came in, blade shrilling. Thonius feinted left and then went right, pausing to rip the antlered headdress off one of the fallen drovers as he did so. As the bodyguard came round for a second try, hefting his cumbersome weapon, Thonius had the antlers held out before him with both hands, like the beast-tamers he'd seen in the circus, warding off big felids with the legs of a stool.

The bodyguard chopped with his chainblade, and fifty centimetres of brittle antler tree sheared away in splinters. The force nearly tore the headdress out of Thonius's hands. Another pass, and now both antlers were cut down. A drunken shipman in the circle of onlookers cheered and clapped, and the bodyguard glanced around with a murderous glare.

Thonius took the opportunity as it was given. He lunged forward and stabbed the sawn-off antlers deep into the slaughterman's neck.

It was horrible and messy. Blood squirted out and drizzled the crowd, which backed away sharply with disgusted complaints. The slaughterman fell on his front, his limbs convulsing. He landed across his own tearing chainblade and a great deal more blood erupted into the air.

All the rough good humour was gone now. No more clapping, no more cheering. This wasn't bare-knuckle chop and punch. A man was dead.

Thonius threw the dripping headdress aside. He started on towards the main street.

But now there were three more slaughtermen running up towards him from that direction. One had a chainblade, another a butcher's axe. The third was wielding a long, bronze-bladed drover lance.

For a brief moment, Thonius considered reaching into his left hand coat pocket and pulling out his ordo rosette. He pictured himself holding it up and declaring: 'By the order of the Imperial and Holy Inquisition, and by the authority of the Ordo Xenos Helican and Inquisitor Gideon Ravenor, I command you to desist and submit.'

Would that stop a lance and an axe and a chainer? Would the sworn and blooded moot-kin of an august and almost deified slaughterbaron even recognise the authority?

Thonius decided the answer was no. He had no desire to end his career with a raised rosette in one hand, a meaningless declaration on his oh so pretty lips and a bronze lance through his torso.

So he reached into his right hand coat pocket instead. All bets were off now.

Will Tallowhand, God-Emperor rest his soul, had given Carl Thonius the Hecuter 6 the day Thonius had achieved the rank of interrogator. Kara Swole had given him a not entirely unpleasant hug, and Norah Santjack had presented him with a silver charm showing Saint Kiodrus inspiring the hosts. Nayl had given him a pat on the arm and a few inspiring words, and Ravenor had given him a first edition of Solon's writings.

The book was on a shelf in his cabin aboard the *Hinterlight*. He still wore the charm. Nayl's comradely pat and heroic words, and Kara's hug, were cherished memories with zero practical application.

On balance, right then, in that dusty side street, Tallowhand's gift seemed the most lasting and provident.

Will had warned him the Six had a beefy kick. Thonius knew it. He'd trained with the gun on the *Hinterlight's* range, exhausting hundreds of clips for ten-zero groupings. This was the first time, in anger.

The Hecuter 6 was a hand-made piece. The body and slide were brushed chrome, the grip satinized black rubber machined out to fit his hand. It formed an inverted 'L' shape because the grip housing, built to contain an eighteen round clip, was longer than the polished body. The safety-off was a steel rocker that the thumb depressed automatically when the weapon was gripped. When it discharged, white flame burped from the snout and the slide banged back and forth, flinging out the spent case with a chime like loose change. The buck-recoil wrenched his wrist. It was so frigging loud. Thonius realised that he'd only ever shot it with ear-protectors on.

The crowd broke and fled. The slaughterman with the lance jerked back four or five metres, his face missing. The man with the chainblade did likewise, tumbling over on the cobbles. The axe man turned to flee. It was all too easy to put a round through the back of his head. Such force. Such monumental destroying force. The axe man spun over, his face hitting the paving first with a wet crunch.

Thonius gasped, and raised the Hecuter to a ready/armed position. His wrist ached. His mind was racing. He heard someone growl a curse, and saw one of the retreating shipmen turn, wrenching an eight-shot heavy revolver from his ermine-edged coat.

Yes, all bets were off.

Thonius didn't wait. He put a bullet through the shipman too.

Kys, already running, jumped when she heard gunfire echo down the streetway. It was distant, muffled. A street away? Two? More? All around her, the moot crowd was breaking and scattering, fleeing the killing zone. Drovers and moot-men ran, panicking. Shipmen and off-world traders were more leisurely, returning to their vehicles, heading back to their ships on the commerce fields. Some had weapons drawn just in case, and the richest had their lifeguard cadres locked and loaded.

The Tusk Verge moot was certainly suspended. There was evidently going to be hell to pay for the disruption.

As she ran, against the tide, Kys could see the warlock in his balloon, heading towards the auction rings and the gates into the pens. She didn't dare risk telepathy now.

'Carl! In the name of the God-Emperor, Thonius! Where are you?'

No response. She halted under the eaves of a barter-hall and self-tested her vox. It was live, all right.

'Carl?'

'KYS? YOU OUT there? I need a hand, I really do!' Thonius called. He was running down the stinking stone stairs into the unlit pens. Above and behind him the street was alive with tumult and firebrands.

He stopped for a moment in the shadow of a drystone wall and reached into his coat for his microbead, tracing the tiny plastek-sheathed wires from his earpiece to the compact set in his pocket. The wires had been torn out, presumably when the drovers had manhandled him.

His heart was still beating fast. He checked his weapon. The tiny LED display informed him he still had fourteen rounds left. And he had another clip in his hip pocket.

The smell and the darkness had become alarming. There was no light down in the pen yards. Just stink. Massive, heavy bodies jostled in the stalls. He was splashing through pools of urine, tripping on raked-up rafts of straw, mud, shit.

'I really frigging want to know the way out of here,' he said.

+Relax, Carl. It'll be all right.+

Thonius smiled as Ravenor's voice floated into his head. He could feel the warm glow off his wraithbone pendant.

A bobbling line of torches was making its way down into the pen yards in the dark. They were coming after him. Thonius could hear shouting voices, gunning chain-blades.

'Help?' he said.

+Ahead twenty paces.+

'Right.' He obeyed. It brought him up against a solid iron gate.

+Open the gate.+

'What?'

+Open the gate, Carl.+

'You expect me to go into a pen full of frigging tuskers?'

+Sigh. Actually, they're demi-pachydrems. Quite placid, despite their size.+

'I know as a fact the average demi-pach on this scum-world weighs in at forty tonnes and has shovel-tusks the size of an ork's bill-hook.'

+Indeed. Carl, you asked for my help and I'm trying. As I sense it, there are sixty-eight of the baron's slaughtermen coming down the pen track towards you, out for blood. I'm not even counting the angry drover-men with them, or the armed traders coming along for the bounty. I'll pacify the demi-pachs. Just get across the yard.+

Carl Thonius sighed and slid back the gate bolt. The sound of it made the herd inside sound and low. Huge hooves trampled forward.

'I–'

+Get the hell on with it, Carl.+

Thonius pushed the hefty gate open and slid into the pen. He leaned the gate shut behind him. The demi-pachs were huge shadows in the chilly night. He could smell their weight, their dung. He could see their snorting breath fuming the cold air.

+Carl? Let's go.+

He walked forward.

Terra, these things were big. Even in the utter dark, they were monsters. They loomed over him. He could sense their parasite-clotted, wrinkled hides. He edged past two or three, then one turned its massive head and he had to duck to avoid collision with a pair of two-metre tusks.

'I'm dead,' he whispered.

+Shut up, Carl. I'm trying to save you here. Keep going. Another twenty paces.+

'Euwww...'

+What?+

'One of these things just defecated on me.'

+It'll wash off, Carl. Come on. Get with me.+

'I see the gate.'

+Good. Head for it. Open it.+

Head low, Thonius scurried through the forest of legs and distended bellies, hearing their multi-stomach gurgle, smelling their constant gas.

He reached the far gate and drew back the slider bolt.

+Wait–+

Thonius didn't. His heart was fluttering with fear now. He so wanted to be out of the pen, away from the gigantic beasts.

+Carl, I–+

Thonius pulled the gate open and dashed out into the drystone corridor outside. He only dimly registered the figures in front of him.

He raised his gun as fast as he was able.

The slaughterman's face was fixed in a grimace, marked with dried blood. The chainblade sang.

The toothed cutter severed Thonius's right arm at the elbow. His whole forearm, the hand still clutching the Hecuter 6, flew off into the dark.

* * *

KYS HEARD THE scream of pain and outrage.

'Carl! By all that's holy, Carl!'

HE'D NEVER BEEN worn. There'd never been a circumstance where it might have to happen. Ravenor didn't even know if Carl Thonius could be worn.

But there was no choice.

The wraithbone pendant shone like fire.

NFFF! PAIN! EXCRUCIATING, dominating... total. I try to blank it, but it's overwhelming. Blood's pumping out of my severed arm. I've fallen down, I'm passing out.

There's a slaughterman standing over me, his murderous chain blade raised, gore flecking from the cycling teeth.

Focus. *Focus!*

This... this is a surprisingly soft place. Warm, inviting, educated, refined. Thonius's mindspace is like a gentleman's club. No, a private dinner party. Every place setting perfect, every line of discourse wise and ironic. God-Emperor, it's so genteel, so polished.

Except for that man at the end of the dining table. The man with the severed arm, spraying blood all over the pressed white table cloth, screaming, soiling himself.

I raise a crystal glass, dignified, and toast. I am the host here. I'm in charge.

The man with the shorn-away arm stops screaming. He looks at me, puzzled, like I'm some gate-crasher.

We look into each others eyes for a moment. There's a door behind him in the wood-panelled wall. A door into a secret room. The man really, really doesn't want me to go in there.

I don't. There's no time. A brute with a chainblade is about to decapitate me.

* * *

CARL THONIUS'S MUTILATED body springs up onto its feet and avoids the downstroke of the chainblade. It circles wide and kicks the chainblade's operator in the face so hard several of his teeth come flying out.

Then there's a man with a knife. Even missing a limb, Thonius's body disarms him easily and leaves the knife wedged under his left eye.

The other two men have lances. Herd lances, with long, broad, bronze tips.

Thonius's body reaches down into the filth and prises the Hecuter 6 from the dead fingers of a severed right arm.

Left-handed, it raises the gun. The grip doesn't fit its hand.

Who cares?

A tight squeeze puts it on auto. The charging spearmen come apart like gristle dolls.

Only then do I sink to my borrowed knees, drop the gun and sag. I've staved off the effects of Thonius's blood loss long enough.

Kys is there. She smiles down at me.

She says 'Gonna be fine. I'll get you out of here.'

And she means it.

THREE

When he woke up, he was flat on his back, with three hard, white suns shining into his eyes, and a tall figure standing over him. The figure was a shadow, silhouetted by the clustered suns.

Although he knew Ravenor could never be a figure, an upright figure, not any more, he was sure that was who it was. It was big and strong, and it was assured. Perhaps this was some lingering part of the strange things that had been done to his mind.

The figure reached up a hand and, with a casual, god-like gesture, swung the suns aside in the sky.

With their light tipped away, he realised they were not suns after all. Just a bank of chrome-hooded photo-lumin surgical lamps on a multi-poise armature. And the figure wasn't Ravenor. Or the God-Emperor.

It was Zeph Mathuin.

The bodyguard was naked except for a pair of white, draw-string shorts and a heavy packing of surgical dressings strapped across his broad torso. Thonius could see the entirety of Mathuin's left arm; the polished mechanisms of a chrome-plated augmetic limb. He could see the old scars where silver metal and caramel flesh folded into one another at the shoulder.

He thought of his own arm and–

The stuff you know.

'He's awake,' Mathuin said, and turned away.

Ravenor hovered his chair across the infirmary to Thonius's bedside.

'Carl?'

Zarjaran, the medicae, appeared from somewhere and checked the diagnostic displays above the head of the cot.

'My head hurts,' Thonius said, his voice sounding to him like it was coming out of distant speakers.

'Naturally,' said Zarjaran.

'I want to sit up.'

Zarjaran reached up to a dangling control box and elevated Thonius's cot into a half recline.

Thonius looked around the room. He'd never been a patient in the *Hinterlight's* infirmary before, except for periodic health checks and shots prior to planet visits. Ravenor was there in front of him, his armoured shell giving nothing away. Mathuin had crossed back to his own rumpled cot and was sitting on its edge, sucking drink from a flask through a plastek straw.

There was an overwhelming smell of counterseptic wash.

'I'm sorry,' Thonius said.

'For what?' Ravenor asked.

'The mess.'

'Things happen in the field, Carl. I'm just glad you're alive.'

Thonius felt as if he might burst into tears. He breathed hard, and felt the tension pull at sutures. He didn't dare look down at his right arm. He wanted Ravenor to mind-speak, so he could hear his real voice and tone and inflection, instead of that bloodless, emotionless voxsponder. But he didn't know if his splitting, psi-abused mind could take it.

'You and Kys got me out.'

'We did,' said Ravenor. 'I'm sorry I had to ware you like that. I would normally ask permission of a friend first, and I don't like to ware someone who's not experienced it before. But it was a necessity.'

'It was peculiar,' said Thonius. In truth, he could remember little about it. The memory of pain eclipsed just about everything else. But he had a feeling of being stretched from within, hollowed out. He was exhausted.

'I'm exhausted too,' Ravenor said. 'It saps me, especially over such a distance. And... in such traumatic circumstances.'

Thonius swallowed. 'My arm. Where... where is my arm?'

'Back where it should be,' said Zarjaran.

Thonius looked down at himself for the first time. His entire right arm was swathed in dressings, with many drug-shunt tubes and wound-drains curling out of it. But they were his fingers protruding from the binding gauze.

'We were able to re-attach it...' the medicae began.

'Doctor Zarjaran is being modest,' said Ravenor. 'He spent sixteen hours on you with micro-servitors.'

Zarjaran bowed his head slightly.

'It's early days, interrogator,' he said. 'But I think the regraft is taking. You might have some long-term loss of function, but the injury was surprisingly clean.'

'Be thankful,' Mathuin growled, 'that the men of the Slaughter Guild take pride in keeping their blades astonishingly sharp.'

Thonius tried to flex his fingers, but he could not.

Then he looked up. 'Sixteen hours, you said. How long have I been out?'

'Two days,' said Ravenor.

'What have I missed?'

'Little. Nayl and Kara are on the surface, looking for Siskind. I withdrew everyone else. Everyone who might have been connected to the incident.'

'What about... Kinsky and his friends?'

'I've yet to talk to them,' said Ravenor.

'He's making them sweat,' said Mathuin.

SOMEONE WAS CRYING. Zael could hear the sobbing sound echoing up through the hab-stack. It was still dark, early. He got out of his little cot into the pre-dawn chill and crept out of the backroom he shared with his sister. Nove's bed was empty. She hadn't been back that night.

Granna was asleep in the family room, snoring a phlegmy snore. Zael could smell the sharp stink of glue. There was a light on, a single glow-globe over the cupboard. It illuminated the little effigy of the God-Emperor that granna kept there.

The sobbing wasn't granna either, though it had been on many nights. It was coming from outside. The stack landing. Zael padded forward, through the kitchen to the door. Through the frosted glass, he could see a figure pressed against the door, head bowed. He could hear the ragged sobbing now. He could even see how each sob gusted brief condensation over the other side of the glass.

'Nove?'

The crying continued.

'Sis? Is that you?'

More sobs.

'Nove? What's happened?'

The crying ebbed. A bare hand splayed flat against the glass, pressed tight, imploring.

'Nove? You're scaring me...'

The door handle turned slowly and released. It did it again. Zael saw the dead bolt was thrown.

Let me in...

'Nove? Answer me. Is it you?'

Let me in, Zael...

Zael remembered the stories going round the stack. Raiders, in the night, knocking up poor families, breaking in...

There was nothing to steal here. But, the stories said, the raiders didn't just want to steal...

'Nove?'

Zael... let me in...

'You're not my sister,' Zael said, backing away. He looked around for a weapon. There was a blunt paring knife on the sink-edge. He grabbed it.

Something to tell you...

'What?'

Something he needs to know...

'Who?'

Let me in... he must know...

'Go away!'

The handle turned again. Then the nurl of the dead bolt began to rattle to and fro.

'Go away!'

The dead bolt began to slide back.

'Go away!' Zael yelled. 'Granna! Come quick! Granna!'

But... oh, now, that was right. His granna was dead.

And this was all... all...

The bolt slunked back and the door began to open.

Zael shrieked.

KYS SLAPPED HIS cheek hard and he fell onto the metal deck.

'What the hell's the matter with you, boy?' she said.

Zael looked up at her, blinking. He was in the corridor. The door to his cabin was open behind him, and he'd dragged most of his bed-roll cover out into the hallway after him.

'I…' he began.

'I was asleep, and I heard you screaming,' Kys said harshly. Then she sighed, and crouched down beside him. 'I'm sorry. I didn't want to hit you. I didn't know what else to do.'

'I…' he said again. 'I had a bad dream.'

'Right.'

Involuntarily, Zael wrapped his arms tight around Kys. She flinched and went stiff. Slowly, though gently, she pried his arms away from her.

'Look, boy. I'm not a people person.'

'My name is Zael.'

'Yeah, I knew that. Zael.' Kys nodded, though until that moment she'd been struggling to remember the kid's name. 'You had a bad dream. We all do. Damn, you wanna try being psy. Then you get bad dreams you didn't order.'

She became aware he was staring up at her. He looked so young. 'It's fine. Honestly,' she said. 'Wanna tell me about it?'

'It was my sister.'

'Throne, Zael, I have sisters. I know how scary that can be.'

'My sister is dead.'

'Oh.'

'She was knocking on my door. She wanted to come in.'

'Right. Real nightmare stuff. I've had shit you–' She stopped and looked at him again. 'You don't want to hear that. You need to sleep. Come on.'

She rose and hoisted him up. 'Pick up your bedding,' she said.

He scooped his bedroll up. She led the way into his cabin. He shrank back when he saw she'd pulled a dagger.

'What's that for–'

'Shhhhh!' she said, a finger to her lips. Warily, she looked under the cot, then threw open the closet, then leapt into the shower room, blade raised.

'Just checking for monsters. None here. It's safe.'

He smiled. 'That was really silly,' he said.

She shrugged and sheathed her blade. 'Frig it, I said I wasn't a people person. Go to bed.'

'Okay.'

'And next time you have a bad dream…'

'Yes?'

'Wake some other bastard, will you?'

'Okay.'

KYS WALKED OUT of Zael's cabin and shut the hatch. She was about to turn away when she paused. She stretched out a long finger and ran the tip of it through the thawing film of frost that surrounded the hatch frame.

She felt the unmistakable buzz of psychic energy.

She walked quickly back to her own cabin and activated the intership vox.

'Ravenor?'

'MAKE IT QUICK. I'm busy,' Ravenor said. He was gliding down the main dorsal corridor of deck three. Kys had to double-time to keep up.

'It's the boy.'

'Zael?'

'Yeah, Zael.'

'What about him?'

'He's borderline psy… maybe nascent. Growing too…'

'I know.'

'You know?'

'Patience, why in the name of Terra would I have brought him from Eustis and made him welcome here if I didn't think he had potential?'

'Well, I wondered...'

'The boy was picking my transmissions up on Eustis Majoris. He's clearly sharp. I want to examine him further, when time permits.'

Kys nodded. 'But, if he's sharp... he could be dangerous. Shouldn't you hand him over to the Black Ships for processing?'

'No. He's sharp, but he's passive sharp. Not active. I can read that much. He's a reflector. An echoer. I don't think he's going to turn into a Kinsky. Or a Ravenor. But I want to know what he's absorbed. Recorded, if you will. Of all the flect users we traced on Eustis, he was the only psyker.'

'I think he could be trouble,' Kys said.

Ravenor swung his bulky chair round to face her. 'I think so too, Patience. But I'll decide. It's my call. He's here because I say so.'

'All right.'

'Now go away,' Ravenor said.

'Why?'

'Because I'm about to speak with the Ministry agents, and I don't want you to kill them.'

'Fine,' she said. And strode away.

THE HATCH HISSED open and Ravenor hovered through. Ahenobarb was sitting at the end of the long conference table, his chin on his arms. Kinsky was leaning back in his seat, flicking nuts from a bag up into his mouth. Lost kernels dotted the floor. Madsen rose as Ravenor entered.

'This is cooperation?' she said.

+Shut up and sit down.+

Madsen sat down immediately, as if struck.

Kinsky flicked another nut into the air. It missed his mouth. Without looking at Ravenor, he said, 'Pull another psy play like that, inquisitor, and I will face you down. Do you understand me?'

He flicked another nut. It went up... and then hovered in the air over his open mouth.

'I believe it's you who must come to understand the way of things now, Kinsky. You are here to help, not to lead. To advise, not to demand. This is my ship. You are guests. This is my case, you are allies of the Inquisition.'

Ravenor let the nut fall. Kinksy flicked it aside with his hand and got up.

'Very slick. Very tough. You want to go now? You and me?'

'Sit down, Kinsky,' Madsen snapped.

'You and me, you frigging crip!'

'Sit down, Kinsky! Now!' Madsen shouted.

Kinsky sat.

'Inquisitor,' Madsen said. 'I wish to apologise for the actions of my team. Kinsky's confrontation just then was out of line, but I'm sure you know how volatile it can be with psykers.'

Ravenor stayed silent so Madsen went on.

'On the surface, our procedures... I understand they sparked a situation. And that resulted in injury to one of your team.'

'It did.'

'How is Interrogator Thonius?'

'Alive. Reunited with his arm.'

Madsen leaned forward. Her eyes were clear and honest. 'I'm glad. Inquisitor, may I talk with you privately?'

'Perhaps. Just be happy I didn't allow agent Kys to attend this meeting. She would have killed all three of you.'

'She would have tried...' Ahenobarb chuckled.

Then he froze and reached towards his neck, gagging.

Ravenor released him. 'She would have succeeded. I have never known anyone as murderous as Patience Kys. You three would be offal by now if I'd let her have her way. Madsen... outside.'

Madsen rose. Swinging round, Ravenor gazed back at Kinsky. 'You bested me before, Mr Kinsky. Well done. But you were right there and I was at my range limit from orbit. Do not... not for one moment... expect a rematch to be so easy. I will burn out your mind in an instant.'

'Whatever,' said Kinsky. The nut he had just thrown up turned in mid-air, shivered, and smacked off his cheek with a bulleting force.

'Whatever indeed,' said Ravenor.

WYSTAN FRAUKA WAS waiting for them outside. Madsen shivered as she sealed the door behind them and faced Ravenor.

'Wystan?' Ravenor said politely.

Frauka deactivated his limiter. He plucked a lho-stick from his card pack and lit it, looking bored.

Ravenor faced Madsen. 'No more chances, Mamzel Madsen. You work with me or I ditch you.'

'I understand. Kinsky is a loose cannon and–'

'No, he is not. He is a powerful psyker who should be enclosed in the bosom of the Guild Astropathicus, and not freelanced as a governmental pawn. Ahenobarb is just a minder. You, to me, are the mystery.'

'Me?' she said.

'You, Madsen. You are clearly in charge of this Ministry team. I know why I should be wary of the psyker, and his brute minder. But they answer to you. Therefore you worry me.'

'I assure you–'

'I don't even know your given name.'

'Lusinda Madsen. Happy now?'

'No. Work with me, in all manner of effort, Lusinda Madsen, or I will eject you and your allies into the void.'

She straightened up and faced him. 'You would not dare. I am here by the authority of the lord sub-sector.'

'Yes, you are. I am here by the authority of the Ordos Helican. This far out, on the verges of Lucky Space, who would know... who would care... if I had you three voided from an airgate?'

Lusinda Madsen smiled then. She said, 'I think we understand each other, sir.'

But Ravenor thought... a *smile*. What a strange reaction.

'THERE HE IS,' said Nayl. He opened the chipped driver's door window of the cargo-8 they sat in so they could get a better look across the crowded street.

'You sure?' Kara asked.

Nayl nodded. It had taken him a few hours of quiet questions and a roll of never-to-be-seen-again cash to get the skinny on Shipmaster Siskind from the traders in Tusk Verge. Trade custom along the Western Banks was notoriously tight-lipped, as Kys's team had discovered, and Nayl and Kara had found on their own foray north. The moot-coast prided itself on being just outside rigid Imperial law, and was never happy to be pumped for answers.

But the uproar during the moot had changed that. Ironically, Nayl had benefited from the mess Thonius had been at the centre of. The locals were in mortified disarray, the slaughterbaron had suspended trading. There was unrest and rancour. The off-world traders felt edgy and vulnerable suddenly, not knowing whether to risk waiting until the moot re-opened or to get out while they were still able. What's more, a shipman had been murdered in the firefight. As a result, the traders were closing ranks, and exchanging protective gossip, tipping one another off to slaughterman guild inspections. Nayl's questions had seemed just part of that process.

'That's Siskind definitely. Red hair, glass jacket, pale tan ATV with red panels on the mudguards.'

'He's rolling,' said Kara.

Nayl saw it. He turned the cargo-8's engine over, got a throaty rev or two, and then edged out from the street-side after the tan ATV as it nudged down the thoroughfare through the bustling pedestrians.

The morning was cold and set fair. An emaciated lemon sun ached through the flat grey sky over the shore. There was a strong wind in off the sea. The town of Tusk Verge seemed dismal and bleak, filled up with people who had no wish to be there.

Siskind's ATV turned east through the town and followed the walled roads up towards the commerce fields. It picked up a little speed as it left behind the more crowded streetways.

'Not too close,' Kara said.

'Oh, please...'

Still, he idled back, and allowed a trader's articulated cargo-12 and a billowing dung-wagon to get in between their vehicle and the ATV.

The dung-wagon turned off towards the highway viaduct. A few minutes later, the cargo-12 pulled to the right and grumbled down a causeway into the eastern loading docks of the moot pens. Nayl drove on through their dust and followed Siskind's ATV out onto the windswept commerce fields that occupied the high pastures above the moot-town. Here, even during the day, canfires burned, marking out landing plots along with heavy-duty mechanised beacon posts that had been hammered into the dry soil. On almost all of the wide plots sat a freighter, cargo doors agape. Inter-orbit lifters of every size and design were ranged along the commerce field plots, often with small fliers and landers parked next to them. Crews lounged about, bored, smoking, drinking.

Nayl eased back again, as if he was about to turn in to one of the plots. The ATV bellied on ahead, heading up to the north end of the landing field.

They followed, slowly. The tan ATV turned right and slewed to a halt in front of the jaw-doors of an ancient bulk lifter that sprawled across its appointed plot like a wallowing hippo. Its entire rust-riveted bulk was raised from the scorched ground on six vast hydraulic legs.

Nayl pulled them over and they sat and watched. The ATV drove up to the foot of the bulk lifter's ramp and paused, allowing Siskind to jump down. Sunlight flashed on the links of his glass jacket. As he began to converse with the dynast-appointed lander man, the ATV revved again and nosed up into the belly of the lifter. Expressing steam, the vehicle's huge cargo doors began to close.

'He's leaving,' Kara said.

'Let's go,' agreed Nayl.

Nayl killed the engine and they jumped out either side of the truck. Siskind was still arguing with the local plot official. A dispute over landing tariffs, perhaps. Kara and Nayl ran up along the adjacent plot, keeping a battered old Latimar Ind bulker between them and Siskind's lifter.

It was a long run. Each plot was about three hundred metres long. By the time they had reached the far end of the plot and had turned in and behind Siskind's vessel, it was raising thrusters and sealing for take-off. Siskind, distant now, was turning from the argument with a dismissive shrug and heading for the gangway. He jogged his way up it, and sealed the hatch behind him. The automated gangway retracted into the bulk lifter's flank and heat-shield armour extruded to cover its socket.

The roar of the lifter's power plant rose abruptly by a factor of ten. There was a fierce downrush of jetted air and AG repulsion that Kara and Nayl could feel even from the edge of the plot. It was suddenly like trying to walk into a gale. Dust and dry grass kicked up in a blizzard. The lifter began to rise, arduously, into the air, creating a heat-haze distortion between itself and the soil.

Shielding his face, Nayl raised the heavy-gauge coilbow he'd been carrying and aimed it up at the ship, into the deluge.

Kara shouted something he couldn't hear.

He pulled the trigger and fired the bow, feeling the solid kick of the coil-spring. A direct hit impacted on the belly line of the ascending cargo ship. A direct hit that went completely unfelt by the ship's crew.

The bow-shot load had been custom made. A wad of adhesive suspension coating a disk of very special material. Wraithbone.

Siskind's lifter rose into the morning air, nose dipped, gouted black smoke, swung heavily to its left and then turned and began to climb on full down-thrust, its burner-flares blue-white. Rapidly, it became just another dot leaving a contrail in the flat grey sky.

Nayl keyed his link. 'Mr Halstrom?'

'Mr Nayl?' the vox contact crackled.

'On your scopes, I trust?'

'Tracking it now.'

THE ALLURE BROKE orbit five hours later. It performed a smooth series of mass-velocity transactions and turned out, sliding effortlessly away from the shoal of anonymous rogue trade ships at high anchor above Flint. To all intents, it was just as anonymous as the rest – none of the trade ships chose to identify themselves electronically. But Halstrom's scopes had followed the bulk lifter to it. It was most certainly the *Allure*.

It powered clear of Flint's gravity trap, bending its course rimward and under the elliptic plane. Cloaked behind extremely non-standard disguise fields, another ship went with it.

The *Allure* was nine astronomical units from Flint and accelerating towards its encoded translation point when its master finally became aware he had a problem.

Bartol Siskind had taken off his jacket of Vitrian glass and hung it over the back of his command seat. The *Allure's* bridge was capacious but low ceilinged. Much of the flight deck instrumentation extended down from the ceiling over the raked crew stations. Siskind took a sip of caffeine and leaned back to study his master display.

He had already received a signal to go from his enginarium, and his course had been plotted and laid down by his Navigator. All systems were functioning well within parameters, and he was getting a particularly fine output rhythm from the principal drive. He reached up and touched a few runes on the screen, tuning tiny, expert adjustments into the mass-drive regulators.

'Translation point in eleven minutes, accelerating...' the Navigator intoned calmly from the adamite crypt recessed into the deck in front of him. Siskind nodded and turned to Ornales, his first officer, about to order him to stow for warp space.

Ornales sat at the position next to him, his face downlit by the massive overhead console that arched down over his raked-back seat.

By the light of the dancing green glow, Siskind could see a perplexed expression on his number one's face.

'What?'

'Are you getting that?' Ornales asked.

Frowning, Siskind looked up at his own master display. A new dialogue box had appeared on top of the scrolling system data. It wasn't especially large. It said: *Cut your engines now.*

'What the hell...?' Siskind tried to clear it. It wouldn't cancel. 'Is this a damn joke?'

'It's external,' Ornales replied, his voice tense. His hands were dancing over his mainboard. 'External source. Pict-only communication.'

'But there's nothing in range...!' Siskind said.

He activated the return mode and typed: *Identify?*

The box blinked. *Cut your engines and heave to now.*

Identify now! Siskind wrote angrily.

There was a brief pause. Then the box blinked again and read: *Heave to. Depower and drop to coasting. By order of the Inquisition. Do not make me cripple your ship, Siskind.*

ONCE THE ALLURE had coasted down, the outlets of the huge drive assemblies at its stern glowing frosty pink as potential power descaled, the *Hinterlight* made itself visible. The *Allure* was a medium-sized sprint trader of non-standard design, heavily modified during its long life. It was long, craggy and bulky, its only concession to elegance the long chevrons of armour ridging its prow like the steel toe-cap of a pointed boot.

The *Hinterlight* was somewhat smaller and a great deal sleeker, shaped like a blade, with the flared bulk of its drive section at its stern. It flickered menacingly into view, appearing on Siskind's sensor panels a few seconds before it was eye-visible. A combination of xeno-derived technology and Ravenor's own mental strength generated the disguise field. It was a system that Ravenor would be forced to have removed from the *Hinterlight* if his arrangement with Preest wound up.

As it visibly manifested, the *Hinterlight* tracked its primary batteries to target the *Allure*. Preest made damn sure the *Allure's* systems got a clear indication of multiple target lock. Neither ship was military, neither an outright fighting vessel, but they were both rogue traders, and where rogue traders went, a decent level of firepower was a professional asset.

Siskind's response, just as obvious, was to make sure his batteries were both depowered and stowed, and his targeting system off-line. It was a clear submissive gesture, an indication of compliance. Even out here, just a few days' voyage from Lucky Space, no one fooled around when the Inquisition called the tune.

An armoured transport shuttle, little more than a gig, dropped down out of the *Hinterlight's* belly hangar, ignited its thrusters in a blaze of blue light, and went flitting across the silent gulf towards the *Allure*. As it approached the other ship, and became dwarfed by its great, battered bulk, guide-path lights began to pulse sequentially along the *Allure's* flank. The gig zipped along after them, tracking in close to the merchantman's scarred hull, and arrived at a hangar dock where the outer hatches and blast curtains were slowly gliding open. The gig paused, adjusted its attitude with a tight burst of point-thrusters, and slid inside.

THE RESEALED HANGAR was thick with swirling exhaust smoke and hydraulic steam. There was a loud, repetitive hazard buzzer sounding, almost drowned out by the huge atmospheric fans under the deck. The echoing buzzer finally cut off and the flashing warning lamps ceased. Overhead floods kicked on and illuminated the gig where it rested on its landing skids in the middle of the primary platform. Several other inter-orbital craft, including the scabby bulk-lifter Nayl had tagged, were berthed in lock-cradles off the platform, connected up to ropes of heavyweight fuel and system-fluid lines.

An internal hatch hissed open and Siskind strode out into the vast hangar flanked by three senior members of his crew. They were all armed, and made no effort to disguise the fact. Siskind was wearing his glass-weave jacket, and a bolt pistol hung in a holster at his hip. Two of his comrades were human – a tall, dark-haired man and a shorter, older, balding fellow – both carrying wire-stocked las-carbines. The third was a nekulli, slender and humanoid, but with long spine-scales flowing back from his scalp. The nekulli's eyes were white slits, his nose virtually absent, his lower jaw thrust forward. Two thin fangs hooked up from this underbite over his top lip. Like all nekulli, he walked with a hunch-shouldered waddle.

The four walked out onto the platform, knee-deep in the repressurisation fog still wreathing the deck, and came to a halt ten metres from the gig.

Siskind cleared his throat. He looked edgy and pissed off.

The cabin hatch on the side of the gig retracted in three, segmented sections. Ravenor's chair hovered out, and sank down to deck level, facing the shipmaster. With a little hiss that made the dark-haired man jump, the chair displayed its hololithic rosette.

'I'm Siskind, master of this vessel,' Siskind said carefully. 'My papers and my letter of marque as an Imperial free trader are in order. If you wish, you may inspect them. Like all true servants of the Throne,' – Siskind stressed that part – 'I have every desire to cooperate and assist the Ordos Officio Inquisitorus. May I enquire... is this a random inspection?'

'No,' replied Ravenor. 'I am Gideon Ravenor, inquisitor, Ordo Xenos Helican. I am hunting a ship called the *Oktober Country*, a ship that I know has had contact with you in the last week.'

Siskind shrugged and chuckled. 'You're after information? That's it? You inconvenience me in the pursuit of my business... for information? Am I accused of any crime?'

'No,' said Ravenor. 'But withholding information from an authorised agent of the Inquisition is a crime, so I advise you to be thoughtful about your next statement.'

Siskind shook his head. He was a handsome man, but there was an unpleasantly cruel set to his features. 'I know the *Oktober Country*. But I've had no contact with it. Not even seen it for, what, three years? There is my information. Now remove yourself from my ship.'

'You are in no position to make demands,' said Ravenor. 'My ship–'

'Will hardly fire on mine with you aboard. I hate to play games, but it was easier to let you aboard. Does the concept of "hostage" mean anything to you?'

'Oh, absolutely,' said Ravenor.

'Shit!' cried the dark-haired man suddenly. Off to their left, Harlon Nayl stood in the knee-deep fog, a heavy automatic pistol aimed at them in a two-handed grip.

Siskind jumped back. To his right, Kara Swole had an assault cannon on them.

'And behind you,' Ravenor added.

All four turned. Mathuin smiled. The barrel-cluster of his rotator cannon cycled menacingly. Siskind and his men had been so intent on Ravenor they'd not even noticed the others slip out under cover of the deck fog from the other side of the gig.

'I was being polite,' said Ravenor, 'but we will play it your way. Harlon?'

Nayl fired a single shot and blew off the balding man's left kneecap. Hit, the man fell onto the deck, shrieking and writhing.

'I think that's established the ground rules,' Ravenor said. 'Now let's get to business.'

I HAD NO desire to waste time. Exposing all of the *Allure's* secrets would have taken months of painstaking research. It was a big, old ship, its history, manifests and logged records lousy with all manner of dubious deals, illegal transactions and outright crimes. Like any rogue trader, in fact. I'd never seen Preest's ship-log, and she'd never volunteered it to me. It was the fundamental understanding on which our relationship was based. Rogue traders, even the best of them, tested the limits of Throne Law. Don't ask and you won't be disappointed. All I'd required of Preest was she keep her activities clean all the while we were associated.

My worthy, long-departed master, Gregor Eisenhorn, had once told me that if you examine any one man, any group of men, any institution, or any world long enough, you will uncover something untoward. I am proud of the achievements of the Imperium, and the virtues of its society, but I am not naive. There is corruption and crime and heresy everywhere. It is endemic. To operate successfully, an inquisitor must learn to be selective, to focus on the principal matters of his current case. To do otherwise leads to stagnation and failure.

Thus, I ignored the forty-eight freight tariff evasions the *Allure* had notched up. I ignored the conviction for grievous assault First Officer Ornales had evaded on Caxton. I turned a blind eye to the fact Siskind had a fugitive murderer working amongst his enginarium crew, and also to the fact that his ship's surgeon had been disbarred from practice due to gross anatomical misconduct. I passed over the fifteen illegal or prohibited weapons carried aboard the ship, the largest two of which were battery-mounted on the hull. I didn't even care about the consignments of yellodes, gladstones and grinweed we dug out of cavity spaces.

I concentrated on flects, the *Oktober Country*, and on Feaver Skoh and Kizary Thekla.

The *Allure* had a crew of seventy-eight, thirty more than the *Hinterlight*. I examined each one in turn, shaking all kinds of petty crime and misdemeanors out of their heads. Meanwhile, Nayl oversaw the phsyical sweep of the ship, and Thonius, from his bed in the *Hinterlight's* infirmary, conducted a data purge of the *Allure's* systems.

'Sir?'

'Go ahead, Carl.'

'There's virtually nothing in the *Allure's* files to link it to the *Oktober Country*. A handful of trade meetings. But I have traced an astropathic communiqué received the day after the *Oktober Country* left Eustis Primaris. It's filed and logged, uncoded. From Thekla. It says what we already know... asks Siskind to make his apologies to Baron Karquin.'

'Thank you, Carl. Keep searching.'

'Sir, the message ends with a curious sign off. "Firetide drinks as usual".'

'Repeat that.'

'"Firetide drinks as usual". Mean anything?'

'Sweep our data core for the term "Firetide". It could indicate an event or time when Thekla and Siskind next intended to meet face to face.'

'That's what I thought, sir.'

'Good work, Carl. How's the arm?'

'Still attached to me. Mr Halstrom's operating keyboard for me.'

'Keep at it. Thank you, Carl.'

I had taken over Siskind's ready room for my interrogations. As Thonius signed off, there was a knock at the hatch.

'Yes?'

Frauka opened the door. He took a lho-stick out of his mouth, exhaled a plume of smoke and said, 'Ready for Siskind?'

'Yes, Wystan. Let's have him.'

I'd saved Bartol Siskind until last, gravely aware of what Duboe had told me under interrogation. Siskind had blood links – remote, admittedly, but still real – to one of the sector's more infamous heretics. For a while I'd kept telling myself it was just a coincidence. Then I'd thought about it more carefully. It didn't have to be a coincidence. Though long-aborted, the Cognitae academy and its mentor had enjoyed a profoundly wide influence. The last time I'd checked – about two years earlier – ninety-four cases under prosecution by the Ordos Helican had involved someone or something with Cognitae connections. As secret orders went, it was one of the largest and most pernicious in modern memory. Also, the Cognitae had prided itself on using and recruiting only the very brightest supplicants. It was no low cult, feeding off the poor and the uneducated. Lilean Chase had not only pulled into her influence the Imperium's finest, she had instigated several eugenic breeding programs that mixed her corrupt but brilliant genes with the bloodlines of the most promising of her students. Her offspring were everywhere, many of them unimpeachable men of high standing. To be a rogue trader, one needed savvy, smarts and panache. Just because Siskind was of her line didn't automatically mean he was a heretic himself.

Siskind entered the ready room. He looked flustered and unhappy. Frauka had given him a smoke, and he twitched it in his fingers.

'Sit down,' I said.

He sat, and had to adjust the setting of the chair. He wasn't used to sitting that side of the captain's desk.

'Bartol Siskind.'

'Inquisitor.'

'I give you notice now that this interview will be conducted mentally. I recommend you relax, or it will be a painful episode to endure.'

He took a drag on his lho-stick and nodded.

+How long have you been master of this vessel?+

The clarity of the first psi-query made him blink. That always happened. No one is ever quite ready for the voice inside your head to be anyone other than yours.

'Fifteen years.'

+Before that?+

'I was first officer on the *Kagemusha*.'

+And how did you come to command the *Allure*?+

Though uncomfortable, he smiled. 'I won it in a card game.'

I verified his truth centres. He wasn't lying.

+How long have you known Kizary Thekla?+

He shifted in his seat. 'Thirty years, give or take. We were juniors together on the *Vainglory* under Master Ensmann. I moved to the *Omadorus* and then the *Kagemusha*, Thekla went to the *Oktober Country* under Master Angwell. When Angwell died, Thekla inherited command.'

+When was that?+

'381. Summer 381. Angwell was old. Four hundred and some. He died of a fever.'

All true so far. Siskind was playing ball. I tried to examine his mind. Curiously, it reminded me of Duboe's. Superficially bright, sharp, fit, but strangely turgid deep down.

+When did you last see Thekla?+

'I told you this. Three years ago, on Flint, at the Winter Great Moot.'

His first lie. It was glaringly obvious. He couldn't hide it.

+When really?+

Siskind sighed. He drew on his lho-stick again, exhaled and looked straight at me. 'Two months ago. Briefly. On Lenk.'

The truth.

+Describe that meeting.+

He shrugged. 'I was in a tavern, drinking to the birth of Bombassen's first son–'

+Bombassen? Your chief engineer?+

'That's right. We were rat-arsed. Thekla came in with some of his crew, bought a round to wet the baby's head. We chatted for a while about old times. Nothing... nothing...' His voice trailed off. This was more truth, but I was annoyed at the opacity now coating his mind.

+You're related, you and Thekla?+

Siskind laughed. 'He's a distant cousin. But our lineage is all frigged-up. You know that or you wouldn't be asking this. Our parents' parents were connected to the Cognitae school raising program. I'm not proud of that. Shit, I'd rather it wasn't the truth. This isn't the first time the Inquisition has pulled me over because of things my frigging ancestors did.'

Also true. True as I could see.

+Thekla sent you a communiqué asking you to make apologies for him at the moot.+

'Yeah. He couldn't make it. But when you've got good contacts with a slaughterbaron, it pays to be civil. He didn't want to piss Karquin off, so he asked me to smooth things out.'

+Do you know why he couldn't make the moot?+

'He didn't say. I didn't ask.'

+Do you know why I'm after him?+

Siskind paused. He breathed deeply. 'Yeah. It's about flects, isn't it?'

+It is. What can you tell me about flects, Bartol?+

'Not much. It's a suicidal trade. I mean, dealing flects is going to bring trouble down on you eventually, right? He wanted to cut me in, but I said no. I move a little grin, sometimes I run gladstones. But not flects.'

+You've never dealt in them?+

'No, sir.'

+Never tempted?+

'By the return? Frig, yes! But I knew it would be bad news. Damn, look at this... I'm being mind-probed by the Inquisition for not dealing them. How frigging bad would this be if I was?'

He had a point.

+Where does he get them from?+

'I don't know. Seriously, I don't. You only get to know if you join the cartel.'

+There's a cartel?+

He flinched slightly, causing the long char of ash accumulated on his lho-stick to tumble off onto the polished chrome floor. He knew he'd just let onto something he hadn't realised I didn't know.

+A cartel, Siskind?+

He recovered smoothly. 'Of course there's a cartel, inquisitor. The flect trade doesn't depend entirely on the *Oktober Country*.'

+I never imagined it did.+

'Far as I know, there are about twenty rogue traders who do the run. The source is extra-sub. It's coming from somewhere out in Lucky Space. And before you ask, I have no idea who runs the operation. Or how it's run. Or anything. You buy into it, that's what Thekla told me when he tried to get me in. It's a contract. You get all the details when you buy into the cartel. There's an up-front payment. A deposit. A gesture of good faith.'

+How much.+

He stubbed the lho-stick out. 'Three-quarters of a million.'

+That's a lot.+

'Yeah, right. That's a lot.'

He was still telling the truth, as far as I could chart. But suddenly I saw the real, bald reason he wasn't a part of his distant cousin's flect trade. It wasn't principle. Siskind couldn't afford it. Three-quarters of a million was beyond his means, and he was resentful about it. The resentment filled his mind in a very readable blur of spiky red.

+What's Firetide?+

He blinked and laughed, about to lie badly. 'I have no idea.'

+Yes, you do. *Firetide drinks as usual...* that's what Thekla said to you.'

Siskind tilted his head back and opened his arms wide. 'You're reading my frigging mind, you bastard! Tell me!'

+Tell me.+

The psychic jab snapped him upright and made tears well in his cruel eyes. 'Okay. O-frigging-kay. Don't do that again.'

+I won't. If you don't provoke me. Tell me about Firetide.'

'I want another smoke.' His mind was muddying up again, hardening to my scrutiny. It was peculiar. I felt my interrogation was going well, but still there was a sense he was giving me answers from a free part of his mind while the rest was impenetrable.

'Wystan?' I voxed.

The door-hatch slid open and Frauka came in.

'Lho-stick for Master Siskind,' I said.

Frauka pursed his lips, and plucked the carton out of his jacket pocket. He offered it to Siskind, who took one. Frauka flashed his igniter and lit Siskind's smoke, then lit another for himself.

'Sometimes, I thank the God-Emperor of Mankind for sealed-unit respiratory filters,' I said.

The comment passed Frauka by. 'I'll be outside,' he said, exiting.

The door-hatch slunked shut.

'You've got your smoke,' I said. +Now tell me about Firetide.+

'It's a festival. On Bonner's Reach.'

+That's out in Lucky Space.+

'Yeah, five days in. From here, two weeks. The last Free Trade station. We used to meet there at Firetide and have a drink or several.'

+Thekla was expecting to meet you there?+

'Hoping is a better word. We've done Firetide every few years. It's a chance for rogues to catch up, away from Imperial scrutiny.'

+Why was he hoping to see you there?+

'Just to catch up.'

I paused. +I contend, Siskind, that the message was clearly an instruction for you to meet him there.+

'Think what you like.'

+He was telling you to come there, wasn't he?+

'Yeah, all right, he was.'

+Why?+

'I don't know. And that's the truth.' It was.

+Tell me why that might have been.+

Siskind looked down at the floor. 'I think he was hoping to recruit me. Hoping to try again. The cartel meets at Bonner's Reach. I've been doing well this season. Thekla believed I could buy in.'

Every word of it was the truth. I couldn't understand why I felt every word of it was also somehow rehearsed.

+Do you think that Thekla, having passed on the Flint moots, might have gone directly to Bonner's Reach?+

'That's likely,' he said.

+Master Siskind, I'm now going to withdraw my agents from your vessel and leave you alone. Thank you for cooperating with the Inquisition. Do not cross us again.+

'I'll try my frigging best.'

+For your information, I have had my people disassemble your communications array and your mass-drive regulators. Nothing has been damaged. I estimate it will take you four working days to refit the systems. My apologies for the inconvenience. But I don't want you following me.+

He smiled. *You're a total bastard,* his mind said. 'Thank you, inquisitor,' his mouth covered.

DRIVE ENGAGED, THE *Hinterlight* began to describe a hard, tight trajectory out and away from the distant sun of the Flint system. The *Allure,* temporarily crippled and adrift, became an increasingly faint hard return on its aft sensors.

Ravenor glided down the midships companionway with Nayl, Kys and Zael trailing behind him. Apparently, Nayl had promised the boy a look at the bridge.

Halstrom was waiting for them at the bridge hatchway. 'Mr Thonius and I have done some research, sir,' he said. 'It took some rooting out of the database, in conjunction with the Carto-Imperialis, but we dug up "Firetide". It's–'

'A festival on Bonner's Reach. Due to begin about twenty days from now,' Ravenor said.

Halstrom wavered. 'Oh,' he said.

'Just because I got there first doesn't mean I don't appreciate your efforts, Mr Halstrom. Well done.'

He beamed. 'Thank you, inquisitor.'

'How's the mistress?' Nayl asked.

'Pissed off, Mr Nayl,' Halstrom said.

'But doing it anyway?' I wanted to know.

'Yes, ' said Halstrom. 'Course is set. Drive engaged. We're heading out into Lucky Space.'

Kys and Ravenor went in through the hatch, and moved across the bridge to join Cynia Preest.

'Thank you, Cynia,' Ravenor said.

'For what, Gideon?' she snapped, gruffly.

'For doing what you didn't want to do. For taking us out into Lucky Space.'

She looked up from her main station grimly. 'I don't like it, Gideon. Not at all. But I am in your service, and while that lasts, I do what I'm told.' She paused and then smiled. 'I understand Mr Halstrom is pretty keen on this whole venture.'

'I think he is,' Ravenor agreed. 'Cynia… you might describe yourself as a rogue trader…'

She halted, mid-action, and looked hard at the armoured chair. 'And? Where are you going with this?'

'If I gave you three-quarters of a million in ready cash, just how rogue could you be?'

IN THE BRIDGE doorway, Zael looked up at Harlon Nayl.

'Why's it called Lucky Space?' he asked.

Nayl grinned a not-at-all-reassuring grin. 'Because, once you're out in it, you're lucky if you last five minutes.'

FOUR

No bugger goes to Lenk any more.

Lenk was the end of the line, the most rim-ward world in the Angelus sub. Once it had been an important trade gateway through to the neighbouring Vincies sub-sector, ideally placed on a stepping-stone line of systems that formed a convenient trade lane down through places like Flint all the way to the sub's capital world. For over six thousand years, it had been a prosperous place.

Then the Vincies sub collapsed, almost overnight. There had been a gradual slump in trade, and a marked increase in lawlessness over a period of years, though nothing terminal. Slowly, the Vincies had become the Angelus's rougher neighbour. But the real collapse had been triggered by a warp storm that had swept, without warning, through a great rimward portion of the sub in 085.M41.

It was a notable disaster. The lethal storm had engulfed eighteen systems, including that of the Vincies's capital world, Spica Maximal. All of the sub-sector's primary population centres and industrial worlds were lost at a stroke. The death toll alone was unimaginably vast. Shorn of its central government, main markets and vital heartland, the sub-sector fell apart. Fifty or so Imperial worlds in the core-ward territories of the sub escaped the storm, but they were all minor colonies or secondary worlds and none had the power or wealth to assume responsibility as a new sub-sector capital. Some attempts were made to align them instead with the Angelus sub – effectively turning the remains of the Vincies sub into a fiefdom of its wealthy neighbour – but it never quite worked. The region fell away into lawless decay, no longer Imperial territory in any meaningful sense. Even the name withered. It was just Lucky Space now.

Lenk's fortunes withered too. The once-proud gateway market, the third wealthiest planet in the Angelus region after Caxton and Eustis Majoris, became a backwater. There was a long period of deprivation, popular unrest, and then a drawn-out, insidious civil war that resulted in a mass migration of its population back into the Angelus sub to begin new lives there.

Now the only trade that went through Lenk was the rogue kind. It became a last watering hole for pioneers and speculators brave or crazy enough to try and make money from Lucky Space ventures.

It had quite a reputation.

As a footnote to this misfortune, the warp storm finally blew itself out in 385, after three hundred years. Left behind in the ravaged rim-ward part of the old sub was a clutch of dead systems known as the Mergent Worlds, the scorched corpses of Imperial planets like Spica Maximal resurfaced from the deluge. They were tainted, of course. Utterly tainted, and utterly prohibited. A fiercely prosecuted interdiction by the Battlefleet Scarus hemmed the

Mergent Worlds away from Imperial and non-Imperial contact alike.

'THE SHAVED HEAD of an old man, from behind, by candle light,' Kara said.

Nayl snorted.

'Not you, old man with a shaved head,' Kara laughed. 'A really old, wizened man.'

'Not bad,' Nayl conceded.

'Your turn.'

Nayl leaned on the iron guard rail and gazed down through the observation bay's segmented glasteel port. 'A citrus fruit,' he said at length.

'That's terrible. And you've used it before.'

'I have not.'

'Have so. Ganymedae. Remember? A waxed citrus fruit, you said. sharp and acid.'

'Can I finish? I hadn't finished.'

Kara grinned, and made a deferring gesture. 'Please, dig yourself out.'

'I was going to say... a citrus fruit, one of the big, fat ones with the amber rind. And not only that, one that's been in the fruit bowl too long and is just beginning to turn. A dusting of grey mould on the skin, a dimpled puffiness.'

She frowned. 'Your metaphor being that it's spoiled?'

'Spoiled. Rotten.'

'It's all right, I suppose. A tad obvious.'

'But "the shaved head of an old man from behind by candle light" isn't?'

'You've got to give me points for allegory.'

'Allegory now? '

'Allegory,' she nodded. 'The old man has seen better days and remembers them sadly. He's worn out. He's turned away, so we can't see his face any more, or even tell if he's alive. He's poor, so he has to rely on candles. Which, of course, adds a poetic flourish about the colour.'

'Poetic flourish my arse. My metaphor was clean and contained.'

'Allegory beats metaphor. Every time. Hands down. I think I win.'

'I think not.'

'You're a poor loser, Harlon Nayl. I've got you cold on this one. Have the grace at least to lose with good manners.'

'What are you doing?'

They both started up and looked round from the rail. Timid and wan, Zael stood in the hatchway behind them, watching them.

'Hello, Zael,' said Kara with a broad smile. 'What are you up to?'

'Just... you know...' He remained in the doorway, as if he felt safe there, and looked around at the gloomy observation bay. The only light, apart from lumin-strips along the edge of the grilled walkway, was coming in from outside.

'What are you looking at?' Zael asked.

Nayl waved him in and pointed out through the port. Nervously, Zael came through the hatch and crept out across the metal observation platform to the rail.

'That's Lenk,' Nayl said.

Outside, cold blackness, pricked by hard star-points and the glimmering, lustrous skeins of distant clusters and more distant galaxies. Dominating the view was a mottled, bruised, orange sphere. It was a world – Zael knew that. A planet, sunlit and unshadowed, suspended by invisible physics in the darkness of space. They were looking down at it, as if from the roof of a hive stack. Zael wondered what his home looked like from this vantage point. Part of him yearned to be back on Eustis Majoris. Part of him never wanted to see it again.

'Lenk,' he said after a while. 'Where's that?'

'Right here,' grinned Kara, as if it was a trick question.

'Are we flying past it?'

'This is a starship, Zael,' said Harlon. 'It doesn't fly. We're at high anchor above Lenk. A stop-over. The Chair wanted to say hello to the Navy Station commander here. He's gone down there with Mamzel Madsen.'

'Why?'

'It's protocol,' said Kara.

'What's that?'

Kara looked over Zael's tousled head at Nayl and shrugged a 'help me out here'.

'It's the done thing,' Nayl said to the boy. 'You know how an important player... a dealer say, makes sure he introduces himself to the moody hammers protecting a down-stack club. It's polite. The dealer makes sure the moodies know who he is, and vice versa. To avoid trouble later.'

'I get you,' said Zael.

'Well, that's all he's doing. The Fleet has a base here on Lenk. It runs operations up into the region we're heading for. The Chair wants the commander to know who he is and where he's going. In case we get into trouble.'

'What sort of trouble?'

It was Nayl's turn to glance at Kara.

'The hypothetical type,' Kara said.

'What's hypothetical?'

Kara crouched down so she was on a level with Zael. She rested her forearms on the rail and her chin on her forearms. 'We're not going to get into trouble. Of any sort. Inquisitor Ravenor–'

'The Chair,' Nayl corrected her.

Kara pursed her lips. 'Right... The Chair won't allow us to get into any trouble. We're safe. You're safe.'

Zael looked round at her. 'I like your hair that colour.'

Surprised, she reached up a hand and touched her short, shaggy fringe involuntarily.

'Thanks,' she said. 'I've been meaning to go back to red.'

'It's nice.'

The boy leant out over the rail and started looking from side to side.

'Careful,' Kara said. 'What are you doing?'

'The planet's not very interesting. What I really want to see is the ship.'

'What?' asked Nayl.

'The ship. I've never seen the ship. I've never seen any ship.' Zael pulled back. 'So what were you doing just then?' he asked them.

'We were playing a game,' Kara said.

'A game? How do you play it?'

'That's a good question,' said Nayl, staring at Kara. 'Some people make up the rules as they go along...'

'Oh, get over it,' she scoffed. She looked at Zael. 'Harlon and I have been playing the game since we first met. Whenever we reach a new planet, a new world, a new place, we get together in an obs bay like this, or get a pict of it on a repeater screen, and we play the game. The idea is to describe the world... but not just what it looks like. Something that also describes what the place is like. It's character. That's how you win the game. Do you know what a metaphor is?'

Zael thought about it. 'When you say something is like something else?'

'That's a simile,' said Nayl.

'Shut up, pedant,' Kara scolded him. 'Zael's on the right track. Why don't you play?' she asked the boy. 'Look down at Lenk. What does it look like to you?'

Zael stared down and screwed up his face in thought. 'An orange rubber ball I once owned.'

Nayl shrugged. Kara cocked her head. 'That's... that's good, ' she said.

'Yeah, pretty good,' Nayl agreed kindly. 'Next time you might want to add some... you know... hidden meaning.'

'Like a baldy bloke with candles?'

'Exactly like a baldy bloke with candles,' Kara said.

'Or a citrus fruit...' Nayl began.

'Over, done, beaten,' Kara hissed. 'Get used to it.'

Zael was oblivious to their sparring. He leaned out again, craning his neck to see the flanks of the *Hinterlight's* hull.

'You really want to see the ship, don't you?' said Nayl.

'Yes.'

Nayl straightened up and looked at Kara. 'What's Rav– The Chair. What's The Chair's ETA?'

'Not due back for another six hours. Halstrom told me Preest was planning to quit orbit at midnight.'

'All right. Can you amuse yourself for a while?'

'Absolutely,' Kara said. 'I've been doing that for years. I'm getting good.'

'Don't start,' Nayl said.

'I'll go see Carl. He could do with cheering up,' she said.

'Fine.' Nayl looked at the boy. 'You're coming with me,' he said.

IT WAS GOOD, but not perfect. Better than that benighted selpic blue jacket at any rate. But still, the lifelessness of his arm creased the shoulder-line of the linen tunic in the most horrid way. He turned three-quarters, then back the other way, studying his look in the full length mirror.

Not good.

Carl Thonius, alone in his cabin, sighed deeply, and began to unbutton the tunic. He had to use his left hand, and when it came to taking the garment off, he had to scoop the shoulders over his head and slide it off his rigid limb.

Thonius had keyed the lights to low and locked the door. He'd put on a slate of his favourite music, but tonight even the light operetta *The Brothers of Ultramar* wasn't doing it for him.

His cabin suite, refined in its decor and usually immaculate, was a mess. Vox-slates were screed across the carpet. He'd lost patience trying to find something he wanted to listen to. His bed, and the dressing chairs and occasional table beside it, were enveloped in a mass of discarded clothes. He'd been through his wardrobe a dozen times, trying everything.

Maybe a full jacket of Gudrunite velvet? Perhaps a blouson of Rustedre shot-silk? What about, damn the season, a long kirtle of the most gorgeous green Sameter clorrie, with ivory toggles and a simply darling gilt brocade hem?

Nothing worked. Nothing hid or excused his damaged form.

At this rate, he'd be wearing a bodyglove. And, from there, it was a short step to shaving one's head and calling everybody *ninker*.

Thonius turned and looked for something else to try on. In doing so, he caught sight of himself in the long mirror, pale and naked from the waist up.

He paused, frozen. He'd always been proud of his thin, hairless, well-exercised form. Lean, he'd call it. Lean and gamine, perhaps.

All he could see was the arm. The dullness of it. The leaden hang. Medicae Zarjaran – may the Emperor bless his craft – had begun a programme of post-op rehabilitation. Thonius counted himself grateful that he could now feel pins when they were stuck into his fingerpads. His digits still refused to move under their own power.

He looked at himself. Keening, the operetta was reaching the most passionate sequence, the loves lost-and-wronged part that he'd always adored.

He stared. Bio-pack dressing was taped around his right arm at the elbow.

With the tenor howling out a requiem for his fallen Astartes brothers, Thonius reached over with his left hand and began to rip the tapes away. His stare into the mirror didn't waver.

He stripped the dressing off and looked at what was revealed. The wound. The slice. Puckered, dead-looking flesh woven together with a million fibre-stitches. Blood and plasma-product still crusted the stitching. Clouds of bruises stained his bicep and forearm.

Staring at it, staring at it, staring at it, he became aware of the pain again: a dull throb, deep set, welling out from below the elbow. Over and over, he remembered the moment of severance. The wailing chainblade sawing around. Impact. Vibration. Shock. Pain. The astonishing notion that a fundamental part of oneself was no longer part of oneself at all.

Blood, in the air.

The smell of blood, the smell of sawed-through bone.

The pain was too much. He had gladstones in his buckle-bag, and lho in his desk, but that wouldn't do. He wanted release, craved it, begged for it.

Thonius took up the tiny key hanging around his neck on a sliver chain, and opened the top drawer of his bureau. He realised he was breathing hard.

The little package, wrapped tight in red tissue, lay inside.

He took it out, and opened it. For a moment, he paused, wiped a palm across his mouth, thought about it. Then he looked down into the flect.

It was nothing. It was just a piece of broken, coloured glass, It was a–

His feet began to tap. His body rocked back and forth. Wonderful, wonderful things happened inside his head.

Beautiful things. Extraordinary things. Reality chopped back and forth, like an automatic sliding door slamming open and closed. Everything was all right. *Everything*. He could see forever. He could hear and smell and *taste* forever.

The fingers of his left hand drummed, like a dancing spider, across the bureau.

The fingers of his right hand twitched.

'Oh my god...' he whispered.

He could see light. A long corridor of golden light. At the end of it was a shape. No, not a shape. He was rushing towards it. A chair. A chair. A chair.

A throne. A golden throne.

The man on the golden throne was smiling. It was a beautiful smile. It made everything all right. The man on the golden throne was smiling and beckoning to him.

For one, perfect moment, one moment of release, Carl Thonius felt immortal.

Bells were ringing.

Ringing.

Ringing.

Frigging ringing.

Thonius snapped up from the flect. He still felt glorious. Blessed. He heard the ringing again. It was the door-chime of his cabin.

'Just a moment!' he called out, and hastily stuffed the flect and its red tissue wrapper into the drawer.

He shut the drawer. With his right hand. He started at that. Emperor above! All of his last few actions had been made with his right hand. It was alive. It was–

Dead now. Limp. Useless.

The door chime rang again. Thonius got to his feet, pulled on his selpic blue jacket, and – with his left hand – activated the 'unlock' stud on his control wand.

The hatch opened. Smiling, perplexed, Kara Swole stepped into his cabin.

'Just came to see how you were doing,' she said. 'So... how're you doing?'

He smiled at her.

'Kara, I'm doing just fine.'

THE FLYER GUNNED out of the *Hinterlight's* main hangar, and skimmed down the body of the hull.

'There,' said Nayl. 'What do you think of that?'

He kept the speed low, the course steady. In the co-pilot seat beside him, Zael gazed out of the port as the dark substance of the ship flowed past beneath them.

'It's big,' was all the boy could really manage.

Nayl took them up the length of the ship and back four times. He could have done it all day. Zael wasn't getting bored.

At length, Nayl said 'Kys told me you'd been having dreams.'

'Yeah, some. Some dreams.'

'Often?'

'Yeah, most nights. Someone knocking on the door. Trying to get in. They want to tell me something, but I don't want to hear it.'

Nayl paused to see if Zael would volunteer anything else. The boy didn't, so Nayl asked: 'Who's the someone?'

'My sister, Nove.'

Nayl leaned gently on the stick and swung the gig around again to head back to the hangar.

'I want you to talk to The Chair when he gets back,' Nayl said.

'Okay. I've been thinking about the game.'

'The game?' Nayl eased back the thrust as the guide signal for dock-entry began to bleep mutedly.

'I said it looked like an orange rubber ball I'd once owned,' said Zael.

'Yeah, you did.'

'You didn't think that was very good, but it was. That's what it looks like. I remember the ball. My sister gave it me when I was seven. A birthday present. It got bounced up and down the stack halls, it got all worn and scabby. All scarred, like that place. But it's gone now. Lost somewhere. Like Nove. That's why that world looks like the ball to me.'

Nayl sighed. 'Ladies and gentlemen, we have a winner.'

FIVE

Cynia Preest sighed gently. Save for her chin, her face was shadowed by the loose, fur-trimmed hood over her head, but in that shadow, Nayl could see a smile.

'I rather thought,' he whispered, 'that smiling was something you hadn't planned on doing out here in Lucky Space.'

'Dear Harlon,' she muttered, 'permit me a moment of nostalgic pleasure. It's been a long time. I'd forgotten the flavour of this place.'

Nayl hesitated. Whatever flavour the shipmistress was detecting was entirely lost on him. As far as he was concerned, Bonner's Reach smelled of promethium, dust, ozone leaking from the ancient void-shields, spice-musks and perfumes, and a general humid, noisome odour of air that had been through the atmosphere processors a few million times too many.

'I don't think I'm really quite getting its charms,' he decided.

Preest rested a gloved hand on his arm. 'It has a certain character, Harlon. A robust vitality. You smell muggy filth, I breathe in vigour, zest, the aroma of a free trade station. I smell the frontier, the challenge of the beyond. I smell a truly neutral place where merchant venturers like myself can gather and do business away from Imperial scrutiny.'

She glanced round at her other companion, who flanked her to her left. 'No offence,' she added.

'None taken,' he replied. 'When were you last here?'

'An age ago. Decades. But it hasn't changed. I'd forgotten it. I hadn't realised how much I'd missed it. Again, no offence.'

'Again,' said the other companion, 'none taken.'

THEY WERE MOVING along a stone jetty from the wharf towards the craggy bulk of Bonner's Reach. The jetty was sealed against the void by shimmering, intersected screen-fields projecting between hoops of infinitely old technology that formed archways along the stone walk. A hundred metres behind them, the great mass of the *Hinterlight* lay at grav anchor in the immense granite basin of a void-dock. A series of mag-baffles and airgates linked the merchantman to the end of the jetty.

Nayl had to admit that what Bonner's Reach lacked in olfactory sophistication, it more than made up for in visual impact. It had taken them seventeen days to reach it from Flint, but the view alone was worth the trip. Bonner's Reach was an airless rock tightly orbiting a feeble, unstable star at the very end of its staggeringly vast lifespan. Long before, before man had begun to walk upright, someone had built a great stone bastion into the rock of its surface. Internal spaces in the bastion were chiselled down into the rock itself. No one could explain its origin, or account for its manner of construction, nor even ascertain its age. Certainly no one could explain why its makers had abandoned the bastion and left not a shred of themselves behind.

Early human venturers had found the place empty and open to hard vacuum. Effective installation of power plants, void shielding and atmosphere processors had made it habitable, and it had remained so ever since.

Because the Reach had no atmosphere, visiting starships, even those of great tonnage, could come in close and sit at low anchor above the Lagoon, a vast crater-bowl that had been scooped from the rock in front of the bastion. Alternatively – for a higher fee – they could berth in one of the many void-docks and quays hewn into the mountainside out of which the bastion grew.

The view from the jetty was uncompromisingly strange. Looking out through the crackling void-fields that kept in the jetty's atmosphere, Nayl could see the vast, blackened elevation of the bastion, seamless stone cut by a non-human hand. Lights, yellow and tiny, glowed at pinprick windows. He could see ships – giant starships – floating out there in the darkness above the hard-shadowed white expanse of the Lagoon. The crater was full of white dust, but it looked like a snowfield, a sea of unmarked snow, dotted like a snow-leopard's pelt with the shadows of the starship anchored above it. Nearer at hand, bulk freight craft and other merchantmen lay sheathed in their void-docks, umbilically linked to the bastion via the ghostly-lit spurs of landing jetties. The sense of scale was terrifying. He was used to looking down on planets from afar, from orbit. Now he stood on the very threshold of one – and not even a large one – and could look around to see great frigates, clippers and sprint traders suckled against its embracing bulk. With a contrasting point of reference like the *Hinterlight* in view, Nayl's mind balked a little at the dwarfing size of the world, and by extension any world, and by further extension, the Imperium.

And then, in turn, his tiny, inconsequential self.

* * *

Patience Kys strolled onto the *Hinterlight's* main bridge, her eyes on the principal display screen. It showed a view out across the Lagoon as captured by the forward pict-systems.

The bridge was quiet. Most of the primary crew-stations had been vacated. Oliphant Twu, Preest's unnervingly reticent Navigator, had been detached from his socket so he could enjoy a few hours rest in his quarters after the lengthy voyage. Kys was glad he was absent. Twu was always unfailingly polite and courteous to any passengers he encountered, but there was a loathsome aura about him that made most people uncomfortable and Kys positively ill. It was the constant, seething turmoil of his mind. It made her feel seasick. In its way, it was as bad as the blunter, Wystan Frauka.

Frauka himself was present on the bridge, though his limiter was active. He had slumped in the second helmsman's throne, one leg swinging over the arm, smoking as if it was his primary function in life. He nodded to Kys as she came in, and his face curled into an expression that she realised, with horror, was probably his idea of an alluring smile.

She ignored him. A trio of Preest's tech servitors was running standard overhauls on some of the tertiary system consoles on the far side of the bridge. She could hear the hiss and stutter of their gas-powered digits as they unscrewed retaining bolts.

Halstrom occupied the shipmistress's throne, maintaining an intent check on both the ship's engineering turn-around and external activity. He looked to Kys very much the part of a shipmaster, confident and proud of his place. Preest so seldom left the *Hinterlight* herself, it was rare he got the opportunity to stand in.

Thonius sat at the primary helm console to his left. He was flicking through hololith displays projected to his repeater screen from the main actuality sphere, manipulating the images with his good left hand, his right bound up in a sling. He seemed bored and preoccupied.

A few metres in front of Frauka, Ravenor's chair sat locked to the deck by its mag-clamps. The inquisitor's unit seemed inert. Fat cables spooled out of the chair via opened access points in its surface armour, and connected to four chunky portable units arranged around the chair on the deck. Psi-booster units. More cables ran from the units to an open inspection hatch in the side of Thonius's console, linked directly to the *Hinterlight's* potent astrocommunication dishes.

Kys walked up to Halstrom and perched her bottom on the edge of his console desk.

'Mistress Preest doesn't approve of people sitting on the bridge stations,' Halstrom began.

'Oh dear,' said Kys. 'Is she on the bridge?'

'You know she's not…' Halstrom began.

'Then I'd say it was up to the acting master who sits where.'

Halstrom coloured slightly and then grinned. 'Point, Mamzel Kys. This is my watch for a change. You're fine where you are.'

She grinned back. She liked Halstrom. Old school, reliable, kinda sexy too, if a girl had a mind to go for distinguished older males. Which she never had. Not after Sameter.

'How are they doing?' she asked.

'They've left the airgate. Heading down the jetty towards the station threshold.'

'They're taking their frigging time about it,' Thonius complained tersely.

Kys looked over at Thonius. 'What's your problem? Got a hot date waiting?'

Frauka sniggered loudly. Halstrom chuckled and made himself busy.

'Screw you, Kys,' Thonius said.

And so the banter begins, Kys thought. Since they'd met, she and Carl Thonius had spent their time sparring. It was part of the team spirit. But, she considered, 'screw you' lacked a great deal of the expected Thonius finesse.

She slid off Halstrom's console and crossed to Thonius's side.

'What's up?'

He shrugged and glanced up at her. 'Sorry,' he said.

'Nothing to be sorry for. You're tense.'

'I don't know why they're taking so long,' he said. He reached out with his left hand and methodically tapped out a control function that would normally have taken him an instant with both hands. The display image dissolved and changed. Now it showed an overview of the docking jetty through one of the *Hinterlight's* starboard pict-sources.

There was the jetty, encased in its gleaming sleeve of void-fields, stark against the blackness around and beneath it. She could see the landing party. Preest – in full robes and finery – riding aboard an ornamental floater carriage that she controlled with an actuator wand in her right hand. Two bodyguards – tall, heavyset men – walked with her, one on either side of the carriage. They were clad in long, quilted coats and ornamental full-face helms, and each carried a long pole upright. The two poles supported a small canopy above Preest's head.

Behind them came a train of six cargo-servitors laden with caskets.

The bodyguard at Preest's right hand was Nayl. The one to her left – nominally – was Zeph Mathuin. But to all intents and purposes, it was Ravenor. The inquisitor was waring Mathuin's body.

'They're just making a dramatic entrance,' Kys suggested. 'You know the mistress. She likes to arrive in style. Regally.'

'Maybe,' Thonius said.

Kys leaned over and tapped a few keys, swinging the image around to show more of the bastion itself. Mysteries and rumours adhered to Bonner's Reach as they did to all outlandish places. Some said the first venturers to come here found unimaginable treasures deep in the bastion's chambers. Others said there were still corridors and halls cut into the rock down there that no one had yet traced or followed. Many supposed that ancient and profoundly powerful xenos technology, left behind by the builders of the place, had been found. One particular, popular story had it that once in a while, a visitor would go missing... lost forever after taking a wrong turn somewhere, or perhaps taken by the spirit of the place as a payment for continued human use of the structure.

Every few minutes there was a brief flash or fizzle of light. These were photonic flare-patterns, beginning to stutter out from the planet's old and dying star. At this early stage, these emissions were just precursor flashes. In ten or twelve hours' time, they would have matured into a full-blown solar storm that would fill the sky with flame and last for three days. The storms happened every thirty-five months.

That was Firetide, when the ships put in at Bonner's Reach and their masters feasted and drank while the heavens blazed.

Kys sighed. Thonius's edginess was infectious. 'I don't know why we can't just march in and flash our warrants and–'

'Look out there, Mamzel Kys,' Halstrom pointed, indicating the main display. 'Look at the ships gathered there over the Lagoon. I see rogue traders, far venturers, merchantmen of all sizes... and that? What's that? And that? And that over there, the disk-shaped vessel? That's two hundred kilometres away, to give you some sense of scale. This is a frontier in both directions, Mamzel. A fair number of the visitors here have never heard of our authority. Those that have care less for it.'

'That's what free trade station means,' Thonius said. 'This is Lucky Space, free space, a gateway. We Imperials are only tolerated visitors here.'

'The stuff you know,' Kys mocked.

'You wouldn't believe,' Thonius replied.

THEY WERE APPROACHING the entry gate at the end of the jetty. Its ancient stone form was decorated with interwoven carved figures that symbolised leaping flame. Heaps of votive offerings were piled up either side of the gate pillars. Dolls, figurines, ritual pots, small tied-up sacks, drinking vessels, ribbons, occasionally an icon like an aquila; and those were simply the ones of human origin that Nayl could identify. Any others were alien objects he could make no sense of. It was customary to leave a token offering at the gate on departure, to vouchsafe one's next voyage.

Two Vigilants awaited them at the gate.

'You ready with the tribute?' Preest whispered.

'The servitors have been instructed,' Ravenor replied through Mathuin's mouth.

The Order of Vigilants administered the Reach. They collected tariffs, saw to the station's smooth running, and to the congress of fair trade. The pair that now approached them were lean and tall, at least as tall as Harlon or Zeph. They walked with an easy, nimble step that told Nayl right off they were consummate close fighters. Each Vigilant wore a sleeveless, antique gown of ribbed armour, marvellously constructed, baggy black pantaloons that were tight-cinched at the ankle, and black felt slippers that were shaped around the big toe. Their exposed arms were either bionic, or encased in some form of skinplant technology. It was a tech-design neither Nayl nor Ravenor had ever seen before. Sheathed over their shoulders they carried ceremonial hand-and-a-half swords.

Their heads were bare and shaved. More of the curiously-wrought skinplant tech encased their necks, so that their heads seemed to be resting on slender columns of intricately inscribed metal. The skin of their faces and scalps was entirely covered in swirling flame tattoos, echoing the design around the doorway. Their eyes were augmetic implants that glowed a dull green.

'Welcome,' said one. Its voice was like silk.

'The immaterium has brought you to Bonner's Reach,' said the other, its tone rasping and deep.

'Free trade is welcome here,' uttered the first.

Perched on her hovering platform, Preest bowed. 'Thank you for your greeting and welcome,' she said. 'I most humbly crave admittance. I have brought a tribute for the welfare of all.'

'Let us examine it,' said the rasping one.

At a signal from Nayl, the servitors brought forward the caskets and opened some of them. Foodstuffs, much of it stasis-fresh, wine and some flasks of amasec.

'This is acceptable tribute,' said the rasping Vigilant.

'Welcome,' repeated the silky one. 'Do you wish us to advertise your presence and identity to the merchants here?'

'I am Shipmistress Zeedmund. Of the sprint trader *Tarnish*. I am here for Firetide, but I also seek interesting commerce.'

'Zeedmund. *Tarnish*...' they echoed.

'I have serious collateral,' she added. 'Make that known. I am interested in genuine business.'

'You appreciate the Code of the Reach?' asked the Vigilant with the silk voice.

'Peace and discourse,' Preest replied. 'And no weapon within the bounds of the Reach with a range longer than a human arm.'

Nayl and Mathuin dutifully displayed the empty holsters at their hips, the ritual sign of unarmed intent.

'You are familiar with our rules,' said the silky-voiced Vigilant.

'You have been here before,' the rasping one said. It was more of a statement than a question. Nayl stiffened.

'I am a trader,' said Preest. 'I go where I please.'

'Voice-pattern records show you to be Cynia Preest, shipmistress. Not Zeedmund.'

'Traders change their identities. Is that a problem?'

'Not at all. We are ever discreet.' The Vigilants stood aside and ushered them through the threshold. 'Enter and make your trade.'

Beyond the gate, they entered a capacious chamber hewn out of the planetary rock. The air was still muggy and over-used. The place was bathed in a yellow, fulminous light from bioluminescent tank-lamps mounted at regular intervals along the wall. Archways led off into other chambers, and at the far end, a well-lit tunnel disappeared away into the free trade areas. More Vigilants appeared, to conduct Preest's servitors to the communal larders where the tribute could be left.

One of them, his voice a whisper, approached the shipmistress.

'Do you require a guide? A translator? Any other service?'

'I will ask if I need any such service,' she said. The Vigilant bowed and backed away.

With her bodyguards either side of her, Preest began to glide sedately down the long tunnel.

* * *

On Bonner's Reach, visiting traders could avail themselves of drink and nourishment free of charge. Indeed, almost all services were free. A berthing fee was required, of course, but once that was paid, a trader could luxuriate in the bountiful hospitality of the station. The level of comfort was designed to relax visitors and encourage profitable, unhurried mercantile negotiation. The Vigilants merely expected a fee equivalent to one per cent of gross on any deal or transaction made within their precincts.

Of course, this apparent largesse was helped enormously by the recognised custom of tribute. Every captain, master or venturer, human or otherwise, was expected to offer something in the way of foodstuffs, liquor or other intoxicants upon arrival.

Preest's tribute was conducted down three kilometres of rock-cut corridors into a handling bay that adjoined one of the station's many food preparation areas. There the servitors set the caskets down as instructed and made their way back to the *Hinterlight*. A Vigilant labelled the caskets with storage instructions. Before long, kitchen labour would sort through the caskets and distribute the contents: perishables into cold stores and stasis vaults, wine to cellars, dry goods to the well-stocked pantries, specialist foods into appropriate containers, and narcotics to the tenders who walked the floors of the free trade salons.

The Vigilant was called away. Two pot-men were having an altercation in the nearby kitchen.

Preest's caskets were left unattended against the wet quartz wall of the handling bay.

The lid of the fourth casket along popped open. Telescopic levers hissed taut, lifting the produce tray up, revealing it to be merely a shallow false top.

Breathing deeply and slowly, Kara Swole slid herself out of the hidden cavity. She had contorted her body into a tiny space. As she emerged, she paused, grimacing, to pop her shoulder joints back into place.

Kara looked around. There was no time to complete a full body recovery here. She reached her hands up and detached the fibre-optic patch from over her left eye. The adhesive took some lashes with it. She rubbed her eye and wound the patch up in its long string of wire, unplugging the far end of it from the inside of the casket. Thanks to the fibre-optic, she'd been able to see a cold-light view of the outside and judge the best time for emergence accordingly.

Keeping a watchful eye around her, Kara tucked the fibre-optic into a hip pouch. She was wearing a skin-tight light-reflective bodyglove with only her head exposed. He thick red hair was slicked into a tight latex net that made her look bald. She opened the next casket along, and removed its false top layer too. Her equipment was stowed beneath. First, a small, prepacked rucksack on a tight fylon harness. Then, a compact vox, and a multikey that slipped neatly into holder loops on her waistband.

Her limbs and back were sore. She stayed wary, expecting discovery at any moment. The thin combat knife slipped into place in her glove's calf sheath. Nearly done.

She could hear footsteps approaching. One last task. Two almost empty tribute caskets would be more than a little suspicious. She tore open the shrink-wrapped packs of dehydrated kelp and shook their dry contents out into the bottom of each casket. Then she tore the top off a water flask and emptied its glugging contents after them.

Footsteps came closer. She pushed the produce trays back into place, closed the casket lids, and dashed into the shadows at the far end of the handling bay. Then, like an arachnid, she went clear up the sheer quartz wall. The palms and soles of her bodyglove were angle-ribbed with razor-steel filament hooks that could find purchase on almost any surface. She reached the top of the wall, slid into a rocky cavity, and lay still.

A troupe of kitchen labourers wandered into the bay below her, flipping up the lids of Preest's caskets to examine the fare. As she watched, they opened the casket where she had been concealed and took out the top tray.

The rest of the casket was chock full of glistening kelp. She heard the labourers scoff and moan. It was typical cheapskate rogue trader behaviour. Come bearing plenty when in fact most of the makeweight was sea cabbage.

Kara grinned to herself.

As soon as the labourers began to heft the caskets out into the larders, Kara began to move again, scuttling across the rock wall and in under the great flinty arch to the kitchen. Her arms and legs were throbbing with pain. Sheer climbing put an enormous stress on musculature, and her body wasn't yet limber from the forced contortions of the casket.

She forced herself on. A cramp in her left calf lost her some grip, but she clenched her teeth and persisted.

The kitchen below her was a vast and dingy haze, steam surging up from a dozen canisters on a dozen stoves, smoke trailing off roast veal and orkunu and marinated sinqua on the fire pits, drums of broiling ketelfish, pans of frying lardons, tureens of potage, steamers of fubi dumplings and blanching wilt-leaf. The roof of the chamber was a thick smog, which suited her just right. Though stone-cut, the kitchen hall was bolstered with thick cross-members of steel that formed ceiling beams. She dropped down onto the nearest one, swathed in oily smoke and vapour. There, invisible to the staff twenty metres below her, she stood for a long while, tension-flexing and relaxing her tortured body. Arms, joints, digits, spine, ribs, pelvis. As if performing to some great invisible audience, she began to stretch and slide, backflip, rotate and split.

Then she lay on her back on the beam, the kitchen clattering and broiling below her. She was still sore – that was inevitable after two hours in the box. But she was at last spry and warmed up.

Kara Swole rolled over, rose and began to run across the beam towards the interior of the station.

IT WAS THE worst dream yet. Something liquid yet solid was pouring in under Zael's hab door. It was black and it was stinking. Like his granna's glue. Like her frigging mind-burning glue!

He tried to wake granna. She was asleep in her chair, snoring, When he shook her, his hands went into her flesh like it was rotten, flybown meat. Yelping out in revulsion, he backed away and grabbed his granna's little effigy of the God-Emperor from the top of the cupboard. Zael held it out at the viscous horror spurting in around the door cracks into the kitchen.

'Go away, Nove! Go away! Leave me alone!'

Something he needs to know...

He stifled a scream and–

WOKE UP.

Zael moaned and turned over in his cot. The cabin was dark, but he had left a light on in the bathroom. Its frosty glow spilled out across the gloomy space.

He was breathing hard. He wanted to call for Nayl, or Kara or even Kys, but he remembered they were engaged on some sort of mission. He wondered if he should try to contact The Chair. Nayl had advised him too, back at that place... what was it? Lenk?

He hadn't. He hadn't dared. He still didn't really know what The Chair had brought him along for or why The Chair considered him special. But he didn't want to spoil things. He didn't want to give The Chair an excuse to ditch him.

And what was this? Wasn't this excuse enough? Zael was having nightmares. His head was on wrong. After weeks, he was still witchy with come-down symptoms.

Zael sat up in the dark. He pushed his pillow across his knees and then leaned his head into it.

He wished, really wished, he could be a person like Nayl. A sorted out, in-control person. Or like Kara. Hell, even like Kys or Thonius.

Zael heard a sound from the bathroom. Like a block of soap falling from the rack, or a rubber ball bouncing in the metal drain-tray.

How could a–

He rose to his feet, holding the pillow in front of him like the most frigging pathetic shield in the Imperium. Water was hissing in the bathroom now, the shower head. Hot water. Steam gusted out of the cubicle, filming the glass door.

There was someone in there, inside the shower cube. Someone fogged by steam and water.

Zael swallowed hard. 'Hello?'

'Zael?' The voiced echoed out over the rush of the shower. Zael heard someone spit out water to say the name.

'Yeah. Who's in there?'

'It's me, Zael.'

'Who's me?'

'Frig's sake, Zael! Don't you know your own sister?'

Zael began to back away. 'My sister… she's dead. You're not my sister..'

'Course I am, little,' said the misty figure behind the glass door. 'Why do you think I've been trying so hard to find you?'

'I don't know…' Zael murmured.

'Everything's joined, little. Everything's linked. Space, time, souls, the God-Emperor… it's all one big, connected everything. You'll understand it when you're here with me.'

'With you? What do you want, Nove?'

'I have to tell you something. Okay?'

'What?'

The shower shut off abruptly.

'Snatch me a towel, little. I'm coming out.'

'N-no! No, don't–'

The stall door opened. His sister stood before him. Fully dressed, soaking wet from the shower, haloed by steam.

And as burst and broken as she had been when they'd found her at the foot of the hab stack.

Zael simply blacked out.

'LET'S CIRCULATE,' CYNIA Preest suggested. Her voice had a sly tone to it. She was enjoying this, and that pleased me. Bonner's Reach seemed to have reawakened Preest's enthusiasm for my hazardous occupation. For the first time in years, she was positive and engaged, probably because at last she had a proactive part to play.

We were standing in the stone entrance arch of one of the principle free trade salons. The scale of the chamber impressed me. It was bigger than the Carnivora, bigger than the interiors of some Ecclesiarchy temples I'd seen. A monstrous chamber hollowed from the planet's rock, lit by huge biolumin tank-lights suspended in clusters from the faraway roof. The other end of the chamber was so far away I could barely see it.

Even through Zeph Mathuin's enhanced optics.

A flight of marble stairs led down from the archway into the floor of the salon. Below us, hundreds – thousands, perhaps – of figures were gathered informally, drinking, talking, discoursing, trading. On our level, side galleries swept away around the walls of the hall. Looking up, I saw further tiers of galleries, twenty or more, circling the chamber all the way up to the ceiling.

The side galleries, enjoying a view over the salon's main floor, were for private negotiations. There were booths spaced regularly around their circuits, softly lit, where traders dined together, gamed, and indulged. A quick muster of my mind, boosted as it was by the amplifiers on the *Hinterlight's* bridge, told me some various booths were vox-screened, some pict-opaque, and most of them were psi-shielded. A trader entering a booth could activate discretionary barriers to keep his commerce private.

We went down the steps into the throng. Preest hovered her way down like some monarch on her archaic floater carriage. It was a business to keep the canopy decorously unfurled above her.

I switched my mind from side to side, like a broom, sweeping up scraps of detail from the scene. Preest was in her element, confident, happy in a way that surprised even her.

Nayl was tense. A passing taste of his mind told me he didn't like it. I could hear a repeating mantra circling in his thoughts... *way too exposed... too many angles... no cover... way too exposed.*

+It'll be fine.+

He glanced at me. His expression was hidden by the visor of his blast helm. I glimpsed his eyes.

'Very well,' he said, reluctantly.

+What's the trouble?+

'Nothing, boss. Nothing.'

We proceeded onto the floor of the salon. I took a selfish moment to enjoy this brief stint of physicality. I relished the body I was waring: its power, its strength, its mobility. Zeph was almost too easy to ware, one of the key reasons I had employed him. Waring others was often traumatic to both me and them, but Zeph Mathuin gave up his corporeal form without any negative resistance. I borrowed his flesh like a man might borrow another's coat. When the time came for us to change back, neither of us ever suffered any consequences more serious than fatigue.

On we moved, through the jostling, chattering floor space of the salon. On every side, rogue traders chatted and bartered with others of their kind. Bodyguard cadres sat around low tables, getting drunk while they waited for their masters and mistresses to finish socialising. Races mixed. I saw eldar, of a craftworld unknown to me, resplendent in polished white armour, engaged with a fat human ox in furs riding on a lifter throne. Nekulli hunched and chattered around a trio of methane breathers who were tanked inside bizarre viro-armours that glistened like silver and exuded noxious odours. A bounty hunter in full body plate strode past us, trailed by his servitor drones. To my left, a kroot cackled and barked. To my right, a trader whose body was entirely augmetic chortled a mechanical chortle as the shapeless ff'eng he was dealing with cracked a joke. The trader was exquisite: his body parts and face were machined from gold, his dental ivory set perfectly in gilded gums, his eyes real and organic.

Some abominable form of opal-shelled mollusc hovered on a lifter dais and fluttered its eye stalks and elongated mandibles at a rogue trader in a red blastcoat. As we went by, I saw that the rogue trader was human except for his transplanted feline eyes. Something humanoid but not human, an elongated figure in a white vac-suit, its skin blue, its neck serpentine, blinked its large mirror eyes at a monthropod and its larvae. The monthropod and its kin curved their tube forms backwards and clattered their mouthparts to pay homage.

Forparsi drifters in gowns embroidered with stellar charts examined the product examples of jokaero technology. A human trader with mauve skin-dye studied an outworld prospector's gem samples through a jeweller's lens. I saw guildsmen amongst the rabble. The Imperial merchant guilds were supposed to limit their activities to inter-Imperium commerce, but it was well known they had no desire to see the potentially vast profits of the outworld markets go only to the free venturers and rogues.

Everywhere, tenders went to and fro. Some were girls, some boys, many were xeno-forms. They scurried to serve drinks and provide other diversions.

Preest held out a hand and stopped one, a handsome, hairless youth.

'What is it your pleasure, mistress?' he asked. 'I have some of glad and some of grin and also fine sniff-musk.'

'Three amasecs,' Preest said. 'Make them all doubles.'

The tender scooted off.

Several merchants made formal approaches to Preest, but she politely expressed disinterest to each after a few words had been exchanged. One, however, was especially persistent. He was a mutant or a hybrid, unnaturally short and wide, a dwarf by human standards. His hair flew back behind him in a great crest. His thick chin sported a shaved-back goatee. He was dressed in a dark red body-glove armoured with suspended metal plates. His bodyguard – a single, unimpressive elquon manhound with dejected eyes and heavy, drooping jowls – accompanied him.

Approaching Preest, he turned her a deft bow.

'Do I have the habit of acquainting Shipmistress Zeedmund?' he said. Though he was making an effort to affect a tone of high-born class, he could not disguise the common twang in his voice, nor the fact that Low Gothic was not his native tongue.

'I am Zeedmund,' said Preest.

'I am most audible to meet you,' said the little master. I tried to scan him, but realised he was wearing some type of blocker. 'Mistress, what say we chivvy us up some appendable tenders, attire ourselves some disgustable comestibles, and revive to a private booth for interculation?'

Preest smiled at him. 'Why... would we do that?'

'It has been brought to my apprehension by the Vigilants that you are in the marketplace, so to speak, for suggestive retail propositioning. In that rearguard, I am your man.'

'Really,' Preest said. 'Who are you?'

'Milady, my mamzel... I am Sholto Unwerth. Do not be deceived by my diminutive stature. I may not stand tall, but I cast, so to speak, a long shadow. And that shadow is entirely made up of trade.'

He said the last with emphasis, as if we should be struck with wonder at his pitch. We were, though it's fair to say not for the reasons he hoped.

'Do you want me to get rid of him?' I heard Nayl whisper to Preest.

Unwerth heard him too. He held up a hand, the chunky fingers splayed. 'Now, now. There's no need for musculature.'

Nayl glared at him. Unwerth tugged his own earlobe. 'I miss nothing, eaves-wise. Ears as sharp as pencils, me. No, no. All fair. If Mistress Zeedmund here finds me an abject increment in her affiliations, and wants no more of me, all she has to overtake is a word in my general. A simple ingratitude from her, and I will be, so to speak, out of your air. Without any requisite for shoving, slapping or harsh language. On the however hand, if what I have so far expleted trickles her fancy, I would be most oblate to dispell some more, at her total inconvenience, on the subject of what I have pertaining in my cargo hold.'

'A moment, Master Unwerth,' Preest said.

'By all means, have a sundry of them,' he said.

Preest turned to Nayl and me. 'He's just the thing. Trust me on this. I know how places like this are. Can't you just smell the desperation? He's so hungry for trade, his tongue's going to be a lot looser than most around here.'

'It's your call,' I said.

'Just hang around and look bored,' Preest said.

'Not a problem,' Nayl growled.

'Master Unwerth,' Preest announced, turning back to face him. 'I would be delighted to discuss potential trade opportunities with you.'

He looked stunned for a moment. 'Really?' he mouthed. Even his manhound temporarily lost its dejected expression. Unwerth recovered fast. 'Well, I'm ensconced by your cordium. It quite inflates me. Let us revive at once to a booth and digress in private.'

He became quite animated, leading us through the crowd and up one of the marble staircases to the first gallery. As he went, he summoned tenders and made a great show of ordering up a handsome dinner. We followed. As it turned to fall into step with us, the manhound gave me a long-suffering shrug that quite warmed me to it.

Unwerth found a free booth and pulled himself up onto one of the seats. Preest stepped down off her carriage and sat opposite him. Already, tenders were arriving with trays of sweetmeats, savouries and drinks. The manhound went to sit down beside its master, but Unwerth glanced at it sharply and hissed, 'Not on the furniture, Fyflank!'

Rebuked, it curled up on the floor outside the booth and began to scratch its neck lugubriously with a hind-claw, causing a slapping ripple to travel up its overhanging jowls.

One of them – Unwerth or Preest – activated a pict-opaque field, and Nayl and I were left outside to guard the carriage. We leaned the canopy poles against the wall. The manhound looked at us, then settled its chin on its paws and began to doze.

I followed Harlon to the gallery rail and we looked out across the salon.

'This is taking a long time…' he said.

'I never expected this to be quick,' I replied. 'Or easy. I have faith in Cynia. We take her skills as a pilot for granted. It's about time we made use of her skills as a trader.'

'Maybe. Kara okay?'

'Yes. I can sense her. She's in and moving.'

'That's something.'

He was about to say something else when there was a sudden commotion on the salon floor below us. The manhound raised its head sleepily. Nayl and I straightened up from the rail for a clearer view

A fight had broken out. The crowds of merchants drew back to give it room, peering at the action. In a few scant seconds, Vigilants had appeared, swords drawn, and formed a cordon around the fracas. I expected them to stop it, but they didn't. They simply kept the crowds at bay. It seemed that any physical dispute was allowed to find its own resolution, provided those involved stuck to the station rules about weapons.

There were four combatants: a slender human trader with a mane of frizzy white hair, dressed in a long, grey blastcoat, his two skin-gloved bodyguards, and a big brute wearing carapace armour that looked as if it had been made from mother-of-pearl. The armoured man was bare-headed. He had a stripe of bleached hair running across his scalp and his face was threaded with old scars. His nose and ears were just nubs of gristle. He was swinging a power maul in his left hand.

The trader, screaming out to the crowd and the Vigilants for sympathy and help, was trying to stay out of the actual clash. His minders had drawn short swords and wore buckler shields on their left wrists. The armoured brute took one out almost at once, leaving the man twitching on the deck, his body crackling with dissipating electrical charge. The onlookers clapped and whistled.

The other bodyguard flashed in, stabbing with his sword and deflecting the maul with his buckler. The sword made no dent whatsoever on the pearl armour. Ducking under a final, desperate stab, the armoured man swung the maul in hard and connected with the minder's face. The minder slammed backwards, turning an almost complete backflip. He was dead, of that I was certain. The electrical charge of the maul was enough to incapacitate, but the physical blow alone had crushed his skull.

More approval from the crowd.

His bodyguard down, the trader turned and tried to flee. The Vigilants pushed him back into the open. As the armoured man came charging towards him, uttering a bellicose yell, the trader frantically reached into his blast-coat and pulled a revolver.

One of the Vigilants turned and broke from the cordon with stunning speed. His sword whistled down in an elegant slice and severed the trader's hand at the wrist. Hand and gun hit the deck and bounced.

A half-second later, the power maul had laid the trader out. Holstering his maul in a leather boot across his back, the armoured man grabbed the trader's convulsing, sparking body and held it up with one hand, the frizzy white hair pulled back to reveal the man's face to the crowd. With his other hand, the armoured man raised a warrant slate that displayed a hololithic picture of the trader's face.

The crowd began to boo and jeer, returning to their business. The cordon broke up, and the Vigilants gathered up the fallen bodies.

'Bounty hunter,' Nayl said.

'Yeah?'

'You saw him flash the warrant. This place is crawling with hunters. They're looking for absconders and evaders. My guess is they locate them here and then either pick them up once they leave or… if they're bold like Worna there… take 'em down in public.'

'You know him?' I asked. It was silly question. Nayl had been a bounty man himself for many years. He knew the industry, and its more notable players.

'Lucius Worna? Of course. Been in the game fifteen decades. Piece of shit.'

'And there are others around?'

'Everywhere. We've been scanned at least six times since we came in. Hunters check everyone out. They never know who they might run into in a place like this.'

I was alarmed. I hadn't noticed. Waring a body like Mathuin, I expended a lot of my power simply controlling the form. It deprived me of the full scope of abilities I enjoyed in person. Suddenly, I felt vulnerable. I understood Nayl's worried state.

This was a dangerous place.

THE SOLAR FLASHES were coming so frequently now that Halstrom had dimmed the bridge screen resolution. He remained seated in the mistress's throne, running and re-running diagnostic checks on the main console display to take his mind off the wait. Ravenor's chair was just a silent shape, immobile.

Thonius had crossed to Frauka, and the two men were playing virtual regicide on a hololith repeater. Kys watched them. Thonius accepted another of Frauka's lho-sticks and they carried on, smoking, playing, chatting quietly.

Frustrated, Kys paced up and down the main aisle of the bridge between the consoles for a while. She was so bored, she even stepped into the vacant Navigator's socket to try it out for comfort.

'Please, don't do that.' Halstrom called.

Kys looked at him.

'Even on my watch. Twu is very particular about his socket.'

Kys sniffed and got out. 'Aren't we all?'

She wandered back to Halstrom.

'You're bored,' he observed.

'No. Oh, all right, yes. But edgy too.'

'I know what you mean,' Halstrom smiled. Almost involuntarily, he flicked up another screen display. 'See that?'

'Un huh,' she said. 'What is it?'

'Haven't the faintest,' he replied. 'Just a bunch of figures and runes. I keep punching it up, looking at it, but... no idea what it means.'

She looked at him. 'You're joking.'

Halstrom grinned. 'Of course I am. It's the atmosphere post-process chart. But the point is made. I'm just filling time. Is it always like this?'

'What?'

'Work. Your work. As a Throne agent. I thought it would be exciting. Cloak and dagger stuff. We don't get to sample it much, us in the crew. You're down on planets, doing who knows what. We're up at anchor, waiting. I got quite excited when the inquisitor said we were going out hunting in Lucky Space. But it's... it's not really what I imagined.'

'Believe me, it often goes this way,' Kys said. 'Waiting, watching, getting jangly with nerves. Sometimes I think boredom is a more serious threat to us than heresy.'

Halstrom chuckled. 'You must have devised coping strategies by now.'

'Must we?'

'Of course.'

'You're the ones who do the waiting usually,' Kys reminded him. 'What do you do?'

Halstrom waved his hand at the console display. 'This, mostly.'

She sat on the arm of his throne. Behind them, Frauka won another game, and he and Thonius celebrated by lighting another pair of lho-sticks.

Kys looked back at Halstrom. 'What else do you do?' she asked.

'We talk,' he replied. 'Reminisce. Preest is good at that. Her stories are wonderful. Have you heard any?'

'No. I don't know her very well at all.'

'Magnus, the second helmsman, he's good value too. I get all my jokes from him. We talk about our lives and where we come from and so forth.'

'And it passes the time?'

'Passes it fairly. We could try that, Mamzel Kys. I know nothing about you.'

'I know nothing about you, Mr Halstrom.'

He sat up. 'Mutual ignorance. I think that sounds like a grand place to start. You first, where were you born?'

'Sameter, in the Helican sub.'

'Ah, dingy Sameter. I know it well.'

'You?'

Halstrom shrugged. 'My family comes from Hesperus, but I was born on Enothis.'

'That's a long way away. In the Sabbat Worlds.'

'Indeed. We travelled a lot. My father was in the Fleet, and I followed after him.'

Kys leaned back. 'Into service, you mean? You were a captain once, weren't you?'

'Yes,' he said. Absently, he switched the display to another diagnostic graphic. 'But it's my turn to ask. Is that your real name?'

Kys shook her head. 'It's my trophy name.'

'What does that mean?' asked Halstrom.

'I thought we were taking it in turns?'

'This is still my turn. What's a trophy name?'

'It's one you get given when you're a trophy. Terra, Mr Halstrom! You think *Patience Kys* is a genuine name?'

'I did wonder. It sounded rather... how can I put it?'

'Ridiculous?'

'No, no... I was shooting for *theatrical*.'

Kys laughed. 'My sisters and I were all given names. It was part of the game.'

Halstrom turned in his seat to look straight at her. 'Game? I get the impression from your tone that this game was far from pleasant. It may be something you don't wish to talk about–'

'Correct.'

'But still,' he shrugged. 'If it's a name that you were given against your will, why would you keep it? Why don't you go back to your original name?'

Kys thought before she answered. Her face went serious. 'Because it keeps me sane to remember where I've been. And I made a promise, a long time ago, that the name wouldn't be forgotten.'

'Oh,' Halstrom said.

'I think that makes it my turn,' Kys said. 'Why aren't you a fleet captain any more?'

Halstrom sat back and closed his eyes. 'I think your ground rules established that there are some things we don't wish to talk about.'

'No fair!' Kys said, slapping him harmlessly on the arm. 'You can't dodge the question.'

'They're pretty,' Halstrom said. 'Are they a recent acquisition?'

He was pointing at the glittering fish scales looped over her throat stud.

'Thank you. Yes, they are. I picked them up on Flint. But you're avoiding my question again.'

'I know,' he began. 'I don't like to talk about–'

Halstrom broke off. There had been a quick, choppy, blurt on the ship's intervox.

Suddenly sharp, he leaned forward.

'What was that?'

'You tell me,' Kys said, rising to her feet. Frauka and Thonius were still playing their game.

Another blurt came across the speakers A scared voice, indecipherable, cut up by the intercom channel switching on and off.

'What the hell...' Halstrom muttered.

'Where's it coming from?' Kys asked.

'Just checking,' said Halstrom, running his fingers over the keys. Another blurt sounded. A frantic scratching and a low moan, broken by the switching click of the system.

'Someone's trying to use the intervox. Fumbling with it...' Kys reasoned.

'I've got the source,' Halstrom told her. 'Cabin eight fifteen.'

'Zael,' she sighed. 'I bet the little freak is having another nightmare.'

'We should–' Halstrom started to say. But Kys was already striding away towards the hatch.

'Relax,' she called over her shoulder. 'I've got it.'

'DAMN.'

'What's the matter, Harlon?' Ravenor asked.

Nayl backed up from the rail, looking round.

'What?' Ravenor asked again from Mathuin's mouth.

'We're being scanned again,' Nayl said. 'I think someone's taken an interest.'

Behind them, the pict-opaque field dropped and Preest emerged. The manhound looked up at her as she strode past.

'Anything useful?' Ravenor asked her.

'Indeed. Let's move.'

Preest stepped up into her carriage and started sliding it forward. Ravenor and Nayl took up the canopy poles and muddled it into position.

As they moved away along the gallery, Unwerth appeared from the booth. 'Mistress!' he called out after them. 'Mistress, are you concumplished that no exhilarated trade may partake between us? Mistress? I am most heartless in my disabusement!'

'Ignore him,' Preest said.

'Fine,' Nayl said. 'I could even kill him, if that would help.'

'No need,' she whispered. They moved down the stairs into the throng of the salon floor. 'Master Unwerth has been most useful.'

'Go on,' Ravenor said.

'The *Oktober Country* is here. Unwerth has been pestering everyone, and tried it on with Thekla earlier today. Attempted to get Thekla interested in the useless gee-gaws in Unwerth's cargo. Thekla gave him the brush off. See, I told you a dunce like Unwerth would be useful.'

'I'm impressed. What else?' Ravenor asked, keeping his voice low.

'I asked him about flects, of course. Unwerth went coy. It's way out of his league. But he knew the basics. The cartel meets in the second salon. That's through here. And the man to speak to, according to Unwerth, is a merchant called Akunin.'

'Akunin? Anything else?'

Preest paused and looked round at Mathuin's face.

'You seem to want the world from me, Gideon. Haven't I just done terribly well?'

'You have, Cynia. And I'm grateful. But we don't know anything about this Akunin. Agents of the Throne can't just march up to people and demand to be cut into the flect trade.'

'No, they don't,' Preest admitted. 'But rogue traders can. You've got the currency orders, Harlon?'

'Inside my glove, mistress,' Nayl said.

'Well, unbutton and make ready. We're about to do business.'

THE DOOR OF Zael's cabin was shut, but not locked. Kys slid it open and looked into the dark.

'Zael? Zael, you freak? What are you playing at?'

She heard a moan from over by the shower closet.

'Zael? Are you all right?'

Another soft moan.

Kys stepped inside the cabin and reached for the lights. She pressed the activator, but nothing happened. Were they broken? Blown?

Kys advanced into the darkness, her eyes adjusting. She could hear sobbing. The air was warm and damp.

'Zael? Where in the name of frig are you?'

Something moved in the gloom at the sound of her voice. She flinched, but it was just a body coiled on the floor.

Kys reached down and found Zael. His breathing was fast and shallow. From the smell of it, he'd wet himself.

'Zael? It's me. It's Patience. Get up.'

Zael just twitched.

'Come on, you frigger. We have to get you cleaned up.'

She picked him up, and steered him towards the shower stall. Zael began to scream and thrash.

Kys slammed his quaking form up against the wall and held it in place.

'What's the matter with you?'

'Don't make me go in the shower. She's in there. She's in there. She's all bloody and broken.'

'Who is? Zael, what are you talking about?'

'Nove.'

'Who the frig is that?'

'My sister.'

'You told me your sister was dead,' Kys said.

'She is,' Zael wept. 'Go in there and see for yourself.'

Kys let him slump. She walked towards the shower stall. The only light in the cabin was welling out from behind the glass.

Kys realised she had no weapon on her at the same moment she realised there was no reason for her to be armed. The boy had suffered a nightmare. That was the end of it. Why was her heart beating so fast? Why was she so scared?

The fish scales. She thought of them at the very last minute. They were sharp, easy to TK. Mr Halstrom had admired them. She mind-lifted them off her throat stud and hovered them in the air.

This was stupid. The boy had been dreaming. There was nothing in the stall.

She took hold of the door handle. The scales were circling in the air.

She opened the door. Inside the shower stall was–

Nothing.

Kys sagged and breathed out. The scales flew back to her throat and fastened themselves again around the top stud.

'Shit, Zael. You nearly had me there. I really thought...'

She looked round and saw the boy was crawling towards the open cabin door.

She bounded across to him and grabbed him by the hair. He squealed. 'Listen! You actually scared me then with your game!'

'It wasn't a game!' Zael whined. 'It was a message.'

THEY ENTERED THE second salon. It was as busy as the first. At a question from Preest, a Vigilant pointed them up towards a booth on the third gallery.

They climbed the stairs. Almost at once, it was obvious the third gallery was quiet, almost empty.

'I don't like it,' Nayl whispered.

'Oh, do shut up,' Preest said.

The booths they were passing were vacant, as if they had been cleared.

A tender hurried past. 'Akunin?' Preest called out. 'Where do I find Master Akunin?'

'Gone!' the tender cried, and in another moment, so was she.

'I think it's time to split,' Nayl said.

'Agreed,' Ravenor said. 'While we still can.'

Two figures stepped out of a booth ahead and blocked the gallery. One was a nekulli, armed with a traditional saw-toothed lance. The other was a human in head-to-toe battleplate, polished a deep, silvery blue. He had a falchion in his right hand.

'About face,' Ravenor hissed. They turned.

Three more figures stood behind them. One was a man of heavy build with sandy-white hair. To his left stood a kroot with a billhook; to his right, a man in chequered leather armour, wielding a boarding axe.

The man with the sandy-white hair was wearing the camo-armour of a game agent and held a huntsman's hooksword. He looked familiar, very familiar, to Nayl. For a second Nayl thought it was Feaver Skoh. But this wasn't the man Nayl had seen in the cavae of the Carnivora. Nayl had a good eye for faces. This man was a brother or close kin. *A dynasty of xeno-hunters,* that's how the Skohs had been described.

'What is this?' asked Preest. Ravenor could hear the tremor in her voice.

The game agent smiled. 'This is the end of the line.'

At the far end of the gallery behind the game agent and his comrades, Ravenor could see Vigilants gathering, forming a cordon. No one was going to intercede on their behalf. As far as the Order of Vigilants was concerned, this was private business, and would be concluded privately, as per the weapon-laws of the Reach.

+Go.+

At the single word, Nayl and Ravenor/Mathuin began to move. Mistress Preest's aristocratic canopy went clattering over as they up-ended it and drew the weapons concealed within its hollow poles. Stave-swords, with handgrips as long as their thin, straight blades, slithered out into their hands.

Nayl went straight for the game agent, who bellowed and lunged to meet him. Stave-blade encountered hooksword with enough leverage to send the hunter stumbling sideways. But the man in chequered armour and the kroot were right behind their boss. Nayl dummied left out of the swooping downward path of the boarding axe, and smacked the pommel of the stave-sword sideways into the side of the man's head. He cried out and fell down on one knee. Then a scything blow from the kroot's billhook ripped a chunk out of Nayl's quilted coat. The coat was lined with wire-mail, and severed metal loops and scads of downy quilting shredded into the air. Nayl leapt backwards out of range of the kroot's next swing, doubled round to slam-kick the chequered fighter in the face before he could get to his feet again, and came up facing both the kroot and the recovered game agent as they rushed him together.

Ravenor moved the other away, taking on the nekulli and the bounty hunter in the polished blue battleplate. Ravenor's stave-sword parried three vicious strikes from the man's falchion, two off the blade and one off the handgrip base. The nekulli tried to flank him while he was occupied, but Ravenor broke to his left, swinging the stave-sword round in a two-handed, overhead slice that described an arc of almost three hundred and sixty degrees. The nekulli staggered back, wobbled and collapsed, his throat slit.

With a furious exclamation, the man in plate charged in, hacking with his sword. His skill and speed were both considerable. Ravenor parried and deflected the rain of blows with a fluid, switching combination of single and double-handed grips, rotating the stave-sword like a quarter staff.

Nayl had never tangled with a kroot before, though he'd had sight of them often enough to know what one was. Rumour said they were a mercenary race or a slavekind, serving some technologically advanced species beyond the Imperial fringes, a species that only a few rogue traders had ever encountered. Despite its size – it towered over him – and its odd, jerky movements, it was formidably fast and seemed to possess unerringly acute senses. With its crude billhook, it managed to smash aside every clean stroke he made against it. It stank terribly of musky, rancid sweat. It would have been match enough for him, but he still had the game agent circling in from the right.

The kroot landed another rending blow that ripped into Nayl's armour coat. He staggered backwards, wrongfooted, and the game agent slammed in, his hooksword striking across the side of Nayl's helmet.

Nayl went sprawling. His buckled helmet bounced off his head across the gallery floor.

'Harlon!' Preest yelled. The mistress was no fighter. She was caught, petrified on her carriage, between the two melees.

The kroot pounced forward onto Nayl and chopped his billhook down. Nayl rolled, leaving the tatters of his coat behind, pinned to the gallery deck. He leaped to his feet in time to meet and block the game agent's sword, turning its blade aside with his blade and bringing the end of the long handgrip round and up hard into the agent's face.

Bone broke, blood spurted, and the agent tumbled backwards with a raging curse. But the kroot was surging in at Nayl from behind.

'Nayl! Nayl!' Preest screamed exasperatedly. She jumped off her ornate carriage and aimed the actuator wand at it. It moved away from stationary with a rapid acceleration, hurtling forward half a metre off the floor.

Nayl began to turn at the sound of Preest's voice. He was stripped down to his bodyglove, and that would not withstand a direct hack from the kroot's razor-sharp weapon.

The unmanned lifter carriage, travelling at nearly thirty kilometres an hour, struck the kroot from behind and bowled him over. He tumbled awkwardly, emitting a strangled squawk, and went sprawling. Nayl came in, plunging his stave-sword down, blade-first, and impaled the thrashing avian to the gallery floor.

The kroot went into death spasms, beak clacking and bony limbs beating the ground. The violent motion ripped the stave-sword out of Nayl's hands.

The man in chequered armour, his face a mask of gore, was back on his feet. He hurled himself at Nayl. The man had lost his boarding axe. His hands clenched around Nayl's throat.

Nayl rolled expertly with the force of impact, going down on his back and propelling the man right over him with his legs. The man crashed over into the nearest booth, destroying the meeting table under his weight.

Nayl was back on his feet in a moment, but now he was unarmed. The game agent came towards him, chopping with his hooksword. Nayl could do nothing except dance out of the way of each swing. Behind him, Preest was still shouting, and Ravenor was trading blow for blow with the battle-plated hunter.

He'd been in worse positions, Nayl thought. But right then, he couldn't bring a single one to mind.

KYS DRAGGED ZAEL out into the companionway. He was muttering, sobbing.

'What do you mean, a message? What's the frigging matter with you?' she snapped.

He murmured something.

'What?'

Zael murmured again.

'I can't hear you! What did you say?'

Zael looked up at her. Blood was dribbling from his nostrils. Kys couldn't remember hitting him. Why was his nose bleeding?

'Nove…'

Wary for a moment, and suddenly terribly calm, she pulled him to his feet.

'Nove is your sister. I'm not your sister.'

'I know. She came. She told me.'

'Told you what?' Kys asked.

'It's a trap,' he said. 'It's a trap.'

'OH, GOD-EMPEROR,' said Halstrom abruptly. His tone was enough to make both Thonius and Frauka look up from their latest game.

'What?' Thonius asked tersely.

Halstrom began punching the keyboard rapidly.

'Something's wrong. I've lost contact with the mistress's landing party.'

Thonius got to his feet. Frauka lit another lho-stick.

'Bad transmission,' the blunter said, carelessly.

'No, no,' said Halstrom. 'We're being blocked.'

'Are you sure?' Thonius said, leaning in over Halstrom's shoulder.

'No, I'm not,' Halstrom said. He depressed another few keys. Nothing happened. 'Bridge controls just went off-line,' he said.

'That's impossible!' Thonius cried. He was nursing his bound-up limb with his free hand, as if it was suddenly giving him pain. 'You've made a mistake.'

'I assure you, interrogator, I have not,' Halstrom began. 'Primary controls are locked out. The entire system is–'

'Who the hell's that?' Thonius said sharply. He was looking at the hololith displays that showed the feeds from the pict-sources overlooking the jetty. A dozen figures were marching down the jetty towards the *Hinterlight's* airgate. They were uniformly tall, and hidden under hooded storm coats. Four of them were paired off to share the burden of two long, and clearly heavy, pannier crates.

'Seal the airgate!' Thonius hissed.

'I can't!' Halstrom replied. 'We're locked out!'

The main hatch onto the bridge rattled open behind them. Madsen strode on deck, escorted by her two Ministry colleagues.

'What is going on?' she asked.

Halstrom began to rise from his throne. 'Mamzel Madsen, you're not permitted up here–' he began.

'Oh, that's right,' she said. Her arm came up and a snub-nosed automatic pistol was suddenly aiming directly at Halstrom's forehead.

'Sit,' she ordered.

Thonius tried to run. Ahenobarb wheeled around and landed a monstrous punch that sent Thonius tumbling across the deck.

'Oh, f–!' started Frauka, dropping his lho-stick. Madsen turned casually and shot him.

The raw boom of the gunshot made Halstrom flinch. Frauka looked down in surprise at the bloodstain soaking out across his shirt, and then toppled backwards over the arm of his seat.

Kinsky, his face a malicious grin, walked up to Halstrom.

'Sit, she said,' he laughed.

Halstrom sat, feeling his legs going weak.

'Y-you can't do this…' he mumbled.

Ahenobarb was carrying a kitbag over his shoulder. He dropped it to the deck, unfastened it and pulled out a metal object that looked for all the world like a limpet-mine.

He twisted the setting dial, and a red indicator light began to wink on its surface. It was a psionic nullifier unit, extremely high powered, with a mag-clamp built into its base.

Ahenobarb strode over to Ravenor's chair, slammed the device down onto its sleek casing, and locked it into place.

Preest was still shouting. *Give it a rest, woman,* Nayl thought. *It's not doing any good.* He leapt sideways from the game agent's darting sword, trying to draw him round so he could grab one of the fallen weapons. Even the kroot's frigging billhook would do.

The game-agent was smarter than that. He kept pressing in, driving Nayl towards the gallery wall.

Preest was looking back at Ravenor/Mathuin. The whirling stave-sword was slowly getting the better of the battleplated man's falchion. A swing, a strike, a brittle flare of sparks.

'For Throne's sake, Ravenor!' she yelled. 'We have to–'

Ravenor suddenly staggered. Was he hit? She hadn't seen him take a hit. Why was he–

Ravenor fell flat on his face. Horrified, Preest couldn't rid her mind of the simple cliché... *like a puppet when the strings are cut.*

The game agent aimed the tip of his hooksword at Nayl. 'Time to surrender, I believe,' he said.

'Oh, I can go all night,' Nayl panted.

'I'm sure. But can they?'

Nayl looked around. Ravenor was face down on the ground, still, dead. The man in the polished blue battle-plate now had his falchion to Preest's throat.

At last, she had stopped yelling. Her eyes were wide, blinking, wet with frightened tears, staring right at him.

'Fine,' said Nayl, raising his hands. 'Fine!'

PART THREE

Lost with all Hands

ONE

The bulkhead glow-globes and recessed lumin panels began to go out. All along the corridor, they dimmed to black. Then the background whir of the atmosphere processors began to fade too. In a few seconds, the air became warm and still.

'Come with me,' Kys said.

Zael followed. He didn't make a sound, as if he didn't *dare* make a sound. That was good. The last thing she needed was a freaking-out idiot.

She went by touch along through the humid dark. The last psi-taste she had felt had been Ravenor… or rather the sudden, abject lack of Ravenor. Kys hadn't realised how much she was usually aware of his presence when he was around. Like a tinitus, like a hum at the back of her skull.

Twenty seconds ago, it had just gone away. As if a switch had been thrown.

Had he suddenly left the *Hinterlight*? That seemed unlikely. He'd have told her, surely? Was he dead? She hoped that was unlikely too. The abrupt loss of contact had been pretty much simultaneous with the sudden cessation of ship systems. Something had gone wrong. And it didn't take a genius to realise the bridge was not the place to go.

It's a trap. Yeah, right.

Groping along in the darkness, feeling for shapes and obstructions with her telekinesis and leading Zael by the hand, Kys suddenly heard a deep, metallic slunk. The ship's internal mag-locks had just disengaged. Invisibly in the blackness around her, she heard all the doors and hatches open. What next? Was A-g going to cut off?

+Thonius?+ she tried.

Nothing.

+Ravenor?+

'No one's listening, are they?' Zael said.

'I'm not so sure of that,' Kys said.

They both jumped as emergency power cut in, flooding the hallway with a cold, green auxiliary glow. Secondary air pumps began to wheeze and stir some breeze back into the atmosphere.

Kys blinked to get used to the new, chilly gloom.

It's a trap.

'What did you mean?' she asked Zael. Wide-eyed, he looked at her and shrugged. 'Nove said it was a trap. We were going into a trap. I think that Kinsky is part of it.'

'Shit,' Kys said. If she'd had her way, those bastards would be dead now. Maybe Ravenor would listen to her next time.

Next time. Ho *ho*.

She wasn't going to die like this. Not if she could help it. She had one trump up her sleeve.

'Zael? Zael, what else did your sister tell you?'

The boy began to cry.

'Stop snivelling, this is important.'

'She was all mushed up…' Zael sobbed.

Kys crouched down and – though revolted by the contact – hugged the weeping boy to her. 'It's okay, Zael. I mean it. We're going to be okay. I promise you. Nove scared you, I know, but she only came back to warn you. She wants you to live.'

'Does she?'

'Yeah, she does. That's why she tried so hard to reach you. All those dreams.'

Zael sobbed again.

'Come on, Zael. Come on. Tell me what else she said. She wants you to know. She wants me to know.'

Zael pulled away from her and wiped his eyes with both hands.

'It didn't make any sense. Not much of it.'

'I'm sure it didn't,' Kys said, rising and turning away. 'God-Emperor, I could use a weapon.'

'The guy has some.'

'What?'

'The guy has lots.'

She glared at him. 'And the guy is?'

'Nayl,' he said. 'He has lots of weapons in his cabin.'

'Nove told you this?'

Zael chortled through his sniffs. 'No, lady. The guy did.'

Nayl's cabin was a few doors along. Like all the hatches, it was wide open now.

'Stay here,' Kys told Zael, and went inside. The cabin smelled of socks and used bodygloves. 'Wash much, Harlon?' she said aloud.

The cabin was littered with armour, equipment and junk, not to mention dirty laundry. She picked over a few pieces in the gloom, discarding heavy blades and team-portable infantry support weapons. She didn't have time to make a thorough search. On the top of a cabinet, she found a Hostec Livery ten-shot; a decent, rugged autopistol. It was wrapped up in its own holster and shoulder rig. Kys strapped it on, buckled the rig about her bust, and drew the auto to check its load. Fat to the max. Nine in the clip and one in the pipe. The loops of the rig supported three more loaded clips.

Kys put the pistol away in its sheath and walked towards the doorway. On the way, she saw a flanged boline lying on a shelf. She scooped it up and, dagger in hand, reached the door.

Zael was cowering in the door frame.

'Zael?'

'Yes?'

'What else did Nove tell you?'

Zael started to cry again. 'She said... she said they would be coming in through the front door...'

THE AIR GATE was wide open. Feaver Skoh smiled as he marched in off the jetty, pulling back his hood.

'Let's go,' he said to his men. They followed in behind him, stripping off their hoods and storm coats and setting down the crates.

His coat off and his tall, thick-set physique revealed in its armoured glove, Skoh adjusted his microbead earpiece into place. Behind him, his trackers were opening the pannier crates.

'This is Skoh. Come back.'

A crackle. 'This is Madsen. Welcome aboard.'

'What's the situation, Mamzel Madsen?' Skoh asked.

Crackle. 'Bridge is locked down, Skoh. Ravenor is tanked and out of the game. Your brother reports he has all three of the landing party prisoner. Just need you to sweep the decks and round up the crew.'

'Read that. Numbers?'

One of Skoh's men slid the custom long-las out of a crate and tossed it to Skoh. Skoh caught it neatly and armed the weapon.

Crackle. 'We estimate forty-nine. Mostly deck hands and juniors. Be sure to round up the Navigator. We reckon the inquisitor's staff members Kys and Swole are both aboard. Both female. Kys is a telekine. Swole is an acrobat. Neither should give you much trouble.'

'Got that, Madsen. Piece of cake. Lock up the gate and move us off. Skoh out.'

Skoh looked round at his eleven-man team. They were all game hunters, experienced men from Skoh's family business. All of them, now the storm coats had been shed, were revealed to be thick-set brutes in various types of camo-armour. Some carried long-las, some autocannons. All of them, like their master, festooned their armour with trophy teeth and scalps.

The outer hatch of the airgate slammed shut behind them. Then the inner skin closed.

'Let's move,' said Skoh, leading them off into the *Hinterlight's* interior.

Hidden behind a bulkhead, Kys and Zael watched them thunder past 'Right, not that way...' she said.

'NO,' SAID ELMAN Halstrom.

'No?' echoed Lusinda Madsen. She poked her weapon against the side of Halstrom's temple and cocked it.

'I think I was clear. I will not obey your orders.'

'Really? Look, Mr Halstrom... you did see what I did to Frauka?'

'Vividly. But I will not assist you.'

Madsen smiled. 'You really don't have much of a choice, Halstrom. It's been a lovely long voyage, long enough for me to penetrate your ship's systems and encode them to my countermand. It's not been easy, I grant you that. Your mistress, and Ravenor... have made the *Hinterlight's* systems ingeniously complex. But that's why the Ministry employs me. I can shut the ship down,

I can start it up. Now sit down, Halstrom, and pilot this thing.'

'No,' Halstrom said.

Madsen looked across at Kinsky.

'Do it.'

Kinsky swayed and fell. Ahenobarb caught him before he hit the deck and lowered him into the second helmsman's throne.

Halstrom stiffened suddenly, and whimpered. Then he sat down in the command throne and started punching keys. The main systems came back to life.

'Commencing undock procedure,' he said, in a curiously flat voice. 'Thrusters live. Helm active. Disengaging airgate clamps.'

'Soon as we're clear,' Madsen said, 'head for the sun.'

'ARE YOU ALL right, Gideon?' Preest whispered.

Mathuin glanced round at her. He was still very woozy, leaning against the gallery wall just to remain upright.

'Yes,' he replied. 'But it's Zeph. Ravenor's not waring me any more. He just... vanished. Like he was torn out of me. Never known a ride to be that tough.'

'Shut up!' instructed the bounty hunter in the blue battleplate. His angular visor was still closed, and his voice came out as a vox-distort through a helmet speaker. He finished securing the set of mag-cuffs around Nayl's wrists. Mathuin and Preest were already bound.

The man in the chequered leather armour stood nearby, watching them. His broken nose was still bleeding, and his face was beginning to swell and discolour. He kept looking venomously at Nayl.

Nearby, the game agent was talking to two Vigilants as more of the Order removed the bodies. The agent was making some kind of formal representation to excuse the fight and express appreciation for the Vigilants' tolerance.

He handed over a bag of coins to pay for material damages. The Vigilants bowed briefly and began to disperse, taking the bodies with them. Tenders arrived to scrub the floor.

The game agent walked over to join his comrades and the trio of captives. He was talking on a compact vox.

'It's Skoh,' they heard him say. 'Power up, we're coming down.'

'Understood.'

The game agent eyed the three of them. 'They all secure, Verlayn?'

'Yes,' replied the man in blue armour, making a tilting nod with his sharp-featured helm.

'You've frisked them too? No multi-keys, hold-outs, concealed?'

'I've frisked them, Skoh,' Verlayn replied, sounding a little piqued that his expertise was being questioned.

'Yeah, well it pays to be careful. Those two–' Skoh indicated Mathuin and Nayl, 'in particular.'

'When the time comes,' the man in chequered armour growled, 'he's mine.' He was still staring at Nayl.

'We'll see about that, Gorgi,' Skoh said.

'Promise it, Fernan! Bastard broke my face!'

'I said we'll see,' replied Fernan Skoh firmly. 'It's my brother's call. You ask him. He might give you the bastard as a treat. Now let's start moving.'

Verlayn gestured with his blade, and the prisoners began to walk. Skoh and Gorgi fell in step behind them.

THEY WALKED THEM along to the far end of the emptied gallery, and then down a main stair onto a more populated level. Heads turned to watch them go by, but they were given a wide berth.

From a gallery on the far side of the salon, Kara got a good view of them. She hurried along the rail, moving on a parallel course, keeping them in sight. They reached another stairhead, and began to descend again.

Kara stepped back from the rail. She tried her compact vox again, but the channel was dead. Something had happened to the ship too.

She slipped on through the crowd, barely breaking step to lift a folded storm coat off a booth bench as she went by. The owner, deep into negotiation with a business partner and even deeper into a bottle of joiliq, didn't even notice it go.

Pulling the coat on, Kara reached the nearest staircase and hurried down through the crowd as fast as she dared without drawing attention to herself.

THE DECK PLATING shivered again. Then another deep boom rolled through the ship.

'We're moving,' Zael muttered.

'Yeah, we are.'

'Was that like that warp thing? Are we at warp?'

'Translation? No,' said Kys. 'Way too early. That's mag-locks uncoupling. Mooring lines detaching. We're barely rolling yet.'

'What are we going to do?' Zael asked.

Now that was a frigging good question.

She started to speak, but another loud boom echoed down the companionway.

'More mag-locks?' Zael asked hopefully.

'No,' she said, grabbing him by the wrist and starting to run. 'That was gunfire.'

More ominous echoes resounded behind them. They ran down the hallway, across a through-deck junction, and on into the ship's servitor bay. It was a large, long chamber with an oily, stained floor. Along each wall, dormant servitors rested in restraining cradles, most of them wired up to recharge transformers in the bulkheads behind them. In the cold green half-light, the rows of frozen, semi-human, semi-augmetic slave units seemed eerie and macabre. They'd all been shut down at a primary level. Red deactivation runes shone on every cradle.

Kys and the boy edged into the chamber. Like the double blast hatch they had entered through, the exit at the far end was locked open. Kys felt her way forward with her telekinesis, sensing the sidebays full of servicing units and tool racks, the dangling hooks and clamps of the overhead maintenance crane-tracks. Hanging chains swung gently in the slight through-breeze.

She felt – then heard – footsteps coming up behind them, running fast. Somehow, Zael seemed to sense them even before Kys, and he pulled at her hand. They moved to the side, off the open deck space in the middle of the chamber, and slid in between cradle racks until they were crouched and hidden in the deep shadows between a heavy monotask unit and the chamber wall.

+Not a sound,+ she nudged.

Zael nodded.

The ringing footsteps came closer and from their hiding place they watched as a man ran into the servitor bay. Kys recognised him. It was one of the junior enginarium adepts... Soben, was it? Sarben?

He was out of breath and very agitated. He glanced about frantically, and then clambered in behind the servitor cradles on the far side of the bay.

Kys wanted to call out to him... even mind-nudge... but there was no time.

Making a low buzz like an angry insect, a cyber-drone flew in through the hatchway. It was travelling at head-height, and as soon as it was in the bay, it decelerated and began to hover gently along, as if sniffing the air.

The drone was small. It had been built into the polished skull of some deer or grazer. The red glow of motion-tracker systems shone from its eye sockets. Under the base of the occipital bone, the drone's tiny lift motor whirred and pulsed.

One of Skoh's huntsmen came into the bay after it. Despite his heavy boots and thick camo-armour, he made no sound. He carried a large calibre autorifle in a confident, assured grip.

The drone drifted ahead of him, whirring and cycling. The hunter, his weapon braced in one hand, bent down and began peering under the servitor cradles near the hatch.

The drone passed the place where the adept had hidden himself and floated on, about to draw level with Kys and Zael. She felt the boy go rigid with fear.

Suddenly, the drone turned and snapped backwards, accelerating round in a wide arc. The hunter was up and running forward. The drone flew in behind the cradles on the far side of the bay and locked onto the cowering crewman.

The adept started to run, breaking cover to flee along the space between the cradles and the wall. The drone zoomed after him. Soben let out a cry and plunged out between two hoist cradles into the open to escape it.

The autogun boomed. Soben flew backwards through the air with a violent lurch and smashed down onto the decking.

The hunter approached the body. His drone re-emerged and flew along at his side. The adept was dead, but the hunter put another round through his head, point blank, just to be sure. Like a game-kill.

The calculated barbarity of the second shot made Zael wince involuntarily.

The drone immediately rotated in mid-air and stared its dull red stare right in their direction.

Instinctively, Kys lashed out with her telekinesis and swung together several of the hooks and lifting chains dangling from the ceiling.

The drone switched round again at the sound, and the hunter wheeled, firing another shot up into the roofspace. He stood for a moment, weapon still aimed, watching the chains and clamps rattling and swinging.

Then he lowered his weapon and headed out through the hatch with the drone at his shoulder.

FERNAN SKOH LED his captives out into an echoing stone vault in the lower levels of the Reach bastion. It was one of the hangar docks for shuttles and lifters ferrying to and fro from the starships anchored out over the Lagoon. A big, dirty-black bulk lifter sat on the apron, its thrust-drive already lit. The side ramp was open.

The mouth of the vault was open to space. Void-shields kept the atmosphere in, but the huge archway afforded them all a panoramic view out over the docks and quays towards the luminous white expanse of the Lagoon.

Outside, the sky was rippling with flame. Though not yet at its full might, the solar violence of Firetide was startling to behold.

'Emperor damn it...' Preest said suddenly.

'Shut up!' Verlayn spat.

Nayl and Mathuin followed Preest's gaze and saw what she had seen. Several kilometres away to their west, a starship was gently clearing its void-dock as it departed the Reach.

It was unmistakably the *Hinterlight*.

'On board, now,' Skoh ordered, and pushed them up the ramp.

KARA WATCHED THEM as they boarded the lifter. A hooter was sounding, indicating the hangar vault should be cleared promptly. Interior hatches and field-protected doorways were already sealing. Processors were beginning to pump the air out. In less than five minutes, the void shields would disengage and open the vault to space, allowing the lifter to take off.

Kara watched the last of the hangar personnel filing out. If she remained in the vault, she would die. But this was her last chance to stay in the game. This was quite possibly everybody's last chance.

Though the hefty bulk lifter occupied the main space of the vault, ancient stone-cut stairs and ramps led up to secondary platform blocks overhead where small craft were berthed. She ran up four flights, and arrived on a wide stone shelf near the roof of the vault where two compact prospector pods were seated in magnetic clamps as they underwent automated refuelling from an energy bowser bolted to the chamber wall. Kara went to the edge of the shelf. She could already feel the air thinning and the pressure dropping. Below her, the lifter hulk was powering its thrusters up to ready. Its side ramp had sealed.

Kara ran to one of the pods and wrenched the hatch open. Nothing. She tried the other. In a storage compartment behind the operator's seat, she found a shabby old vac-suit, worn and battered. The breather unit switched on into life at the second try. Its luminous dial showed about thirty per cent capacity. What was that? An hour? Ninety minutes if the suit had been well maintained. *Well maintained, my arse,* Kara thought. It clearly hadn't. Maybe the unit would give her as little as thirty minutes. Which wouldn't be anything like enough.

There wasn't even a way of telling if the suit had been compromised. Maybe it had been slung behind the seat because it had a tear or a puncture. Or a holed inner glove. Or a perforated throat seal. Or a faulty pump. Or bled-to-hopeless batteries.

Kara stripped off her borrowed storm coat and began unfastening the suit's corroded side clasps. She'd soon find out.

THE BUZZER SOUNDED one last time, barely audible over the mounting drone of the bulk lifter's engines. Deck lamps around the apron's edge were pulsing and flashing.

Then the vault's void-shields disengaged. There was a great swirl of dust as the vault's vestigial atmosphere rushed out, taking all sound with it.

Suddenly silent, its thruster jets blazing, the bulk lifter rose up off the stone apron and began to climb slowly, sedately out of the vault.

Pitted and rusted, the rough surfaces of its upper hull slid slowly past under the stone shelf.

A single figure, the firelight flashing off its visor for a second, leapt off the shelf and fell away, arms outstretched, tiny, towards the massive vehicle moving out below.

TWO

The violent combustions and flares of Firetide lit up the whole sky as if the entire galaxy was burning. The flickering brilliance cast strange, jumping shadows from the bastion and its surrounding peaks out across the dust of the Lagoon, which now looked yellow in the changing light.

Still only moving at a low, coasting speed, the *Hinterlight* moved well clear of the Reach's void-dock area and soared out over the brilliance of the Lagoon, passing other ships resting at low-anchor. Astern, but moving much faster and accelerating on seventy-five per cent thrust, the bulk lifter left the hangar in the cliff-like wall of the bastion and gave chase. The distance between the vessels began to close.

On the *Hinterlight's* bridge, Madsen settled into the primary helm position beside the central command throne from which Halstrom was running the ship. A particularly brilliant solar surge caused the main pict-source displays to distort and fizzle. Madsen winced at the glare and adjusted down the display resolution to dim the effects.

'All right?' she asked Halstrom.

Halstrom's brow was furrowed, as if he was concentrating hard. Every few moments the muscles of his face gave a tic or a little spasm.

'Kinsky?' she repeated. 'Everything all right?'

'Yes,' Halstrom's voice replied, flat and dead. 'He's fighting me, that's all. Every step of the way.' Kinsky's body lay limp in the chair of the secondary helm station behind them. An unfinished game of regicide glowed on that station's display screen.

Kinsky's mind was inside Halstrom's, forcing the *Hinterlight's* first officer to pilot the vessel. Kinsky was a terribly powerful active psyker, but he had nothing like Ravenor's finesse or training. He could not ware subjects, he'd never developed the technique. But he could get inside their heads, and essentially hijack them. None of Madsen's team had decent shipmastering skills, so Kinsky was coercing Halstrom to use his expertise. It was difficult. Halstrom was resisting. Kinsky couldn't apply too much pressure for fear of burning out the shipman's mind altogether. It was a frustratingly difficult, painstaking process.

Frustrating for Mamzel Madsen too. She was a first class tech-adept and code writer, but she had zero helm training. She was beginning to wish they'd brought a pilot too. She had assumed that a gun to the head of Halstrom or Preest would be incentive enough when the time came. Now just driving the *Hinterlight* was occupying all of Kinsky's mind, when he could be put to good use elsewhere.

Ahenobarb stood behind Kinsky's recumbent form, watching over him as he always did. Every now and then he cast a look in the direction of Thonius. Thonius had recovered consciousness but remained where he had fallen, gazing wretchedly at the interlopers. A huge bruise from Ahenobarb's fist blotched the right side of his face.

Thonius was desperate to act, but quite at a loss to know how. He was unarmed and weak, and the fall had badly jarred his damaged arm. Pain was throbbing through it so acutely he had to keep blinking tears away. Every time he moved even slightly, Ahenobarb or Madsen looked his way. He doubted he'd even manage to sit up without them noticing. And if he did…

Thonius looked at Frauka, flat on his back on the deck beside Kinsky's chair. The blood stain across the front of his shirt was huge and dark, and a pool of blood was spreading wide across the deck under his torso. Frauka had never been a friend really, but he'd been alright. No one deserved that kind of ruthless demise.

For the umpteenth time, Thonius cast a look at Ravenor's inert chair. He gazed at the psionic nullifier unit mag-clamped like a giant barnacle to the front of the chair's casing, wishing it, willing it to fall off or deactivate. Mentally, he turned over every possible idea he could think of for removing the nullifier. Every scenario ended with him dead on the bridge floor.

Aching pain was weakening him. Thonius began to wonder if he was simply not brave enough. He'd always thought of himself as brave, until the heathen moot on Flint. Look how bravery had abandoned him there. He fought off the memory. He was an agent of the Throne. Bravery was expected of him. Maybe he should just get up and have a go, damn the consequences.

Then he thought of Halstrom. Halstrom had been brave. He'd refused to cooperate, even with Madsen's gun at his head. And look how much good his bravery had accomplished.

A vox-chime sounded, and Madsen looked to her console.

'*Hinterlight*, go,' she said.

'Lifter. We're inbound for rendezvous. Request you keep your course and speed and open your hangar.'

'Stand by, lifter,' Madsen said. She looked over at Halstrom. 'You hear that?'

'Yes,' said Kinsky via Halstrom's leaden, weighted voice. His fingers moved heavily across the command console keys. 'I'll hold this vector steady. Open the port hangar and light the guide paths.'

'Good,' Madsen said. She turned back to her console and tapped in a series of instructions. 'Lifter? This is *Hinterlight*.'

'Read you, *Hinterlight*.'

'Port hangar is opening. Link your transponder to the guide signal and get aboard. Make it quick, please.'

'Understood,' the vox answered, distorting a little in time to a brighter than average solar flare outside.

'You've got them all?' Madsen asked.

'All three.'

'Soon as you're aboard, have them taken to the light cargo holds on four.'

'Light cargo holds on deck four, got it.'

'And get the lifter prepped for turnaround. We're on a clock here.'

'Understood, *Hinterlight*. Lifter out.'

Madsen closed the channel and lit up an auspex display that showed a small, blinking rune closing in on the port side of the larger icon that represented the *Hinterlight*.

'They're coming in,' she said.

'I know,' Halstrom said, with effort.

There was another vox-chime, but it was from the internal intercom system.

'Madsen? It's Skoh. We've finished our sweep. Got most of them.'

'What does "most of them" mean, Mr Skoh?' Madsen replied, acidly.

'Forty-six persons, including the Navigator. No sign of the females you mentioned.'

'I'm coming down,' Madsen said. She got to her feet and looked at Ahenobarb. 'Watch him,' she ordered, indicating both Kinsky and Halstrom.

'Always,' the giant answered.

Madsen looked at Thonius and gestured with her pistol. 'On your feet, interrogator. Time to join the others.'

Thonius got up slowly. It was a painful process.

'Madsen?' Halstrom asked without looking round. He was still staring intently at the readout displays, his fingers moving with over-careful precision on the controls.

'What?'

'Take him with you,' Halstrom replied, gesturing at Ravenor's chair with one hand. 'I don't want him here. Makes me uneasy.'

'Over here,' Madsen snarled at Thonius. He limped over. 'Disengage him and bring him.'

Thonius nodded. He crouched down and disconnected the psi-booster cables from Ravenor's chair and closed the access ports. Then he reached under the chair body and deactivated the mag-clamps that held it fast to the deck. Even with one hand, it wasn't difficult to push the chair around on its frictionless grav plates.

For a moment, Thonius looked at the nullifier clamped to the chair's body. It was within reach. How did it detach? Could he do it with one hand, with a simple tug? Could he do it before they realised? Was he brave enough?

'Don't even think about it,' Madsen said. She was staring at him. Mocking. She knew exactly how brave he was.

And that was not remotely enough.

* * *

The hold space of the bulk lifter was a battered, worn, poorly-lit box of metal, its floor and walls scarred and dented by centuries of cargo handling. Nayl, Mathuin and Preest sat in one corner against the wall in a silent huddle, watched over by Verlayn and Gorgi. Free from the weapon restrictions of Bonner's Reach, Verlayn was covering them with a laspistol, and Gorgi had an autosnub. Gorgi had stopped fiddling with his damaged face, and was now scrubbing petulantly at the bloodstains down the front of his chequered armour with a cloth.

'Here's an idea... give it a rest,' said Verlayn from behind his helmet.

'Here's another... shut the frig up,' Gorgi replied.

In the aft portion of the hold, blast hatches led through to the drive chambers. Forward, a flight of metal-mesh steps led up to an open hatch through which they could just see a cockpit area, lit by instrumentation. There were two flight crewmen up there, and Fernan Skoh sat at the top of the steps behind them, loading a bolt pistol.

The ride was rough. Every few seconds, the lifter lurched or shivered. Fragments of metal junk and pieces of cargo packing rolled and skittered back and forth across the oil-stained hold floor.

'Coming up on it now, Fernan,' Nayl heard one of the flight crew call.

Skoh got up and leaned in through the flight deck hatch. He'd holstered his bolt pistol and was holding on to the hatch frame with both hands as the buffeting and jarring increased.

'We're riding something's mag-stream,' Preest whispered to Nayl.

'Shut the frig up,' Gorgi said, aiming his snub at her.

Skoh was talking to the flight crew. Nayl strained to hear.

'...as soon as we're down. You understand? Full spec turnaround and repower. I want this bird ready to fly again in thirty minutes.'

'No problem,' said one of the crewmen.

'Better not be,' said Skoh, turning and sitting down again on the top step. 'This is our ticket out when that hulk starts its death dive.'

THE BLAZE OF Firetide was now approaching its maximum burn. The whole sky was writhing with incandescent flame patterns and scorching blooms of light.

Running lights blinking, the bulk lifter edged in. It was a big craft, but entirely dwarfed by the spaceship it was closing upon. Moving sedately, the *Hinterlight* was a colossal form ahead of it.

Beneath them, the white dust of the Lagoon displayed their comparative shadows, big and small, both jumping and twisting in the light of the overhead storm. The crater rim was coming up, a vast, jagged curtain of sheer black mountains. At their current rate, they would clear the Lagoon in four minutes.

The bulk lifter sped in closer, dropping thrust to match the *Hinterlight's* pace. The massive void-hatches of the *Hinterlight's* port hangar bay were open, and strobing guide lights lit up the gaping mouth.

Expertly, the bulk lifter shimmied in closer, and then banked around on a flurry of attitude jets, hard burning, and entered the bay.

The void-doors began to shut.

The *Hinterlight* turned its nose and began to climb in a slow, westward turn. It passed over the ramparts of the crater wall, and then its massive thrust-tunnels fired in a great sheet of light and it began to power up and away into the illuminated heavens.

* * *

'WE'RE HEADING INTO space,' Zael said.

Kys stopped and turned round to look at him. 'How could you know that?' she asked. Until less than a month before, the boy had never even seen a spaceship. He didn't understand how they worked. He couldn't recognise the tremor of translation if it jumped up and bit him.

'I just know,' he said. He tapped his forehead.

'Nove tell you?'

He shuddered. 'No. Well, maybe. Not in person. I just keep hearing things.'

'Like what?' Kys asked.

'Like... *gravity well exit.*'

How would he know a phrase like that, Kys wondered? She waved him on. The low-deck corridor ahead was gloomy and creaking as the ship's mighty frame responded to the vast influence of gravity.

'Where are we going?' Zael asked.

'Enginarium,' she replied. 'If we can't stop the bastards taking this ship, we can maybe stop them using it.'

Kys raised the pistol she'd borrowed from Nayl's cabin and led the way down the darkened tunnel.

AHENOBARB KNELT DOWN and stroked Kinsky's limp face. He produced a cloth from his belt and dabbed away the perspiration from his partner's brow.

'You're sweating,' he remarked.

'The bastard's making it hard for me,' Halstrom replied from the throne behind Ahenobarb. 'Once we're done with this, I'll kill the frigger myself.'

'But you're okay?' Ahenobarb asked. He could hear Halstrom's fingers clattering over the main command controls.

'Yes. We're clear now. Commencing climb into gravity well exit.'

* * *

THE LIGHT CARGO holds were towards the bow section of deck four. The *Hinterlight* had two principal holds, a legacy to its days as a trader, to accommodate gross cargo. But often, a free trader was required to ship smaller masses of high-cost goods – fine wines, artworks, precious stones. The small cargo holds were built for that purpose, a series of armoured chambers that could be locked off, sealed and, if necessary, environment controlled individually.

Feaver Skoh's hunters had rounded the crew of the *Hinterlight* into small cargo five. The entry hatch was still open, and two of the huntsmen stood sentry at the doorway. Inside, thirty-eight terrified personnel were huddled together.

Skoh himself was standing in the gangway outside when Madsen arrived. The rest of his gang loitered around, leaning against walls, smoking lhos, chatting. Skoh was talking to Duboe. He'd just released the cavae master from the *Hinterlight's* holding cells.

Duboe was thin and filthy. There was a wild look in his eyes, and he was compulsively rubbing his wrists, free from their shackles for the first time in a long while.

They looked round as Madsen approached. She was walking behind Thonius, who was pushing Ravenor's chair. Thonius was sweating and pale. Though frictionless, the chair had been hard to manoeuvre and direct with just one hand after all. He was shaking and exhausted.

Duboe slid past Skoh and strode towards Madsen.

'You bitch!' he yelled into her face. 'You frigging bitch! You knucked up my mind!'

Madsen recoiled with distaste from Duboe's wretched breath.

'Get over it, Mr Duboe,' she admonished. 'It was necessary.'

'Necessary? Frigging necessary?'

'That's enough, Duboe...' Skoh said as he approached.

'No!' Duboe cried. 'Bad enough that this freak mind-frigged me every day!' He kicked the side of Ravenor's inert chair. Thonius winced. 'No, she and Kinsky came at me too. They fried my mind, Skoh! Fried my frigging mind!'

Skoh looked at Madsen. She met his stare. 'You know what's at stake here, Mr Skoh. We tolerate your little commerce on the side. Greedy? Maybe... frig, we pay you handsomely enough. But I guess the flects are too choice an income source for the likes of you to ignore.'

'The likes of me?' Skoh said quietly.

Madsen gave him a withering look. 'Contract thirteen is all that matters. We pay you well for your services. More than enough to cover the risks involved.'

'The risks are great, Mamzel,' Skoh said. 'Running a Fleet blockade...'

'Oh, tell it to someone who cares!' Madsen snapped. 'We're only here today, in this fix, because your hungry little sideline in flects almost gave the game away!'

Skoh shrugged and looked at the deck. Madsen turned to face the edgy Duboe. 'And for what it's worth, Mr Duboe... of course we screwed with your mind. Yours, Siskind's, every other bastard who mattered. Those were my orders, that's what I ensured Kinsky did. We had to make sure none of you idiots gave the game away to the frigging Inquisition. Ravenor is a bastard, a blade-sharp bastard. Any hint of the truth, and he'd have been on us. We had to be sure that anything he learned from mind-searches just drove him further and further into this trap.'

Duboe glowered at her, but nodded.

'No one wants the frigging Inquisition on his back,' Skoh conceded. He smiled at Madsen. 'And my congratulations, Mamzel. It's a fine trap you've devised, beautifully executed. Taking the bastard's team down on Eustis would have created a terrible problem. Questions, follow-up investigations... But if his ship goes missing out here, out in Lucky Space, lost with all hands...'

'I'm glad you appreciate the finer points,' Madsen said.

'You still frigged up my mind,' growled Duboe.

Skoh turned and slammed Duboe up against the wall.

'Live with it,' Skoh said into Duboe's face. 'If you'd run your end of the op better, this would never had been necessary.'

Skoh looked over at Thonius and the chair.

'Who's that?' he asked.

'Ravenor himself,' Madsen replied. 'And one of his lackeys.'

Skoh walked over to Ravenor's chair. He knelt down and embraced its hull, laying his head against it. 'You hear me? You hear me in there, you little crippled bastard? You've cost us plenty. You're going to die for that. You and all your frigging crew. All your friends. You're going to die in the heart of the local sun. And when it happens, they're all going to be as helpless and frigging useless as you.'

He rose, and waved over two of his hunters. 'Put the cripple in a hold all on his own,' he said. The hunters began to steer Ravenor's chair down the gangway into one of the empty holds. Skoh grabbed Thonius by the shoulder. 'You're going in with the others,' he said, and frog-marched him into small cargo five.

He kicked Thonius as they reached the door, and Thonius went sprawling onto the small hold's deck. He screamed in pain.

Madsen joined Skoh at the hatchway.

'Forty-six, you reckon?' she asked.

'All told, Mamzel Madsen. Eight fatalities during the sweep. Some knucks don't know when it's a good idea to surrender.'

Madsen scanned the miserable faces in the hold. 'I don't see Kys or Swole. Or, for that matter, the boy.'

'We weren't told about a boy,' Skoh said.

'A kid, from Eustis Majoris. His name's Zael. He's not here either.'

'The kills my team made were all adult males...' Skoh began.

'I thought you were meant to be expert huntsmen,' Madsen mocked. 'There are two adult females and a kid loose somewhere on this ship.'

Skoh flinched slightly, his professional pride wounded. He called his men close in a huddle. 'Munchs, Dreko – Guard the prisoners here. The rest of you... section this ship, deck by deck, tight-hunt order. Two women, one boy. I'll give a bonus payment for each head you bring me.'

The nine game hunters nodded and hurried away down the hall. Madsen could hear the zip of las-weapons charging up and the whirr of cyberdrones being launched.

Madsen looked up at Skoh. 'By the way, you're brother's coming aboard just now.'

'He got the others?'

'All three,' Madsen smiled. 'Trap's closed.'

'MR THONIUS? MR Thonius?'

The voice penetrated Carl's dream. It had been a nice dream. He'd been in an up-hive outfitters on Thracian Primaris, being measured for a suit of the most gorgeous plum tarnsey. But the bloody tailors had kept sticking their pins into his right arm.

Stab, stab, stab...

He woke up. Faces peered down at him. One of them was the medicae, Zarjaran.

Thonius woke up fast. He was in the cell. He was a prisoner.

Zarjaran examined his arm. 'You've burst some stitches, Mr Thonius,' he said. 'There is some weeping around the wound, and some tissue tearing.'

Thonius looked around. He saw Magnus, the second helmsman; Cliesters, the enginarium chief; Kobax from the ship's galley; the Navigator Twu, wrapped in a blanket.

They were all frightened. Them and all the others. Scared to death.

They were staring at him because he was the only member of Ravenor's personal cadre to be captured with them.

They were expecting something of him. They were expecting something ridiculous. Like he'd get them out. Like he'd somehow be able to do something amazing and free them all.

'Help me up,' Thonius said. Zarjaran hoisted him a little.

Thonius looked at the open hatchway of the hold. Two of Skoh's huntsmen stood in the frame of it, weapons ready.

What kind of frigging miracle did these people want from him?

He wasn't that brave. He'd never been that brave. He was Carl Thonius. He wasn't a hero at all.

THE PALL OF vapour filling the port hangar began to disperse, and the lumen strips on the interior hatches went green, indicating atmospheric equalisation. The whine of the bulk lifter's thrust drive shrank away into the silence of system shut down.

On the top of the battered lifter, Kara Swole raised her head and slowly unwrapped her arms from around the bars of a lateral stanchion which she'd been clinging on to for the duration of the flight.

She was shaking badly. The old vacsuit had done its job, but only barely. Its insulating sub-layer was poor, and her core temperature had dropped sharply. With trembling fingers, she unsealed the helmet and took it off, her teeth chattering. Her cheeks and lips felt raw with cold.

From below, she heard the lock mechanism disarm on the lifter's side ramp. She pulled off the rest of the thread-bare old suit as quickly as she could. There was no time to warm up, no time to feel sorry for herself.

The compact rucksack she'd been carrying ever since emerging from the crate in the kitchens of the Reach was still with her – she'd strapped it around her belly and fastened the baggy vacsuit up over it. Kneeling, her hand still shaking, she put the rucksack down and peeled open the seam-seal. Inside it, side by side, was a matched brace of Tronsvasse auto-pistols. She'd been carrying them concealed as a back-up for Nayl's team, though given the brutal efficiency of the Vigilants she was glad she hadn't been forced to produce one. She was fond of her hands.

Even if they were shaking like hell now.

She slipped the pistols out and checked the loads. Each handgrip held a clip of thirty caseless rounds.

Below her, with a grating rumble, the lifter's side ramp began to unfold.

First out were two men in dingy flightsuits. They hurried into view on the hangar deck and made their way over to the banks of crew service machinery built into the hangar wall to begin a turnaround prep for the lifter. It seemed to Kara that the lifter wasn't intending to stay long.

'Let's go,' Fernan Skoh said with a nod of his head. Gorgi and Verlayn flanked the three prisoners as they came down the ramp, Skoh at their heels.

'Any time now,' Gorgi muttered to Nayl. 'Soon as Skoh's brother gives me the nod, I'm going to mess you up bad.'

'Really?' said Nayl, without interest.

'Shut up, Gorgi,' Verlayn said.

'You shut up!' Gorgi said. 'I'm gonna take my time and mess this one up real nasty for what he done to my face.'

'What?' asked Nayl. 'Improved it?'

'You bastard!' Gorgi barked.

'Shut up, Gorgi,' Skoh said from behind.

'Yeah, shut up, Gorgi,' Nayl agreed.

Gorgi snapped. He lashed out with his left hand and smacked Nayl hard across the face.

'Gorgi!' Skoh snarled.

But the man already had his autosnub pressed to Nayl's forehead.

'You frigger!' he screamed. Two shots rang out, their sounds magnified by the large chamber. Gorgi's head broke apart in a pink mist and he tumbled backwards like he'd been yanked on a chain.

'Emperor!' Preest shrilled in dismay.

More shots rained down from high above them. Most were aimed at Verlayn, and they dented his battleplate with enough force to knock him down.

Nayl looked round. Up on the back of the lifter Kara Swole was unloading serious fire, an auto in each hand. Mathuin grabbed Preest and pulled her down to shield her. Sprawled, but far from dead, Verlayn blazed back at Kara with his laspistol. Fernan Skoh broke and ran back under the lifter, out of the field of fire. His hands still cuffed, Nayl threw himself after Skoh. He caught up with him beside the lifter's rear port landing gear and felled him from behind with a two-handed smash, his fingers laced together. Skoh went down, and his bolt pistol skittered away across the metal decking.

Firing sideways with both autos, Kara leapt along the length of the lifter's top-side as Verlayn's desperate las-shots sparked and careened off the bodywork around her. The two flight crew over by the hangar wall came running back, pulling autosnubs and adding to the hail of fire coming Kara's way.

Nayl hit Skoh with both fists again, but Skoh rolled and kicked out, snapping Nayl's legs away. With his hands bound, he couldn't compensate his balance and fell badly. Then Skoh was on him, kicking him and bending down to jab in punches. Cursing, Nayl grabbed Skoh's torso armour with his cuffed hands and threw Skoh head-first over him.

Shots dented the hull plating around Kara, and one sliced through the fabric of her bodysuit on her left thigh. Another, one of Verlayn's las-rounds, zipped past less than a hand's breadth from her cheek. With a squeal of alarm, she ducked and widened her arms, firing the weapon in her left hand at Verlayn, and the one in her right at the crewmen. The latter jerked and tumbled over dead. The decking beside Verlayn punctured and holed.

Nayl scrambled up, but the cuffs made him clumsy and Skoh was faster. The game agent threw a punch into Nayl's face that dropped him again, momentarily unconscious. Skoh bent down and picked up his bolt pistol.

The clips in each of Kara's guns were nearly spent. The firefight had only been running for a scant fifteen seconds since the first shot, though it felt like an eternity. She'd been really hosing. She took her fingers off the triggers for a split-second, ignoring the rounds exploding all around her, and took aim to make her last few loads count. She fired the left handgun, a single shot at Verlayn. His polished blue armour had withstood the caseless punishment, but now she hit the left eyepiece of the battleplate's visor. Verlayn's helmet snapped back and he rolled over. Then she turned both guns on the remaining crewman and blew him apart.

'Zeph!' she yelled, and hurled one of her autos into the air towards him.

Nayl came round just as Skoh put a boot on the chain of his cuffs and pinned his arms to the ground. Skoh pressed the muzzle of the bolt pistol into Nayl's left eye socket.

Leaping up off Preest, Mathuin reached upwards with his cuffed hands and caught the spinning autopistol by the grip. He swung it round and shot Fernan Skoh through the heart from twenty metres. Skoh lurched backwards off Nayl, slammed into the lifter's landing leg, and fell on his face.

'Holy frigging Throne...' Preest murmured, dazed and terrified.

Mathuin looked down at the weapon he held. The clip was out. That shot had been the last one in the mag. 'Indeed,' he agreed.

Kara clambered down the side of the lifter. Blood was running from the gash in her thigh. Under the lifter, Nayl rolled Skoh's body over and found the mag-key for the cuffs. He freed himself, picked up Skoh's bolt pistol and limped back to join the others.

Kara jumped off onto the deck and smiled at him. He saw her face was pinched with cold, the lines of her nose and cheekbones florid with sunburn. The vacsuit's faceplate hadn't been up to much either, especially for someone riding a lifter bareback through the Firetide storms.

Nayl embraced her and held her tight for a moment. 'Glad you could make it,' he said into her hair.

'Not the easiest thing I've ever done,' she replied.

They got the cuffs off Preest and Mathuin. Preest gave Kara a hug too. 'I thought we'd left you behind,' she said, her voice brittle with relief. 'I thought we were going to die.'

'Oh, have faith, mistress,' Kara smiled. 'You had Nayl and Mathuin with you, the toughest sons of bitches this side of Macragge. They'd have thought of something.' She looked at the two men, who were busy collecting weapons and ammunition from the bodies. 'Wouldn't you?' she said.

Mathuin shrugged. 'No, I thought we were going to die too.'

'I had a plan,' Nayl said.

'Sure you did,' said Mathuin.

'I did,' Nayl grumbled.

'What? Goad that Gorgi guy into giving you a head-shot?' Mathuin sneered.

'It was a start. I was improvising.'

'Look,' said Kara. 'I don't want to play the doom-sayer… especially as Mathuin has that role covered. But we should book. This lifter was clearly expected. We've post-poned death, not escaped it.'

Preest looked at her. The shipmistress was badly rattled, Kara could see that. This kind of stuff was definitely not what she'd signed up for. It was like Majeskus all over again. The fragile excitement she'd generated in herself at the start of the Reach expedition was evaporating fast. She was a trader, a void-voyager, not a Throne agent.

'It'll be fine,' Kara said, reloading her autos, and felt stupid saying it. Preest just nodded.

'Let's move,' Nayl said. He'd armed himself with Skoh's bolter and Gorgi's autosnub tucked into his belt. Mathuin had taken Verlayn's laspistol. He handed one of the autosnubs the flight crew had been carrying into Preest's hands.

'I don't care for guns,' Preest said.

'Humour me. Just put it in your pocket.'

Pinching the weapon between finger and thumb as if it was a scorpion-ant or a fresh stool, Preest reluctantly dropped it into the deep slash-pocket of her gown.

They left the hangar and slipped down the main access hallway of deck two. A glance told them all auxiliary systems were operating. The cold green light, the feeble air-push.

'My darling's running on back-up,' Preest said.

Nayl nodded. 'It's a certain someone has taken control of the *Hinterlight*. Question is, how do we take it back?'

'Kill 'em all?' Mathuin asked.

'Thanks for that, Zeph,' Kara smiled.

'Actually, that was top of my list of workable plans,' Nayl said.

'We have to–' Preest began, and then stopped. She was scared, shaking. She cleared her throat before continuing. 'We have to assess status,' she said.

She led them away from the main access into a warren of sub-corridors that threaded the space between the primary holds to bow and the enginarium and drive chambers to stern. Progress was easy. All internal doors and hatches were locked open.

'Just down here,' she said.

'What are we looking for?' asked Nayl.

'Diagnostic stations,' Preest said. 'There are about thirty located at various points on the ship. They're for maintenance. Senior personnel can check all aspects of ship's status from any of them.'

They reached a cross-junction in the dim sub-hallways. The diagnostic station was a shielded drum rising out of the deck at the centre of the cross. Preest slid back a cover to reveal the console.

'It needs the ship's master keys to operate it,' she said.

'How do we–' Nayl began.

Preest removed her preposterously dangly earrings. The master keys, Nayl realised, were the main parts of each. She slid the keys into the paired sockets and turned both simultaneously. The console display shivered into life. Peering at the display, Preest began to touch some keys.

'Shit,' she said.

'Shit?' repeated Nayl.

'I see what they're doing,' Preest murmured.

'Which is?' Nayl asked.

'The bastards,' Preest added.

'Which bastards?' Nayl said.

'Damn it, that's clever...'

'What is?' Nayl asked exasperated.

Preest looked at him at last, and pointed at the screen. 'Someone's rewritten the authority codes of my darling ship,' she said. 'Clever, clever, clever. Basically, they've shut down and locked all my darling's primary systems – all of them, from drive and life support right down to lighting – and initialised all the secondary and auxiliary systems in preference. The *Hinterlight* is working on back-up, and that network has been entirely secured.'

'Can you countermand?' Nayl asked.

'No, that's the point. The clever part. This *is* a countermand. It's personally encrypted. Whoever did this was a genius. They've taken over the ship using my own back-door.'

'So, what you're saying... is that we're totally screwed?' Mathuin said.

Preest took a deep breath and removed her keys, shutting the console down. 'No, Mr Mathuin. Nearly screwed, but not totally.'

'Spit it out, mistress,' Kara snapped.

Preest smiled at her. 'My dear, no shipmistress worth her salt, no rogue trader, leaves herself open to this kind of piracy. I have secret, core-level protocols to overwrite this kind of crap. Whoever did this hasn't found those.'

'So, that's good?' Nayl ventured.

'Get me to the bridge and I'll punch in a few codes that will unlock the entire system,' Preest said.

'I'm thinking the bridge is probably not an option at this stage,' Nayl said.

Preest nodded, as if she had expected that answer. 'All right, get me to enginarium basic on deck six. Right down at the stern. Main cogitator is housed under the bridge itself, but there's a redundant secondary cogitation stack concealed behind the principal drive chambers. In case of emergencies, damage to the main cogitators or whatever. I can work my magic from there.'

Nayl nodded. 'Good. Great, in fact. But that's a long march from here.'

Preest shrugged.

'Right,' Nayl said. 'Zeph... get the mistress down to this back-up stack. Can you do that?'

'I can try,' said Mathuin. 'What will you be doing?'

'Me and Kara will be heading upstairs to work to the original plan.'

'Kill 'em all?' Kara asked.

'Kill 'em all,' said Nayl.

RAVENOR HAD BEEN pushed into a small cargo hold forty metres down from the hold containing the rest of the ship's crew. It was dark. The door was sealed. The light on the latched-on nullifier flashed in the gloom.

The hold's hatch opened and green aux-light fell in at a slant. A figure filled the doorway.

'You're a bastard. A frigging bastard...' Duboe said as he shuffled into the hold space. 'You hear me, you frigging bastard? You frigging knuck-wipe? I hope so. I hope you do. This is all 'cause of you.'

Duboe faced the chair. He raised the boarding axe he'd pulled from a wall mount. With both hands, he turned the heavy weapon so the back of the axe-head, the pick, was lowered.

'A good deal, I had,' Duboe burbled. 'A good trade. Then you and your freaks came in to frig it up.'

'You know what?' Duboe asked, as if somehow expecting Ravenor to answer.

'You know what? This is payback time'

Duboe hefted the axe up and slammed it against the chair's hull. Sparks flew. The blow had barely made a scratch on the chair's surface. Duboe struck again and again. Apart from a few very slight scratches, his attacks had made no dent, though they had pushed the frictionless chair across the chamber.

Cursing, Duboe put his foot against the chair and kicked it over against the far side of the hold. It slid away and came to rest, bouncing off the wall.

Duboe ran at it and delivered another massive blow. He began to hack away with the boarding axe, driving the chair against the wall so it couldn't roll away. Chips of paint began to fleck off the chair's chassis, and dents began to appear as Duboe threw blow after unrelenting blow at it.

THREE

The Hinterlight thundered on into the blistering flares of Firetide, its real-space thrusters powering it away from Bonner's Reach. Already, the Reach was just a tiny, tumbling rock behind it. The solar storm had set the void ablaze. Gigantic forks of plasma and photonic energy lashed and slapped the vacship's hull like striking lighting, causing the vessel to buck and shake.

It powered onwards, despite the onslaught, heading towards the unstable star.

Like a phantom, running with shields raised against the storm, a second spaceship closed in behind it.

Madsen and Feaver Skoh strode onto the *Hinterlight's* bridge.

'Who's he?' Skoh asked, gesturing to Ahenobarb.

'Muscle,' Madsen said. She walked over to the command throne and looked at Halstrom. His face was now contorted in a grimace of pain as he operated the helm.

'Are we course-set?' Madsen asked him.

Halstrom looked down at his display with difficulty. 'Not quite. Another fifteen minutes. Then we'll be sliding into the star's gravity well.'

Madsen smiled.

'I'm reading a ship,' Halstrom added. 'Sprint trader, on the auspex, less than one AU aft of us.'

Madsen studied the helm display. She activated the main-beam vox and tuned it to a tight band. 'This is *Hinterlight*. Identify yourself.'

'My good woman,' the vox crackled back, 'this is the *Oktober Country*. Put Feaver on.'

Madsen turned to Skoh and he leaned forward. 'Thekla?'

'Good afternoon to you, Feaver. Everything in place, I trust?'

'Of course. We've got them all locked down and the bastard's ship will soon be heading for the heart of the sun.'

'I am pleased. I'd hate to have to start shooting at you.'

'That won't be called for, Master Thekla,' Skoh said. 'Fifteen minutes and we're done.'

'Excellent, Feaver. I look forward to welcoming you aboard. *Oktober Country* out.'

Skoh straightened up and looked at Madsen. 'All set,' he said.

'Thekla sounds like a live one.'

'He is. But we're set.'

'Known him long?'

Skoh shrugged. 'Sixty, seventy years. A working compact. Thekla's been good to my family.'

Madsen nodded. 'Was it his idea? The flects? Or yours?'

Skoh wiped his mouth with the back of his hand. 'Neither. I think it was Akunin or Vygold. One of the original contractees. Thekla came in later. By then, all of the captains had seen the earnings from flects. We started to carry them every time we took a contract thirteen run. The returns were huge. Better than the Ministry pays us.'

Madsen shook her head, wondering. 'Screw you,' she said.

The vox-chime bleated.

'Madsen. Report.'

'Is Master Skoh there?'

'Yes. Why?'

'Let me speak to Master Skoh,' the voice said.

Skoh walked over to the console. 'Let me,' he said. 'That's Rainfold, one of my crew.'

Madsen shrugged and stepped back.

'Rainfold? This is Skoh. What's the deal?'

There was a long pause. 'Chief, we went down to the hangar deck. Your brother had been a long time bringing the prisoners up.'

'And?'

'Chief, they're all dead.'

'The prisoners?'

'No, chief. Your brother and his crew. All of them. The prisoners are gone.'

Skoh's eyes narrowed.

'Skoh, I'm sorry,' said Madsen, stepping towards him.

'The kills are confirmed?' Skoh said into the vox. Like he was talking about antelopes.

'All confirmed, chief.'

Skoh coughed quietly. He paused a long time and then said, 'Alert all hunt teams. Add the prisoners to your list. Hunt them down and kill them all.'

FIRST THE DRONE went by, then the hunter. The only sound they made was the low buzz of the drone's motor, and that was lost in the background noise of the ship's real-space drive assemblies. The hunter paused for a second, panned his lasrifle around, then carried on down the corridor and disappeared through the next hatch frame.

Kys and Zael emerged from behind some vent ducting. Visibility was poor down in the sub-decks, and the air was hot and dry. They were approaching the main heat sinks for the gravity generators and the corridor was lined with red insulating tiles that looked the colour of meat in the emergency lighting.

Heading towards the stern, they switched left through a low-ceilinged power-convertor chamber. It was even hotter in there, and cakes of dry dust clung to the magnetic vanes of the floor-to-ceiling convertor cylinders. Everything was vibrating slightly, resonating to the throb of the giant drives nearby.

At the far end of the chamber, they came out into another tiled hallway and started to move along it.

'Oh!' Zael said suddenly. Kys glanced behind her and saw the drone rushing towards them at head-height, sensors glowing. Twenty metres behind it down the corridor, the hunter appeared, raising his weapon.

Kys threw Zael down onto the deck and dived flat herself. Two las-rounds whined over them. The drone had also zoomed over them, and was turning back tightly to make another pass. Running forward, the hunter adjusted his aim.

Kys didn't have time to get a decent shot at him. She seized the returning drone with her telekinesis and applied all the force she could. Already rushing back in the direction of the hunter, the drone accelerated and smashed straight into its master's astonished face. The impact knocked him over onto his back.

As soon as she was sure he wasn't going to be getting up again, Kys rose and started hurrying Zael on towards the enginarium.

* * *

'Run,' said Mathuin.

'I don't care for running!' Preest protested.

'You said you didn't care for guns,' Mathuin said, dragging her after him.

'I don't care for either!'

There had been one, maybe two, of Skoh's hunting cadre in the outer enginarium bay, and Mathuin knew they'd been seen. He forced Preest to run across the large maintenance shop that separated the outer bay from their destination, the much larger vault of enginarium basic. The shop was a dirty, stained workspace, cluttered with portable machinery and tool-benches. Cogitators lined one wall, racks of machine parts and cartons of spares the other. There was a split level gallery above them with a lifting hoist.

No way were they going to get all the way to the hatch at the far end before trouble caught up with them. Certainly not if that was what Preest thought 'running' meant. Mathuin skidded to a halt and pushed her down behind a stack of bulk-format battery cells and turned back to face the door they'd entered by.

'Stay down!' he hissed.

Almost at once, a figure appeared in the doorway. Mathuin raised his laspistol and fired off a trio of shots that impacted around the hatch frame and discouraged the man from coming through.

In response, a salvo of rounds from a lasrifle came cracking in from outside the hatch. Mathuin ducked. Most of the shots impacted against tool benches before they reached him. Dislodged tools clattered onto the deck. A couple of shots went right over him and made it clear to the far end of the shop where they branded scorch marks on the wall.

Mathuin swung up and fired again. Again, the hunter in the doorway ducked back. A cyber drone came swooping into the room. Mathuin blew it to pieces in the air.

But the slight distraction had given the hunter time to get a better position in the doorway. And he wasn't alone. His lasrifle licked out a fierce, prolonged blurt of fire that forced Mathuin back into cover and allowed a second hunter to roll in through the hatch.

The las onslaught halted. Mathuin began to lift himself up for a return shot when the second hunter opened up on him from the cover he'd found inside the hatch. This man had an autocannon. He hosed the shop with a furious rapid fire of hard slugs. Mathuin ducked again.

The bullets smashed benches over, dented locker doors, shattered the screen of a portable codifier and struck a power-pod trolley with enough force to make it roll sideways.

Hands over her ears, eyes shut, Preest shrieked in terror. Shots were hitting the weighty battery cells they were sheltering behind, rocking them. One cell fell off the top of the stack with a resounding slam.

The huntsman with the lasrifle had taken advantage of the suppressing fire his colleague was providing, and had got into the shop too. Las-fire now joined in support of the cannon. More wholesale destruction. Chips of metal were being blown out of the floor. More glass exploded. Despite their serious weight, another battery cell was knocked off the stack. Their cover was being taken away.

'Can't stay here!' Mathuin yelled above the gunfire.

She nodded and followed him. They started crawling on their hands and knees back from the battery stack, keeping it between them and the shooters for as long as possible. Preest flinched at every close shot. They reached the power-pod trolley that the bullets had pushed along. Mathuin grabbed it and wheeled it around. It was heavy on its greased castors, but he could manage it. Through brute effort, he rolled it until it was completely between them and their assailants.

The pod began to shake and buck as shots smacked into its far side. Mathuin had to keep a tight grip to stop it being wrenched away. Still on their hands and knees, they began moving back down the shop towards the open hatchway to basic, Mathuin dragging the pod after them as mobile cover.

They reached the hatchway and Preest scurried through. Mathuin followed her. They were inside the gigantic vault of enginarium basic, the vast, flask-shaped forms of the principal drive chambers towering over them.

'Can you get the hatch shut?' Mathuin yelled. Shots were zipping through the hatchway over the pod.

Preest shook her head. 'I told you... everything's locked out.'

Mathuin put his entire, formidable strength behind the pod and gave it a colossal shove. It trundled back into the shop, knocking into benches.

The hunter with the cannon rose up, firing freely at the pod, assuming Mathuin was still behind it.

From the upright cover of the hatch frame, Mathuin blasted the hunter with his laspistol. He convulsed and fell, his still-firing cannon raking the shop roof.

Mathuin swung back into cover as the lasrifle opened up on him again. He grabbed Preest by the hand.

'Come on, mistress. More of that running you dislike so much.'

They ran across the open floorspace of the vault towards the giant drive chambers. The train of Preest's gown billowed out behind her. A few sporadic las-shots flew out of the open hatchway. Another twenty seconds, Mathuin estimated, and the remaining hunter would realise they had left the hatch area and come down through the shop after them.

Enginarium basic was cool and echoing. The principal drive chambers were cold and inactive. They were what powered the *Hinterlight* through translation point and into the immaterium. At the moment, the ship was cruising on the power of its real-space engines, which were housed in a separate section of the enginarium two decks above them.

Preest led him in under the massive frames that supported the drive chambers. The architecture of basic was of a cyclopean scale: massive bulkheads, support fairings and cross-members. This part of the ship had to endure particularly extreme pressures and stresses, and was also thickly shielded.

Mathuin glanced back, but the hatch to the machine shop was no longer in sight. If the hunter was in basic with them, then that was just bad luck. He'd probably called in support too.

They went down a short flight of open metal steps onto the chamber's sub-floor, and Preest brought him over to a circular console station growing out of the deck near the drive vault's rear wall.

'This it?' he asked.

She nodded and began sliding the armoured hoods back from the station's panels. Mathuin kept watch. They were dreadfully exposed. Apart from the bulky console itself, there was no cover. Hostiles could approach across the main floor above them. Then there were the gantries and walkways higher up around the drive chambers.

'Hurry up,' he said.

She inserted her master keys, turned them and woke the console up. It came to power, the screens of the codifiers flickering into life. Data scrolled across the screens. Mathuin heard the cooling fans in the consoles base begin to whir as the powerful cogitation stack, a duplicate of the vessel's main data processing device, began to get warm.

Preest's hands clattered over the keypad. She adjusted several brass dials. 'Here goes,' she said.

She entered a series of complex numerical sequences. Nothing happened for a moment. Then the cold auxiliary lighting across the vault dimmed and the main lighting blinked back into life. Getting used to the sudden glare, Mathuin realised he could hear the main air scrubbers working again too.

'Well?' he said.

Preest peered at the screen. 'Hmmm,' she said. 'Interesting...'

MADSEN SAW THE lighting on the bridge flicker and change. She got up and looked at Skoh.

'That's not good,' she said. 'Kinsky?'

Halstrom's fingers were repeatedly pressing the same keys. 'We're locked out. Bridge stations are dead.'

'God-Emperor, no...' Madsen said.

'See for yourself,' Halstrom said. 'The ship just reverted to primary systems. But the helm's down... engines have just shut down too. We're drifting. I can't get her back.'

Madsen sat at the helm position, twisted the main display round so it was facing her, and began to work the instruments in a determined way.

'What's going on, Mamzel?' Skoh asked.

'Shut up and let me think,' she said.

The hailing chime sounded. Skoh opened the vox. '*Hinterlight.*'

'*Oktober Country*. Skoh, what are you playing at? That hulk of yours just went dead in the vac. Your drives have shut down. You're not even holding a stabilised course.'

'Stand by, *Oktober Country*. Temporary glitch. We'll have it sorted soon. Out.'

Skoh walked over to Madsen. 'Well?'

'Preest. It's got to be that damn shipmistress. We know she's loose.'

'What's she done?'

'She must have a... let me see... my guess would be a back-up data stack somewhere. Something not on the specs, something I couldn't find. That bitch. She's brought it online and countermanded my countermand.'

'Beaten you at your own game?' Skoh said.

'No,' Madsen insisted. 'She may have shut us out of the master control system temporarily, but she hasn't got control back herself. I'm not that stupid, Skoh. Operators like Preest customise their ships in all sorts of non-standard ways. Redundant back-ups, hidden cogitation caches, sub-written code systems, encrypted high-functions...'

'Get to the point,' Skoh said.

'I knew she'd have something, that's the point. I didn't know what, but it was a fair bet. She's the type. So I wrote reactive clauses into my countermand. The idea being if she tried to undermine my codes in any way, they'd lock everything up. Yes, we don't have control. But neither does she. Both primary and default secondary systems have closed down and locked.'

'Well,' said Skoh, 'that's frigging great. We'll just sit here then...'

'No, we won't,' said Madsen, rising to her feet. 'All we have to do is find Preest and her back-up stack, shut it down, and my codes will revert control back to us.'

'So where is she? This is a big ship. Lots of area to cover. It could take hours for my men to find her.'

'Yes, I've noticed their efficiency already,' Madsen sneered. She looked at Halstrom. 'We do this the quick way. Kinsky?'

Halstrom's body shuddered. He went limp and slumped back in the command throne. A bead of blood began to trickle from his left nostril as his head lolled.

'Find her,' said Madsen. 'Get inside her frigging mind, force her to disable her stack, and then kill the old bitch.'

Sprawled in his seat, Kinsky's body twitched and shivered like a dreaming dog.

FREE. ALERT. ALIVE. Kinsky's mind rushed out from the bridge, surging down hallways, sliding like a wraith between decks. He left a wake of hoar-frost behind him. He was angry now, aching and drawn from the effort of over-mastering Halstrom's mind.

But this... now this is what he did. Searching, tracking, killing. This is what he liked.

As he sped on, he extended his awareness. He could taste the entire bulk of the *Hinterlight*, its hollowed metal form, every sub-duct, every cross-spar, every rivet. It was like a three dimensional schematic to him. And inside it, tiny pinpricks of life heat, the feeble mind-fires of the other humans aboard. Puny little dots. A handful on the bridge, a heavier cluster down in the light cargo holds. Others, spread singly or in small groups through the remainder of the big ship... Skoh's hunters, no doubt.

And two, far down at the stern, in enginarium basic.

Kinsky's mind began to accelerate. Corridors and downshafts flashed past, hallways blurred by.

He was hungry to kill.

'DID YOU FEEL that?' Zael asked, his voice tiny.

Kys nodded. They'd reached the entry bay into the real-space drive section of the enginarium. A short way ahead of them, the deep, split-level drive chambers had just suddenly stopped throbbing with power. The real-space assemblies had inexplicably shut down.

But the abrupt silence hadn't been what Zael was referring too.

'Yes, I felt it,' Kys replied. 'Something's moving.' She shuddered and rested a hand on the wall. 'Really powerful, really raw...'

With total confidence he was correct, Zael said, 'It's Kinsky.'

'LISTEN!' NAYL WHISPERED. Kara stopped and cocked her head. She was still getting used to the resumed lighting levels and the elevated noise of the air processors. For a moment, she couldn't detect anything else.

'There!' said Nayl, raising a hand. A sound. A steady, metallic beat, like a hammer on an anvil. It reverberated down the ominously empty corridors.

'It's coming from down there,' Nayl said, and raised his bolt pistol to lead the way. They crossed a junction and entered the bare metal deck space of the light cargo holds. The pair had already dismissed the light cargo area, and agreed to press on towards the bridge. But now the hammering drew them back.

It was getting louder. On either side of the wide hallway, broad hatches stood open, leading into empty sub holds. The hammering was coming from a sub-hold ahead of them on the right. And now they could hear mumbling too. Kara drew both her autos and thumbed off the safeties.

'LITTLE BASTARD! LITTLE freak!' Duboe grunted, chopping the axe down. Sweat was pouring off him, staining his filthy clothes. Parts of the axe head had broken off. He swung it again. The front casing of Ravenor's chair was pitted and dented, like the hull of a ship after a meteor storm.

'Little frigging bastard!' Duboe raged and struck yet again.

At last, the axe head punched a hole in the chair's casing. Duboe had to wrench at it to pull it free. He gazed in sick wonder at the small, raw-edged perforation. He bent down and put his mouth to the hole.

'Gonna have you out of there soon, bastard. Gonna drag you out and mash you up. You hear me? You hear me?'

WEAPONS RAISED, KARA and Nayl crept closer to the hold door. The metal-on-metal slamming had stopped for a moment, but now it began again.

'Cover me,' Kara started to say.

Nayl cried out a warning. Two of Skoh's hunter pack had suddenly appeared in the doorway of another hold forty metres away down the hallway. They began to open fire. Shots sang past the two of them. Nayl raised the bolter and fired back, running into the cover of a hold doorway to his left. Kara was too far over to the right hand side of the hallway to make it too.

'Get in there!' Nayl yelled. 'Before they hit you!'

DUBOE HEARD THE sudden exchange of gunfire right outside the hold door. His heart began to race. Axe in hand, he lurched back into the shadows to hide.

KARA FIRED A couple of shots in the direction of the hunters, and then dived into the sub-hold. Rounds exploded against the deck and wall where she had just been standing.

She got up and looked round, guns raised.

'Oh my Emperor!' she exclaimed. In the far corner of the hold, Ravenor's chair was wedged against the wall. It looked like someone had attacked it with a pneumatic hammer.

'Ravenor?'

She only realised Duboe was there at the very last moment. He came out of the shadows with a bestial roar, hefting his axe. She tried to evade, almost made it, but the haft of Duboe's axe cracked across her forearms.

Kara went down, diving, wondering if her arms were broken.

They weren't. Bruised, most certainly. And the impact had smashed both guns out of her hands.

Still on the floor, she rolled violently to her left as Duboe's axe hacked down at her. It scored the deck plating. Bellowing, he struck again, and she lunged into a forward roll under the scything blade. The roll took her up against the hold wall, and she pushed off from it like a swimmer on the turn, backflipped high in the air onto her feet as Duboe's murmuring axe kissed empty air. Now she was upright, hunched low, facing him.

'Duboe. You ninker. Who let you out?'

He sliced the weapon at her again. She danced back. They circled. Another stroke, another sidestep. Round and round. She had to disarm him, put him down hard. He was gone, she realised. He was virtually frothing at the mouth.

He lunged again, with a speed and ferocity that astonished Kara. She tried to duck, but he caught her a resounding blow with his left elbow and she staggered backwards, her feet slipping out. She virtually fell across Ravenor's chair.

Duboe came at her, howling, axe raised.

She looked round frantically for a weapon, something to throw, anything.

There was a hefty-looking metal unit clamped to the front of Ravenor's chair. She twisted the dial, wrenched it free and hurled it at Duboe's face. Instinctively, he chopped with his axe, connecting with the missile in mid air, and sent it banging away across the hold floor. He raised the axe again.

+Kara? Get out of the way.+

She dropped. Blunt as she was, she felt the awesome surge of psi-power unleashing from the battered chair.

The walls of the hold were suddenly fuming with ice particles.

Duboe left the ground and flew back ten metres into the far wall. The chipped axe clattered from his hands. He remained pinned there by invisible power, like a specimen insect, two metres off the floor. His mouth opened and closed. His eyes bulged. He gasped.

+Duboe. Who's the bastard now?+

Duboe screamed. Ravenor's mind crushed him. Every single bone in Duboe's body shattered as it flattened into the wall.

ZAEL GRABBED KYS by the arm. 'God-Emperor!' he cried out, his voice echoing around the eerily quiet real-space drive chamber.

She'd felt it too. It was so violent, so awful, worse even than the rushing horror of Kinsky's unleashed psychic power. She crouched down and hugged the boy to her protectively.

'It's all right,' he whispered.

'Yeah?'

Zael nodded. 'I think someone's about to have a really bad chair day.'

'HOLY CRAP,' MUMBLED Kara, getting to her feet. The terrible psychic-force had ebbed away. Duboe's ghastly, formless corpse slid down the hold wall like soaked wallpaper.

'Are you all right?' she asked Ravenor.

'No,' he said. His voice was strangely distorted. Duboe's attack had damaged his voxponder. 'There's no time, Kara. I'm needed elsewhere.'

'But –'

'No buts. We're all dead if I don't act. Guard me here.'

'Absolutely,' she said. There was no response. She knew he was already gone, his mind running free.

She collected her pistols and went to the hold doorway. Outside, the firefight was thicker than before.

'Harlon!'

'I hear you!' he shouted from the hold doorway opposite. He was cracking bolt rounds down the hall. A heavy return of fire was coming their way.

'I've got the boss in here!' she yelled over the gunshots. 'What's our current?'

'Frigging awful!' he bellowed. 'There's at least four of the bastards down there now, with good cover. We're not going that way.'

Kara swung out of her doorway and let rip with bursts from both pistols.

'I've got to guard Ravenor here!' she cried as she dropped back. 'I think you should double back and see if you can reach the bridge!'

'And leave you here?' he questioned.

'That was the plan, remember? Let's stick to it.'

'But–'

'Just move your arse! I can deal!'

He looked across at her. 'You sure?'

'Frig, yeah. It's me, remember.'

He smiled. She'd always liked that smile. 'Get to the bridge. Kill 'em all,' she said.

Nayl nodded, changing clips. 'See you later, Kara Swole.'

'You know it.'

'Cover me,' he said, rising. Kara leant out of the doorway and rained caseless rounds down the hallway with both guns. Behind her, Nayl started to run back down the way they'd come in. The storm of pistol fire made the hunters down the hall duck for cover. Then they started to fire back again with renewed vigour.

'Here we go,' Kara said to herself.

* * *

'SHOULDN'T WE DO something?' Medicae Zarjaran asked. Thonius wanted to shrug, but he knew it would hurt his arm. Outside the doorway of the hold where the crew were imprisoned, their guards were engaged in a blistering exchange of fire with someone. Two or three more of their kind had come to join them. Smoke from the intense weaponsfire was fogging the deck.

Was this salvation, Thonius wondered? Was this death? Should he get up and try to do something? That was what Zarjaran had meant. Not 'we'... 'him'. *Carl.*

He could try and attack the guards from behind while they were occupied with the firefight. Sure he could. Give him a damned Leman Russ tank and a squad of Astartes, and he'd be right on the job.

'We should just keep our heads down,' he said.

'Really?' Zarjaran asked. He had a look on his face. 'But I thought–'

'Thought what?' Thonius asked.

'Nothing,' said the doctor.

Thought I was a hero? A hard-bitten Throne agent? Think again.

MATHUIN WAS GETTING really edgy. 'For Terra's sake, mistress... sort it out!'

'I can't!' she said. 'Whoever did this has been very canny. We're blocked. They can't get into the ship's master controls any more than I can.'

She looked up from the cogitation stack suddenly. 'What was that?'

Mathuin looked up too. He hadn't seen any movement. Was that hunter catching up with them at last...?

'Like a wind,' Preest said. 'Like a monsoon wind. A rushing noise. I...'

Her voice trailed off. She looked down in horror at the surface of the stack console. Frost coated it. Coated her fingers, her gaudy rings, her velvet sleeves.

'Oh dear God-Emperor preserve me...' she stuttered.

+He's not listening.+ Kinsky's voice boomed in her head. She looked up into the lofty spaces of the vast enginarium. There was nothing there.

Kinsky, moving like a missile down from the roof, looking into her terrified, blinking eyes. He made his rushing mind-form thorny, the better to gouge through her flimsy mind walls.

Something hard and furious struck Kinsky's mind from side on, and sent it sparking away across the enginarium vault. In pain, bleeding psi-force, Kinsky recovered, forming into a thought-armoured ball, tendons of razor-string lashing out around it.

+Kinsky.+

His assailant appeared. It took the form of a marine predator, a great saw-toothed fish, shimmering with inner light. It swam down around the material stanchions of the nearest drive chamber, topaz energy shining from its deathless eyes.

+Ravenor.+

With a beat of its tail, the twenty-metre fish swam through the air towards the twitching armoured ball. Kinsky shimmered, re-composing his non-corporeal guise into a giant mantis, shining in a pearlescent light the colour of his psychotic eyes, its massive claws snapping.

+You wanted to go, Kinsky, Let's go.+

Ravenor's tail slammed round and he surged at the psi-form, eyes rolling back as his great jaws gaped to bite.

'WHAT THE HELL is that?' Preest stammered. Mathuin looked at what she was pointing at. The air was shimmering, unfocused, above the main space of the enginarium bay. As they watched, a dent appeared in the decking, then another, another two, in the plated wall. Something invisible tore through one of the metal walkways along the flank of the second drive chamber and it disintegrated, shearing apart, cascading sparks as it tumbled the nine metres to the main deck. Gigantic toothmarks hammered into view on one of the side ductings. It tore loose, venting columns of steam, and flew into the air. High up, it seemed to strike something and bounced back onto the floor with a dreadful clang. Stripes of ice tracked across the deck and vanished as quickly as they had been made. Corposant flames erupted along the railings of an upper walkway.

'I... I don't know,' Mathuin said. Something was messing with his inner ear and his kinaesthetic sense, and from the look on Preest's face, she felt it too. Suddenly, he could smell flowers.

'Lavender!' she cried.

Then salt. Then charcoal. Then stagnant water. Then blood.

'Throne!' Preest said, covering her nose and coughing. A huge raking split appeared across the length of the deck plating, showering metal shards in all directions.

'Preest... mistress...' Mathuin said. 'You have to concentrate. Shut all this out. Get the system working again.'

She looked at him. 'But–'

'Do it!'

She bent down and began working the keyboard. A grazing dent the size of a demipach cratered the far wall of the vault.

'Ignore all this! Do it!' Mathuin cried.

Then a las-round missed Mathuin's head by a few centimetres. More followed.

The hunters had found them.

FOUR

'Skoh! Report your damn status now! My Navigator reads your ship as lousy with psi-force!'

Skoh pressed the 'live' stud on the vox console. 'Stand by, Thekla. We have a few problems, but we're dealing.'

'I want that ship burning, Skoh!' Thekla's voxed voice crackled. 'Burning and gone, with all its crew! That was the whole point of this protracted exercise!'

'Tell him to shut up,' Madsen said.

Skoh breathed deeply. 'We're getting there, Thekla. A few unforeseen set-backs. Please, stand by.'

He cut the channel.

'Well? This is your plan, Mamzel Madsen. Impress me.'

Madsen was with Ahenobarb, bent over Kinsky's body. The psyker was jerking and thrashing in his stupor.

'Gods!' Ahenobarb said. Ugly red weals like a bite mark had just appeared on Kinsky's throat. Bright arterial blood began to leak out of the psyker's lips. His jaw clenched.

'Rav... en... or...' he gurgled.

'Damnation,' said Madsen.

'Mamzel,' Skoh said, 'it appears this oh-so-perfectly wrought trap of yours is coming apart at the seams.'

'I–' Madsen began.

'Shhh!' Skoh interrupted. He raised a hand and listened to the voices of his men coming over his microbead earplug. Then he turned and looked at her. 'I think you should sort things.'

'What? Kinsky is–'

Skoh slid his long-las out of the leather boot on his back and armed it. He didn't aim it at her, but the threat was very clear. 'I'm taking charge, Madsen. You've ballsed it up this far. My men report they have the shipmistress and one other cornered at the far stern. Get down there. That's clearly the location of her back-up. Get down there and make things good so we can resume control, dump this hulk into the star and be gone.'

Madsen drew her autosnub and glanced at Ahenobarb. 'Eight,' she said. 'You're with me, Ahenobarb.'

'I think that's best,' Skoh replied.

Madsen and the giant hurried away out of the bridge hatch.

LAS-BOLTS AND SOLID slugs were impacting all around them. Preest and Mathuin had to stay low behind the console, parts of which were shattering off under the gunfire. There were at least five of them out there, Mathuin reckoned. Three on the deck, two on the gantries. They had them pinned. He couldn't raise his head enough to squeeze off a shot, let alone allow Preest to complete her work.

They were just waiting to die.

KARA SWITCHED NEATLY out of the doorway and rattled fire from both guns. This time she aced. One of the hunters, approaching over-confident, went over.

But she was down to her last two clips.

She looked across at Ravenor's chair. Battered, holed, it was silent, as if it was empty.

I BECAME A CYCLONE, sweeping away the shoals of his mind-darts like leaves. Kinsky dropped low beneath my storm-force bow-wave and lunged upwards with a mental lance. I changed into a glittering avalanche that fell on him and snapped the lance, but Kinsky slid away like oil and drove the broken-off spearhead into my side. Psi-energy drizzled out, spattering like blood. I shook off the pain, turned and exhaled a gout of pyrokinetic flames that ignited Kinsky like an oily slick.

Flames roared up, pink-hot, sour, fierce. I heard him scream. For a second, I believed I had beaten him.

But then he rose up out of the flames. He wore his human form for a second, laughing at me, arms wide, his hateful eyes becoming little secondary mouths that laughed along. The fire slid off him harmlessly.

So be it. The fight was not over. We threw mind-traps at each other, traps of increasing complexity and ingenuity; bright, intricate things that snapped open, bit shut, became spiked, became corrosive. He and I brushed them aside, and the blizzards of thought daggers we launched once the traps had failed. Then we closed again, our non-corporeal forms shifting and changing rapidly as we tried to out-think one another and prepare for the other's next ploy. Undecided, our ectoplasmic shapes bent and twisted and malformed, rupturing like the skin on boiling milk, puffing out like cysts, spurting like soft lava.

Kinsky suddenly became a bruised, squid-like form that lashed at me with twenty metre-long tentacles. I had already raised overlapping shields of mind-plating, but they buckled under the blows, so I slid the plates apart and then closed them like a vice on the tentacles when they whipped in again. Several snapped. Dark clouds of inky pain and anger squirted from the severed ends. While he was still reeling, I rolled my non-corporeal form into a porcupine ball and launched a shower of quill-shots at Kinsky, pinning the Ministry agent's mind against the sliding fabric of space-time.

Howling, Kinsky tore free. Reality was so badly damaged where I had pinned him, the noxious, infernal light of the warp shone through the punctures.

Kinsky pulsed, reforming. For a moment, he was humanoid shape again, then that split apart as something vast grew up out of it. A thing of smoke and darkness, beaked, eyeless, a primordial ravager from ancient myth.

Nothing seemed to stop him. He was a monstrously powerful psyker. I had the edge in terms of training and practice, and this gave me real finesse. But I was nothing like as powerful as Kinsky's crude, unstructured mind. I would not lose to him. I refused to be bested by such a feral mind.

But steadily, he drove me back across the enginarium.

THE HINTERLIGHT SHUDDERED violently. On the bridge, Skoh saw hazard alerts begin to light up all the station displays.

He looked at the nearest one as another thump shook the deck. What was that? Were they being fired on?

The scope said yes. Two hits, amidships. Starboard hangar voided, hull damage. Fire in the real-space drive chambers. Locked open doors had slammed automatically as the emergency safety systems had cut in.

Astounded, Skoh activated the main-beam vox. 'Thekla? What the hell are you doing?'

'Firing on you, of course,' the vox gurgled. 'I'm tired of waiting, and I'm worried that inquisitor bastard has got loose.'

'Thekla!' Skoh snarled. 'Cease fire!'

The *Hinterlight* bucked again. 'Can't do that, Feaver. Sorry. I have to make sure that ship and its crew are dead, and if you won't be a sport and dive it into the star for me, what can I do? Nothing personal.'

Another brutal shudder. Klaxons sounded. Skoh could smell smoke now.

'You bastard, Thekla,' he said.

'Whatever. I recommend you get off that death trap, Feaver, my old friend. I'll be waiting to pick you up. But hurry... I intend to make short work of that ship.'

The vox went dead. As if to prove the shipmaster's point, the *Hinterlight* shook again. Skoh picked up his long-las and headed for the exit. There was an escape module compartment close by, at the end of the midships companionway. He was halfway down it, when Harlon Nayl came through the end hatch.

They saw each other at once. Both started to fire and move simultaneously. Firing his long-las from the hip, Skoh hurled himself to his right towards the cover of a bulkhead. Nayl's bolt pistol came up blasting. He threw himself into an almost full-length dive towards a side hatchway.

The two powerful weapons blazed at each other up and down the companionway, raising a veil of smoke and riddling the wall-plating with dents and holes. Neither man had much in the way of cover. Nayl's bolts chipped and whined against the thick bulkhead concealing Skoh. The hunter's las-shots fireballed and deflected off the hatch-housing where Nayl was tucked in.

Stalemate... at least until one of them ran out of ammunition. Skoh didn't believe they had that long anyway. Thekla's batteries would have the *Hinterlight* dead in just another few minutes.

He had a better idea. Ignoring the bolt rounds slamming against the bulkhead, he popped the powerclip out of his rifle, and replaced it with another from his belt. Special load, hot-shot, useful for when big game got really big.

Under these circumstances, at this range, the round would go right through the hatch-housing. And the idiot standing behind it.

AGAINST THE DAZZLING backdrop of the Firetide storm, the *Oktober Country* closed in, its weapon turrets flashing every few seconds. Neither ship was a military class vessel, and neither possessed the sort of Fleet-grade weaponry that could annihilate a rival instantly. But like most rogue traders, the *Oktober Country* had enough firepower to take care of itself. Its sustained bombardment would eventually blow Preest's ship apart.

Drifting, helpless, shieldless, the *Hinterlight* soaked the damage up. Sections of plating blew out like foil. Scabbed patches of hull crackled with shorting power sources or glowed red-hot.

Inside, significant chunks of the ship were obliterated, holed to space. Others were auto-sealed, ablaze.

Madsen was still heading for the stern.

'We should just... just take that bulk lifter and go,' Ahenobarb ventured.

'Go where?' Madsen replied. 'That's hardly an option. God-Emperor, I can't believe Thekla could be this insane!'

'What do we do, then?' urged Ahenobarb.

'Carry on. We deal with Preest, shut down her tinkering, then we've got control back. I can raise the shields. Stop that madman from blowing us apart.'

Ahenobarb looked doubtful, but he was used to following her orders.

The deck shuddered under another impact. 'Come on!' Madsen said.

She had been intending to short-cut down through the real-space drive chambers, cutting a good five minutes off the journey, but the doors to the drive room were sealed.

'That chamber is blown out!' Ahenobarb moaned, and started to look for an alternate route.

Madsen looked at the doorpanel display. 'No, there's still pressure. But there is fire. It's worth it.'

She took a multikey out of her hip-pocket, pressed it to the hatch control and overrode the lock. The hatch swung open. Heat and scorching smoke swept out. Fires were blazing through the long, double-storey drive rooms, and alarms were singing all over the place. Coughing, Madsen led the way out along the main gantry walk, ignoring the heat from below.

KYS AND ZAEL had felt the first brutal impact of Thekla's attack, and quickly found themselves driven back through the drive chambers by the inferno kicked off by a damaged power-capacitor. Attempting to exit, they'd discovered the section hatches had locked automatically.

They retraced their steps, desperate to find a hatch that would open to them. It was getting hard to see, to breathe. They clambered their way up the hot metal of one of the gantry ladders to escape a new wall of flames that had sprung up, but now fires were licking into the upper levels of the chamber too.

'Back! Back!' Kys screamed at Zael. 'We have to go back and–'

'Behind you!' Zael yelled suddenly.

Ahenobarb appeared from nowhere, out of the smoke. He swung at her. Kys tried to draw her pistol, but his fist hit too hard, too soon. She went down on the gantry mesh, her gun falling away down into the flames.

Ahenobarb bent down to pick her up. She only had her boline left. She drew it and stabbed it into Ahenobarb's calf.

He bleated with pain. Tearing out of his hands, Kys punched the blade in under his nose.

Ahenobarb fell backwards, over the rail, into the boiling fire beneath them.

A bullet hit Kys in the left shoulder and spun her back down onto the gantry decking again. Starkly lit by the flamelight, Madsen advanced towards her, gun raised. A section of the gantry behind Madsen folded and toppled away into the inferno.

'I told you what I'd do if I saw you again,' Kys said, struggling up to meet her.

'What? Kill me?' Madsen answered. She sneered and raised her auto.

Kys turned. She had no weapon. There was a bloody hole in her left shoulder.

Madsen began to fire.

Kys flipped the fish scales off her collar stud telekinetically... one, two, three...

Spinning, whirring, they sliced into Madsen's windpipe.

Limbs flailing, weapon firing, Madsen fell backwards off the broken gantry and plunged away into the firestorm.

'Come on,' Kys yelled, staggering back to Zael. 'Come on!' They ran as the drive room began to collapse around them.

THE BRIDGE WAS empty. Kinsky's body lay in the second helm station. Halstrom lay in the command throne. The display screens and hololiths showed how the *Oktober Country's* guns were punishing the *Hinterlight*.

Kinsky twitched in his coma. A smile twitched on his lips. It had been a hard fight, certainly the hardest psi-duel he'd ever fought in his life. He had to give Ravenor that much. But it was at an end now. Far away in enginarium basic, Ravenor was down, dazed, pinned, and Kinsky's non-corporeal jaws were closing around the inquisitor's throat. As a final, artistic flourish, Kinsky's mind-form sprouted venomous teeth to deliver the coup.

With a ghastly intake of air, Wystan Frauka sat up. A bubble of blood bulged at his nostril and popped.

Slowly, very slowly, he pulled himself upright and bent over Kinsky.

'Hey,' he said. He slapped Kinsky's cheek. 'Hey!'

Swaying back, Frauka produced his lho-stick carton and his lighter. He stuck a stick in his mouth and lit it. When he exhaled, smoke puffed out of the hole in his chest too.

'Frig! These things'll kill you,' he said, to no one in particular. Then he leaned over.

'Hey,' he said again, kicking at Kinsky's leg. Kinsky remained still.

Frauka reached up and deactivated his limiter.

Suddenly, shockingly, sucked back into his own skull, Kinsky thrashed and woke up. Feebly, he reached out, and looked up at Frauka's face.

Frauka took the stick out of his mouth, exhaled, put it back between his lips, and lent down. He took Kinsky's skull in his hands and wrenched it around. Kinsky's neck snapped with a pop.

'And there you go,' Frauka said. He switched his limiter back on, took the lho-stick out of his mouth, and fell over.

FIVE

Suddenly Kinsky was gone. His psi-form melted, the ecto-plasmic structure of it thawing away like snow. He was dead. I was in no doubt about that, though I had no idea how.

My mind was lacerated, damaged from the fight, but I knew I could not submit to unconsciousness yet. I could sense the terrible damage being inflicted on the defenceless ship.

I looked down at enginarium basic around me. Mathuin and Preest were still pinned down behind the stack console by Skoh's hunters. I stabbed out, and each hunter was felled by a psychic-dagger. Dead or unconscious – I didn't much care which – they dropped where they were.

+Cynia!+

'G-Gideon?'

+Get up! You're clear! There's no time! Get up and override Madsen's codes... Quickly, woman!+

She and Mathuin rose. She started working at the console. Struck again, the ship rolled badly.

'What the bloody hell is happening to my darling?' Preest wailed.

+Just override the codes! We need to get the shields raised!+

She did as she was told. But even if she was successful, there needed to be someone on the bridge to get the shields up.

I soared out of enginarium basic and hurtled up through the decks, through bulkheads, through cabins open to hard vacuum, through chambers gutted by fire.

I swept through the light cargo holds, burning out the minds of the hunters about to overwhelm dear Kara as I passed.

+Get my chair to the bridge!+ I left the command ringing in her head as I flew on.

Up through spinal, through the lateral halls, along the midships companion way. There was Nayl. Without even pausing, I slammed Feaver Skoh into the wall as I went by. He fell heavily, unconscious.

I entered the bridge. It was in uproar – klaxons, alarms, red hazard lights and runes on almost every display. There was Kinsky, dead in one seat, Wystan Frauka sprawled across him, dead or dying. In the command throne, Halstrom. He looked dead too.

His breathing was shallow. His mind had been badly abused.

+Halstrom! Halstrom!+

He twitched, but he did not wake.

I had no other option. I had to ware him.

He cried out as I went in, waking with the shock. Using his expertise, I studied the main console. Still locked out. The auspex showed the *Oktober Country* all but alongside, firing still.

With Halstrom's fingers, I opened the intercom.

'Preest! Are you done yet?' My words sounded strange in Halstrom's voice.

'Nearly, she says,' Mathuin answered. A pause. 'Try it now.'

Nothing.

'Correction,' Mathuin added. 'Try it now.'

Primary control had just been restored. I hit a series of controls and raised the shields.

Not all ignited. Thekla's attack had already vaporised some shield nodes and power feeds, and those that did come on were weak. Still, the vibration from the bombardment abated slightly.

I tried to probe Halstrom's beaten mind, to work out what he would do.

The shields, like most of the ship's systems, derived their power from the ship's primary reactor, which drove the real-space drives. But the fire in the real-space chambers had cut that back by about seventy-five per cent, taking the *Hinterlight's* motive power away with it. Instead, I woke up the secondary reactor, whose only function was to power the currently deactivated warp drive. I transferred that power into the primaries and immediately boosted their shields by forty per cent. It was unorthodox practice, risky too, but an old and very workable Fleet captain's trick, courtesy of Halstrom's experience.

I became aware of Nayl as he came up beside me.

'Halstrom?' he asked.

'No, it's me,' I said.

'Ah. Thought so. Guessing that was you who suckered Skoh outside too?'

'Yes.'

Nayl nodded. 'Thanks for that.'

I was working too hard for decent conversation. Despite the boosted shields, large parts of the starboard flank, the focus of Thekla's onslaught, were still vulnerable, lacking as they did any remaining shields to reinforce. The *Oktober Country* would still kill us in short order, unless…

Another little trick from Halstrom's mind. With what little motive power I could squeeze from the damaged real-space drive, I got the ship moving and turning. We slid through coruscating flame walls of the solar storm, turning hard to port. Thekla's ship spurred after us, still firing its fusion batteries.

'Can you… fly this thing?' Nayl asked.

'No. But Halstrom can.' Turning her hard, I was presenting the *Hinterlight's* undamaged port side – and active shields – to Thekla's ruinous guns. Of course, with very much less motive thrust than the *Oktober Country*, it was going to be near-impossible keeping it there. Already, Thekla was steering out under us to come around at our wounded quarters again.

'Harlon… see what weapons we have left,' I said.

He crossed to the fire control station and started to fumble with the unfamiliar function controls. I kept the turn tight, rolling the ship to keep the full shields pointing at Thekla's dogged attack.

'Frig all,' Nayl said at last. 'Most of it's shot out. Forget lasers, fusion beamers. I've got one missile battery under the prow that's still live.'

'Arm it and target it on the *Oktober Country's* bridge,' I said. It was getting hard to maintain control over Halstrom. He was fading fast. I could feel perspiration dripping off his brow as he struggled to stay conscious.

'They'll be shielded,' Nayl scoffed. 'Especially around the bridge section.'

'I know, Harlon.'

'They've been whaling on us for a good ten minutes. We're junked. They're still at optimum. We're not going to achieve anything firing at their bridge except wasting our last missiles.'

'I know. Please do as I ask.'

'Very well…' he shrugged.

Halstrom was slipping away. I made one last effort to turn the ship and then stepped out of his mind. Released, he fell back in the chair. Non-corporeal, I looked at the displays. We'd turned hard, but in another sixty seconds, the *Oktober Country* would pull clear and resume firing on our damaged sections.

'Armed and targeted,' Nayl reported.

+Harlon, when you hear me give the word, fire. No questions.+

He nodded.

I left the bridge.

Through plating, through insulation layers, through inner and outer hull sections, through raised shields, into open space.

Firetide swelled around me, as far as my mind could see. An ocean expanse of flame and seething discharge, crackling and shimmering. Behind me, the wounded bulk of the *Hinterlight*, sagging and wallowing in the storm. Ahead, the great, dark shape of the predatory *Oktober Country*, roaming in for the kill, weapon banks flaring and spitting.

It was a gigantic sprint trader, ornate and exquisite, one of the most ancient human ships I had ever seen. I could smell its great age, the dusty odours of its long, rigorous life, the musky, spiced auras of the far flung places it had visited, the xenos perfumes of its more ungodly voyages.

I could taste the steely resolve of its ruthless master.

I swept on, through the cavorting radiance of the storm and went in, through its shields, its hull…

Thekla stood on a raised platform, studying his actuality sphere. Target runes were clustering around the graphic of the *Hinterlight*. He was a tall man, regal, in a selpic blue coat furnished with gold braid and a silk cravat. His face was an organic tracery of inlaid circuitry. MIU linkage cables tracked out from the base of his skull, from under the powdered wig he wore, and connected his mind to the sprint trader's systems. His hands were augmetic. He was shouting orders to his bridge crew.

There were thirteen of them, arranged around the edge of his platform, operating polished brass stations. Helm, sub-helm, system-control, vox-and-com, navigation supervisor, ordnance officer, defence officer...

Defence officer. I plunged into the man's mind.

+Now, Harlon. Now.+

'The *Hinterlight* has launched missiles, master!' the ordnance officer called out beside me.

I heard Thekla laugh. 'One last effort, eh? Rather too little, too late, I think.'

The defence officer was fighting me. He struggled and contorted.

'Lefabre? What the frig's the matter with you, man? You're twitching around like an idiot!'

I was hurt, weak. The man's mind was strong. At this range, and through the turmoil of the storm, my abilities were desperately limited, especially without the boosting relay of a wraithstone marker.

But I would not let him go. Frantically, I blew out his neural system, and forced his twitching hands onto the brass levers of his station.

And cut the *Oktober Country's* shields.

In the last millisecond of his life, Thekla realised what was happening and screamed out a name.

My name, in fact.

Eight missiles, in tight formation, screamed in silently out of the storm and vaporised the *Oktober Country's* bridge, taking everyone with it.

SIX

'READY FOR THIS?' Kys asked.

'Yes, I am. Quite ready,' Ravenor replied. His voice still sounded odd, anguished almost. There had been no time to repair his chair's damaged voxponder.

The hatch opened. Ravenor slid forward into the bare cell, flanked by Kys and Carl Thonius.

Feaver Skoh shivered and looked up at the trio. He had been stripped naked, and chained to the wall.

'You,' he murmured. They could smell his fear. He had been expecting this.

'We are going to have a conversation,' Ravenor said. 'How pleasant it becomes is up to you.'

Skoh shrugged. 'I've got nothing left,' he said. 'Ask what you want, inquisitor.'

'Where do the flects come from?'

'The Mergent Worlds,' he said simply.

'The Mergent Worlds are out of bounds. Forbidden, interdicted by the Fleet,' Kys said. 'How can that be?'

Skoh looked at her. 'Rogue traders go many places that are forbidden,' he said. 'The very best can get wherever they want. If the return is good enough.'

'The best?' Thonius asked. 'Like your friend Thekla, you mean?'

'Thekla, and the others.'

'A consortium?' Ravenor said. Skoh shrugged again.

'Thekla... and Akunin?'

He nodded. 'Akunin, Vygold, Marebos, Foucault, Strykson, Braeden. Those are the ones I know.'

'What is contract thirteen?' Thonius asked.

Skoh blinked, amazed.

'I heard you and Mamzel Madsen talking,' Thonius explained.

'And it was in Duboe's mind,' Ravenor added.

'That frigging idiot. All right. It's... it's the reason the flect thing began in the first place. Contract thirteen is an off-books arrangement between the rogue consortium and the Ministry of Sub-sector Trade. The terms of the contract are simple. The traders go to the Mergent Worlds and recover tech salvage.'

'What do you mean by "tech salvage"?' Kys said.

'Whatever they can find. Spica Maximal is the target of choice. Hive cities, population centres, whatever, all just resurfaced from the warp storm. They're loaded with stuff. Hive towers of the Administratum, full of codifiers, cogitation banks, out-use terminals. That's what the Ministry wants. The consortium hauls it back, holds filled to bursting, and delivers it to Petropolis. In return, the Ministry pays. Pays pretty well. And also supplies the consortium with times, dates and codes to help them get around the fleet interdiction blockade.'

'Why does the Ministry want the tech?' Thonius asked.

Skoh shook his head. 'I don't know.' He winced as Ravenor squeezed his mind with a psi-tweak. 'Really, I don't! I'm just a game agent. I ride with Thekla.'

'Make that... rode with Thekla,' Kys smiled.

'Whatever. I relied on him for a lift out to the ripworlds. More often than not he was going that way because he was on a contract run. I got to see what he did. I was there. But I don't know why. Tech... tech stuff is valuable, right? Isn't that why?'

'Perhaps,' Ravenor said.

'What about the flects?' Kys said.

'They were there. Everywhere. I mean, on a place like Spica Maximal, they were all over the ground, far as the eye could see. When we found out what they did, we brought them back with us. The Ministry paid good for the contract cargoes, but it got that a trader in the consortium could double, triple his earnings running flects on the side. That's... that's where I got into it. The side action.' Skoh looked down, as if he was ashamed. That seemed unlikely. Just caught.

'The Ministry didn't object to the flect trade?' Thonius asked.

'At first. But they tolerated it. Everyone was happy.'

'Until my team opened it up, through Duboe and yourself,' Ravenor said.

Skoh nodded. 'Yeah. That's why we got into this. You had to be silenced.'

'Because my interest in the flect trade had put me close to something much bigger?'

'Yes.'

'And the parties involved couldn't very well move against an inquisitor on a world like Eustis Majoris. Not without blowing everything. So they decide to lure me out to Lucky Space, dropping hints and clues to keep me interested. And out here... I could be disposed of, and no one would know better.'

'That was the plan,' said Skoh.

'Madsen's plan?' Kys asked.

'Madsen's plan,' Skoh agreed. 'But Kinsky made it work by thinking ahead of you. Duboe, Siskind... whatever it took. Planting clues, shielding other memories. Drawing you on.'

A sudden chill wrapped the cell. Frost crackled up the metal walls.

'One last thing...' said Ravenor.

'Oh!' gasped Skoh. 'Shit, please...'

I SLAMMED INTO his unhappy mind, turned away his surface thoughts and buried my mind in his memories. From the first scent of the synapses, I knew everything he had told us had been the truth. But I went back. Further.

Spica Maximal. Mergent World. Lately resurfaced, dead, from the horrors of the warp storm, like lost ships dredged up, dripping and rotten, from an ocean depth. I was Feaver Skoh, crunching down a blasted slope with others of Thekla's landing party.

Before me, a vast wasteland of jet cinders and blackened material, twisted, bulbous, shattered, crusted. The sky was domed and full of rushing, splintered cloud. A sun, red as a blood-shot eye, was rising in the firmament. There were buildings ahead of me, towers and spires and cyclopean citadels, all ruined, all made of solidified night. A burned city. A murdered hive. I walked down the vast towers, and saw their countless windows, row upon row, tier upon tier, deadlights like eye sockets, giving back no reflection, stained by unimaginable ages spent in consuming darkness. The crazed black soil under my feet was covered in a myriad shards of broken glass. Imperfectly, like a deranged mosaic, they reflected back Skoh's image.

For a moment I shivered. I was back in Bergossian's dream, the dream that had nearly dragged me to my doom in the deadlofts of Petropolis.

But this was no dream. It was Skoh's memory of Spica Maximal. Bergossian, poor lunatic Bergossian, had seen it in his visions.

The visions of the flects.

They were under my feet. The endless, shattered pieces of glass blown out from the numberless windows of the great hive. Each one charged with power from the long ages they had lingered, submerged in the warp. Each shard was loaded with a reflection of something.

And some things were too terrible to look upon.

This was what Skoh and the other freebooters had collected and dealt. Broken glass from the ruins of a warp-engulfed hive.

I withdrew from his memory. Skoh slumped back, gasping.

'That is all,' I told him.

'I... I have one question. About my brother. Who killed him?'

'He was shot by my warrior Zeph Mathuin during combat,' I said. 'But Mathuin serves me, so the actual answer to your question is... I did.'

'WHAT HAPPENS NOW?' asked Harlon Nayl. No one answered immediately. Nayl stood on the *Hinterlight's* bridge. Aided by her servitors and her freed crew, the shipmistress was trying to repair some life into the wounded ship. She was crying. The damage was immense.

Halstrom, along with Frauka, was down in the infirmary. Last Nayl had heard, Zarjaran was fighting to save both of them.

'Now?' Ravenor replied. 'Harlon, this isn't about the flects any more.'

'Got that much,' Nayl smiled.

'We have been presented with a strong possibility that the local Imperium authorities are trading in heretical technology. The lord sub-sector's private ministry, at least. I don't know if the corruption goes right up to the lord sub-sector himself, but the chances are high. We have a much, much bigger deal on our plate.'

'We're going back to Eustis Majoris, then?' Kys asked.

'Yes,' said Ravenor. 'But now we have an advantage. Our adversary thinks we're dead. Without Thekla to contradict this fact, we can return in disguise. Disguise is essential. I have no way of knowing how deep this corruption runs. Maybe into the Officio Angelus itself.'

'The *Hinterlight* isn't going to get us there,' Mathuin said. That was true enough. So badly wounded, the *Hinterlight* would need months to limp back to a safe harbour outside Lucky Space and begin repairs. Besides, there was a real chance that Preest, shaken and tearful, would refuse another mission for the ordos.

'I... I have an idea...' Nayl began.

ZAEL STOOD ALONE on the observation deck, gazing out at the storms of Firetide. They were fading now, the solar storm dying away. Still, the flashes outside jumped his long shadow back and forth across the deck.

'We're going back,' Kys said as she joined him.

'Back?'

'To Petropolis. That all right?'

Zael nodded.

'You're all right with that?' she said.

'It'll be good to see home again.' Zael walked away from her and exited the deck.

'He's more than nascent,' Kys said to Ravenor. The chair coasted up beside her.

'Much more.'

'Passive like you thought?'

'Yes. Mirror psyker. From what you told me, I think he's very rare. I think the flects he's used have touched off something in his mind. Empowered deep potentials. He's not active at all, but I think he might become a powerful reflective. I think I might be able to teach him to far-see. To predict. To foretell.'

'Yeah, I felt that too. It's like he knows what's about to happen.'

'Not knows, so much as... echoes. The damned flects have woken something in him, but it's something quite amazing.'

'I hope he thinks so,' said Patience Kys.

CARL THONIUS SIGHED. His arm really hurt, but this would make it better.

They'd gone over and searched the *Oktober Country* before imprisoning its surviving crew and allowing it to tumble away into the star's gravity well, undirected and helm-less, tracing the doom it had reserved for the *Hinterlight*.

Thekla's holds had been packed with flects. Raw ones, not even yet packed into their red-tissue wraps.

Carl had one cupped in his hands. It felt warm. He opened his fingers and looked down.

AT THE END of Firetide, a bulk lifter had flown into Bonner's Reach. Transponder codes identified it as belonging to the *Oktober Country*. Hooded, cloaked, three figures left the lifter and hurried to an arranged meeting in a private booth on one of the first salon's upper galleries.

A diminutive figure entered the booth, as pict and psi screens folded down around him.

'I am Sholto Unwerth, and I requent your fulsome advantages,' he said.

Harlon Nayl pulled back his hood. 'Master Unwerth, we have a business proposition for you.'

SOON

Late winter time, Petropolis, Eustis Majoris, 402.M41

'That's a lot of trucks,' Junior Marshal Plyton said, looking down out of the windows of the Department of Special Crimes. Secretary Limbwall scurried over and joined her, peering out at the lorries far below, caught on the rockcrete plaza in a downpour of acid rain. Burn alarms were sounding.

'Yeah, what are they here for?' Limbwall said.

Deputy Magistratum First Class Dersk Rickens tapped his way over, leaning hard on his cane. He peered down at what his underlings were looking at.

'That? That's the new codifiers they've been promising us. Upgraded units, more powerful cogitation. They've been shipped from a provider planet.'

Down below, servitors began to unload crated cogitator units from the trucks.

'Rejoice and be merry,' Rickens said, walking away. 'Departmental upgrade. Think yourselves lucky.'

'Excellent!' Plyton exclaimed.

Limbwall clapped his hands.

Far below them, elevator banks began to carry the units up to their floor. Boxed, the cogitators they brought were still damp from the humid atmosphere of Spica Maximal.

Excited, Plyton hurried towards the elevators.

On the ledge outside the window, a perching sheen bird watched her go. It blinked.

One perfectly machined mechanical eye opened and closed. It cocked its head. It waited in the pouring acid rain.

Looked back.

And blinked.

ABOUT THE AUTHOR

Dan Abnett lives and works in Maidstone, Kent, in England. Well known for his comic work, he has written everything from the *Mr Men* to the *X-Men* in the last decade, and is currently scripting *Legion of Superheroes* and *Superman* for DC Comics, and *Sinister Dexter* and *The VCs* for 2000 AD.

His work for the Black Library includes the popular strips *Lone Wolves, Titan* and *Darkblade*, the best-selling Gaunt's Ghosts novels, and the acclaimed Inquisitor Eisenhorn trilogy. He was voted 'Best Writer Now' at the National Comic Awards 2003.

RAVENOR RETURNED

BY DAN ABNETT

The Black Library's best-selling author is back with the continuing story of Inquisitor Ravenor and his deadly warband in the grim far future. Following on from *Ravenor*, this story continues the action-packed adventures of Inquisitor Ravenor and his team as they investigate the spread of the substance known as 'flects'. But with corrupt Imperial officials to deal with, the time for clandestine investigation may be over!

ISBN 1-84416-184-6

www.blacklibrary.com

THE EISENHORN TRILOGY

BY DAN ABNETT

In the 41st millennium, the Inquisition hunts the shadows for humanity's most terrible foes – rogue psykers, xenos and daemons. Few inquisitors can match the notoriety of Gregor Eisenhorn, whose struggle against the forces of evil stretches across the centuries.

Eisenhorn collects together the novels *Xenos, Malleus* and *Hereticus* along with two linking short stories into one awesome volume.

ISBN 1-84416-156-0